# Also by
# Brandon Rolfe

Countdown To Doomsday
The Analyst

# THE DROMYRK FILE

BRANDON ROLFE

Published by Dolman Scott Ltd in 2016



ISBN 978-1-909204-94-2

eBook: 978-1-909204-95-9

KIndle: 978-1-909204-96-6

**Dolman Scott Ltd**
www.dolmanscott.co.uk

# Dedication

To my veritably steadfast 'Watson' ANNITA

# PROLOGUE

**Germany: 1916**

The steeples were the first to catch the eye with their twinkling sunlight, before sprinkling it down onto Berlin's skyline below them. Sparkling red roofs and green cupolas beckoned the train eagerly, to hurry it on towards the city. The view brought Dromyrk out of his thoughts, away from the hum-drum rhythm of the swaying carriage, and he sat up. He stared out for several moments at the rapidly approaching metropolis. But he was seeing more than the country's capital before him. He was seeing a crucial crossroads, where decision would see professional success either ensured or dashed. This was it. Make or break time. The rising sun's golden rays broke through the cracks in the skyline, to bestow their solar blessing on the rooftops.

'Now or never,' muttered Dromyrk at the sight of the important appointment rushing on closer towards him. He took in a deep breath, exhaling slowly in a long drawn out stream to relax his nerves. As the train's undulating shadow raced across flat meadows and uneven embankments, it suddenly began to cleave off two new portions of shadow. Objects passing across overhead. At the same time a new sound – a snarling whining sound – was just becoming audible above the roaring clatter of locomotive steel. Dromyrk looked up. The Albatross 111 biplane swayed across into view, followed by the older Fokker E 111 monoplane. With the grace of great yellow birds, all wire and canvass, they waltzed from side to side in agile display for the spectators gaping in awe below. As the wings 'waddled' up and down in farewell gesture before moving off, the sun caught the glinting menace of the twin Spandau machine guns mounted directly behind the whirling propeller. Quite remarkable in that these guns were synchronised to fire their deadly venom *between* the propeller blades, rather than rely on deflector plates on the propeller, as earlier planes had done.    Nevertheless, a grim reminder that these two gaily painted flying machines were *fighting* machines – birds of death. Superior engine-power, capable of 166m.p.h., and deadlier missions, had them rapidly leaving the train behind, diminishing to dots towards the south eastern horizon – and the enemy – France.

Dromyrk stood up from his seat to reach up for the luggage rack. The leather valise came down first, then his brass-bracketed leather bag with its gold-lettered inscription: **Olaf E Dromyrk MD.** Just newly qualified, at Vienna's University Medical School, he was here to take up official duties in the *Psychiatrische Klinik*. In complete contrast to family tradition, where both his father and grandfather had chosen to specialise in surgery. The Faculty's *Privadozent* in neuropathology, Dr Freud, however much he may or may not have realised it, had been more than a little responsible for forging his decision in this 'wayward' choice of specialisation. Lingering spots of uncertainty were pushed to the back of his mind. In distraction, he watched the *Landwehr* Grenadier put on his leather strappings with their ammunition pouches and checking the bayonet in its sheath, before taking down his steel helmet and Mauser rifle from the luggage rack. The helmet was the old pre-1916 spiked crown type, its ominous point protruding through a tear in the dull field grey camouflage covering. Barely in his twenties, the soldier's constant defiance of death in the trenches had etched his face with age beyond his years.

The long metal serpent of a train slid slowly into the station, flapping open its hinged 'scales', to disgorge its human parasites onto the platform. Dromyrk stepped down onto the crowded platform and looked about. He dodged smartly aside to narrowly avoid being struck by a butt as the young soldier swung the rifle up over his head and onto his back. Standing outside the exit, Dromyrk looked around to take in the new surroundings.

The morning's golden sunlight bearing down on him emblazoned his own golden features. A rich thatch of lank blond hair, combed back and parted in the middle, was matched with a thick brush moustache. His strong long-boned face, with cold blue eyes sparkling like cut glass, had the pale golden glazed complexion of the fresh outdoor kind that typified his Scandinavian race. Over six feet tall, with generous limbs and large hands more suited to wielding a whaler's harpoon than a medical bag, he was an imposing figure. Yet in spite of what could initially be a daunting image, there was a quietness in Dromyrk's expression and manner that was attributable for his ease in winning over the trust of difficult patients. Perhaps like a priest, but a healer of minds, rather than souls.

Feeling his bag being tugged in his hand, Dromyrk looked round and down. 'Cab, Herr Doktor?' Tiny in comparison, the cabbie pulled with two-handed persuasion without waiting for Dromyrk's answer. He had seen the doktor's bag. His wrinkled face, gaunt with prominent bones and sunken eyes like knots, was worthy of an ancient tree-trunk. Dromyrk saw a work-battered life before him; some bronchial carcinoma problems as well. Behind that he saw inner worry having its toll on the old man. Nodding and giving a soft smile, Dromyrk released his bag into the cabbie's hands. Swaying and hobbling along with a stiff-jointed gait not unlike a penguin, the cabbie loaded the bags onto the carriage. He then climbed up into his seat, behind the horse, and took up his reins and whip. They moved off.

Watching the myriad of grand stone edifices and bronze memorials floating past them, Dromyrk could not recall exactly how long it was since he had last seen them, except that he had been a lot younger. One thing was certain, though --- horseless carriages had been hardly more than ghost whispers of speculation in those far gone days. Now it was virtually a jousting tournament between growling machines and snorting horses with fear in their eyes. It was a saddening foresight that this 'race' would not have a winning horse.

The more he looked out, trying to identify passing landmarks, the more he felt lost. His vague memories of the city were proving to be deceptive. Several minutes afterwards, he almost regretted dismissing the cab, stepping down into imaginary threatened exposure from all that around him. With honking motors, stamping dray-horses and gigantic brewery waggons narrowly missing him, rushing in from all directions as he crossed the unfamiliar square, his passage was slow – and dangerous. Animals and engines were united in common onslaught against him, it seemed, from the noisy river of traffic flowing around him. He had silly fleeting moments of seeing himself entering the hospital as a casualty case rather than as a new member of staff. Almost granting his wish, the great Mercedes roared past on its 60hp four-cylinder bi-block engine, sparing him only by inches, its polished brass accoutrements flashing warning to other 'suicidal' pedestrians. Waving away the exhaust fumes he stepped up onto the haven of a pavement.

He should have remembered and recognised the mental hospital from its massive bulk. It stood out from the lesser structures; imperious without being palatial. But he didn't. Instead, it was the large fluttering white butterfly that arrested his attention in his sweeping search. The nun's white headpiece flapped in the breeze as she wheeled the patient, huddled low in the wheelchair, across the hospital forecourt. The corridors were bleak, with dark-tiled walls. Their mood was reflected in the wan faces of patients found sitting about, listless and 'lost', round every corner. Dromyrk's heavy stride rang out resolutely on the stone floor so that fuddled minds looked up, and 'out', from inner illusory worlds, expecting to see the familiar tray-loads of cups  of horrible medicine that was forever forced down their throats. But the tall gentleman was not wearing a white coat – wasn't carrying any of that horrible hospital stuff – wasn't in a reckless hurry, unlike the usual doktors who rushed past, anxious to get to who cares where, in this damned place. Curious eyes lost their interest in Dromyrk and returned to their inward-focused glazed stares, where the mind saw only what it chose to see.

Dromyrk stopped a *Krankenschwester*. Her bust was overdeveloped, her teeth surprisingly neat, in a face of pocked skin that saw no cheer beyond her routine nursing duties. The enamel bed-pan she carried was empty, newly washed, but a faint odour of its recent faecal contents still clung to her uniform. 'Guten morgen,' said Dromyrk.

'Guten morgen,' replied the nurse, hurrying on past without stopping. She frowned with open frustration when Dromyrk stepped back after her, to ask her something. 'Die Professor Bernheim?' she repeated, after the gentleman's query, clasping a hand to her furrowed brow. She half turned, pointing in a vague direction behind her. 'He's over in – No, wait – let me think – I don't know. You'll have to ask someone else. Sorry.' She apologised once more. 'Sorry.' She hastened away. A porter came along pushing a trolley laden with bed linen sodden with excrement and urine. He didn't know either. He couldn't help the gentleman. 'Sorry,' he said, trundling his trolley-load on along the corridor.

Dromyrk knocked on the open door of a small office. The hospital *Sekretarian*, bent over a desk covered with paperwork, looked up. He removed his silver pince-nez. An official smile squeezed its way into the pale round face, between the jet black moustache and the sharp goatee beard. When the man stood up, his height was little greater than when he had been seated. 'Can I help you, Herr ---?' The frigid tone was far from helpful to those members of the public intimidated by the hospital's oppressive atmosphere.

'Doktor Dromyrk. I have an appointment at ten thirty,' said Dromyrk. 'With the Clinical Director.' He slipped the letter out of its envelope. The Secretary reached out with a rigid official arm to take it. The pince-nez came up again for official scrutiny. 'Ah, Ja. With Die Professor Bernheim, I see.'

'Ja. That's correct,' said Dromyrk.

'Danke.' With an official flurry of wrist and fingers, the man re-folded the letter and handed it back to Dromyrk. He consulted his watch.

'Ja, there is still time. I will take you there. You may leave your baggage here. If you would care to follow me, Herr Doktor Dromyrk.' The man led the way briskly along the dark corridor. With his stiff straight back and his official status, he saw himself to be as tall as the doktor. Passing the Neurosurgery Theatre and then the Electrotherapy Unit, they finally reached the relatively light atmosphere of Psychotherapy Wing B. Dromyrk waited in the ante-room, while the man entered the sanctum of the inner office, to notify the Professor. After several minutes, the door opened and Dromyrk was bade to enter by the Secretary, who then took his leave.

The room was not as Dromyrk had visualised it. The one bookshelf had more space than books on it, and there was little in the way of academic material, papers, instruments or otherwise, between the four walls. Only a single folder on the plain wooden table. The table, with two straight-backed pinewood chairs, made up the furnishings. It was like an over-furnished monk's cell. Dromyrk saw it as a work-place, rather than the study of one of Germany's most renowned specialists in psychiatric medicine; who had worked under a previous 'great', Wernicke, no less, assisting in his monumental research on *Die Gehirnkrankheiten* – brain diseases – before eventually going on to mount his own pedestal of honour in the field of neuropsychiatry.

The Professor, himself, fitted Dromtrk's anticipated image even less. Looking younger than his four and sixty years, the thin pallid face seemed deprived of an inner vitality. Long thin hands stretched out motionless upon the table seemed, like the face, drained in their paleness. The hair was grey. Dromyrk felt himself slightly dismayed at the message of tiredness and stress sitting before him.

'Bitte nehmen sie platz,' said the Professor.

Dromyrk took this stiff invitation to be seated, attentive of the clever blue eyes reading through him in turn.

Bernheim spoke quietly in a clear cultured voice, smiling at intervals a thin gentle smile, asking Dromyrk a number of basic introductory questions. The folder was flipped open and Bernheim peered down at its contents for several seconds before looking up at its subject, Dromyrk. 'Of Swedish nationality, born in Uppsala, you nevertheless studied your medicine abroad, and not in your own country?' He took another look at the papers. 'Initially at the Salpetriere in Paris and then the University and the General Hospital in Vienna.' Bernheim paused here to make plain the exasperation and anger on his face. 'You chose to study in *Paris? – France? France!*

'Yes,' replied Dromyrk, feeling his uneasiness grow as his confidence began to slide down. He chose his words carefully. 'The Salpetriere has adopted some intriguing, indeed, *fascinating*, exploratory diagnostic approaches in the treatment of nervous diseases --- and one wasn't at war with France – *then*.' A small pause, in hope of his last remark not having gone too far. 'One goes where lighted interest and opportunity beckon; and these two schools, in my opinion, have made considerable advances in exploratory teaching methods, where clinical research is made to work *with*, and not *apart from*, general prognosis and general patient care. As for instance, Doktor Freud's innovative neurological approach to treating aphasia -----'

'And you do not consider any one of our *German* medical establishments, *this one* for instance, to be compatible in their teaching programmes?'

Dromyrk knew that, as medical men, they both had the same answer to that, and saw no need to give one --- one that could hurt a teeny bit. 'My father and my grandfather also studied at these schools.' He smiled back, hoping that would suffice.

'So you had the privilege of studying under Meuller, at the Salpetriere, nevertheless?'

'Under LeClar would perhaps be more accurate; most of the time, anyway.'

'You didn't work with Meuller, then? Perhaps you didn't appreciate or *agree* with his *Teutonic* principles? You found them to be somewhat inflated, perhaps?' Bernheim's searching eyes glinted wickedly as he leaned back in his chair, tapping the desk.

Dromyrk was a little surprised at the hard edge coming into the Professor's attitude, finding the questions beginning to hedge him into a corner. As much as he was aware of Bernheim's mental cat and mouse games, and had expected a certain measure of questioning, somehow this seemed to be wandering off the track. He immediately regretted this thought lest Bernheim's acute observation had caught it betrayed in his expression. 'It's true I was not completely swayed by his clinical insights. But it was more a matter of being assigned specific clinical schedules, and just as luck would have it, those were mainly with Professor LeClar.' Dromyrk remembered how Meuller could be quite unquestionably meticulous in formulating his theoretical programmes, while his strength as such, was matched by his inability to communicate with, and convey his principles, to lesser-minded students. He seldom had the patience to lower himself to a level whereby he could understand what it was that his students couldn't understand. LeClar had been the much better tutor. Understand the *student's* problem, understand the *patient*, was how Dromyrk saw it. 'It was luck more than logical bias.'

'I don't recall inviting luck into the conversation, Herr Doktor. So perhaps you would care to expand on that theory. ' It seemed an odd remark to Dromyrk. A testy, even childish sort of remark. He wasn't sure if he understood, or even recognised, the Professor's method of approach.

As Dromyrk went on to answer more questions, he was sensing more and more that his words meant little in their primary context to Bernheim. It was as if the Professor's soft-voiced questions were on an entirely different level from those behind the eyes that peered out, stripping all that before them. He noted how the Professor's smile came out and faded periodically, irrespective of what was said. Like the lighthouse beacon going on and off as it went round and round. There was also a barely noticeable uncertainty, if not a lack of direction, in the questions. Like a rudderless ship going all out at full steam to nowhere in particular. Dromyrk tried to push to the back of his mind what it could indicate, all things considered, in terms of neurotic symptoms.

He noted the 'secret' fidgeting as a sign of the agitated reaction that bred violent eruption. But if it was just Bernheim testing him, it was a damned good performance.

Dromyrk blinked slightly as Bernheim suddenly lurched forward, to thump the table violently. 'And do you believe you have this patience? This *valuable* patience, Herr Doktor?' Before Dromyrk could answer, Bernheim had swept the folder across the table, and leapt to his feet in an angry motion that almost knocked his chair over. Striding over to the window and turning around he clasped his hands together tightly. Dromyrk saw in his nervous pacing to and fro a mind that was equally at unrest, darting in and out of stability from one moment to moment. 'Can you honestly – can you *sincerely* – bring yourself to say that you have the patience to look into the troubled mind and so understand the suffering? Can you really say that you have the right to go tearing someone's soul apart from the mind? And what of the searing pain you cause the sufferer when all your claims of cure are no more than futile bleatings? And can you put the soul and mind together again after your brutal barbaric ravagings? *Can* you, Herr Doktor?' The words were no longer questions, but impassioned pleadings. The beginnings of a sob had come into the man's voice, and moisture had begun to well in the corners of the eyes.

Not a muscle flinched in Dromyrk's face. He stared on in impassive silence at the 'patient', intrigued as to what would happen next. At the same time, he had a sinking feeling in his stomach that his time had been wasted in coming here, to start a new job. If Bernheim was teetering on the verge of a mental breakdown, from over exposure to patient/doctor 'transference' in his work, and all the symptoms were there, then that job was as good as having flown out the window. The hospital would hardly concede to its eminent Psychiater having fallen ill in such a manner. This would be denied; staff would close rank and the offered post cancelled. Or postponed. His journey wasted.

Concentrating on watching for Bernheim's next action, Dromyrk only just caught the movement on the opposite side of the room in the edge of his vision. A door, of what had been mistaken  for  a cupboard, had opened. A tall man, not as tall as Dromyrk, walked slowly, but purposefully, into the centre of the room's little drama. The room now held a distinct aura of great authority from his presence. Of solid build, he was sternly attired in black morning coat, black waistcoat and trousers, with stiff wing collar and red silk cravat studded with a fiery red diamond. A hard jaw structure gave the face its firm expression. The face was clean-shaven but for the generous side-whiskers reaching down to the chin edges. There was strength in the face; greater strength in the eyes that held Dromyrk in their scrutiny. But there was no hostility there. The look was considerate, as it was kindly, in its examination. Just like the tiger using its teeth to carry the cub by its neck flesh, thought Dromyrk.

Staring intently at Dromyrk, he reached inside his coat for a cigar case. Dromyrk stared back at him, then at the first man, then back at this commanding new arrival. His face lit up, and his eyebrows rose, as realisation began to dawn. He stood up. The man looked over his cigar as he lit it, nodding at Dromyrk to answer the question before it was uttered. *Professor Bernheim?'* said Dromyrk. A long stream of smoke , blown out slowly, was sufficient affirmation. The Professor's eyes twinkled. But Dromyrk could not be sure which way that went. Was the Professor pleased at his little ploy fooling him, or was he displeased because his new member of staff had not tumbled to it soon enough? Bernheim was well aware how such an exposure of Dromyrk's confidential material to a patient could be felt as a personal affront. It was his habit to stimulate reaction in patients through mental prodding. Even in members of his staff. As head of the establishment, he was in a position to do so. In just the very way in which a patient, in a moment of devious cunning, was apt to try reversing clinical procedure by throwing back personal questions, in an attempt to disarm the doctor. Best that this new young member of his staff should be made to realise this now. But he saw no such offence register in Dromyrk face. Good. For the moment, anyway.

His eyes still on Dromyrk, while moving his head slightly to the side, Professor Berheim directed his words behind him, at the 'cupboard': 'All right, Janik'. A white-coated man emerged from the side-room. *Die Psychiatrieschwester* – psychiatric nurse. Not particularly clever-looking, but having that quiet assurance of being able to quell a hysterical disturbance with a gentle firmness that was beneficial to the patient. Bernheim gave the nurse a brief glance, pointing with his cigar in the direction of the other 'Bernheim'. The nurse placed his hands lightly on the man's shoulders, now slumped in shivering resignation, and guided him carefully to the door. Just as the door was being opened, Bernheim stepped over to the patient, to talk softly to him. This had a calming effect on him, so that his shivering gradually subsided. Bernheim closed the door quietly behind them, and turned around to face and attend to his new member of staff.

'An interesting case,' said Dromyrk, collecting the scattered papers on the table and putting them back in the folder and closing it. A thin act of stalling, to gather his wits, that didn't elude the other's astute observation.

'And beyond *"interesting"* – your *diagnosis?*' There was a relaxed manner in Bernheim's words that had no need of formality to force its point across. It was the mark of a true man of science who relied on the logic of his principles. He had come a long way in overriding the almost 'superstitious' resistances of his generation's outmoded reactionary thinking, to the present day's advanced scientific theories. In the same way that his physical health and vibrant personality belied his age. A most laudable bridging of the past to the present.

It was this very characteristic that had attracted Dromyrk to the idea of working under Bernheim, with his fresh-minded consideration for embracing new clinical techniques. He bore this in mind as he shaped his diagnosis in a way that he thought would best suit the Professor's modern opinion. 'His disavowal and displacement mechanisms are quite evident in the way he puts across his command of medical matters, to reverse roles and put himself in the place of the doktor. He would appear to know some basic medicine.'

'As indeed he should. He took his degree only four years after I did, here, in Berlin,' said Bernheim.

'He's a doktor?' said Dromyrk.

Bernheim smiled and nodded. 'Doktor Leifsmann, M.D., no less.' He saw the suspicion forming in Dromyrk's mind, with its question creeping into his face. Shaking his head, before taking a long draw on the cigar, he exhaled the smoke slowly up at the ceiling. 'No, he is not a burnt-out member of staff. Nor did he suffer some phantom contagion from those in my charge, as others, perchance, might allege.' Human sounds from other parts of the hospital floated in from the corridor to puncture the room's bubble of pensive silence.

Bernheim put aside his playing with his cigar for a moment to take a more serious look at the young man standing before him. 'Granted, the work, with its nature of extending problems, can have its heavy toll on the mental faculties. Or perhaps as Doktor Leifsmann was more pointedly putting it: *can* you continually ravage the minds of others, foraging among the disarray of madness for a limbo of sanity, while keeping disciplined order in your own mind, Doktor? Remember, apart from working here, you'll be working in three other centres as well: The Queen Charlotte *Asyl* (Asylum), the military hospital at Beelitz, not far from here, and the city *Gefangnis* (prison). I think you'll find the latter to your interest. Some case histories can tend to be fascinating there. Did you ever have the chance to work with the criminally insane in your training, at all, Doktor Dromyrk.'

'Not on a scale worth mentioning – no. But it sounds most intriguing. Most intriguing. I'm looking forward to it.' In fact, Dromyrk was becoming a little impatient at all the small talk delaying their getting down to the basic issue of discussing work. But he didn't consider it polite or wise to hurry the Professor out of his casual conversation.

Bernheim sensed the other's restlessness and shifted towards the door. 'But enough of this idle chatter. If you'll follow me, Doktor Dromyrk, we'll go and see some cases. Leifsmann first, I think.' He stooped to pick up a piece of cloth, that Dromyrk hadn't noticed, lying under Leifsmann's chair. He handed it to Dromyrk. 'You'll be needing this.' The cloth had a lump of white wax stuck to it. Closer inspection showed that it had been kneaded so as to give the rough semblance of a face.

Dromyrk was puzzled by the Professor's remark. 'Really?

Bernheim took the cigar from his mouth to smile broadly. 'You'll find it *speaks*.'

'Ah,' said Dromyrk with a slow dawning nod. Leifsmann's comfort cloth.

'Ah,' repeated the Professor, with deliberate drawn-out softness, indicating that the other's tardy conclusion had been noted. Returning the cigar to his mouth, he turned and they went out the room.

When they had virtually ran out of corridors to pass through, with only a blank wall left to loom up ahead of them, Professor Bernheim suddenly stopped. 'This way,' he said, opening a grey metal door out into an inner courtyard. They stepped out and walked towards what was the hospital's only recently added extension of wooden outbuilding. 'Specially  built to house our new x-ray unit. We were one of the first hospitals in the country to have installed one. Before the hospital governors decided, in their quiet wisdom, that the hospital should go completely *Psychatrisch*, of course. It's remained here ever since, for screening out-patients only. You know, of course, of Rontgen and his ingenious device – you know, the physics professor from Wurzburg? Well, apparently he used rays emitted from a high voltage wire sealed in a vacuum tube, or something of that sort, to scan the skeletal structure *through* the living flesh, no less. Most ingenious. But uncontrolled exposure to the rays can be harmful, I gather, so they're best kept here, in this building, out of the way of the general public, over in the main building. At least that was the original reason for its being erected. But I have to confess to poaching the territory for my own use. I find that the disturbed mind is more readily receptive to external stimuli when given the peaceful environment of isolation. The defensive shutters are more likely to be raised when removed of the hostile hubbub of a crowded hospital. So I've taken over the rest of the annexe mainly for seeing my more sensitive patients. The only people complaining are the hospital governors, for having to spend more money on larger building plans than were originally intended. But that's the least of my concerns.'

This innocent talk, with its 'displacement' context was not fooling Dromyrk. It was making him nervous in waiting for the next probing remark.

Bernheim pulled open the door to the wooden structure, standing back and bidding Dromyrk to enter first. 'Two generations of surgeons preceding you, and yet you leave general medicine , to come into what is still regarded by some as a somewhat *dubious* branch of the profession, Doktor Dromyrk?' The Professor paused in the doorway to take in another searching scrutiny of the 'raw material' he was taking under his wing, to be honed into a proficiently functioning unit. 'You make heavy statement in your letters of application over Doktor Freud's theories, Ja?'

Dromyrk was tongue-tied for a moment. His lecturer, and mentor, Doktor Freud, at the University had virtually opened a floodgate of innovative thought on the human psyche, giving flow to such a torrent of varied avenues of query, that he didn't know where to start in answering the Professor's question. 'Indeed, yes. Perhaps none too surprisingly in these unsettled times of war, he gives a most uniquely empathic insight to that mode of narcissism peculiar to the traumatised soldier. In fact, just before leaving Vienna, I was privileged to know that he's preparing a paper on the subject.'

He found himself gesturing vaguely in a nervous moment's blocked search for words among the massive reserve that he held in mind. 'I find the field most invigorating. I believe that serious study of traumatic neurosis will render invaluable inroads to both the understanding, and the therapeutic potential, of free association by the patient for releasing repressions of the subconscious.' Dromyrk wanted to continue, but slowed down in his mind, finding himself on 'borrowed ground' – what he'd been told – theoretical principles – brilliant, but *theoretical*, nonetheless.

'Hmmm.' Bernheim knew when he was being 'entertained'. The young man was doing his best to impress. 'And so you would accord these new *theories* – these *techniques* – yet in their infancy – the credence of sound scientific principle?'

There was searching challenge, if not direct opposition, in Professor Bernheim's words. Dromyrk was unsure for a moment, wavering in his choice of response, lest it should be the wrong one. Nerves braced, he took the plunge. 'As the basic platform for establishing an entirely new mode of tackling psychoneurotic syndromes – I don't know. I couldn't be certain for the moment. No more, let's say, than I could fault his theories from what I understand of them at present.' Dromyrk cursed himself inwardly in thinking that he had virtually diluted, if not completed negated, the enthusiasm of his previous statement. The old fox didn't miss a trick. The Professor laughed. But it was a quiet measured laugh that betrayed nothing of its inner judgement.

Their footsteps, clumping on the hollow wooden floor, were the only sounds to be heard. All else was silent, peaceful in its isolation away from the noise of the main building, just as the Professor had said. Reaching the small cubicle that was his office, Bernheim took a clipboard from a row of clipboards on hooks on the wooden partition. He perused it for a brief moment then handed it to Dromyrk. 'Leifsmann, ' he said. 'The third door along. Go along and have a look at him. Come back and tell me what you think.' He turned away to sift among the papers on his desk. Sensing that the Professor had left something unsaid on his mind, Dromyrk lingered on for a moment.

Professor Bernheim had no more to say. Or if he had, he refrained from doing so, busying himself with his work on the desk. It wasn't an air of disapproval that Dromyrk detected in Bernheim. More a sound of reservation. He judged the Professor as one who did not chide unduly. Bernheim was more inclined to calm down disturbances, rather than stir them up. His genial manners were really skilful manoeuvres to douse silly bickering arising among rival staff. With his robust personality this would come across as natural among the weaker-minded. He was a man who, when he spoke, spoke clever words that were appreciated by other clever men. For the less clever – the patient – he would lower himself a level. His opinion and counsel in matters of all sorts were greatly valued. Hence he was favoured equally among patients and colleagues.

Dromyrk walked off to cubicle three. He wondered at his tiny inner twinge of guilt. Was it unwise to have held back his exact feelings? He was intending to set up his own clinical research programme to verify, one way or the other, Freud's postulations on the field of psychoanalysis. He wondered if they would prove to be sound.

Dromyrk entered the cubicle, where Leifsmann was swaying in silent agitation in his chair, under the quiet scrutiny of the same psychiatric nurse standing beside him. A small kidney-shaped tray with a steel syringe sat alongside the patient's medical notes, both waiting ready on the table. Dromyrk ran his eye quickly down Leifsmann's case notes. Chloral hydrate -- for sedating the patient's hysteria. The dosage was more than Dromyrk would have preferred to  prescribe. But he didn't voice this to the more experienced nurse, who was closely watching what he saw to be a new still-wet-behind-the-ears doktor. He smiled a polite dismissal to the nurse. With the man now gone, Dromyrk sat down before Leifsmann, pushing the syringe away to one side. He wanted to see if he could establish connection with that disturbed mind, without the bridge being partially blocked off by heavy sedation from the drug. This, after all, was his first *real* patient.

Two days later, Dromyrk attended the Beelitz military hospital. 'War' was all around him, in the long dark wards, with its woeful legacy of wounds and horrific bone-jutting amputations poorly concealed by bandages, where tincture of iodine seeped through. Low moans of anguish from pain afflicted, not by nature's devious pathology, but by man's very anger of steel upon fellow man. But Dromyrk was interested only in those who had 'nothing wrong with them'. Grey ghosts of their former selves, these much harrowed figures were bereft not only of body parts, but of an inner vitality of life. Theirs was an ailment of relatively recent nomenclature: shell-shock. The easy tag applied from want of a more explanatory term, by those who knew none better. In many a general's eyes, of course, they were malingerers, deserving no better a remedy for their cowardly skiving than the bullet by a firing squad. But Dromyrk, if he heeded Doktor Freud's clinical tutorials, saw severe neuroses. Organically sound muscles 'refusing' movement to limbs and tongues (paralysed/mute), with eyes and ears giving no response to incoming stimuli (blind/deaf), was indicative of hysterical conversion.

The shocked brain, where it witnessed or experienced incidents so horrific as to be unbearable, would 'diverge' by converting these blocked-out memories into physical pain or fault in order to render them in a more 'acceptable' form.

The *Obergefreiter*, clearly not such a case, limped up to Herr Doktor Dromyrk, to hand over his medical notes. The corporal was eager to return to a frontline fighting unit and needed a doktor's approval for his discharge from the hospital. Pale, brooding, with a thick brush moustache, he stood to attention while he looked on. Dromyrk could feel  his eyes boring into him, as if he knew him. An undue strangeness began to stir his memory as he read the medical file: Corporal/Signals Runner/16th Bavarian Reserve Regiment/shrapnel wound to left thigh (Somme)/awarded Iron Cross 2nd Class/zealous request for posting to frontline fighting.

Of course, it was all coming back to Dromyrk now. Quite remarkably, he had only just been passing through, in Munich, when the first encounter had occurred. He saw it now. Two years ago, 1rst of August, in front of the *Feldherrnhalle*, in the city's *Odeonplatz*; the long awaited announcement that at last Germany was mobilising for war; this giving rise to the gathered crowd's jubilant singing of *Die Wacht am Rein* and *Deutschland uber Alles*. And as the  unbridled beast of mass hysterical fanaticism shifted from mere voice to riotous jostling,  Dromyrk had seen, there in its midst,  this same weird individual lowering himself to his knees in an ecstatic outpouring of thanks to God for being born German in this time of glorious war. The man had then gone on to deride the tall Swede, Dromyrk, who was standing over him, for not being as blessed in his birth. But Dromyrk had sensed that behind the mousy-haired small man's mocking there lurked an envy for the greater 'Olympian' stature that was the Swede's 'blessed' birthright.

Dromyrk looked up from the file, at the narrow-shouldered *Obergefreiter*, into the dark cold staring eyes. A weird haunting look. Where irrational fervour beckoned for enlightenment in the darkened recesses of the mind, there was much temptation to enter.

Suddenly, all the uncertainties Dromyrk may have held over the route of his future career fell away, giving place to positive resolve. He *would* make his life's work a study of the mind. His specialist field *would* be psychiatry. This very fundamental resolve of work mode that would affect his future had been brought about by this small, daunting presence standing before him. Dromyrk looked back again to the front of the file, at the corporal's name:

**Unteroffizier: HITLER. Adolf.**

# 1

**London, 1943**

The air raid warden watched a 'lump of darkness' shift against the greater mass of darkness as a figure came round the corner at the street's far end. With house lights blacked out and street lights dimmed or knocked out by Jerry's bombing, you developed ruddy cat's-eyes to catch movements like that on nightshift. He followed the dark shape's slow progress down the street. Even at that distance, strength was discernible in its motion – a young man's strength. But there was an odd jerk to the gait that suggested injury. Not too odd a thing then, what, with this ruddy war taking a fair nick out of the country's young lads. The limping figure stopped every few yards, to half turn and then move on. Obviously looking for an address.

Suddenly, as if to help in this search, giant fingers of white light shot up into the black sky. Great seemingly solid beams, sent out by massive 60 inch diameter searchlights with rhodium-plated parabolic mirrors, criss-crossed each other, scraping the darkness in search of their prey. The lights, with their peak power of 8 million candela, had previously used heat and sound locators, which had been slow in 'pinning' a target, so that thousands of rounds were lost before an enemy plane was downed; now they were fitted with 48 inch radar 'mirrors' to automatically target enemy aircraft more efficiently, and so down them using less ammunition. Sure enough, as the street's only two figures lifted their heads up to listen, there came the just audible ominous drone. It was becoming louder. Another wave of Dornier17s, now opening their bomb bay doors in readiness for dropping their deadly loads of high explosive bombs, 4 tons per plane. Scary rumour was that these planes were now equipped with the means for sending 3080 lb bombs to specific targets, using some form of radio-controlled guidance. Where he had failed to destroy the country's air power two years earlier with his valiant 'Valkyrie' onslaught of 109E-4 Messerschmitt fighters, Goering was now using 4000lb Amatol bombs, with their 3000lb explosive mixture of ammonium nitrate and TNT, as well as 18 inch thermite incendiary bombs to wreak havoc on the civilian populace and so bring the country to its knees. The white beams swung about trawling the night, giving momentary glimpses of giant whale-like barrage balloons. The hydrogen-filled monsters suspended there on their cables with a mind to catching an erring enemy pilot off guard. The darkness was further interrupted by the sudden breakout of brilliant flashes, followed seconds later by the muffled rumble sound of anti-aircraft batteries firing their 28-pounder guns. The Royal Albert and King Cross docks, away to the east side of the city, it seemed, by the look of it. Not having beaten the RAF's control of air space, Jerry was now trying to break the country's morale by destroying its docks and factories. Tracer bullets now joined in, lancing up into the sky in long arching sprays of bright diamond spots, seeking out targets you couldn't see. Low rumbling 'sploomfs' of exploding bombs could now be heard amidst distant orange flashes as the bombers vented their fury on the enemy below.

With danger far away across the city and not his immediate concern, the dark figure turned away from watching it and resumed searching along the street for the right door. He halted abruptly at a new  sound catching his ears. A shrill high-pitched whistling --- 4000lbs of steel and explosives screaming down in rapid acceleration, in sure deliverance of woeful destruction. The man's leg injury made it difficult to dive to the ground, so he hunched his shoulders and drew his arms around his head for protection instead. A slight flinching of the arms as the ground shuddered from the bomb's explosion some streets away. He looked up, angry, at the sky. Don't they teach you Krauts to stay in formation and not stray off-wing, over here, you damn stupid bastard!

The steel ARP helmet came up slowly from its shielding angle in the shadow of the doorway. Satisfied that it was safe to come out, the warden straightened up and stepped out from the doorway. 'You're either very brave, son, or you gave up spelling lessons too soon. B-O-M-B --- BOMB!' said the warden. But the young man walked on past him, not heeding the remark. Try again. 'What number are you looking for?' Still no answer. Old experienced 'night eyes' noted the hesitation building up in the other's gradually slowing steps, pausing and going back two  doors. A flickering of lighter flame to check the brass plate. **Dr O.E. Dromyrk. M.D., F.R.C.Psych**. Going out again before the warden could shout to put it out. The right door at last. A nervous jab at the doorbell. After an eternity of waiting, a thin sliver of light sliced the night as the door was opened cautiously. Low inaudible voices filtered up the street and then the door opened wide. 'Close that bloody door, please, unless you want Jerry to think you're inviting him in for a bloody cup of tea, thank you!' cried the warden from up the street. 'God knows, I could well do with one meself, in this bleedin' cold,' the old man muttered to himself, rubbing his hands up and down his arms, as he huddled back into the meagre shelter of the doorway.

The lady housekeeper, factotum, made no display of seeing the young man's nervousness as he entered. Not even half his face being burnt off and covered in a grotesque mask-like plastic skin shifted her passive expression. She was long hardened to receiving all 'sorts' in to see the doctor. Her mode of attire was just as quiet; a two-piece tweed in light beige checked pattern. Faded to a sombre shade through long use; but that was the better alternative to one of those ghastly utility suits you were supposed to go for with your ration book coupons. She led him down the hall to the consulting room. Knocking on the polished black door at the same time as opening it, she ushered the man in. 'Mr Guther,' she announced to Doctor Dromyrk.

The decades didn't tell too unkindly on Doctor Dromyrk. Just near to ending the fourth one, now in his forty ninth year, yet with a waistline that had defied expansion, and his blond hair allowing greying strands to blend in softly without encroaching, he was 'half his age'. The strong 'harpooner' face had taken on a maturity of years, while still retaining its open freshness. Where the new patient had more or less expected heavy frowning, hairy tweeds and goatee beard, or black suit and starched wing collar, he was surprised at Dromyrk's green corduroy jacket and gold and red paisley pattern cravat. But most of all by the psychiatrist's warm smile. A smile from a small 'harmless' person was one thing; but from such a large strongly built person, where the brain automatically registered possible 'hostility', a warm smile was most beguiling. Hence it was Dromyrk's best 'opening tool'.

Dromyrk rose from his chair, looking at the man for a brief moment, before looking to the woman. She left the room. 'Flight-Lieutenant Guther,' said Dromyrk, returning his attention to the man. He said no more, letting the man stand there in his initial unease, taking in his surroundings in a long slow stare around himself. Dromyrk didn't hurry him. He appreciated that the man needed to settle himself, *find himself,* in this new situation. Coming here, stepping through that very doorway, had taken a certain degree of courage. The threshold to be crossed that divided recovery from gradual inner character disintegration of the psyche. Dromyrk studied the man in the silence poised between them. The plastic made it a little awkward to read the man on that side, but there was much to be discerned in those eyes, the natural cheek and other 'things'. It was evident that much more than just the surface had been scarred.

Dromyrk pointed to the chair. Guther's reaction was as expected. Dromyrk recognised the man's hesitance. It wasn't so much the chair, itself, as an object, that was causing his nervousness; it was the *getting into the chair.* Like getting into the pilot seat of his Hurricane. His plane had been caught in the crossfire between the dorsal mid turret machine-guns of the Lancaster bomber he was escorting and the three-gun salvo of bullets from the 109E-4 Messerschmitt. The 7.92mm bullets from the twin Rheinmetall-Borsig machine-guns mounted in the forward fuselage, and the 20mm burst from the Oerlikon cannon in the propeller hub centre had ripped through his centre fuselage's thin skin of doped fabric and plywood, shattered his leg and exploded one of the two main 34.5 gallon fuel tanks, setting the plane and him ablaze before he could get out. He couldn't clearly recall exactly *how* he had escaped – he'd been jammed between the seat and the control column – 'I don't  remember getting out, or even pulling the cord to open the parachute – but I must have done – obviously.' That last word coming out with delayed pained difficulty.

'*Obviously,*' repeated Dromyrk, giving calming confirmation to the pained disbelief he saw was searing the other's mind. A moment's sober reflection saw the likely answer, with those bullets piercing the firewall of duralumin sheets and asbestos panels, between the engine and cockpit, and tearing into the reserve tank in front of the cockpit, exploding its 28 gallons of 100-octane fuel and throwing the pilot out into the night. What further miracles occurred in the dark to save the man was God's business alone. What horrors the mind couldn't face, it pushed away, beyond immediate recall. But carefully, little by little, it could be prised out. Dromyrk's head gave a slight bobbing motion as he measured the other's pain and the work it placed ahead of them.

'I've only a vague memory of coming to when I was being hauled aboard a torpedo boat – apparently off the Dutch coast – some miles out from Zandvoort, I think someone said. Fortunately it was one of ours.'

'Of course.'

'I learned later that the Lancaster had bought it too. None of the crew had survived. I was supposed to have been guarding them; instead I let them all be shot up. They yell at us in briefing to stay in close formation when escorting bombers – but damn me, I had to stray off-wing—so that we all got damn shot up. I lived and they died – poor bastards.'

Dromyrk knew this, not just from the medical file and Flight Commander's notes lying there before him, but also from the raging conflict going on behind the man's eyes. He idled over the first few pages of the file. 'What did your MO ---' he said, looking down at the file, ' --- Captain Melrose --- make of your situation?'

'Should all be down there, in front of you, damn it. He said he'd done all he could do for me. Sent me for  --- you know.' A resigned shrug and a mock horror tapping at his 'mask'.

Apart from Guther's nervous shifting in his chair, Dromyrk noted how he continually gave a cringing look up at the ceiling light. This especially so when the lights flickered as a bomb exploded somewhere nearby. 'Yes, it can be a little glaring,' said Dromyrk. 'Shall I turn it off?'

'Yes.' The curt response was more of a pleading sound than it was word. *Those flashing guns, three of them, all spurting their deadly burning hot lead venom at him – missing at first, the bullets tearing past the Perspex cockpit — then closer, ripping into the plane --- and him.* Guther was now rocking, if only slightly, but plainly agitated, in his chair.

Dromyrk was up quickly, but smoothly, to turn off the light switch at the door. He went over to the far corner. 'I'll put this side lamp on.' He made a point of turning the lamp's shade away to lessen the brightness. 'It'll balance the one on the  desk  without there  being  too much light.' He went and sat down again at the desk, ready to switch on the lamp, but looking at Guther for approval. Guther's nodding was a mixed battle between yes and no, finally subsiding so that Dromyrk switched the lamp on. Considering the man's horrific experience of mangled bones and burning flesh, his shunning the light was understandable. But there was more to it than that. Only time would see to unravelling that.

The hands on the dial of the desk's ormolu clock moved on and on round, but very few words came out of Guther. He was clearly trapped inside his trauma. But he kept on glancing over at the corner light. At least that was what Dromyrk thought at first. Until it occurred to him that Guther's focus of interest was on the small table *beside* the light. The glinting steel chessmen. Of course! He should have seen that. 'Perhaps you'd like to ---' Dromyrk inclined his head, pointedly indicating the chessmen. With new-found energy, that seemingly came out of a somewhat dead horse, Guther was up and out of his chair. They sat down at the chess table. Opponents mustering for battle anew. But Dromyrk saw it to be a battle of a *different* sort. It would not be the first time that he had used this strategy of informality to 'open up' a taciturn patient. The game afforded the patient diversion from head-on collision with his inner problem. Yet by its very nature of involving the patient in direct conflict in battle, it could also, to a degree, give a measure of the patient's psychic readiness to confront that inner 'enemy'. Dromyk reached out with two closed fists, one concealing a queen. Guther picked an empty palm.

Dromyrk watched the black bishop, knight and queen move in on him in rapid, ferocious attack. He saw Guther losing the queen and knight unnecessarily; and the bishop after that. They were reckless moves. They were *suicidal* moves. Dromyrk stole a glance at the troubled young man. He saw victory imminent in three moves. But he wasn't at all heartened by what he foresaw as Guther's black 'imminence'.

A wailing siren signalled the end of the air raid. But they'd be back and more people would die.

# 2

Dromyrk paused outside the Ministry building to stare down the street at the demolition squad newly arrived to tackle the wreckage from the previous night's bombing. The three-storey house, now bereft of its gable-end wall, was like a woman shamefully removed of her dress, all privacy exposed. A mountain of debris was piled at the foot, masonry and timber splintered like matchboxes crushed underfoot. Goering's foot. To some, the view may have looked like a doll's house, with its rooms now openly displaying furniture and domestic oddments, pictures as yet undisturbed on the the wall and one chair remarkably teetering on the ripped floor edge, one leg out in space. But to Dromyrk it resembled the ailing mind in therapy, the subconscious compartments being brought to the surface in cathartic release. The demolition men set about clambering carefully over the heaped rubble, listening intently for sounds of anyone fortunate enough to be still alive and trapped underneath.

Dromyrk turned away, facing again the grey stone entrance, with its wall of sandbags on either side and two naval guards. The younger sailor stiffened to attention with his Lee-Enfield rifle as Dromyrk approached. But the older one didn't see a uniform or a face he reckoned was official, and so continued smoking his short stump of Players Navy Cut fag. He was right. The big blond bugger didn't spare either of them a glance, walking past briskly up the steps and in through the double swing doors with their 'bomb-proof' paper-taped glass panels.

'I swear, George, one of these days, you're going to land us in the slammer. He could have been *anybody*! Any bloomin' brass hat! Even bloomin' Monty, 'imself, on his day off,' said the younger sailor.

'With that hair, son, he'd more likely have been Rommel. Mind you, the Hun would have to have been on stilts, I reckon.'

'How do you figure that, then, George?'

But George's attention was now held by the cute heart-shaped face and golden curls dwarfed beneath a harsh steel helmet looking out from the hatch of a 'rhino'-bodied 3 ton steel-plated Daimler Dingo scout car. The young WRAC, leading a convoy of three 7 ton Daimler Mk1 armoured cars, all driven by giggling females, smiled and winked at him as she drove past. He watched them negotiate a twisting way through the bomb wreckage strewn across the road, passing close to, and narrowly missing, one of the tarpaulin-covered bodies laid at the roadside. Aye, lad, these pretty lasses were making their mark on the war effort with their ancillary duties, filling out their khaki trousers better than a man could --- even if they still couldn't drive right. He promptly flicked his cigarette end away and came sharply to attention, as a dark-coloured shape wielding armfuls of gold braid rings loomed up suddenly in his corner vision.

Inside the building was the usual warren of dull passages that typified these places, with their confusing identical doors, whereby the stranger dithered over choice of compass or diviner's stick for guidance. Dromyrk had been here before, so just missed needing either. Aside of his professional work, he was now on secondment to the War Office and so was becoming familiar with its maze-style building interiors.

The office was small enough. Any smaller, and the spiders may well have ridden 'piggy-back' for want of leg room. Dromyrk unslung the gas mask from his shoulder and hung it by its long string on the hat and coat stand, beside the other one. The damn things had been an absolute nuisance when you first started to carry them around with you; but since it was official ruling not to be without one, you just got used to them until they grew on you, like an additional appendage that you took with you wherever you went. And what else but that some bright ministerial spark should see that 'baby' wasn't left out, getting his very own Mickey Mouse version. Dromyrk sat down at the curt hand gesture of an indication from Colonel Rutkin. Very few spoken words at the opening moments was the usual form for these little clandestine meetings in these stuffy little rooms. And this one was no different. Dromyrk was accustomed to 'preparatory' silences in his professional capacity and waited patiently as Rutkin turned to the filing cabinet in the corner. The cabinet poked out a rude tongue of a drawer and Rutkin flicked the file tabs with a feverish speed, muttering under his breath. Not finding what he wanted, he slammed the drawer shut. Dromyrk afforded himself a private smile at the cabinet's reluctance to surrender its secrets. Just as he would have done at a patient's initial difficulty in 'opening up'. The Colonel tried another drawer. Finding what he wanted, he swirled round triumphantly, closed the drawer and opened the file, all in one swift motion.

Standing there, examining the file, Rutkin was not likely to strike you as a champion mauler of the wrestling ring. Extremely thin, 'giraffe'-necked, with slender long legs and arms, he looked taller than Dromyrk, although he wasn't. The face, thin and solemnly pale, was not a soldier's face. It carried a look of reticence with him peering sleepy-eyed through heavy metal-framed spectacles. The kind of face you would expect to be forever buried between the musty pages of a heavy academic tome; another of those brilliant university dons swapping his gold and fur-collared doctoral gown for His Majesty's dull khaki tunic, you might think. Another Rupert Brooke, perhaps? But no. Rutkin had been an Army lad through and through from before the time he had first taken the open razor to his chin's soft bristles. The nearest he came to having something in common with the likes of that muse of the trenches was his having crawled through the mud, forever bloodied, be it Passchendale or the Dardanelles.

But there was a quiet strength there that commanded respect. And that wasn't just because of the two pips and crown that said colonel.

The coloured  campaign strips on his chest said more. He may not have known how to juggle his iambic pentameters and iambic hexameters to compose a sonnet, but he *had* known how to turn a bayonet and a Mauser M96 pistol held to his throat to his advantage and go on to single-handedly take out two Turkish machine-gun posts. A deceptively passive appearance. Which was to a soldier's advantage, in that it caught the enemy unawares.

Colonel Rutkin sat down. Engrossed all the while in the file, he thrummed away noisily on the table as he read on. Dromyrk waited patiently. The dossier that Rutkin was reading was a personality profile of Hitler that the War Office had primarily asked Dromyrk to compile when they had first approached him. Having done that, he was now officially engaged in lending his expertise and advice in different aspects, usually psychological, that could affect the country's war effort.

Still looking down at the file, Rutkin leaned low over it on spread-out hands, making ready to pounce and say his piece. 'I can imagine, Doctor Dromyrk, that you've already been over this,' Rutkin said, tapping the thin typed sheets, 'with my predecessors.' He straightened up to look Dromyrk squarely in the eye. 'But I wonder if we can just go over a few points one more time, for my sake. You don't mind, do you? It's just that when this was passed on to me by –eh -- , it was in something of a hurry.'

Dromyrk recognised Rutkin's avoidance of dropping a name. It was the cloak and dagger procedure that he was becoming familiar with, where one was told only what one had to know, and no more. A modus operandi of caution, of safety.

Rutkin lifted up a couple of pages with his finger, then let them drop. 'I know it's all here, in black and white. But like I said, I'd appreciate it if I could just run through a few things with you --- get it straight from the horse's mouth, so to speak.' Rutkin tapped on the table for a long thoughtful moment, then sat solidly upright, pushing his chair back onto its hind legs for a further few seconds, to stare searchingly into the other's eyes. This was no parade-ground-stamping, screech-voiced

NCO sitting before him, house-trained to jump to commands. Hell, no. This was a fully-fledged shrink --- no doubt with a brain clinically divided up into countless little shriek rooms of patients' under-the-sheets oedipal horrors – or something like that. The Colonel wasn't yet quite sure which way his feelings fell with this idea of working with a mind doctor. The only doctor he could see that could be useful to a soldier, was one who hacked off the remains of your shattered leg, where howitzer shrapnel had decided that you only needed one. But he had to follow orders. He broke eye contact and let the chair back down. 'Is that all right with you?'

Dromyrk felt the other's silent scrutiny switch off, knowing that it wouldn't be the last. He nodded. 'Of course. Ask away.'

Rutkin perused a page for a couple of seconds, then looked up. 'And you actually *know* Hitler? You actually worked with him personally – in confidence? Is that right?' A faint lingering of mistrust vied briefly with surprise in the words. Rutkin couldn't keep back his mixture of feelings. It didn't help that this man wasn't British. Rutkin's mind flicked through the file pages for a moment, trying to recall the name of the Swedish town that the Doctor had originally come from in that 'neutral' country, but gave up. The faint, but still traceable, foreign accent in the Doctor's words didn't help dampen these feelings any.

Dromyrk didn't miss the latent message in Rutkin's words. 'I *knew* him, yes. But *distantly*, as a doctor, and even then, only in secondary observation, in attendance with Professor Bernheim. I was still very much in a privileged learning role at that time, as Professor Bernheim's assistant. He tended to the patient, while I looked on. To begin with, that is.' Dromyrk reflected back on how he had first tended personally to Hitler in Beelitz's military hospital in '16. But that was not the Hitler that Rutkin was rooting after. That wounded soldier at that time had only been a lighter shade of the evil dark shadow that was now falling across Europe, blacking it out. But for a few inches more, that shrapnel wound on the leg could have been a critically ruptured femoral artery; a fatal wound that would have changed everything. Dromyrk recalled how, even in those early days at Beelitz, that weird corporal had voiced self-discovery of his messiah-style invincibility, on account of Fate having intervened on his behalf --- his having been spared from death, whilst every one of his signal-runner comrades had been killed  outright by  the howitzer shell  exploding in the trench. Whilst, in fact, he had not been sole survivor, it obviously gave him delusional impetus to claim so, and eventually persuade himself that it had been so. And yet, still not satisfied, Fate had to twist the irony yet again. Returning to the frontline, to Ypres, Hitler had received his second Iron Cross, 1st Class, before being hospitalised again, this time outside Stettin, in Pomerania. He had been  temporarily blinded,  not killed, alas, in a mustard gas attack. Whilst it may not have been obvious then, in retrospect it was apparent that these bellicose experiences, his wounds, his casting death aside, had not weakened the man, but rather, had served to *strengthen* the man's belligerent resolve.

'Ah, yes --- Bernheim,' said Rutkin, cutting into Dromyrk's thoughts. 'This Professor Bernheim – you and he were close-working colleagues, right? And *he* knew Hitler, right?'

'Again, only on a professional basis. He was initially approached by Doctor  Bloch and Doctor Morrell, Hitler's personal physicians, for advice on a subject in which the Professor  could offer prime specialist guidance. Without question, the best in the country, in fact, as far as I was concerned then. Bloch and Morrell were pleased. Hitler was pleased. So the Professor and I  took it from there, attending the patient.'

'It's written down here that you "*attended the patient*", yourself, alone, without the Professor, on a multiple of occasions,' said Rutkin, stabbing the file with his forefinger.

'Well, yes, that was more or less how it was, when Professor Bernheim was busy, and had enough trust in my proficiency, from what I had learned from his clinical sessions, to let me  handle the situation on my own,' said Dromyrk, distant images clouding his mind. He was agreeing rather than give room for argument, so allowing Rutkin a free run with his questioning. It would serve as a rough measure of the Colonel's behavioural pattern. That was going to be useful if they were to work as a team. A War Office missive, delivered by a gauntlets-and-goggles Army despatch rider had informed him of this earlier that morning.

'If I'm to understand you, you're saying that this Professor, the best in the land, could ignore the Fuehrer's personal needs, and send in his second best, instead? Is that what you're telling me?'

'From what I'd learned from the Professor, there are ways of quelling histrionic outbursts of the high-minded – and he wasn't yet Fuehrer in those earlier sessions. On the other instances, my observations were from a distance, while Professor Bernheim would have me work later on his clinical notes.'

'So, if I'm to understand you, Bernheim lent a confidential ear to the Fuehrer's inner woes, passing them on to you, in turn, for you to analyse. Correct?'

'Yes, more or less.'

' "More or less" he says.' Rutkin sat back in his chair, tapping his teeth softly with his forefinger knuckle, emitting a soft 'Uh-huh.' Staring pensively at Dromyrk, he went on tapping his teeth, letting out another soft 'Uh-huh.' Rutkin wasn't quite sure yet if he liked Dromyrk; not that it mattered much, soldier to soldier, where rank ruled the day. But this was a civilian. Not just a civilian, but a 'special' prime catch, and orders from above said that the Doctor was to be 'accorded appropriate authority'. That meant nodding dutifully to all the medical mumbo jumbo coming his way, regardless of whether or not he only understood part or none of it. Well, the Doctor, so far, wasn't domineering or prickly, in the least, unlike what he had expected him to be. He had to admit that. Be wary, nevertheless. Realising that he was fidgeting with the file's corner, he stopped abruptly. You never could tell how these shrink blokes read into your small 'invisible' actions. One blink too many and they knew which of your socks had a hole in it. He resisted an urge to shift his buttocks to a more comfortable position on the chair. Rutkin looked down at the file, before throwing a sharp demanding glance at Dromyrk. 'And so ----?'

At Rutkin's prompting for more information, Dromyrk's mind raced back through the years to distant grey images. That sullen pale face with its broad cheekbones and small staring eyes – dark eyes that glinted with a neurotic glaze of paranoid foresight. His brooding expression had not carried any real semblance of authority. But behind it a lowly corporal was conceivably aspiring after promotion and greater power – imperial power. Not unlike his Gallic predecessor had done a century or so before.

Dromyrk remembered how in those early days, in the Beelitz hospital Hitler had been inclined to isolate himself from the camaraderie that generally arose among the wounded confined to their beds in crowded wards. Even in the shoulder to shoulder closeness of the trenches, it seemed, Hitler had maintained his stand-offish manner. And now, almost three decades later, he was employing exactly the same technique of personal remoteness today. This was to give off an image of the deep-thinking leader in the lonely tower of solitary command. By granting private audience only rarely, he created a sense of awe among those few 'privileged' to approach him. Dromyrk saw that Rutkin needed all this material condensed. Short, straight-to-the-point words. 'He has a highly unstable, neurotic, disposition --- paranoid.'

Rutkin frowned at this last word, not wholly believing his ears. '*Paranoid*? You're surely not trying to tell me that he's a timid little man hiding under the bed in fear of ----'

Dromyrk let out a sigh, waving aside Rutkin's misunderstanding. 'An all too often misconception of the term; caused by the layman's too frequent an application of the term to only one side of the double-sided syndrome. Whilst it *can* mean excessive fear, it can, at the opposite extreme, manifest itself in the individual as a colossal swelling of ego, giving feelings of immense power and righteousness – of his being totally invincible. Of megalomania.'

'Righteousness? So the monster thinks he has the right to do what he's doing? Is that what you're saying, Doctor?' Rutkin couldn't hold back a smile of cynical distaste.

'See it more of a case of his not knowing *wrong* --- as in malignant narcissism. It's the psychosis commonly found in violent criminals and tyrannical personalities, where there is generally a distorted view of reality and failure to develop a sense of morality. Compounding this can be various factors ranging from pathological self-absorption and antisocial behaviour, to persecution complex and unrestrained aggression.' Rutkin felt that this last piece was nothing new to him and was becoming impatient, his time being wasted. Dromyrk saw this, but continued. 'There will be a lack of empathy for others, and general absence of genuine emotion in the individual, with no real sense of self. In all, total identity diffusion.' Dromyrk recalled how, when examining Hitler, he had seen through the man's faked expressions, and mimicking of feeling to suit the situation. 'This state of mind is responsible for desensitizing Hitler from any sense of guilt over his horrendous actions. His malignant narcissism makes him totally devoid of conscience. This is why he's not – nor never will be – deterred by public outcry from other governments. He's not even put off by the threat of censure, or punishment or retribution. How can he be, when he knows, in his messiah mentality, that he is infallibly right!' Dromyrk saw that Rutkin was not at all happy with these words and needed bolstering. He decided that a different vein of 'prognosis' was necessary to stop Rutkin's face darkening any further. 'It isn't unknown for the malignant narcissist to harbour a siege mentality behind the grandiose façade of fearlessness. In argument such an individual believes himself to be invariably right. No-one else can ever be right. But when confronted by solid *physical* correction, this blinkered view, as in Hitler's case, allied to unchanging stubbornness, is likely to cause inner conflict, resulting in psychological disintegration and eventual destruction.'

'Y-e-s.' Rutkin's answer came out slowly as he sat back, tapping his teeth again, plainly wanting all that lot expressed in simpler terms.

'In other words, Colonel, walking into a wall, instead of walking through the doorway. The wall tells the individual that he is utterly wrong, leaving no chance of argument. This contradiction, the wall, which shouldn't be there – which *can't* be there – but *is* there, causes confusion. Small at first, but increasing as more of the 'impossible' breaks through, so that self-belief diminishes, with the breakdown and eventual self-destruction setting in.' A little too simply put, Dromyrk thought, but it would suffice for Rutkin's kind of war *outside* the mind, with its bullets, bombs and bayonets.

'Hmmm, so all we have to do is put up the right 'wall' to stop the maniac. I had thought that was what we've been trying to do all this time. 'If Rutkin had been expecting some kind of psychiatric magic spell to solve the 'problem', he was disappointed. He leafed through the file to newly-added pages at the back. These pages were not Dromyrk's work. They were copies of American OSS records of secret Gestapo files. 'He's certainly terrified of the Jewish situation. Never mind what he says up on the political platform; I mean he's personally frightened. You do know, of course, that when he was born, his name was Schiklgruber?

'Of course,' said Dromyrk.' It was an open secret that Hitler's bastard father, a customs officer, was Alois Schicklgruber. Less open was the rumour that the grandfather was a Jew from the Austrian town of Graz, on the River Mur. Dromyrk remembered Dr Bloch's confidential 'asides' to Professor Bernheim that he'd had to purge Hitler of 'contaminated' blood, using both leeches and syringe.

Rutkin looked up at Dromyrk. 'Yes, but were you aware that the grandfather's grave, indeed, the whole graveyard, was completely destroyed, every trace of it removed, and all parish records burned, by secret order from Hitler?

'I recall the rumours. But otherwise, no, I can't say that I was ever aware of that as a substantiated fact.'

*Substantiated fact? Jesus!* Rutkin felt a burning sensation inside himself that wasn't down to indigestion. It was a growing dislike for what he thought he was hearing. He slapped the folder shut and sat back to stare hard at the Doctor. How do you read the mind of a mind reader? 'Correct me if I've got it wrong, Doctor, but am I to understand that you're defending the heathen monster? How do I get this feeling that you're somehow putting up a defence for that bastard with all your Freudian inroads? Are you trying to tell me that there's a legitimate medical excuse for all his diabolical desecrations? That maybe it's because he choked on the milk from the wrong breast and so suffered a bout of hiccups? Well *are* you?  Because if you are, we'd better get it right out in the open, here and now.' Rutkin was now tapping the desk hard, with fingers that looked as if they would have been happier gripping something heavy, like a massive .455 Webley service revolver.

Dromyrk sighed once more with his inner patience. He'd foreseen something like this happening, and it had. The prejudicial wave coming over the layman, to cloud judgement. Ignore the wounded soldier's different colour of uniform, to apply bandages, and you're seen as colluding with the enemy. Perhaps that was too simple an example, when compared to psychological issues. But the gap in understanding had to be closed, nevertheless, if he and the Colonel were to work together. Dromyrk couldn't stop a tiny smile when, looking at Rutkin thumping the desk, he saw the distraught infant likewise banging the toy train it couldn't understand when it wouldn't work. 'What we're looking at so far is the basic psychopathology of the man; the inner workings, if you like. Just like your own UXB people need to be familiar with the inner layout of that very dangerous unexploded bomb, and diffuse it safely.  To know the nature of the danger. To  know the enemy. I'd hazard a guess that there's a handful of generals out there, on both sides, with their opposite number's photograph getting more attention than that of their grandchildren. That's the general answer to your question, Colonel. On the personal side, as a doctor, I must determine the infection potential of any newly found virus. If I find that it has the pandemic potential to wipe out a country – a continent – then it is my duty to destroy that virus. To know *why* the psychotic patient swings his axe at your head is not to *welcome* or *condone* such action, but rather to know how best to predict and *stem* such an urge in that disturbed mind. Or how to judge which way to duck and avoid the axe's blow, as perhaps, you, yourself, would say. You know this as well as I do – or in this military aspect, *better* than I do. I hope that makes it a little clearer for you, Colonel.'

'Right.' Rutkin stared on for a few moments longer, before his uncertainty allowed a forced smile to crack across a face that seemed a little harder than it had some minutes before. His finger pressed a button underneath the desk. 'Right, right,' he said, jumping both out of his thoughts and out of his chair. He picked up the folder. 'I think we're done here.' Directly on cue, the door opened and a plain-faced WREN stood there. Dark brown spectacles made her plainer. 'There you are, Havers,' said Rutkin. 'Take Doctor Dromyrk along to Ops, will you.' Rutkin looked at Dromyrk. 'I'll be along in a minute, Doctor.'

When the door had closed, Rutkin, standing there, said: 'Well?' seemingly to an empty room.

'Seems okay.' The muffled effect of the hidden speaker only told you that the voice didn't sound English. The door opened to let in another soldier. The uniform was darker, sharper creased, festooned with bright insignia, in typical U.S. Army style. An overall smartness that made every G.I. look like a general, while our fighting lads, in their baggy khaki and anklets, resembled walking potato sacks. Triangular tri-coloured sleeve patches bore cannon and thunderflash of the 2nd Armoured Division. This was a heavy division, comprising two armoured regiments of four medium tank and two light tank battalions of three companies each. A gleaming silver leaf on each shoulder said Lt-Colonel. Not quite six feet, but thickset. The deep tanned face was handsome, if ever a rough bark tree trunk could be said to be handsome. On a bad day, a scowl from it would have had the Boston Redskins cowering in their changing room for the whole game.

Lt-Colonel Brentford Louis Bretzler was with the Division's Field Intelligence Unit. Slicing the blue paper seal on the Chesterfield packet with his fingernail, he tapped out a cigarette. 'Put a tail on the guy, just the same.' The words came out with the rich hard-edged cut of the Mid-West. A slim Manhatton Bendix lighter glinted in his hand, then spurted a flame. He blew out the smoke first. 'Just to be sure.'

'My thoughts exactly,' said Colonel Rutkin. He moved towards the door. 'I'd better get along to the Operations Room, before he starts questioning things and getting suspicious. He's only been given half the story'

'Buddy, if I know my shrinks, he'll already be doing that.' The American saw the frown on the other's face as it questioned this last remark. Letting out a low laugh, he touched Rutkin's arm. 'Relax, Colonel. You're not trapped in a room with a loony meathead. The step-mom teaches that shaboggle stuff at Harvard. Nurtures her very own brood of tomorrow's mind-pluckers. Damn near takes over the house with her discussion groups on 'spare' weekends. It's close odds on the old man quitting the house to take up residence in a padded cell or a wooden box, R.I.P'

The door closed behind them.

# 3

The military-green Austin10 Cambridge staff car swept along the graceful curve of the road winding through the forest of green conifers. 'Should be round the next bend, I think, sir.' Red plume and Black Watch badge bobbed on the corporal's tam o shanter cap as he said this into the rear view mirror for the benefit of the passenger in the back seat. As it was, he hadn't the faintest idea if they were nearly there or not. But he had to say something to keep the man happy, seeing as how he kept checking his watch.

At last the trees around them fell away, giving sight of a small copse of stone 'trees' ahead of them in the distance. Tudor-style 'corkscrew' chimney turrets giving off lazy twirls of smoke to the sky. Vertical streaks glinting in the sun were the tall windows that broke up the surface of the red stone mansion. Lindwell Hall. Away to one side, across the empty landscape, two tiny figures were diligently working away, one of them at some form of agricultural contraption. They were both women. Not by their shape or movement, but by their colours. Green jumpers, brown cord breeches and black 'wellies'. The 'uniform' of the Womens' Land Army.

This forming of a womens' army had come not a moment too soon, in 1917, when the country was in a desperate situation, its morale critically low. It wasn't enough that Kaiser Wilhelm had fiercely dented Britain's confidence with his devastating penetration of Scapa Flow and destruction of its *safe* Home Fleet. This by torpedoes from German submarine U-17, under the command of Kapitan-Lieutenant Prien, on October 1914. After three grim years of holding out against enemy blockading of British ports, and critically high rate of our ships sunk by U-boats, the country's food stock was then down to a critical three weeks. We could not afford to rely on the country's food supply being imported. We would have to produce this from our own soil and effort. The massive deployment of our men and horses in foreign battlefields meant that only women were left to carry out this urgent new task. So the new Land Army came into being. Laying aside needles, thread and ironing boards, women were taking to the great outdoors on a massive scale, to tackle the land with spades, pitchforks, tractors and threshing machines. These women were now an important integral part of the war effort, right on the heels of the men's active fighting force. Their battlefield was the farms and market gardens, with an extra six million acres of land being converted for cultivation to produce enough food to feed the Armed Forces and also the Home Front population. But in addition to essential food for the people, vital materials were also being supplied for the war machine. A smaller select army of lasses, given the task of managing forests and running sawmills, was producing timber for part-structuring our fighters planes, bombers and other aircraft, and wooden-structured minesweepers. Special charcoal, necessary for the manufacture of high explosives, was also being obtained from alder buckthorn bushes.

A high spiked wall hid the select dwelling, except at the gateway, where the building leapt out in bright patches of sandstone, to penetrate the surrounding grove of snow-sprinkled larches. The large building had reproduced itself in countless little chips covering the driveway and scattered up the stairs under the stone portico. They parked beside the matt grey Plymouth P11. The white star on its side marked it as strictly U.S. Army property. Dromyrk followed the corporal into the house. Entering the hall, they brushed under palms held in the jade grip of two grimacing Chinese warriors mounted upon two wider-grimacing jade dragons. A narrow carpet of raw sienna ran down the centre of the polished teak flooring in front of them. Broad staircases on each side of the hallway ran up to the balcony, where an ancient crest emblazoned the balustrade centre.

Somewhat incongruous in this setting was the khaki-clad figure seated at a modern metal table, gulping down a mug of tea. The private put the mug down hastily and got up to approach them, asking to see their passes. The corporal was annoyed by this, on account of his rank. But he held back from bawling the private down. Because there was an officer over at the French window watching him. One of those swank Yanks. They showed their security passes.

Lt-Colonel Bretzler casually ambled over to the little group. He spared a few moments for an openly humorous inspection of the red cockade, then the regimental tartan trousers, before raising his eyes to meet those of the bearer. 'Pants today, instead of the kilt? Makes sense, I guess, with this lousy weather. Go grab yourself something to drink, Jock. There's tea and coffee in the kitchen, way back there, somewhere. At least it's what you Brits call coffee. It's the one that tastes worse than the tea. Tastes more like burnt-out Detroit engine oil.' He watched the corporal walk away, then turned round to face Dromyrk, pointing behind him, over his shoulder, with his thumb. 'Great guys, those Jocks --- those bagpipes sure scare the hell out of me – never mind the Krauts!' His 'Hollywood-white' teeth suddenly flashed out a diplomatic signal of friendly fire. 'Glad you could make it, Doc.'

Dromyrk caught the subtle teasing note in the jovial words. If Rutkin was one to hold down his rising vexations behind an officer's self control, this one, in contrast, would be batting his sore points sky high right out of the stadium – officer's self control be damned! As they walked up the left staircase, Bretzler pointed to the brightly painted heraldic shield. 'Great things these old family name tags, with their Latin mottos --- tells you things,' said Bretzler, transferring his look and innuendo from the crest, to Dromyrk. 'Like your name, for instance. I've been giving some thought to that, along with some reading. Let's see now – Drom – that's *dream*, right? Then Myrk  -- that's a distorted derivative of *dark*, right? That's dark dream, or nightmare, if I've got my numbers right. So if I'm on target, I'd say your folks, way back, were well ahead in the game as shrinks. I'd guess as a mixture of soothsayer and herbalist mind healer. You don't have any records of old great granddad being burnt at the stake, do you, Doc?'

Dromyrk smiled, nodding to himself in inward appraisal at the Lt-Colonel's effort. 'The concept is not entirely without premise, I grant you. However, I find it hard to imagine you mounting your earnest search into my family's entomological origin solely for the purpose of leaving it "way back there," when the focus of your real interest is much more recent. *Here, in person, in fact.*'

Bretzler let out his characteristic soft chuckle. 'Touche, Doc. Boston Redskins,One; London Shrinks, One.' Jeez, but how these Brits put their words, even if he was a Swede. He had to admit that he sure liked the smart way they put their words together in precise syntax formation. Just like those machines in the bowling lanes dropping their polished nine-pins down in their right places. Whoa, buddy. Careful there. Got to be sure of the guy first. 'Okay, okay, Doc. But like I was saying, we're sure more than happy to have you here. A lot of our guys are getting the shakes. The nerves in a hell of a  shattered  state. Some  near  breaking point, I'd  say.  And  these are not rookies, fresh out of college, with 'Fraternity Alpha' initiation candles still dripping  wax  from their bare asses. These are old hands – the tough guys, back from one mission too many not a second too soon.' Dromyrk saw a serious look cut through the otherwise casual expression on the American's face. He'd worked with Americans before, as patients, not many, but this one, even in his military role, was proving to be intriguing, purely as a character study. 'We need your professional touch, Doc, in looking the guys over.'

'From what you're saying, I'm assuming the situation to be somewhat more acute than what I had gathered from Colonel Rutkin's briefing.' The operational details given to him by Rutkin  at yesterday's meeting had indeed been very sparse. Whether this was from a soldier's form of getting bluntly to the point, or because Rutkin was not yet sure if he could fully trust him, was not yet clear to Dromyrk. It was little wonder that Rutkin hadn't thought to use even less words by tapping out instructions in Morse code with his pencil. But then this was an SOE (Special Operations Executive) training school, so perhaps this was to be expected. Winston, himself, had given the 'green light' for setting up SOE, declaring an urgent need for 'dirty tricks', if we are to win this war. MI6, alas, had not been so happy, looking down on the new lot's amateurish status and disapproving of their cloak and dagger skulduggery as being below that of good old professional intelligence gathering. They had nevertheless acted as overseer of SOE's efforts up until '42. Now SOE was its own boss, running its own missions totally independent of the other intelligence agencies. It was virtually answerable to no-one but the PM. And Winston wasn't asking any questions.

A number of these secret training centres (hush-hush whispers said six) had been set up outside of London, safe from the bombing, but still within reasonable travel distance from the city. Through early liaison with America and Canada, SOE had set up a training centre for special agents in Oshwaka, near Toronto, and so was partly responsible for the subsequent setting up of America's OSS, Office of Strategic Services. Further cooperation with the American Forces had seen two airfields (Tempsford and Harrington) specially assigned to SOE for dropping 'Joes', as the Yanks were apt to call them, from specially modified aircraft, into enemy territory. This centre used the Harrington airfield, (USAAF 179 Airfield Code HR) which had been built courtesy of US Army Engineers. Thanks, guys; we Brits very much appreciate your help.

'Through here,' said Bretzler, pushing in a panel of false book-spines that was a door. 'Clever lot, those ancient aristocratic guys, building all these secret passages. Not only did they dodge the king's heavy man when he came to fill his tax loot-bag with gold sovereigns,  they could also dodge the nagging wife and slip off for a sly one with the buxom broad in the village tavern.' He glanced over his shoulder to catch Dromyrk's attention. 'But I guess things'll be a little more liberal in your country, Doc. With all that easy partner-swapping and bare-but birching in the snow. Mind you, it beats me where the fun comes in, with the frozen balls falling off.'

'Our laws do have their points of censure, I can assure you, however well they may elude the foreign eye. As for your fear of losing those *frozen assets* --- perhaps we have our way of eluding that also.'

'Oh, yeah?' But Dromyrk didn't go on to enlighten Bretzler on that point. 'You don't say a lot, do you, Doc? I tell you that for free. But I see your technique. You observe and absorb. Like a sponge. You're taking all this in, the fun, along with the serious, making whatever it is you can of the total fudge with your analytical mind. And not giving out one word of a clue. Good, good. That's what I like to see. That's why you're here. You'll see why in a minute.'

As Dromyrk followed Bretzler through the dark, he could tell that it was a narrow passage from the wooden beams brushing his shoulders. Bretzler opened another door in front of them and they were in a small room with dim light coming from somewhere. A faint draught brought a mouldy smell to the nostrils. Bretzler fumbled for a few moments until there was a click. A screen lit up before them. 'The original owners, centuries ago, liked to spy on their guests. They had their very own peep show through a hole in the eye in the oil painting on the other side of this wall. Now it's our turn to do some spying. With the help of our technical wizards and their fancy optical gadgets, we can improve on the original peep hole's narrow field of view, with a panoramic view of the whole room, camera obscura style.' He stepped aside, to let Dromyrk have a better view. 'What do you think?'

The room, a 16th century drawing room, was spacious, with books taking up one whole wall. Morose faces looked down from the other walls, their stares forever suspended, along with polished blades that were a little too large to be cutlery, mounted between them. But Dromyrk's attention was drawn to the six live occupants in the room. Four men and two women. Two of the men were in earnest conversation, leaning in to speak in low tone. Each of the other four seemed barely aware of those around them. Seated back in their own dull leather armchairs, they were indrawn, their minds elsewhere. Even at this distance, Dromyrk could see the subtle signs of nervous tension. Agitation in aftermath of harrowing experience. His eyes still on the screen, he half turned to Bretzler. 'I'm to work on these six?'

'These and another five. They're still in the process of debriefing, following their recent mission, and then further training and briefing for separate missions in France and Holland. We need to be sure that they're up to the task. That's where you come in, Doc. Assessing their mettle. When we drop those 'Joes' through that freezing black space in the plane's floor, out into the night, there's no turning back. And we can't afford to be dropping duds. One dud can put a whole mission in the ditch. Contacts, networks, lives, months of preparation --- the whole damn lot --- *caput!*'. Bretzler stepped forward, to peer more closely at the screen. 'This lot here --- we were lucky to get them back. Perhaps I should say that *they* were lucky to get back. Pulled them out by the hair, more or less. There should have been another one. He didn't make it. Best information we have is that he's dead, or mortally wounded, but not quite dead. Between these two options, hell would be a better place if those SS torturers get their hands on him.' Bretzler switched the screen off and turned away in quiet anger. 'The Krauts, damn them, were already waiting for our plane to fly in onto the tiny field strip near the small village of Pillac, in the Vaucluse province. Even with the local Resistance giving us covering fire, it's a damn miracle how we still managed to take on our load and get back into the air.' He paused for a moment. 'But then, maybe it wasn't luck --- maybe it was *arranged.*'

'Arranged? Are you implying that ---?'

'That's *exactly* what I mean, Doc. Maybe there's a spy on the loose somewhere along the line in our lot. That'll be another one of your tasks --- rooting out the bastard. You can do that can't you? With all this new body language and quiet signs your lot go on about? Was it not Freud who said there's no such thing as a real slip of the tongue?

That everything that comes out has a definite target, no matter how roundabout and accidental it happens to sound? But then, you're not going to answer me on that question either, are you, Doc? Another of your trick cards, held close to the chest.' He was right. Dromyrk didn't comment on the remark.

Going back downstairs again, they were confronted by a small man in the hallway. Bright rosy patches on the cheeks spoke of a life spent in windblown open countryside. 'Colonel?' The accent was openly foreign. A man proud of his country. With that nasal tone, French, perhaps, Dromyrk figured. With the man clearly knowing the Lt-Colonel, the querying note in his voice was plainly asking after the identity of the stranger, blond, like German, accompanying him.

'Ah, there you are, Palpiere.' Bretzler looked from one to the other as introduction between them. 'This is Doctor Dromyrk. He's joining the team. Doctor Dromyrk, this is Al Palpiere. Al runs our ---'

'*Alphonse*, Colone!'

'Sure, okay. *Alphonse* does his invaluable lot in making sure our guys get the French angle right before flying out on their missions. Can't have them ordering Old Kentucky bourbon and knickerbocker glory in the Café Parisienne, when it's maybe Gestapo Gretel wearing the waitress's apron.'

Palpiere had previously worked in the fields and vineyards of Toulain in the Bassin district, until the Boche had decided to take his job, his village, his country and his *libertie* away from him. Now his bitterness was driving him to reverse all that by his training these men and women, down to the smallest detail, how to take on the natural mannerisms of ordinary everyday French folk. This was essential if they were to avoid detection as enemy agents. A single word or gesture out of place, and kindness would be the choice of being blindfolded or not, when put before a firing squad. The Frenchman's attention was held by the docteur. 'Dromyrk? That is ---?'

'Swedish,' said Dromyrk.

'Ah, oui, Suedois --- *Swedish*.'

Dromyrk detected the faint contempt in the man's words, especially the last. This derision, directed at Sweden's remaining neutral in time of war, was ignored by Dromyrk, in the same way that he tolerated patients' occasional outbursts of hostile remarks. There was nothing else he could do. But his country was doing a considerable lot in its own way for the Allied Forces. Through its non-hostility to Germany, it was avoiding invasion and any subsequent military suppression. Hence it was free to act as it wanted. It was thus able to provide the neighbouring Scandinavian countries with vital supplies. By allowing Germans to use the country's telephone and telegraph systems, Swedish sources were tapping into thousands of messages sent by Germany's Baltic Fleet, and so passed on valuable intelligence to the Allied Forces. It was also giving training to thousands of Norwegians and Danes preparing to reclaim their land. The country, because of its 'neutrality', was also a great sure haven for Jews. A great many thousands of these persecuted people were being smuggled in from Denmark, Hungary and other Nazi-vanquished lands, to be given open asylum in Sweden. All this deadly mischief and more, Sweden was carrying out under Hitler's very nose. Inasmuch as Dromyrk knew of his country's laudable effort, how was he to explain this to the embittered Frenchmen facing him? Hence his letting it go. He was long since quietly hardened to patients' subconscious 'transference' of anti-parental hostilities onto himself.

Bretzler was enjoying the moment of coolness between the other two. He interrupted their awkward silence. 'Is Major Drummel around?'

'No. The Major has gone to ---, ' Palpiere paused, '—to check the night flight time for ---' Palpiere paused again to look with uncertainty at the docteur. He wasn't at all sure how much of their secret programme he could reveal in front of this Nordic-looking stranger.

Bretzler nodded his assurance. 'It's okay.'

Palpiere continued, only a little bit more assured by the Lt-Colonel. 'Major Drummel has gone to the airfield to set the last minute timings for Operation Zeta.'

Bretzler turned to Dromyrk. 'Major Drummel, one of your guys, runs the show here.' Anxious to get on with things and not waste any more time, Bretzler started to edge away. 'Okay, Palpiere, I'll let you get on with whatever it is you're doing, while I show the Doctor around. Come on, Doc, I'll take you round the place, with all its wacky departments and even wackier people. Boffins and weirdoes. Yeah, we've got plenty of those.' Stepping out into a cobbled stable-yard, its stables now converted to hush-hush war effort workshops, Bretzler looked up at the main building's face. 'I swear when this lousy shit of a war is over and done with, half of the mad crew in this place will change back into those goddam gargoyles with a mere magic puff of smoke.' But the stone faces simply glared down at Bretzler, sticking out their tongues at this crude sentiment. One couldn't expect anything better from a foreigner --- a *Colonial*, at that!

# 4

*He turned over with a hard rightward pressure to the control column to bring the Hurricane's port wing up to right angles with the horizon, and some foot pressure to the starboard rudder pedal to keep the nose from rising. The port wing fell over until it was parallel to the horizon again, but now upside down. Pulling the stick back, the nose fell towards the ground, going down vertically on the Messerschmitt 109s escorting the twin-engine Dornier 17 bombers directly below. For bombers, they were damn tricky buggers to hit, their narrow fuselages giving you less of a target to pin down on your sights. Speed built up rapidly from 300mph -- 360mph – 380mph -- to just over 400mph. Tipping the ailerons, he turned the plane from side to side in the vertical plane. He placed the sight's red dot in line with the port side engine of the Dornier about three hundred yards below him. He pressed the red firing button on the stick, and through the inch thick Perspex windscreen saw the double tracer streams of bullets from the wing-mounted .303 Browning machine-guns slicing empty air just left of the bomber's engine. Pushing the stick more forward, his plane was past the vertical and gravity tried to throw him out of the plane, pushing him up into the cockpit's Perspex canopy. Tight harness dug hard into the shoulders. Blood rushed to the head, and his vision went red. The tracers were now striking the Dornier's engine, sending metal fragments flying off it. Fright seized him inside. His plane was getting too close to the bomber. He was going to crash into it. Pulling frantically on the stick, he was away just in time, missing collision with the bomber's starboard wing. Foot down, and tipping the ailerons, he banked the plane to port, pulling hard on the control column, so inflicting tremendous gravity strain on the Hurricane's frame. Great force pushed him down hard into the  cockpit seat once more. His vision went black. Long seconds of alarming blindness, then easing the stick so that sight returned. He banked the plane onto its port wing-tip to pull it round, then completely over, pulling back hard on the stick in a tight loop-over turn, blacking out again for an eternal few seconds, then tipping the ailerons to bring the plane upright once more. The Hurricane climbed slowly. Turning left slightly, he suddenly saw it. Red tracer cannonade coming towards him from the centre of the Messerschmitt 109's bright yellow nose hub. He turned the Hurricane sharply over onto its back and dived. The Messerschmitt copied the turn, its cannonade still cutting the air alongside him. Still in a furious dive, eight hundred, nine hundred, one thousand feet, Hurricane, followed by tracer bullets, followed by Messerschmitt. God alone knows how he wasn't hit. Easing his dive, he turned the plane onto its side, pausing there a second, then pulling the nose up, to come round in a complete barrel-roll. Where the hell was the 109? It had vanished. Gone off to catch some other nervous pilot by surprise with its poison spray. He continued to weave about the open sky, as he'd been instructed, as all new pilots were instructed, but wherever he turned, wherever he dived, fear, disguised as tension, was his companion.*

*Watch out! Two Messerschmitts coming out of the sun rapidly in a sharp curving attack towards him. Finger down hard on the button, his Browning machine-guns thundered in double judder, their .303 bullets ripping off pieces of tail that hurtled past, rasping on his fuselage port side. The 109 shifted to port. Its tail structure broke up, a large mangled piece, with glaring swastika emblem, raced back, bouncing off the port wing. Duck! His head ducked in reflex as the jagged fragment flashed past, somersaulting as it touched, but miraculously didn't smash cockpit's Perspex. The green and yellow fuselage fell away below. The other Messerschmitt banked steeply to starboard and over onto its back. He turned the Hurricane over and upside down likewise, firing at the 109's blue underbelly. The North Sea was now over his head as he pushed the stick forward, while keeping his sights on the 109. The Hurricane's Rolls-Royce*

*1,050 h.p. Merlin engine spluttered and stalled, its carburettor temporarily denied its vital high-octane fuel. The propeller idled helplessly for a second. Rumour from Intelligence was that the Messerschmitt engine had an injection fuel system, giving guaranteed constant flow of fuel even on an upward climb, unlike our Spitfires and Hurricanes that used a sump pump system, causing stalling in a loop climb. But that was strictly 'hush-hush'. Mustn't dampen morale. The hell of a harness dug hard into his shoulders. Flames leapt from the 109 yellow nose engine. Suddenly a loud bang from behind him. A large hole gaped on his port wing-tip, ragged fingers of torn fabric sprouting up around its edges. He broke away from the Messerschmitt, pushing the stick to the right, turning steeply to starboard and pulling the control column back hard so that he blacked out for a long moment. Easing out again, he saw two, no, three, 109s flash past his tail. Where the hell did they come from! But they didn't hang around to attack him further. Blasting a hole in his wing had been enough for them to move on, hungry for the kill. 'Nearly lost you there, Red One --- Keep searching around you everywhere, for God's sake.' The radio's crackling words from Red Leader were replaced, after moments of spluttering static, with on-and-off bursts of imminent danger alerts from different units, each held in their own gripping moments of life and death urgency: 'Watch your tail, Bonzo.' --- 'Where are you, Dodger? Bloody well stay on my wing' --- 'Bandits at two o'clock, Jimmy.' --- 'Behind you, Harry, behind you!' Jerry also shared frantic moments over the radio: 'Achtung. Achtung drei Spitfeuer unter, Achtung, Spitfeuer.' Someone was even playing chess! 'Queen's knight to bishop three.'*

'Queen's knight to bishop three.' Doctor Dromyrk voiced his move aloud so as to cut into Guther's faraway thoughts.

*Black menacing shapes flashing past around Guther, in criss-cross mode of a typical aerial dogfight, faded as he came out of his confused reverie. Disturbing staccato gunfire gave way to what* he began to recognise as the psychiatrist's voice from what seemed a long way off across a small chess table. He also heard another voice which he came to realise, surprisingly, was his own. 'You hang on in there through sheer fear – the old adrenalin and blood pumping their way round like hell. It's either you or him. If he doesn't  go down, it's your plane that goes down.' Looking down dreamily at the array of pieces, Guther moved his pawn with a heavy slowness. He looked up at Dromyrk. 'Flying out at the start of a mission always gripes your guts. But seeing Jerry there in front of you, coming towards you at four hundred miles an hour to kill you, really grips your inside,' a long anxious pause, 'until you pressed the button to get him first --- before he gets you. Before he gets you.'

Dromyrk saw Guther's words come out with struggling difficulty, between pauses of nervous breathing. There was also a glistening patina of sweat coming out on Guther's forehead. With this, and the facial twitches, Dromyrk tried to measure the degree of torment seizing the man's mind. There was evidently much horror there, re-running itself over and over again, like an endless reel of film. He moved his bishop, warning Guther of looming checkmate in three moves, to prompt the other danger in his mind. And waited. But Dromyrk wasn't expecting a landslide of traumatic revelations to come pouring out of Guther like toppling dominoes. Not at this early stage. But every little psychological prodding helped. Guther was fighting a brave solitary campaign against his inner enemies. But until he found the strength to bring this out in spoken form, to be shared with his doctor, his battle was far from won. He watched Guther's attention on the chessboard lessen as it strayed inwards, elsewhere, once again.

*He saw the Spitfire go down in flames on his right, just as a Messerschmitt 109 hurtled past in half roll, climbing away from its kill, into the sun. Pushing the stick left, he banked to port, away from the Lancaster bomber he was escorting, to chase the bastard 109. Closing in to about two hundred yards, thumb hard on the red firing button, he sent out a fierce juddering two-second burst of bullets. Fragments of wing flew off the 109 and its engine started coughing out black smoke. But it was still there, stubbornly refusing to go down. Another two-second burst, the wing gun-ports spurting out their .303 tracers. Red flames now erupted on the engine, spreading rapidly, to engulf the wing, so that the Messerschmitt dipped, to take a corkscrew twisting dive, down, down, down out of sight.*

*Suddenly a large explosion, wrenching the control column out of his grip. The whole plane was juddering around him like a wounded beast in its last throws. Flames shot up everywhere in the cockpit. He tried to open the canopy. Jesus! It was jammed! Corrigan hadn't fixed the fucking faulty catch! Tearing off his harness for better movement, he managed to force the canopy back. He reached for the stick, to turn the plane on its back. His leg was trapped! It looked odd? Bones somehow pointing about at odd angles and blood pouring out all over the place. How did that happen? He couldn't think how, with nausea rising up inside him. The heat was so great so that he fell back in his seat, feeling he was about to pass out. A moment of fright seized him. Death was about to take him. He passed out. He was conscious again. He was free of the plane and falling rapidly. Down, down, down towards the sea. A tug at the parachute's rip-cord and his descent slowed with a joint-jerking jolt. The parachute splayed out around him and the lifejacket kept him afloat in what was not cold water. One of his flying boots was hanging off --- or was it part of his leg that was hanging a funny way? A horrible sickening smell came to him. Burning flesh? From where? At the corner of his vision, a swollen blubbery mass of dead flesh that had been his outer face. Hundreds of searing needles stung what was left of his face underneath. A piercing pain in his left leg and hip. He couldn't pull the parachute harness because of pain in his arms and hands. Everything hurt. He lay back. The sky was peaceful and sleepy. They were hauling him into the boat. Was it a fishing boat or a gun-boat? He couldn't be sure. His mind was groggy, confused after-shock. Their voices sounded foreign. French, was it? Or Dutch, maybe? Asking him if he was all right. Saying something about water.*

'Are you all right? asked Dromyrk. 'Would you like a glass of water?'

Guther struggled to find his way out of his inner mish-mash of confused memories. He shook both his head and his hand, dismissing Dromyrk's offer of a drink; he didn't need it. He was all right. But this was incorrect. He was far from being all right. Very much so.

Dromyrk saw Guther's delirium of jarring mental images escalating to the more disturbed state of outer agitation. First the faint twitching of fingers. This becoming whole hand jerks. Spreading to arm shifting. Shifting restlessly from side to side in his chair. Just as if he was fighting the enemy on all fronts, having nowhere safe to turn to. This  caused memories of another 'trapped soul' to jump up in Dromyrk's mind. The decades fell away. Berlin.  He hadn't quite believed it when Professor Bernheim had first told him. But he had seen it for himself  later, whilst  waiting in attendance in the vast Reichstag antechamber. A glimpse through the massive 17 ft high doors into 400 square metres of sanctum sanctorum that was the Fuhrer's own office. What he saw within hardly matched the almightiness around it.  Pathetically puny was a more fitting description. Hitler, in histrionic tantrum, was beating his fists on the vast desk, screaming in rage, before planting himself against the wall, his arms spread out in plaintiff posture of the ever suffering martyr. Seen more deeply, it was a child's tactic to summon the doting mother's protective sympathy. Working on the notes given to him by Bernheim to analyse, and Hitler's earlier medical history passed on to them by Dr Bloch, Dromyrk got his first real insight into that brooding dark mind. These hysterical outbursts were a common occurrence when Hitler's authority was challenged, so that he had to play the long-suffering martyr. He was caught between a domineering father and a loving mother whose excessive attention had critically hindered his emotional development. With the mother not intervening when the father had beaten him, he had hated the mother as much as the beatings. An inner conflict of allegiance between mater and pater that had greatly distorted Hitler's judgement of absolute values. Mentally torn between opposing forces, an ogre personality was evolving. Hence his calling Germany, 'Fatherland', where a pathological urge was decreeing a need for self-supremacy over all others – a need to challenge, override and annihilate all opposing forces – a need for war.

Dromyrk got up promptly and stepped over to Guther, to pull up his eyelids for a brief look at the eyes. He then went over to the steel-framed glass medical cabinet perched on top of the lacquered Chinese corner cabinet. Opening the glass and steel door, he took out the small phial of chloral hydrate and the steel syringe. As well as the small bottle of antiseptic and a small cotton wool swab. Putting these down on his desk, Dromyrk flipped Guther's file open to check his medication dosage. He then drew 6mls of chloral hydrate into the syringe. Guther's restless movements made it awkward to remove his arm from his jacket. But taking a strong grip of the patient with his large 'harpooner's' hands, Dromyrk managed this, pulling up the shirt sleeve to dab the arm with the antiseptic swab. Holding the arm firmly and pressing with a strong thumb to bring out the vein, he inserted the needle.

Withdrawing the needle, Dromyrk took another look into Guther's eyes. Satisfied, he went back to the desk to press a button to summon Mrs Morton. He returned the needle and phial to the cabinet.

Guther's agitated movements were gradually subsiding. The door opened and Mrs Morton came in. 'He's in no state to leave just at the moment,' said Dromyrk. 'We'll let him sleep it off on the couch in the drawing room. We'll need a blanket.'

No further words were necessary. She understood. 'I'll fetch one,' she said, turning to go back out.

'Have you lit the fire in the drawing room?' said Dromyrk. He was thinking how cold the large Edwardian room could be without a fire, especially in this weather.

She stopped. With her back to him, she clasped her hands together tightly, her lips taking on a similar tightness. Her mind fought with annoyance at his silly question. Of course it wasn't lit. With coal rationing as it was, you had a better chance of seeing as much as a spark in the grate with one of those incendiary bomb things coming down the chimney, heaven forbid. He was always telling her to spare the coal. Now here he was asking her if the fire was lit. You couldn't help thinking that he didn't appreciate the trouble she went to, in keeping the larder stocked as best she could, with this terrible rationing. Him being big, he  had a big appetite, so she had to go to great lengths to provide for his meals. You had to search around for the right shop for what you wanted, to make it worth your while joining a long queue. One egg a week allowed per person, and he'd had that, as well as three ounces of the four ounces of bacon allowed. His one shilling and ten pence of meat ration had gone on a large chop, so she would spend her ration money on a larger amount of cheaper meat, so that she could make a stew for both of them. She would have to walk further now, seeing as how Heckill's had been hit – half the street with it – nothing but bricks left where the shop had been. Poor Mr Heckill and Sally had been killed. But where was she going to get his eggs from? One tin of dried powdered egg per month may have been all right for some folk, but she didn't like the taste, and she didn't think that Doctor Dromyrk would either. She had to feed the Doctor proper. Maybe that small grocery shop in Pentin Street --- she couldn't remember the name --- would be worth trying. But the Number 17a bus was not going that way now, after Tuesday's bombing damage to the roads, so it would be quite a long walk. She turned round slowly to face him, her expression only slightly less fraught. 'No.'

'In that case we'll be needing a heavy blanket. Better make it two.' He went over to Guther, looking down at him, measuring the 'load'. He looked over at Mrs Morton. 'If you could just hold that door open for us, please, Mrs Morton.' She went back to the doorway, to hold the door back wide to allow the Doctor to pass through with the patient's arm over his broad shoulder.

Passing along the hall between closed doors, the 'crump' of bombs exploding in the distance was more subdued. But the lamp on the slim walnut side table still flickered nervously.

5

You could well say it was a 'weapon' of sorts that was proving its value in its own little corner of the war. An American invention, using only several pounds of silvered-brass tubing, its power was constantly growing across the country. Originally from Clarinda, Iowa, Major Miller was now a household name, very much 'adopted' by the country, his brainchild appreciated as much, if not more, by civilians as by the military. The truly unique 'Glen Miller sound' of tenor saxophones harmonising with clarinet, to give the now familiar low slow-melody *Moonlight Serenade*, floated out softly from the Rainbow Club's ballroom, catching Lt-Colonel Bretzler's ear in the main dining room.

Bretzler listened to the music, serious thoughts suspended for the moment, his mind stolen by the romantic mood. In much the same way as close-clutching couples on the dance floor were caught up in heartfelt emotional thoughts. Provided entirely by the American Red Cross, the Rainbow Corner Club, just off Piccadilly Circus, in Shaftesbury Avenue, was a much welcomed haven for GIs in war-torn London. This was where the young servicemen, tired and partly homesick, could come to soothe 'duty nerves' or escape boredom, drinking coke, playing pool, jiving to juke boxes, scoffing hamburgers and jitterbugging to big-band swing music. All the dazzling commercial trinkets being showered on a depressed ration-bled population. Our own girls frequented the club, each eager to snare her very own dark-tanned 'Adonis model' and greatly enhanced by this exciting new fast-paced music and lifestyle from across the Atlantic. Little wonder that every handsome GI that a girl attached herself to casually mentioned that he just happened to own a string of Texas oil wells or a vast cattle ranch in Montana stretching from horizon to horizon. This glimpse of a bright rich American swinging lifestyle --- of how things could be --- of how things were *going* to be, after this war was over and done with ---- was providing a significant uplift in the country's otherwise bomb-battered sunken morale. Thanks, Glen.

Bretzler smiled as he watched the other soldier at his table make his ravenous attack on the one and a half inch thick T-bone steak that would have fed a British family for more than a week and still have more than the bone left over. 'Doesn't this music grab you, Frank,' said Bretzler, watching the beef gradually disappearing between deft strokes of fork and blade that reminded you of a samurai's swordplay.

Captain Falzoni, seemingly oblivious to all but that on his plate, managed to eat, laugh and speak at the same time, without looking up from the important business that was his food. 'Sure,' replied Falzoni, through a mouthful of the best Texas beef and French fries. 'Sure, and I'll get on that floor and take me a dame --- when I'm finished here. And then you'll have to call in the MPs to control the frenzied mob when those dames come crowding over, fighting to get to me.' He paused for a backhand wipe of his mouth and a swig of Tennessee bourbon. 'Don't you fancy one of those English cuties for yourself, then, Brent? Seems as if there's plenty to go, all round, fair share.' With his handsome Italian features of dark complexion, perfectly sculptured strong Roman nose and chin, and a rich thatch of shiny black hair, the Captain reckoned that he had the dame-grabbing sexual allure to have more 'cats' purring on his arm in one hour, than Charles Boyer could have swooning after him in all of his smoochy films.

Falzoni, just like Lt-Colonel Bretzler, was also with the Army's 2nd Armoured Division. The Division had sustained its own share of heavy fighting. To the forefront in ground combat operations, as part of the Allied Task Force Operation Torch, it had mounted an early offensive in North Africa, landing at Casablanca in '42. Fighting through to '43, the Division had moved south, giving support to the 1st Armoured Division, in its amphibious attack on Sicily, with landings at Gela and then Licata. They had met heavy head-on defensive from the newly-formed Hermann Goering Panzer Division and the 15$^{th}$ Panzergrenadier Division. The Luftwaffe gave air support to the German ground forces. The Panzer division's two battalions of 99 tanks and the Panzergrenadier division's 3 regiments of grenadier infantry and 1 battalion of 60 tanks had engaged with the 2$^{nd}$ Armoured Division in fierce fighting through to Palermo. The Panzerkampwagen VI Ausfurung H tank – or 'Tiger' – weighing over 50 tons, with its 12 cylinder 650hp Maybach engine, and its 88mm gun – more powerful than anything we had – was a most formidable resistance force to fight against. With that and an overhead hornet's nest of Junkers Ju87 Stukas screaming down in vertical attack, their undercarriages permanently lowered to catch the wind and sound like Wagner's feisty maidens emptying their lungs to high heaven, you just had to keep your head down and push hard, to force Jerry back. But superior Allied air and naval strength had finally forced the Panzer Division to fall back to Messina. We'd lost a lot of good guys in those assault operations. Falzoni had taken *his* share of the scrapes, with a scar for memento, where an exploding mortar bomb had ripped his tunic-top and belt off, the belt buckle, not the bomb, gashing his side. Falzoni's restricted window view of Palermo, from the Unit's field hospital tent, was that his dad's original hometown looked like it could do with a few repairs.

Major Bretzler, for his part, had his gold leaf replaced by silver leaf, in his promotion to Lt-Colonel. Shortly after that he was transferred to 'other duties'.

With the MO ticking Falzoni off the sick list, he was now on furlough (leave) in London. The Unit's PR Officer, Major Hennely, had instructed all the guys going on furlough to make a special effort to be diplomatic with the Brits. With his mind on that thought, Falzoni tapped his blouse where the inside pocket had two pairs of nylons. He knew how to make a special effort to be 'diplomatic', all right. Latin charm on its own was fine, but when backed up by good old glamorous GI uniforms and generosity of stockings, perfume, chocolates, cigarettes and other goodies, you had an absolute winner. Forking up the last French fry and popping it in his mouth, he placed the fork back down beside the bare bone and pushed the plate away.

Bretzler watched the Captain slowly stroke his chin absent-mindedly, and then fondle his Yale graduation ring, his thoughts far away. Across the Atlantic, perhaps? It wasn't just Dromyrk who could read minds from physical behaviour --- well, maybe better, Bretzler conceded. He ventured the guess. 'So what do you think your old man thinks of his prize son, Franco, Giuseppe, Attorney at Law, invading sunny Sicily, the very land that spawned his own mom and dad?'

Falzoni stopped rubbing the ring and looked across at Bretzler, surprised at the question pin-pointing the very subject he had been thinking of, namely being back home. 'I'll know the answer to that when we're finished here, and get shipped back home – *if* I get back home.' He took another sip of bourbon while he thought. 'There again, the old guy never was one to confide his inner feelings with any of the family --- almost as if he didn't have any emotions – only the stamina to work hard all his life. That in itself must warrant some merit, I guess.' Falzoni thought of his dad, Enrico Falzoni, a fresh young Italian immigrant of seventeen years, with almost nothing but his second-hand shirt and pants, stepping ashore onto American land in 1904. Setting out soon after as a street vendor of fish on a wheelbarrow --- the business expanding through the hard years to a flourishing family-run catering corporation operating across the states. Where his elder brothers and sister had 'slaved' all those years with 'Pop' to build up the business, Frank, being the youngest, was allowed by the old man to 'escape' and go to college to study law.

At the same time, Bretzler's thoughts went a generation further back, to his grandfather pulling up his roots in the small Rhineland town of Braubach, that nestled quietly on the river bank 400 ft below Marksburg

Castle, south of Koblenz, with a mind to replant the Bretzler family roots in the New World as the 19th century was drawing to an end. Disembarking onto Ellis Island, New York's newly formed immigrant reception and inspection station, Erst Joachem Bretzler, newly qualified veterinary surgeon, clutching his leather bag of surgical instruments, was already planning to head purposefully for his next and final destination --- the Union's leading dairy state of Wisconsin. With horse-drawn transport rapidly being replaced by the internal combustion mode as the new century approached, horses as a main source of a veterinary surgeon's income was lessened. But for dairy products in a growing country's growing population, career prospects were very promising. The son, Theodore Arthur Bretzler, chose humans for his probes and needles, qualifying as a dental surgeon, so that he was now principal partner in a prosperous multi-partnered practice in Milwaukee, and part-time lecturer in dental medicine at his alma mater, the city's university.

With vets and dentists having landed on their feet and settled their lot, Bretzler wondered for a moment what he, of the third generation, was going to be doing after this Hitler mess was finally swept aside once and for all? He hadn't decided yet. He couldn't quite see what 'hat' he would be wearing, job-wise, when that finality came about. Bretzler shut his mind off from that distant issue, to look across at Falzoni. 'You mentioned earlier that you had folks here.'

'That's right,' said Falzoni, pausing as he tapped all his pockets, looking for something. 'Yeah, that's right.' Another tap, just to be sure. Nothing. 'Say, could you toss me one of those, Brent. I seem to have run out of mine, or left them somewhere.'

Bretzler picked up the packet of Chesterfields, jerking it, so that the cigarettes poked out. He let Falzoni take one then took one for himself. Gold glinted in his hand and a thin flame jumped up from the Bendix lighter. 'You were saying.' He picked a flake of tobacco off his lip while he waited.

'Yeah, as I was saying – it seems there's a brood of the Falzoni Family here, on this little island.'

'Only "*seems?*" You're not sure?'

'Yeah, well, like I said before, the old guy doesn't give out much of that sort. What gems of the past he may let slip are as rare as those pearls you expect to find in your plate in the oyster bar, in Luigi's, in sunny San Fran.' The Captain paused to draw on the cigarette, and then breathing out the smoke, leaned back in his seat to continue. 'Bonnie Scotland. In Edinburgh, or *Edimboorg*, as the old guy would say. I've got cousins up there. Not sure what the tribe total is, but apparently two of the guys are in the Army, one in the Royal Artillery, serving with a twenty-five-pounder field-gun crew – 'somewhere where it's all happening' in Africa. That'll be El Alamein, where we were. Who knows, maybe he was among those mad drunk Brits we saw at Benghazi, not far from Alamein, when we were leaving the area. The other brother is with a Black Watch unit – 'somewhere in the East'.'

Falzoni thought for a moment. 'Crazy thing is, though, while these guys are out there fighting for their country – begging your pardon – their *King* and country -- their old man is taken away by cops in the middle of the night, and transported to a detention camp, on some remote island, or other, the Island of Men.' Falzoni expressed his confusion with a screwed-up look. 'I mean, what sort of name is that? Sounds real loony. Sounds like a sneaky hideaway for ass-poking faggots.

'The Isle of Man,' corrected Bretzler. He was aware of the island's function as an out-of-the-way '*holding centre*' – it sounded better like that – for non-naturalised male aliens whose countries of origin were those of the Axis Powers. The information was mentioned briefly in his files from Colonel Rutkin. From what he remembered vaguely, two towns on the island served this purpose – Peel and Douglas, situated on opposite sides of the island. Peel facing out to the Atlantic, and Douglas facing 'inwards', towards England's mainland. In Douglas, men of German and Austrian origin were 'accommodated' in ordinary private houses that formed Hutchinson Square, several streets inland. The Italian men had their quarters in apartments – Metropole Mansions – looking out on the promenade --- and the Royal Navy's sheltered fleet, anchored just off shore. A good view for a spy. Not that there was any reason to fear that. Treatment of the internees was humane, the only sign of military detention being the barbed wire fencing along the pavement edges --- and the one or two soldiers standing casually on guard smoking --- and holding Lee Enfield rifles. Churchill, in a moment of indecision over who was who in this mass of aliens, at the outbreak of the war, had, as a safeguard, ordered his officials to "bag them all."

'It seems the King was a bit annoyed,' said Bretzler, 'when he came to learn of guys risking their lives on the front line, while their dads were locked up, all because of their foreign origins, and ordered Churchill to release them. At least, that's how it landed on my ears.'

'I wonder how long a train ride to Edinburgh is. Any idea?'

'Listen, buddy, I hope you're not getting any ideas about going up there for a good old cousins-across-the-Atlantic get-together. I need you here, Frank. We've got important things to see to. You don't think I had your CO instruct the MPs to drag you away from all those wild dolls-and-drinks parties in the camp -- that you just *absolutely* hate -- and drive you up here, VIP style to London, just so you can smoke my cigarettes, borrow some fast bucks, and wave to His Highness Georgie-boy on his balcony at Buck House. Face it, pal – you're select material – and I'm the one that selected you. I'm officially allowed one fruitcake sidekick to run with me on this assignment. Out of all the files of known personnel I've been through, the dog-tag with your number on it comes up spinning three bars jackpot.'

Falzoni held a hand up in a limp mock Boy Scout salute: 'Jawol, Oberstleutnant!'

As they rose and made to be on their way, the big band, on cue, broke into another of Miller's bouncy numbers backed by a female vocalist's words: 'Pardon me, boy, is that the Chattanooga choo choo? ------'

Half an hour later and half a mile across the city, the music that Bretzler and Falzoni listened to – were forced to listen to – was of a slow doleful

'Palm Court' strain scratched out on violin strings by an elderly ladies quartet sitting partly camouflaged by large green palm fronds shifting around their heads. As a dark figure loomed up silently beside him, Bretzler pushed his empty glass away. 'Two more highballs,' he said without looking up. The figure didn't move away. Bretzler looked and saw it was a different waiter. Another bent, crack-faced old guy, like the one who'd brought their drinks before. The hesitance on the old guy's face sure as hell meant that he needed a change of words, like all these slow Brits did. 'That's whiskey and soda. And I want to see a couple of Titanic icebergs in them, not goddamn frozen raindrops.' But it wasn't an Anglicized translation that the old man wanted; he was now perfectly well acquainted with these new American terms, with all these young American soldiers pouring in, eager to spend their ample bright dollars-worth of dull English pounds. God knows, our own fighting lads would have had reason to look fresher, brighter, with that sort of money in their pockets. The cracked face broke out another wider crack at the sight of that thick roll of notes unfurling in the American officer's richly-tanned hands. Bretzler handed the funny Brit money over. 'And have one on yourself, old timer.' No further bidding was needed, the old man snatching the money and empty glasses in virtually one movement and hobbling off under the swaying palms.

Colonel Rutkin's striding into the room was a welcome interruption to their restless waiting. They rose to greet him.

'Colonel.' There was question in Bretzler's voice and his raised eyebrows. As far as he'd understood, Rutkin was supposed to be bringing someone else with him.

Catching Bretzler's query, the Colonel half turned towards the doorway, his look implying beyond it, saying: 'Gone to ----' What he meant was clearly awkward enough for him not to be able to finish the sentence.

'We call it the *can* back in the States, Colonel,' said Falzoni, giving out a broad smile that was as much cheeky as it was cheery. These crazy Brits with their coy manners hidden behind their stiff upper lips.

Rutkin swung back round stiffly to look the 'other' American straight in the eyes. It was all becoming a bit much. First the Swede, then the American – German, now another American – Italian this time. 'Falzoni – that's Italian, isn't it?'

'Yeah, that's right, sure it is. But, say, don't look at me like that, Colonel – I wave the good old Star Spangled Banner just as high as the next guy.' The irritation in Falzoni's words was only discernible if you knew him well and were familiar with his moods. Back in the States foreign names were the ordinary everyday thing and commonly accepted thing, sliding into every slot and profession without as much as a blink of the eye. But here, in this crazy little island with its crazy insular society, completely cut off by the sea from all other cultures, anyone that wasn't tagged Smith was as oddball as a monkey walking down the street wearing derby and pants. Although, in time of war, that sea contributed a  vital defensive factor. Falzoni looked from Colonel Rutkin to Bretzler, his growing smile relaying its message of more mischief. 'And take Colonel Bretzler here; did you know that  his old man back in the States sends old Adolf a Rhode Island turkey hamper every year come Thanksgiving Day?'

Bretzler flashed a cautioning glance at Falzoni. He could well imagine Falzoni, as an attorney, dismantling  witnesses' statements because they didn't know which way to duck serious questions disguised as humour slammed at them.

'Does he, indeed?' Rutkin's response was as cool as it was aloof, showing no emotion, to take up the ball in the Captain's game of verbal tomfoolery. 'And no doubt the recipient of this generous annual gift dons an Uncle Sam top hat in honour of the occasion?' Make no mistake, as superior ranking officer, Rutkin could have barked the American down – both of them, but we were supposed to  be  cooperating  with  our US  allies, in return for their invaluable supply of troops, weapons and what seemed to be a never-ending abundance of everything else they were  pouring onto our besieged island. Everything grew on trees, it seemed, over there.

Falzoni smiled at Bretzler. So the stuck-up Colonel Rutkin wasn't that stuck-up that he couldn't give his own mould of back-slap repartee. He was about to give more lip to Rutkin, knowing that his 'near insubordination' always upset Bretzler, when he stopped. All three of them looking towards the doorway, at  Colonel Rutkin's colleague making a late entrance. A WAAC NCO. It was a long room so that the doorway was a fair distance away. Walking this distance under the steady scrutiny of three men, all officers, two of them American, and her having only two stripes on her sleeves, would have given a lesser lass a self-consciousness that would have been betrayed in her movements. But her brisk steps showed none. Inside those uniforms were three men and she was a woman. Other girls may have needed those gruelling years at a Swiss finishing school to acquire their self-assured finesse, but her mamma's example and daddy's ever sympathetic ear had sufficed as her mentors in social grace. She came up to them, stopping before them, totally at ease.

Falzoni didn't find her to be appealing. For a start, not enough stacked up in front on the 'balcony' he  reckoned.  Maybe  it  was  the  way  these  crazy Brit uniforms pulled in long and straight, leaving nothing much sticking out front or back.  And  the  crazy  stooge-style  stripes  round the wrong way, pointing downwards. The face didn't impress him either. Too long and not a speck of dame's paint anywhere. He liked a broad that had a round cutie-shaped face, like those Hollywood glamour models had. At least her hair was blonde. But still definitely not his type of bird. Nah, somebody else could have her.

'Corporal Leighton-Lagrishe will be joining our  team,' said Rutkin in his usual brevity. They all sat down.

As  they  settled  into  their  chairs,  and  Rutkin  continued  the introductions, Bretzler missed out on her first name, his attention being totally on her. Unlike Falzoni, he was very much taken in by her. Where Falzoni had failed to see, Bretzler was seeing beyond, in depth, so that she was stirring him inside. He almost felt guilty, somewhat transparent, at thinking she could see how he was emotionally  moved by her so quickly. Corporal Leighton-Lagrishe was a very attractive woman, but in a very different way from what Captain Falzoni would ever appreciate. Her strength of character was of the kind that only an English upper-middle-class upbringing could breed, so that she was at ease with anyone, be it beggar or brigadier. He saw her deferring to 'superior' officers only because of military protocol. Glossy folds of her golden hair were neatly entwined at the back of her head in a French pleat style that Bretzler found most attractive. Facial make-up was not necessary where an affable personality beamed out on you through intelligent pale, 'pearly', grey-blue eyes. That he could see all this in her, in spite of the uniform which, like Falzoni, he thought was severely spoiling, was absolute verification of her loveliness.

'It's Selena,' she said with a soft laugh, when he asked her, seeing that he had missed Colonel Rutkin's words, him being somewhat --- 'far away'.

Bretzler had half expected her to speak in a shrill, almost horse-whinnying manner that the upper-class often affected to mark their difference. But she didn't. He was glad. If she had spoken that way he would have seen it as a kind of weakness that needed to hide behind a social barrier. She spoke in her own relaxed manner that said she had confidence in herself, without needing her class for back-up. That warmed him to her even more. Their attention on each other at that moment made them feel that they were the only two there. 'With a name like that your old man must at least be sharing an ash tray with Churchill. Mind you, it would have to be a big one, considering those prize-size Havanas Winston smokes.' said Bretzler playfully, to draw her in.

'Daddy doesn't smoke,' she returned, with a matching playful note in her voice. 'And before you say it, no, we don't have our own family-appointed bishop in our own family house private chapel. That would be more C of E. and we're R C.' A jaunty twist of her head to look at him sideways with a twinkle in her eye: 'But there is Uncle Gerald, with lots of gold braid on his sleeves and cap, at the Admiralty.' She smoothed her skirt, with an over-to-you motion.

'I'll file that under Reconnaissance as a dummy run,' he said, sitting back and 'examining' her openly with what he hoped she understood to be his warm friendly smile. He hoped his warm expression was conveying a more intimate message. Inhaling on his Chesterfield, he noticed her looking at his cigarette and the packet. The look was that of curiosity --- possibly intrigued by the American brand; of mischievously wanting to try one. He offered her one, but she smiled, shaking her head and whispering a soft: 'Thank you, but no.' This was still an official meeting, however informal it may have looked. The American officers may well smoke, but she could only imagine Colonel Rutkin frowning hard at his lowly corporal joining in.

Falzoni was now 'tuned-in' to the subtle interplay between the woman and Bretzler, and watched them with amusement, waiting for 'developments'. Colonel Rutkin was also sensing that the meeting was straying from its primary focus of importance. His words were falling on deaf ears. That he was being ignored, however inadvertently, was annoying enough, but he reminded himself that more urgent issues were at stake and needed to be discussed. Controlling his irritation, he rapped the coffee table hard with a knuckle to reclaim everyone's attention. All three looked round at him. 'Thank you,' he said with a gruff hint of annoyance in his voice and a cutting glance round at them all. Falzoni returned the look with his usual nonchalant broad smile. She sat back to listen, crossing her legs the other way round. Bretzler's only movement was to take a slow draw on the cigarette. He blew the smoke out. 'Carry on, Colonel,' he said.

'As I was saying, Corporal Leighton-Lagrishe will take over the duties of E. R.' --- a brief look at his notes ---'Yes, E.R. – Ethel Rosemary -- Waites, as of twenty four hours from now. Miss Waites has ---'

'That's Thursday,' said Falzoni, happy to supply unnecessary information, if only to rile the pedantic Colonel.

'Thank you, Captain. Yes, that, indeed, would make it Thursday, as you so rightly say.' A nod and a controlled smile of 'gratitude' at the Captain. 'Miss Waites has been assigned to Camp Bailey so as to allow the replacement to slot in as inconspicuously as possible. As her predecessor was civilian, Corporal Leighton-Lagrishe will carry out her duties out of uniform; this to make the changeover as minimal as possible, thus arousing less curiosity and ensuing questions.'

Falzoni's smile spread again. Gee, but doesn't the guy put it across real swell. Maybe I should try spilling it out that way – all honey-tongued smooth – to the judges back in the old town. Could maybe earn me a hell of a lot more dollars a lot more quicker. The cigarette tip glowed brighter as the Captain warmed to these thoughts.

'As it happens, I already know Doctor Dromyrk,' she said. She'd given the casual piece of information to lighten the concentrated expressions Bretzler and Rutkin had assumed. But it seemed to have had a different effect on Bretzler.

'I see,' said Bretzler, stretching the syllables out. His head had tipped back a fraction, to match a faint note of – was it dismay? -- in his voice.

She wasn't sure of what her ear had picked up, but she responded to what she thought it sounded like. 'Oh, no, don't misunderstand me – I wasn't a patient. Good heavens, no. No I was simply acting out mother's wishes and accompanying a family friend – more Aunt Helen's friend, actually, --- to Doctor Dromyrk's surgery. Over several months – perhaps nearer to six – if I recall correctly.'

'There was no one else to escort her? The husband?' Rutkin's putting aside military issues to enquire into a private non-military matter was peculiar enough to signal a break in the meeting, so that seats creaked as positions shifted and legs stretched.

'No. As far as I gather, I don't believe things were doing too well in that area, alas.' She had said enough on that subject, and their interest in it was waning.

Except for one. 'The old tomahawk dance round the totem pole, in other words.' The expression on all three faces was the same as they looked round at Falzoni. What the hell was he talking about? Taking a long draw on the cigarette, he exhaled the smoke slowly, enjoying keeping his audience in suspense. 'Battles more ancient than Time itself – marital disputes – decree nisi – property wrangles – alimony settlements – and all the rest. Great dollar reapers for the legal eagles holding the reins on both parties. Not that I'll be making that my specialty. Hell, no, I'll be going into Criminal Law when I get back and set up my practice –– when I get enough clients to set up practice –– if I get enough clients to set up my practice.'

They returned to putting their heads together on what was really important. But minds had been distracted by the side-line interruption so that there was the collective feeling for running through each point quicker and so end the meeting. Then they could get out of this place with its crazy crackpot quartet music. Maybe they should play it to Germany's Lord Haw-Haw. That would shut him up. Little wonder that this hotel had been old Rutkin's choice of venue.

Eventually they all stood up. Putting on his cap, Colonel Rutkin looked at Lt-Colonel Bretzler. 'I can rely on you to pass on the necessary to Dromyrk?'

'You can leave it with me, Colonel. I'll see to it.'

'Good.' Rutkin now looked to the Corporal. She had been collected from her barracks and driven here in his staff car. Now he would have to have her taken back. He waited for her.

'It's all right, sir,' she said. 'Colonel Bretzler has offered to drive me back to my barracks.'

It was Falzoni's turn now to look at Bretzler. 'It's okay, Frank, I haven't forgotten this swell, quaint, old English pub you've newly discovered outside of town. I'll get you there and drop you off. Trust me, buddy. I'll get you there. But you'll be riding in the back of the Jeep, where your hands can be no trouble. The Corporal's riding in front with me.'

'Sure thing, Brent. So let's get going. Hey, and say, Brent, can you lend me fifty bucks.'

6

Doctor Dromyrk stepped in through the Belsize Hospital entrance, leaving outside a scene of structural wreckage in exchange for the human wreckage all around him inside. Those who couldn't manage to stumble along on their own feet, with minimal help from another, were carted along on stretcher trolleys. Blood, injury and pain were evident either way. The typical aftermath of another night's bombing, with Fire Brigade and Rescue Teams bringing out what living forms they could from beneath the mass devastation of buildings. Stepping carefully around those  laid out on the floor, through lack of space, Dromyrk made his way along the dull corridor, with its dull green-tiled walls, heading for the Psychiatric Unit.

Sister Nolan came round from behind her wooden table to meet him. 'Good morning, Doctor Dromyrk.' She held out the brown folder.

'Good morning, Sister.' He took the folder. 'Thank you.' He looked at the name. 'Margaret Pomfrey.'

'Room three,' she said, in her dry Irish accent, with a typical saving of words. She had lots of duties to see to and didn't waste time with long speeches. Wedded totally to her professional work for  forty-six spinster years, she had never known socialising with polite small talk to have done her any good. She had already turned away, back to her work, before Dromyrk could get out a word.

He looked up from the folder, at her flapping headpiece, as she bent over the other files on the table. 'I seem to recall that this was one of Doctor Eldridge's patients, Sister.'

'Doctor Eldridge was taken to Saint Mary's last night for emergency operation. A bombed factory wall collapsed on top of Doctor Eldridge's car. Nurse Eldridge survived the accident but suffered cardiac arrest before reaching the hospital. Resuscitation failed.' No more words. A sharp concise delivery, without looking up from the files. The ingrained effect of handling a daily oncoming march of death and human desecration whilst remaining totally devoid of emotion.

Dromyrk breathed in and out for a silent moment of taking in this news. 'I see.' He spared a quiet smile for the back of the woman's head, and seeing nothing more was forthcoming, turned and walked away in the direction of room 3.

The room was an improvement on the commotion in the corridors only because it was quieter. But it was just as bleak. Empty but for two wooden chairs, a table and a vase of faded waxed crepe paper flowers , the room gave off an infectious gloom with its dull old furniture pieces that looked as tired and worn as the patients who used them. The air-raid blackout curtains didn't help much either. Heavy and black, they were just the thing to induce dark broodings in a disturbed mind.

Dromyrk didn't like the room at all. Definitely not his choice of setting for seeing a patient. He would have much preferred one less depressing for the task of easing the patient out of morbid solitude. But the suggestions he had voiced on this aspect had not travelled far. Sensible as they had been understood to be, the hospital was pressed for space – every cubic inch of it – in these pressing times of mass bombings with their heavy toll of casualties.

Dromyrk tried to pull the thick drapes a little further back, to let in more light and dispel what little he could of the dismal atmosphere. The raised cracks in the drab linoleum creaked under his feet as he stepped over to the empty chair. He sat down to face  the patient.

A maelstrom of neurotic unrest was instantly discernible behind those sickly green eyes, behind the lost expression on the pallid face that was ravaged in years beyond its bearer. But looking older than her forty-one years was only half the toll levied by her inner turmoil. Dromyrk detected, in the forefront of all those confused emotions, a simmering anger. It was coming forth in words that hadn't yet left her dry lips – in bursts of fury that hadn't yet glinted in her eyes. It had to be extricated and brought out from its dormant pose, not by scalpel or forceps, but by a careful cajolery that was the shrink's tool. By a smoothness of words more silken – some would say more devious – than that of the skilled diplomat. Dromyrk had effectively forged himself this very skill over an anvil of nearly three decades of quelling patients' silent wailing. Professor Bernheim had once remarked that doctors wore their bright white coats over their more sombre attire for the same purpose that pirates kept their black Jolly Rodger flag concealed up until the last moments before attack --- to hide the fact that they were plunderers --- physicians and surgeons robbing the body of its dignity of privacy --- psychiatrists purloining those most fiercely guarded of all secrets.

She was nervous at his coming into the room – at his being there. Dromyrk watched her shift about uneasily in her chair and waited for her to settle down. It didn't ease matters any that he wasn't her regular doctor so that he was not familiar to her. Above the smell of hospital disinfectant he caught a faint whiff of urine coming seemingly from the patient. She somehow sensed he was aware of this and sharply pulled her hospital dressing gown more tightly around herself. That was a good sign. Where there was still a degree of concern over personal cleanliness, suicidal motive had not yet arrived on the doorstep.

'Good morning, Margaret,' said Dromyrk. 'I'm Doctor Dromyrk. Doctor Eldridge isn't able to see you today. So how are you feeling today, Margaret?' He smiled as he gave this friendly question, at the same time reflecting on its banal stupidity. He could see and knew only too well how she was feeling and it certainly wasn't sunshine happy. With her sitting there tensed with worry, shifting restlessly and constantly wiping her sweating palms on her gown, he saw an overlap between severe anxiety neurosis and personality disorder. Her mind was deluged by a lifetime's never-ending flood of irrational worries, making her anxious, irritable and distracted in response to her surrounding environment. Overactivity of her sympathetic nervous system and increased tension of the skeletal muscles would almost certainly be causing a degree of insomnia. What few hours of sleep she was able to snatch would most likely be disturbed by morbid dreams, if not nightmares, and intermittent waking -- the waking spells, with their crushing melancholy, being barely an improvement on the nightmares.

Dromyrk read through Eldridge's notes to see this confirmed. The medical file also stated that the patient suffered from periodic panic attacks//headaches// depression// obsessive compulsion// hyperventilation syndrome with its fear of heart disease, giving palpitations, fatigue, attacks of breathlessness and illusionary inframammary pains. Eldridge had put her on antidepressants. Good.

Dromyrk reflected back on how, from his early work with Dr Freud, theoretical explanations that had evolved since then, however varied, were basically agreed that the stresses and difficulties brought on by anxiety neurosis arose from child-parent relationships in early childhood or even at birth. Problems from a lifetime away stored, unacknowledged, in the dark vault of the subconscious. For these problems to be resolved, it was imperative that they should be acknowledged – that they attract attention. Dromyrk likened this to a red flag being waved to attract attention and so summon help in a distressed situation. However, if the immediate background to the flag is also red, the signal for help may not be noticed. So rather than alter the background, the flag itself must be of a colour to contrast with the background. Hence the cry for help from the subconscious must manifest itself on the conscious level by way of a neurotic symptom that clashes with the social environment; that stands out as 'odd' or phobic behaviour compared to that of others -- in order to be noticed – and so eventually resolved. This concept, from a young and as yet still wet-behind-the ears intern, had afforded

Professor Bernheim some measure of humour, as well as his quiet nod of approval.

'You're not the doctor.' The words blurted out in a struggle that carried as much relief in them as there was protest. Dromyrk appreciated the effort made in getting them out. The patient suffered from a severe persecution mania that bombarded the mind virtually unceasingly with attacks of guilt that made the ancient Spanish Inquisition seem like a nursery game in comparison. Each day, upon waking, the patient's mind would inevitably engage in an inner 'courtroom battle' over the moral issue of her thoughts that would determine whether or not she was eternally damned. Trivial perhaps, to the 'sane-minded', but not so to the troubled mind made to back into a corner by pressure from all directions. Watching her facial muscles twitch and the small shakings of her head, Dromyrk knew how this pressure could escalate to the point of anguish where the patient was almost unable to hold a thought in mind at all, for fear of it being a damning one. How many patients over the years, when at last relieved of their problem, had confided to him that, in moments of anguish, they would have preferred the mind of a dog, so as to have been spared their mental torture?

'You're not the doctor,' she said again, with a pained childish insistence.

'So what did Doctor Eldridge say to you, Margaret? Can you remember anything at all that he said to you that made you happy?' His deliberate use of the word 'happy' was a test – a challenge – on the strength of stricture of her thoughts which were *forbidding* her to be happy. But as he was saying this, Dromyrk was thinking back on another patient who had put the same protest to him.

*'You're not the Doktor!' Hitler had thrown the same accusation at him – albeit loaded with more piercing authority. It was the second time that Dromyrk had made a clinical visit, on his own, to the man who claimed to carry a country's destiny on his shoulders. Not long after having been appointed Bundeskanzer – Federal Chancellor – by Reich President, Hindenburg, Hitler had now taken it upon himself to assume the title*

*of Fuhrer. He barely recognised Dromyrk as the young assistant who had accompanied Professor Bernheim on previous clinical sessions. This was to be expected, where the man's attention was permanently focused on his own performances. When surrounded by milling throngs of adoring young fraulein, the compliments he paid them meant less than the fanatical rapture on their faces meant to him. That was the differential factor separating the neurotic from the psychotic – when the neurotic feels like God, he knows it's an irrational delusion; when the psychotic feels like God – he knows he is!*

*The man's torrent of high-pitched words at last muted down in accepting that Dromyrk had indeed been assigned to see him by Professor Bernheim. A sudden reversal of opinion that typified his erratic mood changes that forever confused those around him. But he wasn't conceding to being wrong. He was never mistaken. It was impossible for him to be wrong. This turnabout was only because it was in keeping with the fact that he needed to see the doctor. 'The good Professor would only send me his best, Herr Doktor Dromyrk. This I know, as your Leader. And you are the best because you are German! You are of German destiny's appointed supreme Aryan race, superior to all others -- and superior to Jews.' The fervour that suddenly glowed in those eyes and shook in the clenched fists was that of the dangerous zealot, Dromyrk noted.*

*'I'm Swedish. I came to this country by way of Professor Bernheim's invitation to work under him'*

*The glow went out of the eyes --- a moment's stalling; avert obstruction – reroute attack. Both hands came up, now opened wide, palms facing out, in a placatory gesture to pat Dromyrk on the arms. But they stopped short of touching, where neurotic compulsion shunned contamination from foreign objects. Dromyrk noted this also. 'No, no, Herr Doktor Dromyrk, you are mistaken. You came to this country because it was your destiny to recognise Germany as the greatest, the strongest, of all nations. You came from Sweden, but your father was German. I know this. I know this. Only a German father could have endowed you with the distinct features – blue eyes, blond hair, strong physique – that are destiny's emblem of the supreme Aryan race.'*

*Dromyrk's faint shake of the head at this tirade only succeeded in bringing on another rabid burst of correction from Hitler. 'No, no, you are of good German Aryan stock. You are mistaken. Just as the Jews are mistaken in claiming that Christ was Jewish. He was born of a brave Teutonic warrior serving in that area of the world. I know this. I tell you this as your supreme Leader, the Fuhrer, as you must learn from your Fuhrer.' As Hitler's frenzied ravings continued, his points of argument changed abruptly, from one to another, without completion and without any logic to sustain them. By this very mode of evading the truth was the Fuhrer able to control his ministers and generals. Brushing aside all that he didn't wish to hear, he could override all problems and protests put to him by his minions. While standing conversing among others, he was totally distanced from them.*

*Dromyrk saw no point in interrupting the man's senseless ramblings. He was here as a doctor, not a politician.*

*It was as he was walking out of the Reich Chancellery, into Vossestrasse, that Dromyrk caught a movement of colours at the corner of his eye that didn't please him. Brown shirts, brilliant red arm-bands with white-eyed swastika and black jackboots. A group of Sturmabteilung – Stormtroopers moving in on him to cut him off at the foot of the broad steps. The heaviest of them, the Obersturmfuhrer, detached himself from the group to approach him. Dromyrk remembered the face, friendly on the surface, as it was menacing underneath, from an earlier encounter. The chin-strap, pulled tight to hold on the kepi cap, didn't soften the image any. Obersturmfuhrer Krunz, if he recalled correctly. On that occasion the man had tried to persuade Dromyrk to join their glorious Nationalsozialistische Deutsche Arbeiterpartei – (National Socialist German Workers' Party) – (NAZI Party). Dromyrk wasn't expecting the man's words to be any different from last time. 'Heil Hitler! Good day, Herr Doktor. You have just come from seeing the Fuhrer, is this not so?' Since these clinical visits were supposed to be low-profile, Dromyrk wondered how this man knew about them. No doubt the answer lay among a host of other dark dealings the man took under his wing. Dromyrk didn't bother to reply. He stared at the man, waiting for him to continue. 'You are in privileged close association with our Fuhrer, Herr*

'When can I go home, Doctor.' Dromyrk looked at Mrs Pomfrey, measuring her plea against her medical history and Doctor Eldridge's notes on her prognosis/progress chart. She was stable so far on her antidepressants, but she could relapse any time. There was still a lot of ground to cover, in an uphill climb, before they were 'home'. 'I want to go home,' she said again.

'We have to make you well, Margaret.  He thought for a moment, before throwing in a testing remark to stir things up inside her. 'What particular thought makes you happy?' He watched the patient wresting with the question. It involved a twin-horned task. Putting a name to that that which would generate a euphoric feeling was task enough for a normal-minded person. But, in the patient's condition, happiness was virtually synonymous with violating the severe taboo restrictions that governed her mind with iron discipline. She was now applying short finger-strokes to the top of her head at the back, where tension from mental pressure was concentrated. 'Would you say, Margaret, that of all the things you hear and read about, it is only the bad ones that go against your beliefs and give you pain that are true?

The patient rocked slightly, giving a nod for a yes.

'And why do you think this is? Why do you think that you never find facts that support your beliefs and make you happy, instead of those that cause you great pain from worry, Margaret?'

Margaret could only manage a pained shake of the head, totally unable to answer. At this stage the patient did not appreciate – let alone *accept* – that the subconscious was trawling the mind's incoming intelligence solely for that which could cause great worry. By giving credence to these points over all others, it sought to give pain enough to draw attention to its greater deeper-rooted problems. The patient had to be guided along a gradual route in order to eventually understand this.

Dromyrk patiently put further questions across softly to Margaret, assisting her along the way with the occasional smile and nod of encouragement, and filling in for her where she couldn't find words to finish a sentence. All the while he stole glances at his watch. As soon as this session was ended, he had to go over to the Ministry of Information. They needed his report on what the country's state of public morale was from all this bombing.

But they were a somewhat stiff-minded lot to put your ideas across to, where a 'spirit of establishment' carried more weight than logic. They had not been fully convinced, three years ago, when he had predicted Hitler reacting with childish revenge, with the total abandonment of military strategy, when our RAF bombers had targeted the Tempelhof airfield and the Siemens factories in Berlin. Churchill had ordered this RAF raid after 515 Luftwaffe bombers had dropped 500 tons of high explosives, 50 'parachute air-mines' and 36,000 incendiary bombs on Coventry, in November, that year, razing the city to the ground. Miraculously, only 568 people were killed, with another 863 suffering injuries. Whilst the Luftwaffe could have continued its concentrated campaign of bombing RAF airfields, so destroying our air force outright, and achieving complete control of the sky, Hitler had ordered this strategically sound operation to be halted. The Fuhrer, in his infallible wisdom, decreed that punishment of Britain's civilian population, rather than destroying military installations, was now the primary objective of his almighty Luftwaffe. Leaving his air-staff generals in much dismay, no doubt – and leaving us with enough planes to fight back. Since then, we had gradually gained control of the sky, it seemed.

There were those among Dromyrk's professional peers who, in studying the effect of blitz trauma, were inclined to believe that the brain can't live in fear forever. Their estimated period for the endurance of fear being limited to 21 to 25 days. That when reaching that point, the mind would be confronted with an ultimate choice between self-shutdown – suicide – or self-adjustment, in order to survive.

But Dromyrk's theories on the subject held greater optimism. He believed in a greater resilience of the public. Inasmuch as individuals may well experience their own morbid periods, nevertheless, as a united body of neighbours, communities, strangers, all pulling together under common threat, there was the underlying mettle to defeat that common enemy. More so, because the impact of the blitz on the populace was spread widely across the whole country, so levelling out the stress. From the collated statistical figures he'd had a chance to examine over at the Ministry, blitz damage was nine  times less than originally feared, thanks to sensible use of Anderson garden shelters and the bird cage style Morrison indoor shelters, as well as those Underground platforms adapted as makeshift shelters. According to Dr Nicholls at the Ministry, we were well on our way to having put out 2.5 million Anderson shelters – as well 22,000 bunks, 123 canteens, chemical toilets and medical kits for those using the Underground as 'home-from-home' overnight shelters.

From the way the figures were going, Dromyrk  saw something in the region of nearly 2% -- about twenty-nine thousand -- being the city's eventual death toll. But unlike fellow psychiatrists, he didn't believe that trauma from prolonged bombing would have so adverse an effect on the population as expected. He frowned for a moment. Was his prevailing optimism due to him simply wanting to see his theories as being correct?

Dromyrk looked at Margaret. She wasn't showing any signs of saying anything further. He was also due to go to Lindwell Hall, and time was pressing, but he didn't want to upset her by prompting her unduly. He checked his watch again.


The US Army jeep, with its strange roofless, doorless open design, was as much an odd sight to staring onlookers, as street damage, human as well as buildings, was to the vehicle's two GI occupants. You didn't see all this damage at the Crailwood Army Camp outside the town. Great hollow-eyed stone skulls looking out at you; others with half their 'skulls' sliced away in horrific operation. 'Hell, and here's me thinking we were stopping counting the broken windows back in the old country.' Falzoni's cynical understatements were always like that, taking you one way or the other; you either laughed or winced in irritation. They would probably have gone down well in a Marx Brothers script but for the serious thought cutting through them. Captain Falzoni twisted around from side to side, taking in the scale of scarring left by another night of bombing. 'And these are the guys that want to go on fighting? Jeez, it's no wonder they want us to help them.' Bretzler answered this with a nod and a hard hand-thump on the steering wheel.

Like a tough wart-hog, the jeep grunted and growled its way round obstacles, before racing on again with angry acceleration. Slowing down they carefully circled round a great red mangled mass that was one of these uniquely British double-decker buses lying on its side. A dinosaur compared to our slim Greyhound coaches. But quaint. The next large body to confront them was real. A brown and white – and red – Clydesdale dray-horse. The waggon was splintered matchwood, its broken bottles spilling coloured liquid that curled round in mixture with the animal's blood. Hoses everywhere – entangled – running straight – bulging from high pressure – half deflated, with tiny fountains spouting out from punctures made by high velocity blasted debris.

But another day was another day for these Brits, with business carried on as 'usual', it seemed. The man Falzoni grinned at, as they passed, was tackling a typewriter perched on top of a makeshift table of a door resting on two wooden boxes. Beside him, another man was standing dictating to a woman wrapped in a fur coat, sitting cross-legged on an office swivel-chair and taking down his words in her shorthand pad. Who the hell needs an office, anyway? 'They damn well don't give up, do they, these crazy people?' said Falzoni, shaking his head.

Bretzler caught a glimpse of the other feeling in his pockets. He held out his Bendix lighter. 'Light one for me too, Frank. I don't know if it's all this smoke around us, but I feel like I could do with a smoke myself. Maybe the Doc would have something to say on that.'

Falzoni lit two cigarettes and put one in Bretzler's mouth, handing him back his lighter. He sat back, blowing out a stream of smoke. 'Ah, yeah – this Dromylik ---'

'Dromyrk.'

'Okay. So what do we know about this guy? The Colonel hardly filled us in on it the other night, and you've told me even less, Brent.' Falzoni reached into the back seat to pull aside a jerrycan and pick up a combat helmet. He tapped the cigarette end's ash into it. 'He's certainly dug himself in well with the top brass. So how long has he been over here, with us, then?'

'He came over in thirty seven.' Six whole years, Bretzler thought to himself. And before that?

Dromyrk, in fact, had experienced an increasing uneasiness developing in him over those last years in Germany. What had been a lifetime's ambition – namely, to work with the country's most revered specialist in mental disorders – he gradually came to see was the one thing – the *only* thing -- that stopped him from being seized and arrested by the Sturmabteilung. And God knows, what after that? His continued resistance, time after time, to Obersturmfuhrer Krunz's pressure to make him join their glorious Party had made him a dangerous enemy of The Third Reich. But so far he had been untouchable, the Stormtroopers kept at bay by virtue of his privileged position as doctor to the Fuhrer. But he had come to appreciate the precarious knife-edge balance this was. Things could change. Just as Hitler's mind was unstable, so was the country becoming unstable. And Hitler's mind *was* the country's mind. Seething unrest was becoming apparent throughout the land. For all its scientific and intellectual progression over others, Germany was developing into a festering bubble of malevolence.

Although Sweden is neutral now, there was no guarantee at that time how the political wind would blow. So there was the choice of returning to his original homeland, or making a complete break of it and leaving Europe altogether. He had no marital ties to hold him down -- Tildi's warm smile now a cold memory pushed to the back of his mind. He sought the wisdom of 'ancients' from his grandfather, father and Professor Bernheim. They were unanimous in seeing it better to have someone on the outside in these dangerous times. Somewhat akin to the scientist monitoring the malignant organism's growth inside the controlled experiment chamber --- from *outside* the chamber. He had thus fled the country, crossing the water to England. Twelve months before his initial inspiration, Professor Sigmund Freud, had sought similar refuge in England.

'I reckon this guy being a regular buddy of old Adolf means that we track his every move closer than Hawkeye and Chingachgook,' said Falzoni.

'*Hawheye and Chingachgook!*' Bretzler looked round in feigned surprise at Falzoni.

Falzoni grinned back. 'My Classical Period reading at college.' He held a hand up in mock Red Indian greeting. 'How.'

'I'd be careful about giving a hand salute like that, Frank. You never know how these people, with their funny ways, might take it as a Nazi salute – especially like the short limp-hand salute that  old Adolf gives when he's pretending to be a nice guy. Could end up stringing you up from a lamppost, partisan-style. Bretzler looked about. 'That is, provided there's still one left standing up straight.' Funny interlude over, Bretzler turned back to the front, serious things on his mind again.

Falzoni's cigarette end brightened as he took another heavy draw and then blew the smoke out. 'So how did it go with your lady aristocrat the other night, then?'

'She's not an aristocrat. She's just –- 'He stopped, unsure how to find a suitable definition.

'Yeah, right – I get it.' He watched Bretzler's face for a reaction. But Bretzler wasn't giving out any sort of expression that was an answer. 'You're serious about her, aren't you?' Still no response from Bretzler. 'Yeah, you're serious, all right. It's hit you like a grade one tornado. Just like that Canadian Red Cross nurse we ran across near to Casablanca, on the road to Marrakesh. Dumb, but she sure had a cute ass. What was that place called – Rala – something?'

'Rabat. And you're going in the wrong direction. Marrakesh is south west, heading inland from Casablanca. That's where we split up, if you remember, with Findlay taking his vanguard reconnaissance unit along that way, while we headed north east, along the coastal road to Rabat.'

'Yeah, that was it – Rabat. Boy, was she trouble!' Falzoni fell back in his seat, coughing out a choking, laughing, mouthful of smoke.

Bretzler kept looking to the front. 'Cool it, Frank. That smoke's going to your head. Didn't your mom ever warn you about that?' He threw his cigarette to the roadside.

'The only warning I'm keeping in mind is Major Hennely's protocol briefing on behaving with the Brits. Especially that bit telling us to watch out for them leeching onto GIs, sucking up all they can from us. And that goes for the broads as well!'

Up ahead they could see a white-helmeted ARP (Air Raid Precaution) warden waving his arms about in his best effort as traffic policeman. He was trying to control the flow of vehicles round what looked like a massive crater some yards beyond him. Even without seeing a UXB (Unexploded Bomb) sign, the ladder propped up out of the large hole, and the cable snaking out of it to connect the man disarming the bomb to the earphones on the UXB sapper's head, was message enough. Life and death was literally balanced in hands of the officer disarming the bomb. Every intricate move of his fingers relayed to the sapper's ears. The last word coming through would mean either a job completed or life ended. The diversion signs that should have been put up further back to stop the traffic coming this way had not been put up soon enough so that a bottle-neck of vehicles was building up. As they began to slow down, Falzoni shook his head at the sight of the warden's helmet. 'These Brits and their crazy tin hats. Reminds me of the little tin bowl old Aunt Carmela carried seeds in to feed the chickens out the back yard, back in Arkansas. Mind you, I guess our guys wore the same shallow crown style helmet in the First World War. Until they saw sense and changed it.'

The jeep came to a halt. As they waited, a tandem bicycle drew up slowly to stop alongside. The 'passenger' was a very elderly gentleman – a business man – judging by his bowler hat, brolly and briefcase. His 'chauffeur' was a young woman, appropriately attired in peak cap and leather gaiters in place of bicycle clips. 'Jeez,'dig this guy, Brent,' said Falzoni, in mock despair. 'Don't these crazy people ever think of quitting? And if that's not enough, they can't even drive on the right side of the road.'

'Yeah, I guess there is that,' said Bretzler slowly, in quiet resignation. Sometimes Frank could go on too long with his crazy meathead ravings. 'Yeah, I guess there is that, Frank.'

7

Major Drummel was a short square-framed figure with a bustling energy that seemed to want to burst out of his constricting shortness. The head seemed out of place – stuck on the wrong body – honed to a sharp hatchet-like front that sliced the trim military moustache in two. His hands and arms moved about everywhere needlessly as he spoke in rapid bursts. What some would see as nervousness. Others, more knowingly, would recognise the Major's agitation in being tied down to a humdrum job, when what he wanted was a shot at the action. Perhaps, in reality, it was a mixture of both. Originally turned down in his application to join a paratrooper unit, it was ironic that he was now responsible for getting others ready for the 'jump'.

Colonel Rutkin, standing before him, looked down at the dark brown, rounded, mass on the table. It reminded him of horrific burnt-out forms he'd seen in trenches long ago. Judging by the crumbs on the tray, it had already been under multiple attack. He reached down for a piece and put it in his mouth tentatively. His expression was one of careful examination.

'What d'you think?' said Drummel in his neat manner.

'A little too rich, for one thing, I would say,' said Rutkin. His jaws passed the 'cookie' around his mouth slowly so that the taste buds could decide. 'They do like their things sweet.'

'True. But otherwise, jolly good.' Drummel was evidently enraptured by this great flood of 'goodies' that was now coming into Lindwell by way of US generosity. Perhaps more accurately, by way of Captain Falzoni's smart 'off-the-camp' dealings. They'd been told to expect a certain degree of loud-mouthed brashness from Americans in general. But this Falzoni was a phenomenon apart. Aside from all the 'cookies' and eye-popping foodstuff that didn't see daylight – didn't *exist* -- in this country, much needed military equipment was being brought in via the amazing, if not questionable, Falzoni supply-line. From where? How? Since that equipment was urgently needed, no questions would be asked. That Falzoni was sure some provider. Drummel could almost believe that if he'd ordered an 82 ton B-52 bomber with icing on top, it would have been sitting on Lindwell's doorstep within the hour. Quite frankly, that smooth-talking American could sell gravity to someone falling off a cliff!

'What did you say it was called?' said Colonel Rutkin, as he dithered over whether or not to pick up another piece of the 'cookie'. He was beginning to like the taste. But he didn't want the Major to think that he was too keen to accept American cooking in place of good traditional English cooking. He stepped back, taking out a handkerchief to clean his fingers.

'Kentucky Mountain Loaf,' said Drummel. 'Quite a favourite over there, I gather.' But the Colonel was no longer interested in American eating habits. His mind was elsewhere. He had turned away to walk over to a table across the room. The small bevel-edged box, compact like a woman's handbag, now held his new interest. But it didn't hold ladies' personal things, and it was made of steel.

'This will be the --- ?'

'Convertor M-209,' said Major Drummel. 'Lieutenant Colonel Bretzler's, own machine. Left it with me. To familiarise with.' Drummel bent over the US Army issue field cypher machine to open it. 'Jolly sophisticated for its size.' The small steel cover swung back to reveal a close-set arrangement of knobs, buttons and numbered wheels.

Rutkin gave the metal casework a brief touch with two somewhat reluctantly stretched-out  fingers. Plainly he wasn't into mechanical things, or how they functioned. Only in how they could be of help to the soldier in the battlefield. Gadgets, to him, were only a secondary form of soldiery. 'Yet another ingenious American invention, for which we must be eternally grateful,' said Rutkin in an openly peeved tone.

'Swedish, in fact, sir. I had in, in fact, thought it was German at first. You have to admit that they're well up in their engineering. Jerries, maybe, but you've got to give them that. Back when I was Production Manager with Huntly and Brenns Engineering, there were two separate occasions when the company would have gone under had we not decided to take on, at my advice, vital components of a German design for our production line machinery. Without those pieces, the assembly-line would have drastically ground to a halt; and probably not without missing an opportunity to cause an accident in the shop floor end-line team. Like I've said, absolutely tip-top engineering. You've got to give them that.' Drummel paused in his little spiel for a breather and a look round at the Colonel. His confidence faltered for a second under Rutkin's iron-faced glower of disapproval at the Major's words. A hedgehog, in the circumstances, would have perhaps curled up into a defensive ball. But Drummel simply gave an embarrassed cough to cover his faux pas. He hastened to repair the damage. 'Invented by some Swedish chap in the States. Very versatile in the field, from what Colonel Bretzler tells me; standard equipment piece, in fact, so that they have thousands in operation. In fact, Captain Falzoni has promised us a small consignment of them.'

Drummel scratched his forehead in puzzled thought. 'To be honest, I don't quite see how he does it – but he *does*, nevertheless. He's a lawyer, isn't he? In civvy street, I mean? I suppose that helps – knowing how to duck and dive between the quartermaster's rules and statutes.'

'I wouldn't delve too deeply into that aspect, Major,' said Rutkin. 'If Winston is none too concerned with rules in his current enthusiasm for dirty tricks warfare, then we should be content to work under his official shadow.' But the Colonel's words were a mixed bag. In the same way that his mind was divided. He didn't like to think, or know, that they were accepting stolen supplies from the American. But he accepted, at the same time, that snatching illicit opportunities, however distasteful, was vital in winning this deadly game against the Hun. It also occurred to him that this two-way swing of judgement was not confined to him alone. There were those he knew at GHQ who did not fully concur with Winston's outlook, whilst still obeying his commands. Just as there must surely be a similar conflict of wills over *there*, in the Reichstag. For a fleeting moment he was both proud and shocked to find himself thinking in unison, so he supposed, with those older hierarchy members of what had formerly been Germany's imperialist Reichswehr, now renamed the Wehrmacht. Professional soldiers like himself who staunchly went by a traditional military code of honour. From reports coming in, these old soldiers held considerable disapproval of their corporal-come-Fuhrer's tactics. But Hitler, it seemed, was inclined to ignore their advice --- at great cost. Come to think of it, Dromyrk's profile predictions of Hitler's various battle tactics had been too often ignored, cast aside by sceptics as mumbo jumbo. And they had been fairly accurate forecasts on the whole. Rutkin bit his lip.

He recalled Dromyrk's earlier remark on knowing your opposite number in the game. Admiral Wilhelm Franz Canaris. For eight years so far, Canaris, was head of the Abwehr (Military Intelligence & Counterespionage ) running Germany's clandestine spy operations in parallel to our own SOE and OSS operations. With Heydrich having been assassinated last year, Canaris now figured as the country's supreme controller of intelligence services. Heydrich had been the restraining power that had held Canaris back up until then. Not only had he been head of the Sicheheitsdienst (SD) the rival intelligence service that spied on everyone else, but as SS-Obergruppenfuhrer, he had been head of the Reichssicherheitshauptamt (Reich Main Security Office; RSHA) with total control of all Germany's security services. Heydrich had thus enjoyed considerable political influence. Perhaps more so because he was in close association with the chief of German police, Reichsfuhrer SS Heinrich Himmler.  His violent demise in Prague, shot down in the street but still alive, had been a much botched-up SOE operation.

Heydrich, the much hated 'Butcher', had died from bullet and grenade shrapnel wounds soon after. The backlash of repercussions taken out on the civilian population had been horrifying. Rutkin shuddered inside at the thought. A much botched-up operation. At least it hadn't been one of his operations. It had been shortly before he had joined the Section.

But Canaris and Himmler did not get on well together. They were bitterly opposed. This from the reports that Rutkin had so far received. A somewhat tricky bird, was Canaris, Rutkin thought. Head of the enemy's undercover operations, yet of yesteryear's code of honour. Not only had he openly denounced Hitler in hostile terms, but he was relaying intelligence material to the Chief of the OSS station in Bern, Switzerland. We were already turning German spies we'd arrested into double agents. So to be on the safe side, it did well to bear in mind that those Swiss clocks could cuckoo in double tone. If it was reliable material, and not a dupe, how long could it possibly be before Himmler persuaded his beloved Fuhrer to put the Admiral before a firing squad? Rutkin wondered if Dromyrk could answer that puzzler, because he, himself, couldn't.

' --- moving this lever and enciphering your message – making sure the letters are in groups of five, using these wheels, then printing them on the this paper strip under the lever. Then radio the  message to your contact  in the field. That's it. Not as complicated as the Enigma contraption, but good for speed. 'Let me demonstrate. This knob here is ---'

Catching on to half of what the Major was saying brought Rutkin out of his inner preoccupation. He waved Drummel's intended demonstration aside. 'It's all right, Major, I'll take your word for it.' Rutkin's interest was apt to fade as promptly as it had arisen. He strode off, causing Drummel to close the cipher machine with a noisy clamp, before scurrying after him. Walking along Lindwell's corridors, they passed room after room of quiet intensity, the figures bent over in learning deadly crafts of subversion and sabotage. How to kill, destroy and survive behind enemy lines.

It didn't escape Drummel's notice that the Colonel wasn't really interested in technical things themselves, in spite of the technical questions he threw out over various pieces of equipment. He plainly wasn't a 'technical things' person. He was a military-minded man, a solid infantry man,  interested in the human performance of those training to use the equipment. He assessed things and personnel according to how soon they could be put into active service. But then Drummel, in turn, had never seen any real active service. His squat stature and flat foot arches had always worked to his disadvantage. Especially with the coming of the war. The  Army Selection Board had not placed him with a fighting unit. Instead, because of his technical background, they had offered him  the  post of Technical Overseer with  a  Midlands light engineering company. Like many other companies,  it  was   replacing domestic productions with those more suited to the war effort.

Formerly making oven-plating and gas-ring tubing for cookers, they were now turning out 0.5" – 6" armour plating, and wheel-track plating, for the 42 ton Churchill tank, along with the 6-pounder turret gun. Sub-contract work for Vickers-Armstrong had them also producing the tubular sections for the tank's Grundlach rotary 360 degrees prism periscope.

But Drummel had not been taken in by the Board's attempt to quell his dissatisfaction by saying that the post would be on a liaison basis with the military. He just couldn't quite conjure up a happy picture of himself surrounded by hundreds of females, their shrill prattle shrieking above the din of already thundering lathes. The Board had relented and assigned him to Lindwell Hall. It was a move nearer to the fighting front. Initial friendly jibes of 'Who called in the Home Guard?' had riled him on his first arrival. But he had hid his irritation and got on with helping fighting men – and *women* – learn a new brand of underhand warfare tactics.

As they moved on towards the Hall's east wing, a new strain of voices came to ear. Faint and coming from a far end side entrance, it seemed. But still recognisable as American voices. Inasmuch as Drummel was enjoying this regular cornucopia of American supplies, courtesy of 'Falzoni & Co', he was nevertheless a little unsure of how things stood now with this new lot joining them at Lindwell. Four altogether. Along with the two Americans, a Swedish psychiatrist and one of our own army corporals – a woman, it seemed. That was it, as far as he knew. And that wasn't much. You could always count on the Colonel to be scant with his operational details. He expected you to pick up the trail like a dutiful bloodhound and know exactly what the hell he was going on about in spite of his not fully saying so. You learned to follow on, like that faithful sniffer, watching out for 'puddles' and unsafe footing that could cost you. Although he would not say so openly, Rutkin was apt to become very much annoyed if he saw that you had not grasped the end point of his instructions. The other points leading up to that end point you had to make up for yourself. That was the measure of an officer's efficiency, as far as Rutkin saw it.

The Major saw that The Colonel had also heard the sound of the new arrivals. He saw it causing Rutkin to think and frown. It served as an appropriate moment for Drummel to voice his own uncertainty. A quick nervous cough before he spoke. 'What exactly is my standing, sir --- here at Lindwell?'

'*Standing?*' Rutkin switched his frown, in a sharp swing round from the approaching voices, onto the squat 'block of khaki', barely five feet tall, in front of him.

'I thought *we* were running the show here at Lindwell? Am I still holding the reins? Or am I being ousted from my post?' said Drummel. 'Perhaps to a new posting elsewhere?'

Rutkin saw anxiety, if not fear, in the man's face. He didn't like that in his officers, however justified it may be. He appreciated the Major's concern with this American 'intrusion' onto their patch. But perhaps he was mistaken. Had he seen something else beyond that in the Major's eyes? Was it hope? He tried to think of something appeasing to say that would quell the man's inner unrest. 'They do, after all, let us use their airfield, which they built, for our operations, Major. We have to remember that before we ---' Rutkin cut himself off before he said something that would sound priggishly anti-American.

'Gift horse in the mouth, and all that – right, I get it, sir.' But he didn't get it, insofar as he still didn't know what his position was to be with Lt-Col Bretzler having issued his own official mandates on  the place. The last forty-eight hours had seen a hectic whirlwind of upheaval with Bretzler implementing an  immediate  shift all round of procedures, in both administration and the  training routines. Virtually like upturning a wastepaper basket, the Yank had thrown out their old running system and replaced it with new schedules that covered everything down to who sharpened the pencils. Witnessing all of this in the midst of its happening, Drummel had had his comments fall on deaf ears. The American wasn't deaf. He just didn't want to hear them. Drummel might just as well have been invisible. Hence Drummel's concern over his position being threatened. He had run Lindwell up until now. So now what?

Rutkin, of course, knew of all these changes even before they had been made. It was he who, in joint-agreement with Lt-Colonel Bretzler, had given the green light for them to be carried out. But in hearing it blurted out, not only from a confused Drummel, but from other surprised members of staff here, it did tend to sound a bit much. He had to play along if only to appease Drummel. 'Good grief! Did he really go that far?' True, we had wanted them to come over as allies and help us win the war; but now that they were over, were they now of a mind to *take over*?  A calming smile at Drummel. 'You'll just carry on as before, George. Help them to slide into their slots here --- *and watch them as they do*. They can, after all, be useful to us. Watch them and listen to what they're saying.'

Drummel didn't need the Colonel to tap his nose, (which he didn't) to signify that this was a chummy pulling together against the Americans. That he had called him by his first name, instead of the usual 'Major' or 'Drummel' had been sign enough. 'What exactly is it I'm required to be watching and listening for, sir?'

Rutkin took in a long deep breath to hide his impatience and irritation with this blockhead soldier in front of him. It wasn't just the shrink, Dromyrk , who could read mind signals in people. The very way that Drummel had added that 'sir', so much like pupil to headmaster, told him that the fool had barely grasped his message beyond the sound of the words. No, this idiot would not receive a posting to an active unit 'elsewhere', as he had again hopefully intoned in his utterance of that word. Since the man obviously understood the working of technical systems better than that of the soldier, it would be better – *safer* -- to keep him with his machines, and well away from the battlefield. Once again, a warm smile of reassurance to the dumb Major. 'You'll know. And remember – just keep an ear to the ground.'

The Colonel was now edging away, checking the time on his watch, while casting a furtive glance in the direction of the approaching voices as they grew louder. It was apparent that he was not in a mood to parley with the Americans. Drummel needed to get another thing clear before the Colonel went. 'Do I watch the Doctor as well?'

Facing away, Rutkin threw his eyes to the heavens in exasperation. He came back down to earth to turn with a polite smile of patience at the Major. 'So how has Doctor Dromyrk been progressing in his debriefing sessions with the men?'

'He's given the all clear on Maxwell and Redfern to go on their missions. '

'And Tolley?'

'It seems he was unsure on Tolley.'

'*Oh*? And did he give any indication of the nature of this?

'I'm afraid you would have to get that directly from him, sir. If he can give it to you in simple layman's lingo, that is. Sorry, sir.'

'Never mind. I'll get back to him on that myself, when I can.' Rutkin really was in a hurry to get away now. Standing at the open doorway, he looked across the open moor at a group of men in training. He couldn't, at this distance, see what it was that they were carrying, but it must have been heavy since it caused them sway and stumble in their combined effort to move across what seemed like open space. But their progress across the 'open' moor was pocked with dull-thudding explosions around them, along with staccato machine-gun fire. This, all the while, being monitored through binoculars held by a distant figure in duffle coat and Marines green beret.  Rutkin looked back at Drummel. 'If you'll excuse me, Major, I have to go now. I have to have a word with Sergeant-Major McCulloch, over there. In the meantime, Major, carry on as we said with --- *you know.*' Rutkin's slight nod was supposed to convey to Drummel what it was he was supposed to know. Turning away, Rutkin suddenly remembered something and turned around to face Drummel again. 'I need to speak to the Frenchman, Palpiere. He's around here, somewhere. I saw him as I was coming in. If you would be so good as to go and find him for me, and bring him to me, Major.' That said, Rutkin was gone out the door before Drummel could get out his answer.

'Will do. Right away, sir.'

Lt-Colonel Bretzler had now come round the corner down the corridor. With his excuse of having lots to do, Major Drummel barked out a curt: 'Got to go,' and disappeared through a conveniently near doorway faster than Alice's Mad Hatter Rabbit could have done. Bretzler could only give his casual low guttural laugh at how his two British counterparts had made themselves scarce with great speed.

Suddenly the light was partly cut off by a large figure standing in the doorway. It stepped inside. A Fallschirmjager wielding the Italian 9mm Beretta Modello-38 sub-machinegun. There was also an FN Browning P-35 9mm pistol on his belt. Although the brown-green camouflage jacket concealed his regiment jacket underneath, you could still identify him as a Luftwaffe paratrooper on account of the chin-strapped steel fallschirmhelm having no projecting visor and deep flared rim that typified all the other German helmets. Bretzler put on his stern look to address the man. 'I'm nailing *you*, buddy, before you vamoose as well.'

The soldier stared back at him, waiting.

'We've got a problem, buddy.'

'Aw, aye? An' whit's that, then?' replied the 'German' in broad Glaswegian accent.

'I'll tell you what the goddamn problem is, Jock. The goddamn coffee percolator has gone and done a runner, just like everyone else around here seems to be doing. That's the goddamn problem.'

'Whit the hell is a percolator — *sir*?'

Insubordination wasn't number one priority in Bretzler's mind so he ignored the remark, with its insolent delay of the last word. But he couldn't get over this pauper-style way of how the Brits lived. 'What is --?' He stopped his words short, to take in again, their primitive ignorance of what was plain ordinary living in the States. Bad enough that they didn't have air-conditioning and indoor toilets. Even the hillbilly folks back home knew what was out there that they didn't have themselves. But these highland guys were another thing altogether. And their heavy rasping accents. Those London Pearly King people sure spoke with a quaint twang; but when Jocks spoke, it was like struggling to get your ears through another tangled mass of Jerry's barbed trench-wire. 'Jeez, buddy, we sure as hell have a problem, all right.'

# 8

It was either remarkable coincidence, or simply that he liked the official air of doing it, that Colonel Rutkin was always last to enter a committee room. He strode into the long austere War Office room in his usual hurried busy-on-the-move manner, letting the door close behind him with a loud clump. Passing between two double rows of military personnel seated in metal-framed chairs, he stopped at the front. He turned around to face his audience. Khaki was roughly balanced by blue, with a darker tinge of brown for our US allies. A fair haze of cigarette smoke had gathered near the ceiling from their waiting on his arrival. Discordant sounds of conversation died down, the American voices last. An outbreak of polite coughs scattered around the room. They waited.

'Peenemunde, gentleman,' said Rutkin at last. 'At least I think that's how you pronounce it – my German being not at all that good.' A little smile, both on his face, and those of the audience, at this little joke of a personal admission. His face quickly went serious again. 'A little village lying just off the German Baltic coast. According to our experts, it apparently sits on an island – Usedorm – near the mouth of the river Peene, on the eastern coast.'

'Usedom,' said someone.

'Sorry?' said Rutkin, looking across the room to locate the speaker. He saw it was Jeremy Withers.

'It's called Usedom,' said Wing Commander Withers.

'Oh, I see. I beg your pardon. You're personally acquainted with the place then, are you, Jeremy?'

'Well, no, not myself personally, John. But when Reggie Heathesome and I took our vacation from Cambridge to do our German summer studies, Reg developed a keenness for sailing, and so headed out that way, to the coast. I don't share his love of the sea, so I preferred staying inland.'

'Must give you some whackoo of a gut feeling, I'll bet, flying sorties 'cross all that sea,' came the heavy Texan drawl from the silver-haired soldier decked in a chestful of campaign ribbons, seated behind Withers.

'I don't like tracer bullets strafing my plane's underside, inches from my backside either, but it doesn't stop me doing my bit,' replied Withers.

'I think he's got you there, Hanny; 'bout evens,' quipped Lt-Col Bretzler, from the front row.

'Anyway, that's how I know the name,' Winters continued. 'Can't give you any more gen on the place, though. Sorry.'

'I see. That's a pity. Thanks all the same, Jeremy.' Rutkin breathed in deeply for a second to pull his mind away from friendly talk, and get back to the others on a more serious issue. 'As I was saying – Peenemunde -- which may at one time have served as an idyllic venue for sailing enthusiasts -- is now a devilish thorn in our side.' A creaking of seats, with attentions all round now sharpened in readiness for heavier words than those they'd heard so far. 'A thorn that we must pull out promptly. If we fail to do this, we'll be in danger of falling back in our effort to defeat the Hun.' Rutkin stood there, nodding his head at those before him, in deadly affirmation of his grim choice of words.

He suddenly looked to the back of the room. 'Lights.' The room went pitch black. Low laughter broke out from different lumps of the darkness.

'Sorry, sir,' said a humble voice from the back of the room. The corporal had failed to turn on the projector before turning off the room lights.

'For heaven's sake, do just get on with it, Corporal,' said Rutkin. He didn't like his little presentations going wrong and was as much irritated as the corporal was flustered. 'What's your name, Corporal?'

'Corporal Harvey, sir.'

'Well get on with it, Corporal Harvey.'

'Sir.'

A moment's whirring from the slide projector, then it lit up. The beam of light lit up the screen perched on the slim tripod, as well as half of Rutkin, caught unawares standing in the way. He quickly stepped out of the way. Scratches and wiry blotches raced randomly across the screen while a large optic bubble danced to and fro trying to find the right focus. Suddenly the screen went dark, focused on what looked like an aerial shot of a landscape, if it was anything, being so obscure.

'What exactly are we looking at?' said someone in the dark.

'What we believe to be the sites of secret experimental work on some new kind of weapon at Peenemunde. Our Intelligence people have long suspected that the Germans have been working on new weapons development. But we never could ascertain the location. Well we now know – in fact, since last year we've discovered that they're working on some kind of flying bomb. Yes, a damned bomb that flies by itself! Absolutely fiendish! From what I gather from MI6 and SOE reports, it was originally called the Vergeltungwaffen – if I can get my tongue round that correctly.' Rutkin looked across to roughly where Withers was sitting in the darkness. 'Is that all right with you, Jeremy?'

'It'll do. It means 'vengeance weapon'.

'I can well imagine Adolf being hopping mad and wanting vengeance, what with his blitz bombing attempt on us having failed,' said another voice in the dark.

'Right. Well this flying bomb weapon is now called the V-1,' said Rutkin. 'And if that isn't enough to have on our plate, we believe they are also working alongside that on a type of rocket weapon. The V-2.' Slides clicked on and off in their turn on the screen, showing shots of what were very inexplicit beyond being tubular shapes, probably metallic, and rounded shapes that could possibly be concrete emplacements. Some 'things' seemed to poke out of the screen – probably the tubular 'things' standing vertical. One seemed to sit at an angle, as if lying on an inclined plane – on a ramp, perhaps? The screen suddenly went blank.

'If that's all there is, it wasn't very informative, I must say,' said someone, accompanied by mutterings of agreement from others.

'Lights,' said Rutkin. The lights came on and the slide-projector's hum cut off. An RAF officer stood up from the front row and stepped over to join Rutkin. Group Captain Tommy Hollings. He put a large illustrated board on the tripod. He looked round expectantly at Rutkin, his cue for the Colonel to let him take over. Rutkin, as if reluctant to relinquish his leader position, hesitated, before stepping away. Just before sitting against a table facing the audience, he turned to hold out a hand towards the Group Captain. 'Group Captain Hollings, for those of you who don't know.' He sat against the edge of the table, folding his arms.

Hollings turned back to the board to point at its drawings. It featured what seemed like a large cigar-shaped structure pointed at one end. A tubular structure was attached a short space above it, at about halfway along its length. The artist had done the rough semblance of a short blunt-ended wing facing out this way; presumably there would be one on the other side, otherwise the 'thing' would be somewhat unbalanced. Hollings tapped the board with the back of his hand. 'The V-1, gentlemen. Die Wergeltungwaffen. Although we've suspected for some time – a long time in fact, -- we were put off the scent, so to speak, because of its rather misleading codename, which was Flakzielgerat – 76. Which I'm told means flak-aiming apparatus.' He grinned over in Withers direction for confirmation of his translation. Withers grinned and nodded back his approval. 'I think you'll agree, not quite the thing to spring up a picture in your mind of a great flying bomb,' said Hollings. 'It's only within the last twelve months, with invaluable help from the Polish Army Intelligence field units,' Hollings continued, nodding in appreciation to the Polish officer seated on his own at the back, Captain Pecri Jalwanowski, 'that we've at last been able to pin down our suspicions on what was going on and where it was going on. We lost a damn lot of time on that mistake.'

In fact, Germany had been working under Britain's 'Intelligence radar' since as early as 1931. A rocket research station had been established at Kummersdorf Weapons Range, near Berlin. Working under the directions of a Dr Werner von Braun, an initial contingency of eighty scientists had grown, after moving to Peenemunde in '37, to a total five thousand personnel in '42. Whilst Dr von Braun was working on the rocket's development, Dr Waltman Thurl was in charge of the flying bomb's development and production.

The Group Captain stood looking at the board with its deadly illustration as he went on speaking.

'The bomb uses a gasoline-powered pulse-jet engine that produces an eleven hundred pound thrust. We now think actual test flights began roughly twenty-four, perhaps thirty, months ago, over the Peenemunde range. It was originally called the Fieseler FL-103, after the Berlin company. It bears no resemblance whatsoever to its 'cousin' the V-2. For a start, it's shorter. And it has wings, which you can see here – well, one at least. The V-2 is plainly a rocket, and much longer I gather.' Hollings paused for a breather. A faint smile of triumph touched his otherwise serious expression as he made to continue. 'But Jerry's game of secrecy ended, alas, in August, last year, when a Mosquito on routine reconnaissance mission flew over Peenemunde.' Hollings searched for a face among the RAF lot. He found it. '*Foley*, was it, Tom?' he said.

'Yes, it was Flying Officer Foley, along with Bob Haines who took the aerial shots. Jolly bit of luck, really,' said Squadron Leader Thomas J Warren. 'Changed our outlook somewhat. Gave us a new scent to follow.'

'Thanks, Tom. Anyway, photographs brought back from that airfield showed evidence of construction activity with circular emplacements on the ground. Our photo experts were not able to define anything out of the ordinary at first. However, later intelligence showed us that rockets had been fired. We think the first V-2 rocket test flight was in October, last year.'

Colonel Rutkin stood up suddenly to interrupt Hollings. 'Some months ago our MI5 analysts managed to elicit vital confirmation of rockets from two POW generals we're holding in one of our VIP detention houses outside the city, not far from here. They spoke freely and boldly of their rockets.'

'But surely they must be bluffing? Mustn't they? I can hardly imagine two officers of such rank freely giving you such information face to face, on a silver plate, so to speak.' This stuffy outburst from a stuffy 'old guard' soldier, Brigadier Roemont.

'That is precisely the point, sir – namely that they were totally unaware that they had given us this information. Their words were in what they believed was private, *secure*, conversation which our analysts listened in on by way of some new-fangled electronic eavesdropping devices, rigged up by our technical wizards,' said Rutkin. 'It is a further interesting point that General Vohlman is of the opinion that Germany is gradually losing the war, whilst General Meinz strongly refuses to concede to such defeatist concept. Such was the intensity of opposing views that the insolent language that eventually arose between them only stopped short of blows being exchanged. They now refuse to speak to each other and are demanding separate latrines.'

'I see,' said Brigadier Roemont, ruefully rubbing his chin. It wasn't only that he had been corrected by the Colonel. He simply didn't hold with this kind of squabbling behaviour between generals, regardless of uniforms, regardless of circumstances.

Hollings took over again. 'We've since had the photo reconnaissance operations cover every square mile of French coast from Cherbourg to the Belgian border. Flights by RAF at Leuchars and Benson, and the 8th US Air Force's 13th, 14th and 22nd photo reconnaissance squadrons. We now have films readily identifying vehicles carrying what looks like long cylindrical objects. Latest material shows rockets lying on trailers near an emplacement. A shot of one of them partly erected gives us an estimate of about forty feet or so in length.'

Two silver stars glinted on the shoulders of the next person who felt the need to speak. US Army Air force Major General Coolson Weighley. 'Hell, I don't mean to sound like some bellowin' longhorn steer, but like the Brigadier was sayin', can we be so sure that this whole Peenemunde show isn't just *that* – a *show* – a damned put-up job? Usin' dummy props an' all to create a distraction from what Jerry doesn't want us to see somewhere else. Camouflage in reverse, if you want.' The Major General had gained his two stars on account of the influential Washington business contacts he made as the country's number one provider of beef. So you didn't need to dig deep beneath the uniform to find the cattle baron. And he treated his staff the same way that he treated his cattle. He waved his hands to reinforce his point. 'We're all usin' dummy set-ups – Jerry's usin' them – we're usin' them. Hell, our reconnaissance flight guys have photographed enough dummy set-ups to put all the Hollywood studios together out of business.' Some polite controlled laughter from the others.

Group Captain Hollings was about to reply to this, but seeing that Colonel Rutkin wanted to say something, he stepped back. His mouth was getting dry, anyway. He poured himself some water from a carafe on the table.

Rutkin paused for a moment, looking down at the floor, to consider his piece, then looked up. 'The idea of this whole Peenemunde situation being a hoax is not one exclusive to this meeting alone. Yes, admittedly there are some who think this is a hoax for the reasons we've just heard, namely, to distract us from important things elsewhere. But also on the grounds that such a large rocket is impractical. But consider this, if you will. If we believe it not to be a hoax a hoax, then we would bomb Peenemunde, certainly. It follows, in turn, the Germans would only want us to bomb Peenemunde if it was not a real important research station.' Rutkin hesitated for moment before giving his next 'reason' – given to him half an hour ago by Dr Dromyrk in advice for this meeting. 'I have it on some authority, that Hitler, in his state of divine omnipotence, would consider it to be below his station for him to consent to his superior Aryan troops hiding behind a shield of deceit, rather than rely on their invincible power to defeat the enemy.' He rubbed his cheek as an inner humour brought on a faint smile. 'Take that as you may, we have another factor to help tip the scales of decision. We've just intercepted, somewhat by chance, an otherwise insignificant piece of evidence that decides the case. An official circular issued by the German Air Ministry for fuel ration allowance to German Air Force experimental stations, in fact. It shows Peenemunde's allowance to be above that of other stations that we know to be genuine. Thus, Peenemunde is not a hoax.'

'Unless *it also* is a damned dupe,' muttered Weighley quietly in his lingering doubt.

Rutkin glanced at Weighly before continuing. 'We also have air-photos of massive concrete structures at Watten, near Calais, and two other places --- all of them connected to railway lines. As far as can be judged, these give strong indication of stepped-up activity. This finalised report, codenamed: 'Landline', to Special Operations Investigation Committee. As a result, the Joint Parliamentary Secretary to the Ministry of Supply, charged with coordinating information about secret weapons, has issued strict orders for Peedemunde to be bombed. The Operation will be called 'Crossbow', as agreed under joint council.' Rutkin paused to push forth his message with a stabbing forefinger. 'We must destroy the V-1 and V-2 launching sites, before they can mount deadly attacks, and cripple, if not totally destroy, our chance of retaliatory measure. Otherwise, their effect on the public is apt to be one of terror, since -- if I've got it right from the experts – these bombs-- unlike planes -- would seemingly suddenly come out of nowhere, to drop their screaming death-loads on the masses below.'

Rutkin stopped there to look around and see what effect his last point was having in the others' faces. He consulted his notes on the table for a moment, and looked up again, to continue. 'Crossbow will be a large-scale joint counter-air and strategic attack operation by RAF and US Army Air Force squadrons to delay V-weapons attacks and limit their effectiveness once the Germans begin to use them. First Crossbow target is Peenemunde.  As far as our calculations can predict, we foresee this calling for many, many, sorties and a colossal tonnage of ordnance.' He paused and took a deep breath, hesitating, before making his next gruesome statement. 'Primary objective is to kill as many personnel involved in V-weapons programme as possible. So living quarters – *civilian,* more than military – will be our primary target.'

'Amen,' said Bretzler, in a low drawn-out tone that was by no means a merry one.

All right, this was war, and killing was the inevitable part of it. As a soldier Rutkin knew that, and had done his share of killing.  But his kind of killing – the killing he *understood* – if killing *can* be understood -- was man-to-man across a battlefield. Who died, and how one died, in that particular theatre of war was left for Fate or Luck to decree. But this standing here, naming from afar, specific masses of individuals, *civilians especially*, to be put to death was moving him inside. He made to finish. 'Two lesser objectives: to destroy as much of the V-weapons installations and documentation as possible – and to render Peenemunde useless as a research station.'

Hollings sensed that the Colonel had said all he wanted to say for the moment, and took over again. 'Bomber Command will be launching roughly five hundred and ninety-six aircraft – three hundred and twenty-four Lancasters, two hundred and eighteen Halifaxes, fifty-four Stirlings – dropping around eighteen hundred  tons of bombs on Peenemunde, eighty-five per cent of this tonnage  being high explosive.' He looked around to see the effect of these figures on the others, then continued.  'We've considered it to be best – *essential,* in fact, -- to use the tactic of pinpoint bombing in this operation, where precision is vital, considering the smallness of the target, in a night-time raid. Just as we did when we bombed the Mohne and Eder dams and the battleship Tirpitz in Hardanger fjord in Norway.'

Rutkin's mind brooded over this mention of May's bombing of the Rhur Valley dams. Reports of the results of this operation were still trickling in, and heavy as the damage had been, it was perhaps not as heavy as they had estimated it would have been. He couldn't help wondering what degree of success would come out of this operation, with all its massive effort.

'We intend to have Bomber Command's Pathfinder Force using one aircraft to control progress of the entire raid, orbiting above the target area,' said Hollings. 'With there being three aiming points, that is, living quarters, rocket factory and experimental station, Pathfinders will use crew shifters, moving from one aiming point to the  next, as the raid develops.'

'Why can't we just shoot the damn things out of the sky, like we've done before?' said the Major General. 'Deal with them when they come. Seems like you RAF lot handled the Hun all right in the Blitz. What's so special about these ruddy things that we can't do the same again? Use all the bombing effort you're mounting for a proper job on Berlin, instead of some little island offshore.'

Hollings was momentarily at a loss, stalled by the interruption. Not just because he was put off what he was going to say, but by the technical nature of the question. His speciality was operational intelligence, so he was needing to refer to someone better qualified. He looked to the front row, at the Volunteer Reserve RAF officer holding the long rolled-up paper tube across his knees. Pilot Officer Knowles, in spite of the uniform, could only look like the brilliant engineer, 'on loan' from Imperial College's aeronautics laboratory, that he was. His specialised knowledge was an invaluable asset to RAF Technical Training Command. You could well expect him to stir his tea with a slide rule. His preference for books, rather than the sports field, at school had seen him labelled as 'Know-all' Knowles.

'Perhaps you would care to enlighten us, now that we're under attack from the 'ruddy things,' Hollings said, with a widening grin at Knowles.

Knowles stepped up to the tripod. Taking spring clips from his pocket, he set about fastening the sheet to Hollings' sheet. It was a cut-away version of the one beneath it. Much like the anatomical drawings of an animal's inside, except that this animal had a fiercer bite. He shifted himself from foot to foot for some seconds to ready himself. 'Sorry, sir,' he said looking at the Major General, 'but this ingenious piece of engineering by far outclasses anything we have for velocity, except, perhaps, for the Hawker Tempest. The V-1 has a velocity of four hundred miles per hour. Our planes are too slow to catch it.' He scratched his chin. 'That is, unless they have a height advantage that would allow them gain speed through gravitational acceleration by diving down on it. And we don't have many Tempests – *do* we?' He looked at Hollings.

'We're lucky if we have even thirty. And so far as I understand, these are assigned to 150 Wing.'

'Like I was saying,' said Knowles, 'no plane we have can catch it, with it travelling at four hundred miles per hour, at an altitude of two hundred to three hundred feet, powered by a pulse-jet engine. Weighing around forty-seven hundred pounds, with a length of just over twenty-seven feet and a width of seventeen and a half feet, it carries a nineteen hundred pound warhead, we think, of Amatol thirty-nine.' Knowles stopped to peer in close at the drawing. Turning round again, he touched the sheet to indicate a point, not that it really mattered to the others. 'This, here, as I've said, is the pulse-jet assembly engine; an Argus design, if I'm not very much mistaken – designed by Lusser, giving it an operational range of round about one hundred and sixty miles, more or less. I've seen his designs – quite clever, really, in their simplicity. Apparently the engine pulses roughly fifty times  per second, giving it ----- if I've  got my information right -- thanks to Captain Jalwanowski's Resistance  contacts  on  site,' a curt nod to the Polish officer,  '--- what I'm told is a distinct buzzing sound. A  sound which  I'm  also  told,  can be heard from a considerable distance away. This could perhaps be a small asset to our pilots in locating it from afar without the need for radar.'

He judged it to be an apt moment for a small humoured piece to ease his listeners' minds from the weight of all these technical details. Another nod and smile at Captain Jalwanowski. 'I'm further told that Hitler, on hearing the sound, considered it to be like that of an insect, so declaring that it should be called the Maikafer. Or May fly.' Not a sound from anyone. Not a single flicker of amusement, or even interest, shown anywhere. Only impatience, with everyone waiting for him to get on with it. An awkward twiddling of his thumbs for a moment in the dead silence. 'Yes, well, I just thought I would mention it. No matter.'

Taking refuge from his gaffe by turning swiftly back to the drawing, he stabbed a finger at it. 'Fuelling is by gasoline octane seven five – a whole one hundred and fifty gallons of it. The engine is ignited by automatic spark plugs about two and a half feet behind the intake shutters – just about here.' He bent for a closer look. 'No, sorry, here.' He straightened up. 'The current for the plugs, of course, coming from a portable starter unit. Highly pressurised acetylene gas is issued from multiple nozzles, three, I should think, in front of the engine to start it.' Knowles turned around facing the others, rubbing his hands slowly together in reflex habit of removing the chalk-dust from his fingers as he normally did standing before a class of students. 'I have to say that I think that the low static thrust of the pulse-jet engine, combined with the short wings causing a high stalling velocity, would make it virtually impractical for the V-1 to take off on its own power over a short distance. In which case I can only see it being launched either from a modified bomber aircraft, a Heinkel, perhaps, or by some form of aircraft catapult mechanism.'

But he erred slightly in his judgement. No aircraft was necessary. Even as Knowles spoke these very words, another one of many V-1 test-flights was being carried out at a remote coastal stretch. Positioned on an inclined ramp, the deadly flying bomb was launched by a Dampferzeuger (steam generator) device using stabilised hydrogen peroxide and potassium permanganate to jettison it off with an initial velocity of 360mph into the Baltic's dark grey brooding sky.

Still rubbing his hands together, Knowles stood for a moment, looking around as if expecting questions, as he usually did with his students. But nobody so far questioned his obviously better knowledge. He went on, turning as he did, for a brief look at the drawing. 'It uses a simple autopilot system – made by the Berlin firm, Askania, we think – to regulate altitude and airspeed. A weighted -----'

'If it doesn't have a pilot, it must surely need some form of radio guidance to direct it to its target, otherwise how would it get there?' It was Brigadier Roemont this time throwing the question. 'All we have to do surely – if I'm understanding this confounded contraption correctly – is to jam the ruddy thing's radio frequency. So what's the problem?'

When Knowles turned around, his expression was a mixture of wry amusement and scientist's irritation at the layman's tardy comprehension. He stooped slightly, nodding his head with patience, as in his lecturer's manner with students. He managed a smile as another train of thought struck him. 'Ah, yes, well that is perhaps the simpler part of its setup. It doesn't, in fact, actually *require* guiding, as such, along its programmed flight. Instead, it need only be pointed in the right direction on its initial launching.' Another thought struck him, amazing him that it hadn't occurred to him before. Simplicity was, indeed, the key word. The thought of it being pointed in the right direction made his mind home in on the concept that should have occurred to him when had said so. 'There is the further possibility that it is launched, not airborne, but from the ground – from an inclined ramp, perhaps. Such a method would eliminate the larger margin of error of the required direction, through unsteadiness, if launched from a moving plane.' The logic was better, but it still niggled Knowles that he hadn't thought of it before.

He pushed the annoyance aside to continue. 'As I was saying, a weighted pendulum in the guidance system stabilises a gyrocompass, whilst also controlling the fore and aft altitude measurements, so regulating the pitch.' He tipped a horizontal forearm up and down at each end. 'In other words --- stopping it from nosing down or nosing up. As for reaching its target, I can only imagine that some form of digital countdown within is how the distance flown is determined. For instance, an anemometer – that is, a wind vane propeller --- mounted on the nose would drive an odometer to give so many revolutions. So many revolutions, in turn, would represent one digit, which, in turn, means so many miles. The requisite number of digits, representing the target distance, is obviously set prior to the launching, with the counter set at zero. On reaching that number, I can only imagine detonating bolts firing, causing spoilers  to jam the tail elevator gears, and cut off the control hoses to the rudder gears, setting the rudder in neutral. The poor bomb, alas, would have no choice, thereafter, but to go into a steep dive.'

Whilst the designers had originally seen their V-1 to be a thunderous beast diving down on the enemy in powered fury, their flight tests were showing that the dive was causing a cut-off of fuel, so stopping the engine. Thus the bomb's intended mighty roar of descent was reduced to one of silence.

Knowles rubbed his hands again, as if in nearing the end of his lecture. 'Apart from the aspect of its great velocity, making it next to impossible for our fighters to chase, its fuselage consists of welded sheet steel. That would make it virtually impregnable to fighters' machinegun bullets. A plane's cannon-fire would do the trick—yes, but there again, if the fighter plane is too close when firing its cannon – the bomb's exploding warhead could well destroy the fighter as well.'

'Hell, what's the use of chasing the thing if, on catching it, we can't shoot the goddam thing because of its steel body. Can't we just tip the goddam thing's wings and send it spinning off into the wide blue yonder?' Bretzler, in his frustration, had intended the remark as a joke.

But Knowles, looking from Bretzler to Hollings, was all at once caught up in the idea, nodding his head and muttering more to himself than others saying: 'Yes – yes – there is the possibility of upsetting the gyroscope's control of flight stability.' Knowles and Hollings both looked over to Wing Commander Withers for his opinion.

'Well, if you think the idea is solid enough,' said Withers to Knowles, 'we can certainly give it a try. I'll see to entering it onto Operational Briefing'

'What kind of percentage are we to expect?' said someone from what was becoming a rising collective outbreak of conversational murmurs.

'*Percentage? Sorry?*' said a puzzled Knowles.

'For the planes lost in the proposed Peenemunde raid,' said Wing Commander Withers. It wasn't him who'd thrown the query at Knowles, but he was just as keen as whoever had, to hear the answer.

Knowles didn't have that kind of information. Hollings had, but he wasn't sure how much he was allowed to say. He looked to Colonel Rutkin.

Rutkin pursed his lips for a moment. 'We're looking at something in the region of about five point nine per cent.' That wasn't the figure that his advisors had given him; they had said their losses were likely to be nearer 6.1%, but Rutkin saw no reason to let on about that figure this early, before the actual mission. He bit his lip.

Bretzler juggled the figures in his head, as no doubt others were doing. He reckoned that would make it a loss of about 35 planes. He didn't say anything. Neither did anybody else. He just lit another Chesterfield, to inhale deeply and blow out another tired stream of smoke – tinged blue in the funny light, like those air guys up there.

The meeting didn't last must longer after that. Its expectant momentum was spent. All that could be said had been said. All those words now needed to be replaced with action.

With casual talk breaking out as everyone began to leave, Rutkin turned to Lt-Col Bretzler. 'Do you, by any chance, play bridge?'

'As it happens, I *am* familiar with both our own version and the English version, for all their differences. Colonel. But I prefer to stick to poker, with the odd cigar and maybe a couple of shots of the old Tennessee bourbon thrown in while stacking the hard bucks.'

'That's unfortunate,' said the Colonel, with what seemed to Bretzler to be genuine regret, much to his surprise. 'Actually we're trying to make up a foursome, that is, myself, Commodore Leighton-Lagrishe and his niece, for a friendly tournament night this evening at the Whitings Club,' said Rutkin.

Bretzler's thoughts of cigars and bourbon dimmed, out-shadowed by a new distraction. 'By niece, are we talking about our very own Corporal Leighton-Lagrishe?'

'The very same. From what Gerald tells me, I gather that she plays a calculatedly shrewd hand  that makes her an ideal half for a formidably winning pair.'

Bretzler's leasure interests now surged in a different direction. He found it easy to agree with the last part of that remark, but not in quite the way that the Colonel meant. 'In that case, Colonel, maybe I'll get to thinking I'll just tag along with you.'

Rutkin's face reclaimed its hard judge's severity. 'We'll need a definite affirmative.'

Definite affirmative! Listen to him! And here was he thinking the old goat's ice was melting inside. 'Count me in, Colonel. Count me in.'

# 9

No matter which angle you looked at them from, you never could have considered Monique ('Monica') Redfern and Selena Leighton-Lagrishe to be two peas from the same pod. You never could have fitted them into that pod even if you'd used a shoehorn. Alike, perhaps, only in that their names were a mixed mouthful of the European and Anglo-Saxon tongues. But they worked together. Selena as instructor and Monica as learner. That would progress later, in the real game, the fatally dangerous game, in German-occupied territory, to Control and agent in the field.

'Let's try it one more time shall we,' said Selena.

'Must we?' replied Monica, not hiding her reluctance.

'You were good – in fact, better there – but let's give it another go. And hold on to it before we lose it. You'll appreciate the benefit that we did.' Tired as she was while saying this, Selena could see that Monica was just as tired – probably more so. It's always that way when you're the learner – the one bearing the unfamiliar harness and being whipped into shape by the seemingly cruel instructor. But in spite of this, she couldn't let Redfern see that she, her instructor, was tired. Otherwise the learner's weariness would set in more rapidly, so shutting down the mind's intake of instructions.

Selena had sometimes wondered over Monica's loquacious manner. She wondered if it would go against her by letting something slip out in when chattering within earshot of Nazi sympathisers. But Doctor

Dromyrk had quelled her fears in this, voicing a different view. Dromyrk saw it to be a positive aspect. A quiet reserved manner was all very fine and polite in the sort of situation that duly expected politeness, he had said. But in enemy territory, where everywhere, everything, everyone, bristled with danger, suspicion homed in quickly on taciturn faces that could be concealing potentially dangerous secrets. Hence Redfern's open talkative personality could serve as 'proof' of her innocence to Gestapo and security patrol inspections.

But Selena had to admit that Monica fitted well into the role that she was being trained for, namely that of the young French woman. With her cute turned-up nose and quaint freckles clustered around her two high-boned cheeks, she looked very much *la femme tres 'chic'*. That and her chirping noisily like a garden finch. These chromosomal 'foreign' features  passed on genetically, through her mother from her grandmother. Monica had faint memories as a child of her grandmother milking those goats on her Pyrenean hillside farm. The dog tending the herd of goats had been a massive great woolly thing almost bigger than her. Or so it had seemed to her at that sensitive age.

With the area being isolated and scarcely populated, the language spoken was very much in dialect. Thus the French tongue that the mother had spoken to a young Monique had not been proper French. But this was an added asset for Monica, and with some rough vernacular swear words thrown in, her verbal image would, hopefully, pass as real. So unlike the proper tongue a non-French  imposter would  learn out  of  a  book.  Thus fooling German scrutiny in the field. Her weak point was her accent. She needed to polish up on that. But that was not Selena's concern. Palpiere would work on her doggedly with that one until he was satisfied that she was ready. For further real effect, Monica would use her mother's maiden name of Berac.  So when ready, Monica would be dropped by parachute into German-controlled Vichy France as Monique Berac.

Monica had first come into the 'game' when summoned one day by an official-looking letter in dull buff paper to attend an interview at some obscure back-of-nowhere address. The building had seemed even more remote by way of it standing there all alone; all the buildings that had once stood around it having been reduced to rubble by Jerry's bombs. It had looked like a school. But it turned out to have been a workshop and clinic of sorts for the prosthetically infirm. On first reading the name on the door, she had closed her eyes for a second at thoughts of the unsightly. But things turned out to be not as they seemed. Very much so. The man leading the interview panel, in spite of being somewhat severely attired in a dark tweed three-piece, had carried a heavy military air. Perhaps that was because it was Colonel Rutkin on one of his rare ventures down civvy street in mufti. The other man, blond and handsome for his age, a doctor, from what she had managed to understand in her nervousness, had not said a single word throughout the interview. He had simply listened to her speaking – as well as watching her hand movements, she sensed. That had struck her as weird and had unnerved her a little. Doctor Dromyrk had since seen her on several further sessions here at Lindwell Hall to monitor her progress. The woman, also blonde, had brought Monica a little more out of her nervousness with her deliberately softer questions. That same woman, Selena, in fact, was now at Monica's table, taking her through the intricate steps of learning Morse code --- the *sinister* side of the craft, with messages doubly-concealed within messages.

'Come on, you can do it,' prompted Selena once again.

Selena and Monica were separated at their table by a large wooden partition across the middle of the table-top. This way the learner could concentrate without the distraction of being under the instructor's critical eye. At the same time as taking verbal instructions from the other side of the panel. It also hid the instructor's frustration at the many mistakes of the learner. For the sake of speeding up Monica's training in preparation for her going on a mission, Selena was employing a technique suggested by Lt-Col Bretzler that had proved successful in his experience with coding machines in the field. Rather than have Monica memorise the dots and dashes for each individual letter, she was having Monica recognise the sound of each letter that was keyed to her. Monica would return the sound, and if correct, Selena pressed the button for a green light to flash on Monica's side. Working on one letter at a time, until it was learned, a new letter was added and repeated with the previous one; this process repeated until all the letters were learned.

Selena took in a deep breath and let it out again in a long drawn-out silent sigh. 'All right, Monica, let's try a new word this time. Your own codename for identification in the field. Is that all right?'

'Yes.' Monica's codename was berger – French for shepherd. Easily remembered from her childhood stay at her grandmother's.

'Ready when you are.'

Monica commenced tapping out the letters on the brass key. **Dash dot dot dot dot**

'No, stop,' said Selena.

'What's wrong now? That was b e, dash,dot,dot,dot dot wasn't it?' said Monica.

'Yes, but try doing it this time without saying the letters out loud. I know that makes it easier for you, but if you try doing in your mind only – yes, it's harder but that will force your mind to work at it harder, knowing it has to do the job. Do you follow me?'

'Yes, I think so.'

'You'll have to do better than *think so* in the field – you have to be doubly sure and *know so*. Right?'

'Right.'

'Good. You'll appreciate the effect it has in building-up your expertise.'

'I hope so,' said Monica. Was that a tinge of peevishness that Selena heard creeping into the other's voice?

'All right, once again; your codename from the beginning again,' said Selena.

Monica's brass key started its clicking dance once more. Dash,dot,dot,dot dot dot,dash,dash, dot

'No,' said Selena.

'What's wrong this time?' There definitely was an open annoyance in Monica's voice this time.

'That's b e p you've tapped out. You've mistaken the letter p for the letter r. I can understand; it's a common mistake for learners because they're so alike, dot,dash,dash,dot for the letter p and dot dash,dot for the letter r. Just remember that r, the letter with the extra leg, is the one that has one dash less. Okay?'

'Okay.'

'Also,' said Selena, hating to go on with another correction, knowing how it would dig into Monica's confidence, 'that wasn't your assigned signature I was hearing on those last two key-taps.' By signature, Selena was referring to the characteristic effect of the individual's hand pressure and timing on the key, so giving a specific sound unique to the sender of the message and recognisable to the recipient as the server's signature. This way, if the enemy somehow acquired the field agent's codename and used it in a false message, the absence of that vital signature would show that message to be false. It required tedious repeated practise of how one decided to hold and use the tapping hand on the key. Selena had instructed Monica how to rest the heel of her tapping hand on the back of her other hand resting firmly on a solid surface to produce the effect that was her signature. Any message sent, using Monica's codename berger, but not employing that specified hand position, would give a different sound, and so would be interpreted as false. 'You can't afford to miss out on that important point. You've got to be on your guard – *always*. Otherwise the whole mission is ruined and we're all wasting our time here.' The last few words let out her frustration.

Selena hadn't meant to put it across so brusquely to Monicaa, but it was too late now that she'd let it out. She bit her lip, but refrained from saying sorry. That would have defeated the purpose of her discipline. Being soft in this game didn't do anyone any good at any time.

'I suppose so,' came the sullen reply.

Selena almost barked Monica down for what sounded like a limpish answer, but decided that ignoring it and pressing on would be better.

'All right, so let's have it again. Remember --- the extra leg --- the one we want, r, is the one with one dash less.' Selena waited. The brass key sat dead. Some muffled muttering from the other side of the panel. Oh God, she's still trying to mouth off the letters silently to herself, thought Selena. The sound of a chair shifting. At the thought of Monica shirking her task and running off in a huff, Selena made to get up and call her back. But the key suddenly started to jerk up and down rapidly with its new message of dots and dashes.

'What on earth ---?' Selena began, then stopped, a smile breaking out on her face as she read on. She burst into a little giggle, just managing to read out aloud: 'Blueberry muffins and real coffee.'

Lieutenant Colonel Bretzler's strong broad face appeared round the corner of the panel. He gave her his best of a flashing white teeth smile. Stealing a quick look at Monica's tired expression, he nodded his inference to Selena. 'I reckon now's a good time for 'school' to take a break for some refreshments. Coffee and cake. You two okay with that?

Monica was about to blurt out yes and jump up in eagerness to get away from her tedious lessons. But she saw the way Selena looked at the American and pulled herself back. She shook her head without looking up. 'No, it's all right, you two go on ahead. I'll practise a little more on these letters first.'

'Okay, kid. I'll steal teacher for a little while. I'm sure she'll slap me down if I get my etiquette wrong.'

They sat down in the kitchen, at a long wooden table that bore scars of centuries, rather than decades, of service to the nobility. Bretzler playfully ran a fingernail along one of the old grooves. 'I reckon this one was maybe made before Washington cut down that famous little tree of his, huh.' He moved to another groove. 'Or this one maybe? Anyway ---' He slapped the table in empty conclusion with a broad hand that carried its own abrasive marks of conflict.

Their eyes met. 'So how is Redfern doing? He said, referring to Monica. 'Has my suggestion been any good to you?'

Selena searched his face for meaning beyond this remark as he looked down at his coffee, stirring it. She couldn't help feeling a little disappointed – *hurt?* – that they were seated here, alone, face to face, and yet here he was, talking of someone else, not of her. Should she feel guilt at this? Shame even? Was it being childishly selfish, she wondered? She poked a finger into the muffin as if it could give an answer that would render her conscience free. She looked across at him, into his eyes as he looked up. 'She's certainly coming along more quickly than anyone I've seen learn previously.' She chanced a smiling innuendo. 'What else have you got to give us, apart from your Mid-West state charm, I'm wondering.' She lifted the muffin up in comic over-inspection. 'We've certainly had a regular cornucopia of your goodies, so far.' The muffin, for instance, would have raised many an English eyebrow as a topic of curiosity prior to Uncle Sam's generous landing of virile young men on these shores, bringing new hope and strength, as well as eye-popping goods and candy --- and trouble for innocent young English maidens. Now, thanks to Captain Falzoni's 'infusion of new life' into Lindwell Hall, the muffin was a much savoured palate's delight.

'It's called American hospitality. We like to help our cousins across the water. Makes the Atlantic seem that little bit smaller,' said Bretzler in his low relaxed drawl.

And that annoyed Selena inside. That the Atlantic division should be reduced, but not theirs, was the irony. That he should be so much at ease, so near, yet so distant in his talk. She wanted so much for their talk to be more personal, if not yet intimate. At their bridge session the other evening, he had behaved so gentlemanly and followed all the demands of etiquette. His concentration had been held all the while by the cards, without him sneaking furtive – hungry – glances at her chest, as most men were inclined to do. If she was honest with herself, she had to admit that she had been slightly disappointed by that. Even when they had gone on to a dance club later, she had been a little let down by his good mannered self-restraint. When the dance band at one point stopped the 'old' music and broke out into the new American-style jitterbugging music, she definitely hadn't wanted him to swing her in full somersault over his broad shoulder, like other G.I.s were doing with their shrill-screaming partners. But she had been thrilled at the thought of being jerked and pulled a little more roughly by those strong arms. But he hadn't. Instead, he'd jived, lively yes, but away from her, with only the odd touch of hands as he swirled her around. He hadn't even shot a quick glance down her blouse when they danced close together to a slower beat.

His mum had obviously brought him up to be a good boy. Her own parents, especially daddy, had taught her to be free and easy in her manner when facing even the hardest of social encounters. That way, there wouldn't be a 'hardest', since all would be equally manageable. And she was. But here with him, his hands only inches from hers, she felt like a gym-slipped schoolgirl making her first-ever recital before the entire school assembly and its VIP visitors on Parents Open Day. Now she was feeling those shivers inside. She sensed that he was not his usual calm self inside – if that was another way of saying that he was emotionally uneasy like she was. In fact, he *was* unsettled. He could handle any broad, but his footing was unsure with this class dame. But his reservations were not just about social etiquette; it was this strange feeling that he had experienced only rarely.

These on-and-.off moods, like heat waves, between them made it downright funny. Not comic funny, just weird – maddening even. She could scream with exasperation. No doubt Doctor Dromyrk would have a convoluted expression of multisyllabic words to explain the syndrome.

'My training schedule with her is almost complete. She'll do well on that side. She can finalise her field training with your lot when we're done. It's Captain Falzoni who's handling her – not *literally*,' she let out a nervous giggle, 'isn't it?'

'Yes and no in that order.' He had smiled for a second at her accidental joke and then gone blank-faced again. He saw her bite her lip in forethought of her next remark's answer. He waited.

'There may be a chance that I will have to jump from a good old plane myself, to work as Field Control for Redfern in the event of her encountering unforeseen problems.'

Bretzler stared at her for a long moment, stroking the bristles under his chin as he thought. 'We'll try hard to not let that contingency arise. Right?'

'Right.' He could at least have shown a little more emotion at the thought of me being involved in danger, she thought.

Their long spell of awkward staring at each other was broken by Falzoni striding heavily into the kitchen. 'Are my ears burning, or is it the air-conditioning that needs fixing in this antique old joint? Not that this old place ever had air-conditioning , except from cannon-ball holes, it's being still stuck in the sixteenth century.' Dragging up a chair, he sat between them, looking from one to the other, smiling. He addressed the Lt-Colonel. 'Mea culpa; sorry I'm late. I was cornered in the Rainbow Club by a guy from Magan boot camp – one of the 1st Division's marine lot. Shenny Hitchpole. Anyway, he wants me to write to his mom.'

'Let me guess --- dame trouble,' said Bretzler.

'On the nail, buddy, on the nail.' Falzoni picked up Bretzler's gold lighter that was lying on the table, to light a cigarette for himself. Bretzler waved away Falzoni's offer of one of his.

'Does she want,' Bretzler nodded with a confidential air at Falzoni, '--- *you know*--?' Plainly he was a bit self-conscious at voicing such an issue in front of Selena.

'No, no, it's not that sort of bother. The trouble is he's already got a girl back in Ozark, Alabama.'

'If that's all, can't he do his own letter-writing to his mom? Unless he's one of our many semi illiterates who've put aside their ploughs and pitchforks  to take up the semi-automatic M-1 Garand carbine?'

'If only it were that simple. Trouble is, he's already tied up ball and chain. Married by proxy. All the contractual agreements duly dotted and signed. Leaving only the you know what to be confirmed in solid act,' he said with a lowering of his last words, as he glanced at Selena, deciding not to give a fingers sign for clarification.

'Don't mind me, I'm one of the gang, as I believe, you guys would say,' said Selena, a little tired of the 'secret gang' antics of the other two.

Bretzler was puzzled. 'Proxy? How the hell can he do that? Is he Asian or something? Hitchpole sounds like the all American farm-boy, straw hat and Levi dungarees, to me.'

'Deep South folks, snake-shaking evangelist fanatics. Or is it some crazy singing-to-tall tress sect? I can't remember exactly,' said Falzoni.

'Like I said, Hill-Billy moonshine hooch and molasses,' said Bretzler.

'Anyway, he wants me to mediate in my professional capacity as a lawyer and handle the legalities --- if there *are* any with that woolly-minded lot --- between the parents, wife and pastor.'

'I wouldn't imagine that being dumped like that, the wife will constitute a whole mountain of problems on her own for you to smooth out. I don't relish the task. You're welcome to it, buddy.' Giving a broad cheeky smile, Bretzler reached over to take one of Falzoni's cigarettes.

'Hitchpole wants me to get an annulment of the marriage so that he can marry this English dame. She's Catholic, like us, and won't make a move with him until his marriage is dissolved. And it can, since the so-called nuptials haven't been consummated.'

'In nomine Patris et Filii et Spiritus Sancti' said Bretzler.

'Amen,' said Falzoni, concluding the blessing. 'I knew you'd understand, Brent.'

It pleased Selena to learn that Bretzler was Catholic. She had wondered about it before, but hadn't dared to broach on the subject in case it frightened him off. A question on that subject, woman to man, can all too often shoo away the potential catch. The two men were now well into their cigarettes and man talk, so that she felt a little left out. She straightened out her skirt with deliberately loud pats to get some attention from the men. But they barely gave her a glance, their sports talk being more interesting. She got up. 'I'd better get back to Monica. I've left her on her own too long as it is.'

She pushed her chair in closer to the table, the legs scraping noisily on the stone-flagged floor, and made to walk away. Bretzler looked up at her. 'Let me know how that *contingency* develops, and I'll see what I can throw in at my end to find a way to get around it.' He held up his cigarette. 'Okay?'

'Okay.'

# 10

'As much as that,' said Colonel Rutkin flatly.

Wing Commander Withers noted the lack of any surprise in the Colonel's low remark. 'You expected this?' said Withers. Compared to Rutkin's deliberately low estimate of 5.9% for bombing results, the actual raid had wrought great devastation on the site, resulting in the higher figure of 6.7% loss of 40 aircraft; 20 Lancasters, 15 Halifaxes, 5 Stirlings. As it turned out, early bombing marking had missed the primary target, the forced labour camp, by 1.5 miles. Adjusting this initial error, the camp was bombed successfully, killing 180 Germans and 500-600 foreign workers, mainly Poles.

Rutkin tapped the arm of his wood-and-canvass folding chair, a self-conscious agitation robbing him momentarily of words. He looked away, out the window, at the Stirling bomber having its outer starboard Bristol Hercules 1650h.p. engine cowling removed, and the engine, with only a single bent propeller blade remaining, sprayed with white foam to dowse the flames that had erupted dangerously from it on touching down on the RAF base landing strip. 'Yes, we had expected a figure nearer to this this --- higher than what we had originally stated.' He stole a guilty glance at the Wing Commander who was standing, hands in pockets, looking down on him.

After a long look, in heavy thought, Withers spun round sharply to look out the window at the commotion of ground crew around the badly shot-up plane. At two mechanics already diligently replenishing the tail turret machine-guns' empty bullet-belts with a fresh load of .303 bullets. 'And the damn ruddy blighters are still coming,' he said, still looking out the window. 'In spite of all our bombing.' Withers looked down, to idly kick away a tiny crushed-up paper ball that had missed its target, the waste basket. 'Not an altogether broadside onslaught, perhaps, but a damaging barrage nevertheless. Enough to nick public morale. All the more unsettling by way of their erratic pattern of staggered delivery and irregular timing.' He swung round again to face the room, sweeping an arm about wide to vent his annoyance at something – anything. 'They simply come out of nowhere, one at a time. There's no solid flying formation to track and focus our guns on. It's like swatting buzzing wasps. Great bloody buzzing things that they are.'

'Quite,' said Rutkin quietly.

'They've obviously become more mobilised; firing the V-1s from transport vehicles,' said Withers. 'A lot more difficult to track down and deal with, now that they're moving about all over the place, it seems. At least our second raid on Peenemunde has put their work on the V-2 rocket back some months. That's if our agents over there have got their figures right. It's something I suppose, to put them on the run.' Bomber Command had, indeed, mounted a second raid on Peenemunde, destroying the site, not only in its military aspects, but at the expense of those 780 or so civilian casualties. It was not just these human statistics that irked Rutkin, since he'd given the green light on the operation, but the goading fact that the threat from flying bombs was not yet entirely thwarted.

Intelligence reports said that scientific and engineering documents on the bombs' progress were stored in other locations apart from Peenemunde and Friedrichshafen in the foresight of the site being wiped out.

'Which can't be seen to be altogether too good a thing if we don't know where they are and where they'll launch from next.'

'No, I suppose not,' said Withers, his confidence crumpled somewhat. He went and sat behind his desk, to swivel to and fro in his chair. He pulled some papers closer to look at them. 'These reports say that rocket production has been moved to an underground location further east; even Poland, maybe.' Leaning back in his chair, the Wing Commander called out loud to the closed door: 'Moley! Tea!' No sooner than the words had left his lips than the door flew open and the airman hurried in with two steaming cups and a tin lid bearing two tea biscuits. Placing them down on the desk, Corporal Moley turned and left promptly.

'Thank you, Corporal,' Withers cried out, once more to a closed door.

Rutkin rose to take his cup, but declined the biscuit.

'No? Oh well, John, I'll have yours. Pity about this wretched condensed milk.' Withers dunked his biscuit in the tea then swore when half of it fell back into the tea. 'Bugger!'

But as they drank their tea quietly, far away across the airfield, and far far away to the east, near Nordhausen, in Germany's Harz mountains, Hitler's emergency contingency plan, in the event of Peenemunde being destroyed, was already underway. This was for production work on the V-2 rocket to be continued underground, in an abandoned gypsum mine, a mile into the mountainside. With Nordhausen concentration camp providing the necessary labour force of 10,000, 90% of whom were non-German. Set up originally by the Fuhrer, the production development plan had caught the eye of SS Commander, Heinrich Himmler, so that he was now responsible for running it.

Rutkin looked up from his tea at the Wing Commander. 'All your bombing seems to be having only a marginal effect on German installations.'

Withers gulped down a mouthful of the brown semi-poison. 'At least we've implemented some modifications to enable our fliers to get at those V-1 blighters.' Roughly 100 aircraft, in fact; Griffin-engine Supermarine Spitfires, deHavilland Mosquitoes, as well as American P-1 Mustangs had been tuned to make them fly fast enough to catch up with the deadly German flying bombs. As well as speed improvements, all planes in RAF 150 Wing Squadron were having their 20mm cannons adjusted to converge at 300 yds ahead. This allowed us to shoot the V-1s, without being too close to suffer backlash of the target exploding. 'Going strictly by confirmed hits, our Tempest seems to be top scorer so far, followed by the Mosquito, the Spitfire and the Mustang.'

Withers clasped both hands round his cup, to take a drink, then looking through the window at the sky as he thought. 'But all in all, I would rate our Mosquito as the all-rounder plane.' In fact, the de Havilland DH98 Mosquito, made almost entirely of wood, to give it high velocity, had the multi-role of fast bomber, fighter bomber, night fighter, maritime strike aircraft and fast photo reconnaissance plane. 'We're sending them out as high speed nuisance bombers, dropping four thousand pound bombs from high altitude, in raids so fast that Jerry's night fighters are too slow to intercept. We've also got them flying over the North Sea, to intercept Heinkels, flying out from Dutch airbases, intending to launch their V-1s from the air. Modified Wellington bombers, acting as Airborne Early Warning and Control aircraft, direct the Mosquito fighters from four thousand feet altitude over the sea.' Withers took another swig from his cup. 'Shows we can still put a sting up Jerry's arse.'

Colonel Rutkin wasn't enjoying his tea enough to finish it. He looked around for somewhere to put his cup, finally placing it on the floor beside him. 'But like you said, Jeremy, they're still coming ------ the blasted V-1s. We can't allow ourselves to be too complacent, to forget that they're still creating havoc.' Rutkin's expression darkened as he went on. 'In spite of our deploying AA gun batteries stretching from North Downs to the south east coast of England and a cordon closing the Thames Estuary from attack, a defence line along East Anglia's coast, and also along the coasts of Yorkshire and Lancashire – they're still coming.'

'Yes,' said Withers, tapping his chin with his cup, his expression slightly fallen. 'I suppose it can be a bit of a dowser if we look at it like that.'

'We have to, Jeremy. Our AA lads have been too quick with their jubilant cheers at what they're thinking are direct hits with the V-1s. It's simply the damned things' engines cutting out on reaching their destinations and falling to earth.' Truth, alas, was that the V-1s were proving difficult to hit on account of their relatively small size and high velocity. Cruising at 2000-3000 feet altitude put them just above the effective range of light anti-aircraft guns and below that of heavier guns. This high altitude and high speed was making it impossible for standard British QF 3.7 inch guns to cope in its traversing and firing action. Nor were barrage balloons proving too effective a defence against the sting of Jerry's 'wasps', since the V-1s had specially modified wing edge cutters for slicing the balloons' suspension cables.

'We need better guns, said Rutkin gruffly.

For what seemed a very long second or two, they sat in silence. Suddenly Withers stood up, so fast that he almost knocked his chair over. 'I don't know about you, John, but this tea, awful as it is, has made me very hungry. What do you say we take ourselves over to the NAAFI canteen to grab something to eat?'

Rutkin had nothing to say to this, but he nevertheless followed Withers out the door.

# 11

Harry Carswell struggled against the khaki–blue tide pouring out of the train along the platform. Outnumbered in his civilian clothes, he edged his way, with one elbow, through the contra-flowing river of sappers, sailors and airmen, while holding on tightly to his large case of travelling salesmens' samples, lest it should be wrenched from his grip in all the bustling. All around the same battle was going on multi-fold for individuals. Shoulder-borne kitbags swinging about narrowly missing other bags and their bearers' heads. Scattered about the mass of uniforms, threadbare civilian clothes in their drabness reflected the sullen expressions of their weary wearers. Here and there children with their ID details written on cards hung around their necks looked tiny and lost, as indeed they were, amidst the teeming crowd of grown-ups, their wailing cries drowned in the noise of the station's overall commotion.

A plainly distressed mother, wielding a battered teddy bear, anxiously sought after her own precious little one. From out of all that milling khaki, a tiny arm stretched out to grasp the mother's hand. That crisis, only one of many, was resolved. Nervous farewells between servicemen and their dearests, kisses, tears welling up everywhere. The public address system, with its unintelligible quacking announcements, would still have been unintelligible even if there had been no noise. Overhead, pigeons fluttered and flapped freely from girder to girder, wondering what all the fuss was about down below.

Climbing aboard the train, Carswell found himself engaged in a new battle trying to make his way along the narrow corridor, searching for a seat in a compartment. A 'million' others, alas, had the same idea, so that compartment after compartment was full as he made his way along slowly, like a contortionist, squeezing, wriggling, past others that had decided to stand, sit and lie in the narrow passage. Doors were slamming closed along the train. The platform gate was closing, when it suddenly pulled open again, allowing two MPs to come through and sprint for the train. A whistle blew somewhere and Carswell noticed the adjacent train beginning to slide away – no, it was his own train moving off, ever so slowly, out of the station.

Clawing his way past body after body, Carswell's relief, at seeing an empty seat through the glass window ahead of him, was mixed with alarm when he saw a similar searcher coming along the corridor towards him. The uniform blazed out its smartness in contrast to the dull khaki around him. It was a Yank. An officer. Sliding the compartment door open, Carswell stepped inside, closing the door again behind him. Looking up at the luggage rack, he was dismayed to see nowhere to stow his case. He would have to sit with it on his knees and it was heavy. He sat down with the case on his knees. Settling into his seat with his not too comfortable load, he allowed himself a private smirk when he saw the American look in then move on.

But the American stopped and turned around, being spoken to by someone out of sight. The two American MPs came into view, talking to the officer outside the compartment. All three looked round in unison into the compartment. One of the MPs reached out and wrenched the door open with a resounding crash. The two MPs stepped in, all resplendent in their brilliant white rounded helmets, brilliant white belts, holsters, baton sheaths and brilliant white anklets and stretch spats over their boots. They stood there tapping their white batons in their hands, virtually filling the compartment, and bristling with martial authority.

Harry Carswell's inside jumped with fright as one of the MPs, staring hard at him, spoke. But no, he was speaking to the man seated next to him. 'Okay, Walker, it's the end of the road,' said the MP. 'Even a lousy worm like you can't burrow your way into that woodwork to escape.'

Walker, obviously a deserter, since he wasn't in uniform, glanced furtively at the compartment's opposite door.

'Touch the handle, pal, and I'll show you the magic trick of turning fingers into matchsticks with a touch of this magic baton.'

'Surely there's no need for that, Officer?' This outcry from the feeble little woman clad in fox-fur coat and hat, and barely thicker than the man's hefty baton.

'Begging your pardon, lady, but this nice young man has been naughty to his Uncle Sam, having thrown away Uncle Sam's nice uniform and not wanting to play Uncle Sam's nice game of bang, bang, you're dead.' The MP bowed his head, with a mocking smile of politeness, to the interfering little bone-bag. He turned to his colleague. 'Cuff 'im.'

Carswell watched the metal pieces, seemingly huge in their nearness, snapping around and ensnaring the man's wrists.

'On your feet, Walker. We're going for a little stroll,' said the MP, still tapping his baton menacingly.

'Where is that, then? The train's moving.'

'Where you can't escape a second time, hiding among civilians, in civilian clothes, like the weasel coward-assed deserter you are. The guard's van. Move it!' Trapped between the two burly MPs as they went out into the corridor, the prisoner had no way to run, back or forward; but nevertheless, as a grim reminder of the futility of such an idea, the one at the back continued to tap the prisoner's shoulder with his baton.

Before Carswell could place his case in the vacant seat beside him, the American officer had stepped into the compartment and plumped himself down in the seat instead. With relative peace resumed in the compartment – and in the mind – Carswell looked around himself at the other occupants. Nine in total, squashed together like tinned sardines; eight seated shoulder to shoulder and one, a soldier in tartan trousers, asleep in the luggage rack. Another British soldier and the American officer seated. Both soldiers were asleep, or pretending to be. Carswell could not believe that they could fall asleep in such a short -- and 'unsettled' – time. But then, with MPs on the prowl, what soldier, regardless of uniform, didn't want to be elsewhere quickly. So their rapid attack of somnolence was pure pretence. How trepidation hastens the senses.

Carswell could smell the American's application of personal toiletries; so vigorous in their freshness compared to the staleness of body odours that was the affliction presently borne by the county's populace on account of severe rationing of much needed, much missed, personal commodities. He breathed in slowly to test the scent. Was it hair cream, or was it body lotion? He chanced a glance round at his fellow traveller. The man's uniform trouser creases were sharp enough to have done for a shave instead of using razor blades.

The officer sensed the furtive scrutiny and turned round full to greet Carswell. Pausing to light his cigarette with matchstick and thumbnail in one hand, as only an American soldier could, he held out a hand to shake. 'Frank Falzoni. I'm up visiting cousins here in Edinburgh.'

Carswell gave his name in return, but it came out in a low scraping effort that the American was unable to pick up. He noticed for the first time that Carswell had a bandage wrapped tightly round his throat, with the tell-tale stain of tincture of iodine coming through just about where the larynx would be. Carswell tried again. 'Carswell,' came the croaking effort. He tapped his throat. 'Sharpel,' it sounded like to Falzoni, but he understood.

Falzoni nodded knowingly, pointing at the man's throat. 'Say, buddy, I guess that sure must have been one lucky chance of Jerry's shrapnel just passing by, rather than stopping, where it could have done more damage.' He tapped his own side where he had been 'touched' by shrapnel. 'I know the very feeling. Got it here. Back in Palermo, where the Second Division was ---'

Carswell cut him off with a forefinger to his lips signifying silence, then pointing at the compartment's opposite wall. What he muttered to Falzoni didn't make sense.

'Didn't quite catch that, pal. Sounded like "waltzing bears". He looked at where Carswell was pointing and saw the notice, partly concealed by a kitbag. 'Right, I get it. Walls have ears. And here's me, the soldier boy, needing to be told that by you. Quite right. Good thinking.' He sat back for a long draw on his cigarette.

'Falzoni?' croaked Carswell. 'That's Italian, isn't it?'

Not that one again. Falzoni noticed glances at him from the others at this remark. He shook his head. Jeez, the Brits sure had the heeby-jeebies on foreign names. Probably bunged up all their philatelists in the Tower for treason. He blew out a long train of smoke. 'Sure was the last time I heard it. Not unless that Sister of Mercy midwife back then misplaced name tags between deliveries and ended up whacking the goddam wrong pink butt.' He held up a mock hand of peace. 'I swear, folks, there's no swastikas on the soles of my socks and no mug shots of Il Duce Musso in my locker. But I can tell you that you can bet your last dollar that I've taken up my trusty musket for cause and country no less than Old Davy Crocket himself.' The sleeping soldiers had no comment to make on this sweeping declaration.

Further verbal raspings to Falzoni from Carswell revealed that he was a travelling salesman representing the firm of Cobb and Son.

'Cobb? Let me guess --- they deal in corn seed,' joked Falzoni.

'Corn seed?

'Yeah; cob – corn ---. Forget it.'

Falzoni's cheerful chatter eventually petered out – perhaps to everyone's relief – when a 'sleeping' soldier muttered that a little peace and quiet would be good.


Finally arriving in London's St Pancras Station hours later, the hectic battle recommenced. This time to get off the train and make one's way – fight one's way -- towards the platform gates and the station exit thereafter, if one was still in one piece. Making his escape from the station and its mad milling crowd, Carswell, headed for a parked taxi, with its massive gas-bag fuel tank made of silk soaked in rubber mounted on its roof. A sure sign of the times of severe fuel shortage, especially for private civilian vehicles. Fully inflated, the bag would have held about 13 cubic metres of gas, obtained from burning coal to make coke in the much needed process of manufacturing iron for the war effort. But it was not fully inflated, Carswell saw. Judging by the amount of deflation, his rapid mental assessment told him that there was still enough gas there to get him to where he wanted to go. He stepped forward and opened the door to get in.

The driver, already in a bad mood, almost exploded with anger at the unclear mutterings from the passenger climbing in behind him. Turning round, the driver was about to shout at the man, when he stopped himself, seeing the stained bandage. 'Could you give me that again, sir; a little slower maybe this time.'

Carswell did better. He handed the driver a slip of paper with the address on it. The driver looked at it. 'Not sure if we can get there all the way. Maybe have to walk a bit. There's been a helluva lot o' bombing in that area. Makes it difficult to get through anywhere on wheels. Don't know if your place will even be there.' He handed the paper back to Carswell. 'But let's see; can only try it.' He started the engine, and letting the clutch out they moved off a few yards, only to suddenly brake abruptly. A bell-clanging fire engine raced past, missing their front by a few feet, followed by a truck carrying an Air Raid Rescue team. 'See what I mean,' said the driver. 'Bloody Huns.'

Back inside the station, Captain Falzoni entered a phone booth. Dialling a specially reserved number, he waited. No voice at the other end. Only a three-click-one-peep pre-arranged security recognition signal. 'Rabbit's in the field,' said Falzoni. He put the phone down and left the booth.

Outside, the two MPs, along with their prisoner, Walker, climbed into a military jeep and drove off. After travelling for about a mile, they stopped and Walker got out. The two MPs saluted him and then drove off again. Walker got into a grey saloon with a US military white star on its door and it moved off.

The old black Ford taxi's meter ticked away as they headed eastwards, dodging and swerving around bomb holes and rubble all the while. Carswell looked out the window on both sides as they sped along. Desolation from bombing seemed to increase as they headed further east. Finally they had to stop where the road was blocked, not so much by bricks strewn across the road, as by houses strewn across the road. They had been blown outwards, the bombing effect being so intense. The driver didn't much fancy having to negotiate a way round the blockage by going down a side street, since the damage seemed to be just as bad there. The best thing for it seemed to be to go further on foot. The Air Raid Rescue and the Fire Brigade guys were already doing their bit, he could see, with heads bobbing up here and there among the colossal wreckage, going about their rescue work.

The driver turned to Carswell. 'It's only another block or so past this one – or what's left of it – if it's still there. I'll let you off here and you can go round down that side street there.' He pointed. 'That way there. It's only about a couple of minutes away.' Carswell paid the fare and the driver opened the door. 'There you are.'

Carswell got out and stood for a moment to watch the taxi reverse with difficulty around piles of rubble, as well as entanglements of hosepipes, and then going off the way it had come. He turned and started to step, and where necessary, climb, over and around the mass of broken stone, to make his way to where his intended address was supposed to be. He passed a man standing crying, looking down at two shapes shrouded by blankets lying at his feet. One of the shapes was barely two feet long. A soft woollen doll partly protruded from beneath the blanket, still gripped beyond death by its infantile owner. Carswell at last reached the address he was seeking. Ternhill Road. The door-bell was not working apparently, and only after half a dozen heavy knocks, and exasperating waiting in between, did the door open cautiously several inches. The suspicious face looking out seemed as narrow as the space it was peering through. 'Yeah?' it said.

'You have a room to let, yes?' croaked Carswell.

The man couldn't understand Carswell's words so that they had to be repeated.

'You have a room to let, yes?'

'Can't yer bleedin' read? What's that notice in the window say, then? Room to let; that's *to let*, not *toilet*. Course we 'ave a room to let!' The man stepped back, opening the door wide enough for Carswell to pass through, but no wider than that for nosey parkers to see into the premises. 'Gawd, that's some scratch you've landed yerself with in the old yodel box. Did one of Jerry's flying sausages stick in yer throat, then? Great bloomin' explodin' sausages they are, an' all. Blowin' the whole place to pieces, they are, as yer can see down there. It's a wonder this place is still standin'. Mind you, I ain't movin' for no-one, I ain't.

The man, landlord of the premises, was very small and thin, with wire-rim spectacles perched on the bridge of his pencil-thin nose. The arms coming out of a dirty waistcoat had their shirt sleeves rolled up to reveal yellowing sweat-stained sleeves of his long-johns coming down to his thin wrists. There wasn't much ardour in washing, with all the brick dust that was forever clotting the air after bombing raids, it seemed.

Carswell stood there patiently listening to the landlord, Mr Rushey, rattling on about house rules and other tenants in the house. A perfunctory glance took in the dark depressing atmosphere of the hallway, with its drab wallpaper, peeling off in supposedly unseen corners. Somewhere, upstairs it seemed, the faint radio voice of Bud Flanagan was singing for a rabbit to '--- run, run, run.' He understood, as he listened, that he was sharing the place with four other tenants. 'Breakfast at half seven to eight. If yer goes out before that, or comes down after eight, then you've 'ad it, see. Take it or leave it. Everybody's got their bath night. Yours will 'ave ter be Friday. Only water-rationin' number of bucketsful to be used. You'll see the notice when you're up there. No baths on Saturday or Sunday. Uses up too much coal.'

Carswell listened on, all the while holding on to his case. His only sign of impatience was his checking the time on his watch. Rushey noticed this and drew himself up for his last piece. 'Rent is three weeks in advance.'

'One week,' rasped Carswell.

'No, I said three weeks. Didn't yer 'ear me?'

'One week!' came the scraping, but firm, reply.

Rushey was about to argue further, when he saw the notes appear like magic in Carswell's hand. It was a very fat wad, and the notes were new and crisp. With all that money, why was the geezer fussing over the small thing of a mere two weeks? He looked down at Carswell's tight grip on that heavy-looking case. That and all the cash he handled easily enough. The geezer's got to be a spiv. Dealin' on the black market, he reckoned. Rushey liked the idea of that. With all this bleedin' rationing, goods were hard to come by once your coupons were used up. So it would not be a bad thing to 'ave someone in the 'ouse who knew how and where to get those little 'extras' for a good price. Besides, goin' by the geezer's eyes, and knowing spivs for what they are, the bleedin' geezer could well 'ave a piece o' lead pipin' up 'is sleeve. So no arguing there. 'Right,' he said. 'One week's rent.'

The money no sooner appeared in Carswell's hand, than it disappeared into Rushey's waistcoat pocket. 'I'll show yer to your room,' said Rushey. 'It's at the top o' the 'ouse.'

The room was no surprise to Carswell, considering what he'd seen downstairs; dreary, like the hall, and tiny like the landlord. With some red and white stripes painted in, it would have done as a sentry box. Carswell looked around at the sparse furnishing. A low short bed with tired-looking blankets, a stool and a small bedside cabinet that was a box with a hinged lid standing on its end. There didn't seem to be a wardrobe or any place to put clothes, until he pulled on a knob on the wall and the wallpapered door opened to reveal a shallow recess that was the wardrobe. 'Right,' said Carswell, turning round to face the landlord squarely. He gave another significant check of the time on his watch.

Rushey got the message and moved away towards the door. 'My name's Mr Rushey. And yours?' The eyebrows on the thin face jumped up to carry the question.

'Mr Carswell.'

'Mr Carswell. Right.' Rushey went to the door and then turned suddenly. 'Oh, yeah, another thing; no tarts allowed in the rooms. We don't want no trouble with coppers, okay.'

'Tarts?' repeated Carswell, smiling – his first smile of the day. 'Okay.'

With the landlord gone and the door closed, Carswell took off his coat and threw it on the bed. He sat down on the stool. Getting up again, he went over to the door, listened for a moment, then locked it securely. He then started to undo the bandage at his throat. It had been irritating him all through the journey. When it finally came off completely, the iodine stain was still there on his throat. But there was no wound. Not a single scratch of injury on the skin. The idea of a bandage had been of his own inspiration and had impressed his superiors.

The purpose of the bandage, implying a wound, was to give people who saw it a false reason for him speaking in a difficult unclear voice. This way no one would ever detect or believe that his accent was foreign – and it was. It was a hard fact that all too often field agents, well trained in their specialised subjects, were uncovered on account of their accents, or misuse of their adopted tongue's idiom. Thus under his guise of a throat injury, he could speak in short, broken, not necessarily grammatically correct sentences, if needs be, and nobody would suspect a thing.

He went over to his case to open it. Taking out the top layer of surgical appliances, he put it on the bed. What was now showing was a large high powered field transmitter. He looked at his watch. It wasn't time yet. Messages in Morse code were to be exchanged only at set times. Still forty three minutes to go. But he could get ready in the meantime. Taking out the long coil that was the aerial, he stretched it out towards the window. Then taking out another long coil, the power lead, he held it in his hand while taking out the bulb from the light socket hanging from the ceiling. He plugged the lead wire into the empty socket.

With nothing else to do but wait, he sat down on the stool again. He was tired after his long journey from the Fatherland. Looking down at the water marks on his trousers, he shook his head, thankful that no one had remarked on it, or questioned it. The faint stains were from the evaporated salty seawater that he'd got on his trousers stepping from the dinghy that had taken him from the U-Boat 570 to the Scottish shore.

He checked the time again. After he had sent his message and taken fresh orders, he would try and get some sleep. Looking round at the rough bed, he wondered if that was a futile hope.

But one thing was certain; to end his night, he would not be standing to attention, like those downstairs, to sing the national anthem's glory to the Englander King George.

# 12

'You felt a recurring animosity towards your father? Would you say this is still so?' Although put across to the patient as a question, Dr Dromyrk's words were lightly assertive and probing in their mode of stirring the silt covering deep-layered emotive memory. Settled in now for regular sessions with Dr Dromyrk, Flt-Lieutenant Guther still needed 'starting-up' as a means of bringing him out of himself.

The patient shifted in his seat, and hopefully was shifted inside as well, Dromyrk thought. But he had to wait – and wait -- through the empty silence. Totally normal, as far as preliminary openings went, they sat staring at each other, the one patiently, the other nervously. Something more than empty silence must have been working in the room, in Guther's head, so that he eventually gave an abrupt shrug. 'I don't suppose we ever really liked each other. Not really.' Guther fidgeted with his right hand, looking round the room, and then back at Dromyrk. 'Does it matter? *That* and all this?' The latter he indicated with a point at his face, while a general sweep of the hand entailed everything else.

'Do *you* think it matters? What would it mean to you if it *did* matter?'

'Means nothing.'

Another try from a slightly different angle. 'What would you say you considered to be something that mattered – say, while on your way here, this morning, for instance?'

Guther could only give an empty shake of the head to this.

Dromyrk saw how Guther took this simple question as a heavy task. He saw the irritability and confusion flickering on and off in contorted exchange on the grotesquely masked white face. Like moonlight passing across an unevenly broken and secretive landscape. A grieving mother would undoubtedly have rushed forward to pull her hurt child to her aching bosom. But Dromyrk simply sat back passively, watching, waiting. The heavy silence between them was only broken by the low-toned engine-gurgling of 'doodlebug' V1s flying overhead, to suddenly cut out, followed by the muffled crump of them exploding on falling to ground. AA guns leant their own staccato tattoo of heavy bangs.

The minutes ticked on.

Dromyrk listened all the while, 'hearing' where he could, through professional instinct, what Guther was 'saying' in his silence. That pained expression on that soundless face was screaming behind those eyes that searched for release. This intuitive insight of Dromyrk's was a build-up of gruelling years of practise stretching back to those 'enlightening' clinical sessions with the horrifically afflicted trauma casualties of that earlier conflict twenty-seven years previous. Alas, many, if not most, doctors who had served in that war had not been successful in grasping the complexities of this new field of mental illness. Those old doctors who had failed to comprehend the needs of the patient then, still failed to cope today. Dromyrk, with his analytical training, and first-hand experience, had come along that difficult road in even stride, a forerunner to the new genre of psychiatric doctor that was urgently needed for today's mentally war-damaged.

Dromyrk looked beyond the desecrated, partly plastic, visage, beyond the mental scarring behind it, in search of more deeply recessed fault. The *genuine* root of the patient's problem was what he sought. Guther's neurotic personality was one that could well suffer serious infliction long before it added military injuries to its psyche. The latter problem being a distraction shield, devilishly contrived by the subconscious, to ward off triggering the release of the real problem buried deep down.

Acute introspection, over the subconscious transference from patient to doctor, indicated this possibility. That, along with the behavioural pattern recorded so far in Guther's medical dossier.

Dromyrk pulled the dossier closer for a few moments of quick perusal. His apparent abstraction was to give the patient some 'space'. He appreciated that Guther's continual refraining from answering questions was not done in deliberate defiance. The patient had to 'bring it all out' by his own volition. Persuasion that went beyond carefully selected soft words of association was not on.

Guther's words, some loud, some almost inaudible mutterings, trailed out between long spells of silence. All the while Dromyrk would listen, responding occasionally with a carefully chosen question to coax out further 'secrets' by way of the patient's innocent words. Other than this, he held back from interrupting the patient, giving guidance only by occasional nods or an attentive 'Mmm.' It was like a slow-motion game of tennis, the ball going from one court to the other, each server trying to anticipate the other's strength and direction of return delivery.

Although the main substance of Guther's reactions came across as rebuff, it was clear to Dromyrk that the man's situation was the reverse. He was plainly crying out for help, under the psychological subterfuge of words that seemingly implied the opposite. If playful words should happen to come out, it was only to hide the inner fear of isolation through misunderstanding and abandonment. At present he was relatively stabilised. The antidepressants were helping him, but not as much as Dromyrk would have wished. Dromyrk studied the intensity of those eyes, the one totally bereft of lashes and lid peeking its hideously comical way through the layer of sallow plastic 'skin'. In spite of medication, the patient could suffer a relapse at any time.

The better half of Guther's face twitched as he struggled to put words to puzzling thoughts. He rocked side to side as if it strengthened what he was about to say. 'I just don't get it.' A hand waved around, trying to find a way out for the thoughts and their words. 'You speak of mental problems being rooted away back in early infancy. I mean how can ---' Another wave of the hand as he paused and struggled to express his thoughts. 'I mean I don't see how that adds up in the long run. How come we don't all wind up with the same mental problems, considering that we all come from the relatively same starting point, so to speak? We all follow the same passage, popping out into the world as babies, and after that what? Babies surely can't be all that different, one to the other, so how come infancy can cause so much different results in adults, like you say. That is what you're saying, isn't it? So how is it then that some people have mind problems and end up in straight-jackets while others are okay?'

Dromyrk couldn't remember, between patients, having put it so bluntly as that to Guther, if he had done so at all, that is. Plainly the man had been doing some reading up on his own. However it was not the first time that a patient had put that question to him. Dromyrk swivelled his chair away slightly from the patient, losing thought of him as he looked out the window, far away to when Adolf Hitler had posed that very same question. But the Fuhrer, in spite of his own psychoneurotic syndrome, had been more interested in disparaging the dubious Jewish doktor, Herr Doktor Sigmund Freud, whose original postulation it was, rather than the medical answer itself. It had been that sunny autumn weekend when Dromyrk and Professor Bernheim had been officially 'requested' to attend the Fuhrer's presence at his country residence, the Berghof. All their excuses of it being an inconvenience to their work swept aside, a very short flight in an exceptionally agile triple-engine Fokker F.XVIII had them touching down on the Berghof's own private landing strip before they had barely time to adjust to the plane's engine drone. Serving as Hitler's quietly salubrious country retreat, away from Berlin's war rooms and iron-handed planning, the Berghof was perched some 3022 feet up on the Obersalzberg mountainside, in the Bavarian Alps, near to the small Bavarian town of Berchtesgaden.

Not so much a single structure, the Berghof was a large compound of some seventy to eighty buildings. Immediately adjacent to the Berghof, a large barracks housed a contingent of SS Leibstandarte Adolfe Hitler troops, commanded by Obersturmbannfuhrer Bernard Frakken. These provided a security patrolled zone that took in, not just that of their Fuhrer, but also the complex of mountain homes of Nazi leaders situated nearby. Anti-aircraft gun batteries and smoke-generating machines were also in place to deal with hostility from the air.

As Dromyrk and Professor Bernheim walked onto the large terrace, Eva Braun gave her attention to her small black terrier, rather than to them, while her sister, Grell, spared them a bleak smile, before turning away. They looked to the figure in the corner for an indication of what measure of greeting they should give the two new arrivals. This man, in light grey flannel suit and large-brimmed dark felt fedora hat, was crouched down on his haunches with his back to them, softly stroking the head of a large German Shepherd dog. The man got up and turned round to face his guests, Dromyrk and Bernheim. Hitler, removed of jack-boots and tunic, with all its military insignia, gave off an image totally contrasting with that of the ogre Fuhrer that was terrorising Europe. Instead, it was that of an affable avuncular image. Of no possible harm or danger to anyone, whatsoever.

But not by chance was this switch of character so. It was simply a devilish twisting of the man's multi-sided charm mask that cajoled naïve masses into seeing him as their benevolent father-figure of a leader. Still patting the dog's head, his hands protected by suede gloves, from his neurotic fear of dirt and infection, Hitler held out a hand in warm welcome. Not quite the rigid straight-arm Nazi salute ritual that Dromyrk and Bernheim had expected. Here, in the peacefully remote alpine atmosphere, Hitler was able to amble casually among farmers in their lederhosen and open shirts, and thankfully accept flowers from children and their awe-struck young mothers. Those not fortunate enough to get close to their adorable leader gaped on from afar, behind the security barrier at the compound's driveway entrance. Here was where he hosted world leaders, who came harbouring suspicions, and lulled them into recognising Germany's National Socialism creating scientific and industrial greatness.

Dromyrk was not too surprised by Hitler's eagerness to take them on a personally conducted tour of his house. The house which he had purchased with the royalties from his book, *Mein Kamp*, after which he redesigned and decorated and furnished with ornaments of his own choice. Or so he claimed. Had Dromyrk not known Hitler's medical history, he would have been surprised, as others would have been, at the man's virtually bubbling pride over his own artistic effort on the house. This from the same self-claimed messiah tyrant who held steel-fisted rule over the country that was itself enforcing tyrannical rule over Europe. That he, of all people, should need praise for his own 'little house'. In Dromyrk's mind it reflected on the child's seeking of parental approval for its simple crayon drawing.

Leaving the terrace's informality of cactus plants and brightly coloured parasols behind them, they followed their host, babbling out his own praise, into the darker austerity of the entrance hall. He took them first to his study, so that he could show off the sophisticated telephone switchboard system. This to demonstrate that whilst away from the capital, he still held Germany in his iron control, issuing his infallible commands to generals and politicians from afar. His intellectual leaning he demonstrated by stocking books on architecture, music, painting and history in the library. Teutonic was the theme broadly pronounced by expensive furniture in the Great Hall, along with its massive red marble fireplace mantel. Dromyrk and Bernheim later learned from one of the domestic staff that behind one wall there was a projector room that screened American films that were strictly banned in Germany. Apart from 18th century German antiques and furniture adorning rooms, there were, surprisingly, also caged canaries in most rooms. Bedrooms were hung with old engravings as well as being honoured with small water colour sketches by Hitler himself. Rumour had it, again from a domestic staff source, that one of Hitler's aides-de-camp, commenting on these paintings, had remarked on the pity that Hitler had not got into art school, whence he could have progressed from water colours to grander oil paintings. That individual, long accustomed to office administration duties at Wehrmacht HQ, found himself promptly posted to a front line fighting battalion. Eva Braun's bedroom suite had an interconnecting door to Hitler's suite. Hitler had not shown them this last feature, that confidential information having come from one of the household staff.

The following morning, at breakfast in the pine panelled dining room, Hitler announced to his guests that whoever wished so could accompany him on his afternoon walk. Among those who gratefully accepted their Fuhrer's generous invitation, along with Dromyk and Bernheim, were Hitler's associate henchmen, Goebbels, Bormann and Himmler. Albert Speer, Hitler's favourite architect and designer of special effects features for mass rallies, begged to be excused. He was having to fly back to Berlin in order to finalise arrangements for the Fuhrer's coming torchlight parade that would be gloriously highlighted by 130 magnificent pillars of 'solid' light from 200 cm dia. Scheinwerfer-43 searchlights of 2.7 billion Hefner candlepower, each powered by 120 kilowatt generators, reaching up 13 kilometres into the sky, to Valhalla itself. Himmler would most likely have liked to have believed in this last piece, steeped as he was in the realms of mythical superstition.

A small distance across the Obersalzberg valley, on a wooded area of the Mooslahnerkopt hill, there was a Techaus (teahouse). Whenever Hitler was at the Berghof, it was almost a daily routine for him to stroll, accompanied by his guests, and guards at a discreet distance, along that wooded path of less than a kilometre to the teahouse. Of some concern to the guards was the fact that at one point the trees fell away to give a space, with a bench for a rest and a panoramic view of the valley below. Anyone seated on that bench provided a conveniently static target for a powerful rifle shot from across the valley. That very thought didn't escape Dromyrk as they passed the exposed spot. Thus the guards, on these walks, forever nervously hoped that Hitler would not choose to take that seat, 'invincible' as he was, even for a few moments.

As they neared the Techaus, Hitler, carefully out of earshot of the others, was plying Dromyrk and Bernheim with what seemed anxious questions about the human psyche and its neurotic traits. Professor Bernheim supplied most of the answers, although these didn't seem to quell Hitler's ever rising dissatisfaction. For every answer that Bernheim gave, Hitler had two more questions to launch at him. It was when they were all comfortably settled in the tearoom and general preoccupation was with the apfelstrudel, that Hitler saw the ideal moment for a casual aside remark to Dromyrk and Bernheim, who were seated nearest to him. He asked the same question that Guther had just put to Dromyrk. Why would that common infantile flaw manifest its blemish in later adult life only in some? Although he had put the question across as a general issue, it was not difficult to note the undertone of personal interest.

Professor Bernheim smiled for a moment while he considered the question. He then turned to the young Doktor Dromyrk, indicating that it was his turn to resolve Hitler's conundrum. After all, he had studied that specific field under the wing of Freud himself.

Dromyrk decided that a light parable was best for shedding light on Hitler's puzzlement. He told him of the two babies born on the same day, at the same time, in the same hospital. Along with these common factors, they also shared a common flaw passed on to them by their grandfathers. The grandfathers, being keen anglers, had left the grandchildren the legacy of their angling thigh boot waders. Each right boot had a hole in the sole. When the babies grew up, one of them became a keen angler like his grandfather and wore the boots. He thus eventually suffered from rheumatism in the leg. The other baby when it grew up, developed a fetish for archaeology, spending his time in the desert far away from water. He suffered no such ill effects of the limb. Thus common flaws in infancy does not necessarily warrant similar problems in adulthood where the social conflicts encountered vary so considerably.

Bernheim beamed his professor's smile of approval at his young assistant's cleverly simple example, concocted so for the layman's benefit.

After some long moments of silence, Hitler could only conclude that both grandfathers must have been Jews in order to have given their grandchildren defective merchandise. The young man suffering from rheumatism must also have been Jewish since he was foolish enough to wear the faulty boot. The other young man would undoubtedly have had a solid Aryan parent to cleanse his blood of its Jewish impurity. With that said, Hitler decreed that no more need be said on the matter. After that, conversation all round fell to a low level that would not disturb their Fuhrer as he decided to take a nap in an easy chair.

Guther listened to Dromyrk relating the same tale to him, taking it in with his own inner 'pinch of salt'. Rocking in his seat and throwing up his hands, he gave a nervous laugh. 'And I don't even fish!'

'And you don't even fish,' repeated Dromyrk slowly in solemn agreement with the jocular remark, seeing that the case in reality was far from funny.

As Dromyrk sat considering the patient's situation, his mind strayed back to what he had been recalling about that day with Hitler. He then thought of Rutkin. Only days ago Rutkin had been querying him, for the umpteenth time, over the feasibility of picking off Hitler with a sniper shot at that exposed spot in the Mooslahnerkopt woods. Sergeant-Major McCulloch at Lindwell had said it could work, but considered putting in a commando unit, trained for that specific operation, to be a plan with better chances. Dromyrk didn't know. He couldn't say. It wasn't his thing. They could decide between them.

His concentration on Guther now disturbed, Dromyrk felt in a hurry to finish the session. He checked his watch. He looked down at the note Mrs Morton had brought in before Guther had arrived. It had been handed in at the door by someone who hadn't the time to spare to come in. Or didn't want to come in. Dromyrk didn't recognise the name.

Carswell.

# 13

It wasn't so much lots of planes filling the sky, as pieces of sky interrupting the awesome massive fly-past of Allied Forces bombers. Like a great blanket being dragged across the firmament, its ripped patches blinking, not from the sun, but from dull sky, bright in contrast to the overall blackout effect of the roaring war machines. On and on they came, seemingly never-ending. Heads everywhere were turned skywards, gazes held by the great droning shift above them, their minds momentarily forgetting the street's devastation from bombing all around them.

Harry Carswell was only one of many standing around, eyes to the sky, trying to pick out and identify different bombers. Lancasters, Wellingtons, Canberras, Stirlings, Mosquitos, Liberators, and perhaps most noticeable in accordance with its Herculean dimensions, the US B-17G, or 'Flying Fortress'. Carswell was caught between admiration for its size and dismay for what damage it could inflict on his country. Luftwaffe reports relayed to his own department in the Abwehr had originally shown the heartening figures of heavy losses of these planes. Two factors prominently stood out as the cause for these losses. The American pilots, obviously lacking German discipline, were having the cavalier tendency to break away from the protection of their 18 plane wedge formations. Hence becoming 'flying ducks' for ferocious Messerschmitt fighters. The Luftwaffe greatly appreciated this reckless bravado of American pilots ignoring their commanders' instructions to stay in formation. Because the B-17G's guns were originally concentrated laterally along the fuselages, the planes were very much open to frontal attack. Luftwaffe fighter pilots were quick to take advantage of this second vulnerable point, attacking the American bombers head on. Thus B-17G losses soared. These losses would have been greater but for the fact that Russia and North Africa were the main concern of Luftwaffe fighter strength at that time.

But the American bald eagle's colossal pride would not allow its feathers to be ruffled for too long. That, and what Carswell understood to be virtually limitless monetary and material resources. So much so that between '35 and '39, some 13,000 or so B-17G planes had been manufactured. More critically, Abwehr reports passed on from Luftwaffe High Command gave alarming details of technical modifications in the plane's design. The vulnerability of frontal attack was now removed by the installing of Bendix remote-controlled swivel-turrets, with double 12.7mm machine-guns, positioned immediately under the plane's nose. This giving the plane a total of 13 guns. To ensure greater precision, computerised gun-sights enabled improved targeting, taking in factors of range and wind speed, so allowing for striking even through dense cloud. Tough and able to withstand enemy fire, it was seen as amongst the most effective bomber of the war; it flew more combat missions than any other bomber, and wherever the theatre of war was, it was there dropping its tonnage of bombs. Thanks to American generosity, 85 B-17G had been transferred to two select RAF squadrons for the purpose of electronic surveillance on bombing raids, carrying enemy radar-jamming devices, air-interceptor-jammers and tail-warning receivers; the swivel-turret under the nose replaced by the plane's own radar.

If this wasn't enough to rattle Jerry, detachable fuel tanks were being developed for fighter escort planes. This allowed fighter planes to escort bombers for a greater distance into enemy territory, and also allowing the tanks to be dropped for the plane's greater manoeuvrability when encountering enemy fighters.

What was worrying Carswell's superiors was that the B-17G bombings, in their colossal tonnage, were causing serious problems with the country's transport system. Causing crippling damage, in fact, to roads and railway lines and fuel supplies; so much so that tanks were delayed from being transported from the factories to the battle fronts.

Carswell knew all this from his Abwehr (Military Intelligence) department's secret files. Angry at the whole situation, he could have cursed every one of those planes as they passed. But there were too many and he didn't have the time. He had urgent work to see to. Reichsfuhrer SS Heinrich Himmler had issued the appropriate department with strict instructions that Carswell would face a firing squad if he failed to obtain the information they needed. Be it on German soil or otherwise, no place would provide hiding-place enough for him to avoid the inescapable penalty of failing in his sworn duty to serve his Fuhrer.

Carswell paused for a last look at the planes. It was a mixture of planes flying without tactical formation. But he knew that when the planes cleared the coastline, they would assemble into their specific official formations. The B-17Gs gathering into packs of 36, formed from three layers of 18 flying one above the other. This was their improved battle-shape for countering attacks from the deadly Messerschmitt 109. Much better than the original 18 plane wedge formation.  He turned and left, almost being knocked down by a motorcycle as he stepped off the pavement. His mind elsewhere, he'd forgotten for a moment that these cursed British drive on the left.

Carswell followed the circular staircase winding down into the Underground's labyrinth of cold stone passages and platforms. Surprise turned to an inner jeering joy at the site of people lying on mattresses and bunks packed tight against the platform walls. Such so-called bravery of the British that they should hide in these lowly subterranean 'caves'. Like Neanderthal Man. But Carswell's glee was dampened by the expressions carried on the faces of these people. Not that of the war-weary, but that of a remarkable chirpy cheerfulness. A weird 'communal' spirit floated among them with their shared jokes and dialogues. The camaraderie of those held in a common cause; under siege they may well be, but theirs was the mettle of resistance in a great united fight. Not that he had seen this on faces in German bombed streets.

Carswell pulled his eyes away from this discouraging site, to set about searching for his contact. Moving from platform to platform, he scanned the figures standing about as they waited for their trains. His eyes fell on and held the tall blond man in a grey herring-bone tweed Raglan overcoat.

The first thing that caught Dromyrk's eye when he looked round was the bandaged throat, then the buff envelope protruding deliberately from the man's gas-mask box – the recognition marker. His attention went to the man's face. Dromyrk's inside jumped. It couldn't be! But sure as hell, it was! It was Obersturmfuhrer Krunz! Older, like himself, Dromyrk saw, but still retaining that same hard face, with aggression spring-loaded in what the unsuspecting would have mistaken for a friendly smile. But the overall menacing image that Dromyrk recalled was perhaps softened by the fact that the man was out of his Sturmabteilung – Stormtrooper's – uniform. In its place he wore a fawn raincoat over a light brown double-breasted suit and a velour-effect rabbit skin trilby. Although now in civilian garb, he had climbed in rank to that of Hauptmann, or Captain.

As Krunz approached, Dromyrk moved along the platform edge to a more empty spot that was reasonably out of earshot with others on the platform. Krunz held out an unlit cigarette in a gesture of wanting a light, as an excuse for standing near to, and talking to, Dromyrk. With both of them recognising each other instantly, passwords were hardly necessary. But Krunz had to follow strict procedure in strict German style. Nobody was near enough to critically judge his accent, so Krunz was able to speak without his now irritating croaking act. 'If you have not a light possible, it is of no matter.'

'I always carry a light for the Underground,' replied Dromyrk. He lit the German's cigarette. A ridiculous fleeting thought of burning the man's face with the match flashed through his mind. He threw the match down onto the line. The frightened little mouse scurried away between the shining rails.

Inhaling deeply on his cigarette, Krunz frowned as he studied a war effort poster on the opposite wall across the rails. It depicted a fat Goering and his Fuhrer seated in a bus eavesdropping on two unsuspecting ladies gossiping in the seat in front of them. Krunz blew out his smoke with a  conniving smile etching out on his face. He directed the smile round at Dromyk in a glinting side glance. He took another deep draw on his cigarette, blowing out slowly to induce impatience in the other and strengthen the effect of his next statement. 'The Fraulein Matilde Mannleifen is well.'

Dromyrk's inside jumped again. He breathed in long and deep, his mind jostling with what it had just heard.

Krunz couldn't resist letting out a devilish gurgle of delight at the effect his news had had on Dromyrk.  'Truly one breathes deeply and gratefully at good news. And this is good news, is it not?' Krunz paused before putting across his punch-line remark. 'And for this one will gladly demonstrate gratitude. *Yes?*'

But Dromyrk was not ready to answer at that moment, his mind racing back through the years – all those years ago.

Tildi had played the violin so beautifully at the Leipzig Conservatoire Festival, where he had first become 'aware' of her. Ever so beautifully. Magnificent as the music had been, it was only noise, compared to her. They had met ever so 'accidentally' thereafter at concerts  held in aid of charity fetes and medical funding. They had become so close that Professor Bernheim had worried over his young assistant's distraction from his work. Dromyrk had not stated any firm words on marital commitment, but he had been meaning to. He had definitely been meaning to.

And then she had vanished.

Her entire family, father, mother, and two younger brothers, had suddenly disappeared. Herr Mannliefen, a wealthy banker of long established professional integrity, was not a Jew, but he had always made it openly clear that he thoroughly disapproved of the wave of anti-Semitism that was spreading across his country like some wretched flesh-eating bacterial infection. Now, if rumours were to be believed, he and his family had been 'removed' from their country. When one was transported, courtesy of the Gestapo, to a special detention centre, it was tantamount to no longer being in that country. Even if it was not a concentration camp equipped with 'extermination facilities', nevertheless, life, as one had hitherto known it, had ceased. One no longer existed. Or so German citizens had come to learn under the rule of the glorious Nationalsozialistische Deutsche Arbeiterpartei, or Nazi Party.

So now that he knew she was well, as Krunz had put it, the question was to what extent? There was no possible answering of this question in Dromyrk's surprised mind. Furthermore, he read extortion in Krunz's manner of delivering the startling news. He would have liked to have pushed the man off the platform onto electrified rails. But that would have been of no benefit to anyone. He needed to know more about Tildi. Common sense said that information wasn't going to be given freely. He steeled himself inside, holding back his newly found anger at the obvious message that Tildi was being used as a pawn. To enforce his compliance. In what, exactly?

Dromyrk was very much accustomed to waiting long periods for patients to say next to nothing. But now he felt an unfamiliar impatience rising up in his need to know more about that on which he had long since given up hope. He looked at Krunz, waiting for an answer.

Krunz nodded, understanding. He indicated with his eyes the Underground line-map on the opposite wall. 'Two stations along,' He said. 'Tomorrow. Same time. I shall be needing another lighting of my cigarette.' Throwing his glowing cigarette onto the track, Krunz turned and made for the exit.

The little mouse came scuttling back along the track, defying death from live rails, as a blast of wind and light sliding out of the tunnel signalled that a train was fast approaching the platform.

# 14

Howling around her like a demented banshee, the wind sliced through between the parachute straps and fastenings that suspended Monica Redfern from the balloon on the end of a cable fed out by a motorised winch 900 feet below. Her instructors had judged her to be ready for this next stage. But right at this very moment she didn't quite share their opinion. With her stomach tied in a knot from nerves, she was caught between fear of the coming drop and shame of releasing her bladder and seeing her piss cascade down on those below. She gripped her straps tightly.

For weeks she had been put through the gruelling training for 'ground techniques' of working with explosives, compass marching, street fighting, housebreaking, lock-picking. Hopefully these would not be necessary. But if so, they would be useful. She was expected, when critical circumstances decreed it, to be able to work on her own in hazardous conditions capturing and interrogating prisoners. Over that time a great deal of data on German military units and weapons had been 'pumped' into her. Now she had passed on to this. Jumping over and over again from six foot high wooden platforms to learn how to land and roll over the right way that was the difference between breaking a limb, if not your neck. They had been forced by a beastly shouting sergeant to swing like stupid monkeys from bars in order to strengthen the limbs, muscles and tendons. So the beast had said.

In a sudden instant of horror, she was plummeting down in terrifying acceleration towards the ground, the wind rushing through her mouth and nostrils, almost choking her in her surprise. As she raced on down, down, down, fright seized her inside at the thought of the parachute not opening. A Dutch parachute trainee had already been killed in his drop from a 'Flying Coffin', the Whitley bomber trainer plane.

An abrupt frame-jarring moment had her pulled back at the shoulders as the silk parachute opened out above her, filling her own personal part of the sky like a giant quivering jellyfish. Relief came in a great gulp, replacing what would have been a gurgling sob. Landscape features, trees, bushes, field boundaries, floated up gently in sharp detail in her slow descent until she realised, in alarm, that the ground immediately beneath her was rushing up rapidly with threatening nearness. Her side to side swinging motion was not making it easy for her to judge the distance. As her feet touched the ground, she let her legs buckle under her and rolled over as instructed. But she felt an absolute idiot as the parachute dragged her backwards across the ground. Tugging on the guide lines, she manipulated the parachute so as to empty it of the air current. Striking the circular release component on her chest, she was free of the damn ruddy harness at long last. Not a moment too soon.

She was pulling the whole parachute lot together and beginning to fold it all up when suddenly the ground behind her was ripping up clods of earth under the impact of machine-gun bullets. Monica's first instinct was to dive down on the ground for cover. But that was simply offering herself as an easy static target, her instructors had warned her. Instead, she dashed off, zig-zagging, to elude the bullets chasing her. The bullets stopped. Panting and standing still to take deep breath, she was suddenly struck from behind, in the kidney area, by a figure that had leaped up out of nowhere it seemed. The man had her down on her knees and putting a hammerlock on her neck, held a commando dagger to her side, ready for an upward thrust beneath the rib cage to the heart.

He released her and stood back to let her get up. She saw it was another one of those beastly Scottish instructors, Sergeant McAllister.

The man stood there grinning with a mile-wide mouth of teeth. He balanced the deadly slim Fairbairn and Sykes dagger, the 'Rolls Royce' of commando daggers, on his forefinger an inch from its steel guard. 'Right,' he said. 'It's your turn. Use yours on me.'

'I haven't got it,' she said, feeling all her aching parts. She couldn't help feeling that she'd left some parts of herself behind somewhere.

'Whit dae ye mean, ye havenae got it? Yer supposed to have it wae ye a' the time.'

She was exasperated with all the buffeting she was getting from jumping and dropping – and hell – everything else. 'Who am I supposed to be fighting with a silly knife up in the air, then? Tell me that.'

'Ye cannae stay up in the air forever, lassie. When ye come doon to earth, you'll find it's a guid wee weapon to hold in yer hand.' Suddenly the dagger was not in his hand, but thudding into the ground, barely an inch from her right toe. 'Use mine, then.'

She stared down at it.

He taunted her. 'Come on, use it. Or are a' you English lassies only guid for eyein' yon fancy Yankee sodgers?'

Monica's eyes flashed at the Sergeant. Grabbing down at the dagger, she let out a cry and stood back holding her hand. 'Now look what you've made me do. I've gone and broken a finger-nail.' Snatching up the dagger and making a clumsy lunge at him, she found herself once more in his death-delivering grip.

Back in Lindwell Hall, Monica was confronted by Selena Leighton-Lagrishe coming out of the Operations/Briefing Room. Dressed in her usual eloquent lines, even though it was khaki, she made Nicola feel mildly absurd in her dirty camouflage-patterned one-piece SOE parachute jump suit and monster size boots. 'I gather that Sergeant McAllister wasn't too happy with your effort,' said Selena.

'At least I dodged the bullets.'

Selina gave a slightly rebuking twitch of her eyebrows. 'You don't really think they were trying to hit you, do you?'

Monica held out her hand for Selina's inspection. She had just come across another two broken nails she hadn't noticed before. Probably from pulling on the parachute straps or gripping them tightly with her nails in her nervousness. 'Look what it did to my nails.'

Selena put away her instructor's face, replacing it with her 'friend-and-supporter' smile. 'Never mind. Put it behind you. Put it down as valuable experience you'll be thankful for later, when you're really in the field. You'll feel better when you've had a shower and changed clothes. What are you wearing tonight?'

Monica ran her hands up and down her arms and sides for a moment, wincing in the process. 'If how my body feels at the moment is anything to go by, it would have to be an all-covering dress to hide my black and blue marks and bruises.'

Selena was alluding to that evening's dance being held in the West End Belmore Hotel Ballroom. It was daddy's birthday, and thanks to Captain Falzoni's entrepreneurial wizardry, a great host of drinks, victuals and a US Army ten piece swing band was promised. He hadn't been able to engage Glen Miller's guys as they were away performing at a G.I. boot camp somewhere else.

It was only to be expected that mother would make noticeable noises of distrust, if not outright disapproval, of this American generosity. Selina could only sigh heavily at this thought. But an uplifting thought was that of Brent Bretzler coming to the dance. He would meet her parents. Mother had given her now familiar sniff of distaste of her daughter 'associating' with this American soldier, officer or not. In her snooty priggishness she used the word 'associating', rather than bring herself to accept that her daughter was in love with Lt-Colonel Bretzler. Well, let her!

'Don't you worry, honey, Brent will have your mom jitterbugging before the band's halfway through its numbers,' Falzoni had said.

Selena didn't quite feel that remark was enough to allay her uneasiness over her mother's possible unkind behaviour. But it was good to have the Captain's whacky encouragement. Falzoni could surely hold an audience in laughter in a morgue. Selena's inner woes vanished when Brent Bretzler came out of the Operations/Briefing Room. He took her by the arm. Giving Monica a nod to excuse them both, he drew Selena away with him. 'Before we hit the big time at your old man's party tonight, I want to take you to a cute little bistro joint I've found, thanks to Frank, in Chelsea. I want us to be on our own, before going on to the party, so I can tell you something. Here's not the place. They do a good number on and off, in French cuisine, for the asking, provided you ask them nicely and with a fat hand of bills for back-up. If we put a step on it, we can maybe get there before the onions get overcooked by an incendiary bomb.'

# 15

The gull screeched out and took off from its rock, frightened by the Royal Navy gunboat surging  into sight round the headland, from out of the fjord. Leaping and diving over the waves ahead of its foaming wake, the 68 foot gun-boat raced along at 40 knots on its routine coastal patrol, threatening all with and its 20mm Oerlicken auto-loading 6 pounder gun forward and its 0.5 inch Vickers machine-gun aft. The moon blinked overhead, as the gulls criss-crossed repeatedly before it. Heads turned up at the birds' irate cries, missing their shadows racing over the curly crested waves. But that wasn't all that the crew's eyes missed, passing off the area as clear, and speeding on up the coastline, letting the birds fall behind in a squalling retreat.

Beneath them, in the fjord's dark waters, a giant reptile stirred from its slumber  and slipped out at a slow 4 knots on its two 375hp electric engines  towards the sea. The submarine was moving out on the next stage of its mission. Once surfaced, it would take power from its two supercharged 6 cylinder 4 stroke diesel engines giving 2800-3200 hp. Nothing else moved and the moon was afraid and was now trying to keep out of sight behind the clouds.

The seagulls had been more perceptive than the humans and were already swirling and squawking round the small island that was coming out of the sea. Rising out of the water as a sharp pinnacle at first, the 'island' suddenly became very fat and swelled up and out of the sea to form an incredible shining grey island 220 feet long. The water cascaded off the submarine's sides and settled beneath it with a roar that met its shifting tonnage. One hundred and four tons of inrushing water welled up and rolled on the surface. Submerged, the U-Boat Type VIIC displaced 857 tons and when surfaced displaced 753 tons so that the difference could be put down as sweat on the long metal hull.

Figures were coming up on the conning tower. One man, the Kapitan, was scanning the sky and coastline with infra-red binoculars. Beside him, his First Officer, was looking up, concerned, at the raucous taunts of the gulls, where a clamorous swarm of them now besieged the submarine, the white flecks hanging around overhead like a swarm of midges. The noisy attack was more than just a harmless plaintive squealing; it could carry far across the water, with the circling white specks helping in turn to attract attention, especially if the moon should come out.

The Kapitan dipped his head forward to bark orders into the speaking tube. Four ratings, one after the other, popped up out of the deck hatch to run along the deck to man the guns. Two of them tending to the 88mm SKC/35 naval gun, the other two to the 20mm anti-aircraft gun. Priming them for firing, they waited in readiness for the British gunboat's possible return or any other enemy approach, sea or air. The Kapitan lowered his binoculars. Seeing his First Officer's worried expression, he followed his prolonged gaze up at the sky. 'One of nature's necessary nuisances,' he said. 'A contingency, not so much unforeseen, as unstated on the strategy table charts in our superiors' operations rooms.'

'Perhaps the Fuhrer will solve the problem,' mocked the First Officer. 'Perhaps he will order the damn birds to report to the concentration camps! They would never dare disobey their Fuhrer's commands!'

The Kapitan gave a grunt of a laugh. 'Ja. Just like he solves everything else.' The bitter irony of the remark  and the laugh said that they both thought the opposite. That that man back in Berlin, waving his arms and screeching his speeches, just like gulls, should declare himself to be supreme controller of the country's armed forces was an outrage. More *pointedly*, his insane directions pointed the very way to sure defeat. The Kapitan's inner rancour came out in his words as he spoke, staring out at the darkness. 'We are ready?'

'Ja, Herr Kapitan. Obermaat Hoffmann is ready with the Enigma coding machine.'

'You have changed code wheels for this hour's message?'

'Ja, Herr Kapitan.'

'How long before transmission?'

The man held his wrist low down to check his watch with his torch. 'Seven minutes and forty three seconds, Herr Kapitan.'

No further words were needed. Minds and machines throughout the boat throbbed and pulsed alike as all waited. Breathing in fresh air was a relief, after hours of breathing in stale air given out by generators when submerged.


*Underneath the Arches* wasn't quite coming off with the comic paupers' message intended as when sung by Flanagan and Allen, now that that it was being hollered out in wide, twanging, American accents, at a fast jiving rhythm, by two females in US Army uniforms. Backed up by blaring saxophones and trumpets, they were making a good effort of sounding like the Andrews Sisters trio 'Brent' Bretzler thought, enjoying it. But he saw the faint frowns of puzzlement, if not quiet despair, on the faces around him. English faces of course. He smiled to himself, and then catching Frank Falzoni's eye, smiled with him. Falzoni was whirling and twisting with Monica Redfern on the small 'postage-stamp' square of dance-floor allotted to one end of the Belmore Hotel's main function room. It wasn't quite clear who was leading who, both of them caught up in the excitement of their movements. But Monica's wriggling body movements caught more attention, from the men especially, with the tight black silk dress hugging her, bringing out her white flesh, to give the 'French' Monique that she was to become.

There was noticeable relief on faces all around when the two girls ended their number and a soft slow solo trumpet rendering of Vera

Lynn's *White Cliffs of Dover* started up as the rest of the band broke up and headed for the bar for a break. Humming and low murmured words began to accompany the music. Frank and Monica left the dance-floor, Monica coming over to join Bretzler and the rest of the party group, while Falzoni made for the bar. There was an abundance of alcoholic beverages available on the party tables, supplied partly by Falzoni, but he just had to be away for a few minutes of free time among other GI buddies.

Bretzler could sense what Frank was feeling, his own feelings drifting that way for some lingering moments. A faint sensation of becoming ensnared, was it? With all these civilians, Selena's family, relatives and friends all around him, and Frank away over there, he was like a fish leaving its shoal to approach that enticing hook. Their announcement, his and Selena's, of matrimonial engagement, had brought out surprise, congratulations – and an only just discernable degree of dismay. The latter from the mother. Uneasy and unsure over how Selena would take his proposal, over mussels grilled with garlic, onions, parsley and breadcrumbs in the bistro, Bretzler had faced a tougher test of nerves facing her parents. His guess over the mother's reaction was spot on. He imagined that she saw it as an 'intrusion, if not a sacrilege, with him, an American soldier, not even a full colonel, entering their upper class social station. The father had been most forthcoming with his welcome. Selena's uncle Gerard, Commodore Leighton-Lagrishe, had been a trifle quiet, if not as gloomy as the sister-in-law.

Beyond a brief 'Congratulations', the Commodore had reserved his words for his close discussion with Colonel Rutkin about something that had nothing to do with a doomed guy preparing to tie the matrimonial knot. As far as Bretzler could make out, before interrupting their private tete-a-tete for handshakes, it concerned the Atlantic convoy situation. The codes for Allied shipping routes had been intercepted and cracked by B-Dienst, German Naval Intelligence, so that rough figures were giving a gloomy total of over 183,000 tons of Allied shipping lost to wolf-pack U-boat attacks. Nor did it help the crisis any that Germany was producing thirty U-boats a month. 'And yet that buffoon, Hitler, keeps on taking U-boats from the Atlantic and re-deploying them to protect Norway and North Africa,' said Commodore Leighton-Lagrishe. 'But at least B-Dienst so far haven't broken into our codes for North Africa. We've still got that edge on them, thank God.'

Bretzler left them to their low-voiced hush-hush 'cabal'. He thought how Selena's family and his were of the same church. That had to count for something. What the hell, he was here to fight Hitler. After that there would be time enough for him to arm-wrestle with the mother-in-law.

Bretzler watched Selena walking around, showing her ring, chatting and giggling among friends. He caught her eye as she looked round from her joyous talking and smiled his love across to her. She stood there staring at him, her heart held by him in a moment of girlish coy rapture, and then went back to join in the squeaks and squeals of female friends.

Frank came back over, and true to form, had soon gathered his now faithful circle of listeners around him for another outpouring of hilarious tales. Outrageous comical slants put on real events in their ferocious fighting in the field that made the life and death balance all seem a great farce. How he had been virtually stripped naked in Palermo when a mortar blast had ripped off his shirt and pants. Only the fact that it wasn't a Sunday had saved the company padre from fainting at his ungodly exposure. And they all laughed uproariously. Even Bretzler, and he had heard the stories a million times since. And he'd been there with Frank in the battlefield, experiencing the real horror behind the jokes. He certainly had to be thankful for having Frank lessen the distance between him and his new family. Most of them, at least, if not them all.

Bretzler looked across to see Mrs Leighton-Lagrishe taking her brother-in-law, Gerard aside for a quiet word. Taking a sip at his bourbon, Bretzler braced himself and started walking over to talk to them. A hand on his arm stopped him. It was Colonel Rutkin. 'Has he gone over?' he said in blunt cryptic form appropriate amidst the party atmosphere.

Bretzler's mind stalled for a second, interrupted as it had been. He remembered Dromyrk. 'Yes.' That was all that was needed in reply. He walked on to join Mrs Leighton-Lagrishe and Commodore Leighton-Lagrishe.

Selina, in a straight-hanging Tunic-style gown in gold lame matching her golden hair, now let down upon her bare shoulders, was talking with her father and Monica. She excused herself to go over and give some support to Brent in his 'confrontation' with Mummy and Uncle Gerard. She bit her lip and fidgeted with the bright beads of her narrow shoulder straps as a separate thought struck her. Back in the bistro, she had held back from matching Brent's proposal with an announcement of her own. She wasn't sure how he felt about children and so had refrained at the last moment from saying that she was pregnant. She knew how Mummy and Daddy, in devout religious observance, would be scathed by her news. If she told them. What would Father O'Malley think? She thought of Colonel Rutkin's statement that she should prepare for possible parachuting into enemy territory to act as Monica's field control. For a frightening moment of clarity she thought of how she could lose the baby active in the field. If she didn't step back from duty on medical grounds, that would be a solution. The fleeting thought burned her inside and she felt like leaning over and singeing her hand in penance on one of the table candle-flames.

Suddenly conversations all around were interrupted by the loud crashing sound of the band starting up again. Falzoni had stepped up and seized her by both arms. 'You've dodged me so far, kid. Brent can have you after; but now I'm going to show you some real boogie-dancing. Let you see what you're missing hitching up with that guy. Come on – let's swing.'

Selena could barely forgive herself inside for thinking that was a good idea, but not for the same reason that Frank meant.

# 16

'Look out!'

Hauptmann Krunz, alias Harry Carswell and Dr Dromyrk jolted to an abrupt halt in automatic reflex at this warning shouted out by the fireman on their right across the street. But it was a false alarm. For them, that is. The warning had been directed beyond them, across the open ravaged space where innocent homes had stood only hours before, at the group of auxiliary firemen and rescue workers standing close to the wall that had suddenly begun to bulge out at its top. The men scattered out the way in all directions, like bull's-eyed ninepins, as the great expanse of masonry bulged, cracked, crumpled and gave way, the upper steel girder, roasted to buckling by incendiary bomb flames, crashing down on top of the great melee of bricks, ash, dust and smoke.

Krunz and Dromyrk promptly moved across to the other side of the street as the great black cloud of dust and floating specks of debris billowed out in their direction. Stepping carefully between snaking hosepipes and around lumps of what had once been some-one's home, they made their way down the street. As like many others across the war-torn metropolis, the street had lost its identity, removed of its face, with its inner secrets of intimate rooms and closets laid bare to open view. The small residents' private park in the street's centre offered a little cheer only in that it displayed no rubble from bombing. Its former pleasantry of greenery had long since been replaced by the dull brown of earth, it having been dug up, like so many other parks in the city, to grow vegetables in the war effort. Short metal stumps all around its perimeter were all that remained of the railings that had been cut by oxyacetylene torches and removed. The railings being used to make planes, ships, tanks and whatever else that could serve in military use. A siren was howling somewhere and another rumble of collapsing masonry nearby was followed by the high-pitched sound of a warden's whistle and pounding boots as, once again, rescue teams hurried frantically to save what they hoped they could.

'I take it you know where you're going in all this – this -- great atrocity of a mess?' said Dromyrk for want of better-fitting words, looking round about himself at the ensuing madness of fellow man. 'Because I, for one, am quite lost. Every street needs a separate map.'

Krunz cast him a sarcastic smile. 'So now you will agree how our two great cities, Berlin and London, are drawn together in their likeness. With all this punishment inflicted on them by our bombers, yours and mine, they are like two magnificent emperors with their crowns knocked askew. It is our sworn mission to rectify the positioning of these crowns to their former glorious status. To have our two countries finally united after the war, in negotiated settlement, to work as one great Fatherland, under the leadership of our almighty Fuhrer.' Krunz looked round at Dromyrk and nodded in inner insight. He managed a short dry laugh. 'But of course it is the destination to which we are now going that you wish to know. Have no fear, we shall be there in a few minutes more.'

They picked their way round the rubble and continued on their way, with structures still falling and the siren still howling all the while.

The small tearoom nestled quietly roughly halfway along the amazingly undisturbed side-street spared, as yet, from all the tumult of horrific desolation of the surrounding area. Run primarily as an establishment for embittered Russian emigres grousing over the 'Jewish Problem', it also served as an initial tryst for those seeking more secretive venues for grinding their political axes. Brought together selectively to form a secret society to share one common grievance and one common goal, these individuals constituted the British Union of Fascists. Members were mainly of the country's upper class that sought alliance with Hitler's Nazi Germany. A clandestine movement monitored by the even more clandestine movements of MI5.

The man pushed aside on the small table what he had been reading and, looking up, smiled at the doorbell's gentle 'ting' as they entered. He rose to greet them. Balding where a blond lion's mane had once flourished, and with fresh florid complexion, the man stirred no recognition in Dromyrk's mind. Dromyrk felt an iron hand grip his and equally firm eyes raking his own face for what answers might lie beneath. He awaited Krunz's introductory details.

'Herr Landor Salmerssen,' said Krunz. 'A fellow countryman of yours, Herr Doktor, and truly sympathetic with our cause as to be fully committed to its ultimate designs.'

After a moment's thought, Dromyrk found recollection of that name. He had no personal acquaintance with the man but he recalled reading of him in Swedish newspapers. One of Stockholm's powerful commercial barons who was always assured of being at the better end of a deal. Totally self-made and denied an education like that of Dromyrk's, he was always able to acquire his intended ends with something involving more than a spitting on and shaking of hands. A radical outspoken loose cannon in his country's politics. In business he had always made no secret of the fact that he strongly favoured forging industrial alliance with Germany.

They all sat down and refreshment was ordered, although tea was the last thing on their minds. Leaning forward with his forearms on the table and looking down at some sugar grains, Salmerssen dallied with them with his finger as he spoke to Dromyrk. 'Mr Carswell tells me that you are in an ideal position for obtaining some useful information.' Joining his hands together firmly and still leaning forward, he looked up into Dromyrk's face, only inches away, awaiting an answer.

Krunz cut in before Dromyrk could form a suitable reply. 'We can well appreciate that the Herr Doktor's position is of a very sensitive nature. Involving personal details more traceable back to the individual than that of scientific and engineering blueprints. But the Herr Doktor has been persuaded that his endeavour should be of the utmost. For the consolidation of all our cause's plans and *personal* plans. You would agree, Herr Doktor Dromyrk?'

Krunz had indeed spoken for Dromyrk, but behind the helpful wording there was the strict imperative from which he was not being permitted to waver. He thought of Tildi and her family – and of his Aunt Imelda, back home in Uppsala, now that Salmerssen was in the picture. Dromyrk held back from answering for a moment, hoping his silence would incite Krunz or Salmerssen to say more, helping him to read their real thoughts, as he did with patients. But neither of them said anything further to that. 'I agree,' replied Dromyrk.

Dromyrk forced out a smile, to meet the other two breaking out around the table. Tea arrived at the table. As it was being poured out, nobody paid any attention to the Air Raid Warden in the street outside. It didn't strike any of them as odd his being there in spite of the street having suffered no bombing damage. He carried the regulation gas-mask box. But instead of a gas-mask, the box held a camera with a 40mm f1.9 short focal length lens that provided good depth of field and sharp pictures.

Colonel Rutkin made his way with practised familiarity through the quiet West End tailor premises with nothing beyond a curt nod at those around him. No words were necessary. But he was not here to be fitted for a garment. Nor was he surprised when the back wall of the fitting cubicle, its pegs laden with jackets for camouflage, swung silently back. He hadn't even needed to touch anything for it to open. That had been done by whoever had monitored his approach.

Rutkin entered the narrow dimly-lit passage, where two servicemen waited on him at the far end. They wore different uniforms, one in dark Navy blue, the other in lighter Air Force blue. The one colour they both shared was the brilliant white of their belts and lanyards snaking down from their shoulders to the butts of the service revolvers held in their brilliant white hip-holsters. The seaman reached out to take Rutkin's War Office ID card and scrutinised it carefully. The airman scrutinised Rutkin. The card was handed back. Giving salutes, the two guards stepped sharply aside. Returning the salute, Rutkin walked on to the steel-plated door at the end of the passage. Once again the door opened up on its own accord before him.

Wing Commander Withers held the heavy door back for Colonel Rutkin to enter. 'You managed to get yourself away, then,' he said.

'Couldn't have made it sooner, Jeremy,' replied Rutkin. 'When Winston decides to reminisce on a personal episode, he likes to make it long-lasting, even when it is absolutely of no relevance to more important matters at hand.'

'You can tell me all about it later,' said Withers, closing the door and following Rutkin into the centre of the secret Operations Room, where there was a steady buzz of things happening. It was only one of many such strategy planning rooms dotted about the country, in the least suspected locations, hidden behind the least suspected of innocent civilian fronts. Whilst newly emerging radar supplied some information of incoming attacks, the main eyes and ears of these centres were those of the fifty thousand or so men and women of the Royal Observer Corps. These, in their vigilance, stood on hilltops and rooftops and other suitable vantage points, on the coasts and inland, armed with binoculars and rangefinders, warning control centres of the enemy's approach.

The room was roughly sixty feet square and twelve feet high, with a large forty feet square table occupying its centre. All around the table were personnel of mixed services, mostly women, moving discs, coloured in accordance with their field units, either by hand or by long croupier-style rakes from time to time according to information coming in. This data was relayed to them, via their headphones, by men in four corner glass cubicles, whose task it was to analyse incoming information and so issue instructions to those at the table.

Rutkin stood beside the table. The entire wall opposite him was a map of the European theatre of war. An Army corporal mounted on a slim rail-run ladder moved to and fro to shift coloured pin-flags according to what was going on over there. Rutkin didn't like how the German flags were amassing round the Allied flags at one point on the map. He looked down in dismay at the table situation as a Wren raked in a disc, to pick it up and drop it in a side tray. 'That's Ronnie Townesend's light armoured expeditionary reconnaissance brigade gone under,' said Withers to Rutkin. The brigade had plainly been no match for General Meiller's spearhead panzer division of monster 50 ton, 10ft by 12ft 'Tiger' tanks.

Rutkin clenched his fist and cursed in low voice. 'Dammit! I warned Winston that I thought it was a dangerous gamble of a position. But Monty had him charmed his way. Dammit!'

They looked round as Brigadier Wallace came over to join them. He pointed to where the corporal on the ladder was moving a flag in Germany. 'Operation Bludgeon,' he said bluntly. 'We mount a massive air and artillery bombardment to disrupt German morale and make gaps in their defences. Lt-General Hogarth will then cross the Rhine on the right of the Allied advance, to seize Mees and Reswel. At the same time, Lawrence's US Eighth Army will attack on the left between Reswel and Duisberg. Troops will cross the river in amphibious vehicles and landing craft, while our engineers will move in with ferries and Bailey bridges. We're then relying on tanks to push the attack forward on the west bank. They'll be helped by a daylight airdrop by General Reynold's US Eighteenth Airborne Corps, made up from the US Seventeenth Airborne and our own Sixth Airborne Divisions.' Brigadier Wallace rubbed his hands together, looking round at Rutkin for comments.

'Hmmm. I would have thought it somewhat unconventional in strategy – putting airborne troops ahead of ground forces,' said Rutkin. 'I do hope you're right.'

'Of course I'm right, man. We think it should prove to be less vulnerable to a punishing counter-attack like that of Arnhem. Armoured and airborne forces will combine with infantry in attack to give us an overall bridgehead forty miles long and ten miles deep, all within twenty four hours. The objective is to encircle the Ruhr's industrial cities, before advancing on to the north German plain and advancing on ultimately to Berlin. We're counting on Canadian forces to cross the Rhine at Emmerich on the far right of the advance, so as to liberate the Dutch territories still under German occupation.'

As the Brigadier went over his proposed field tactics, Rutkin tried to think of a parallel version of the tactics that he could concoct and pass on as dummy plans to Dr Dromyrk.

A very young lieutenant had come out of one of the cubicles to approach Brigadier Wallace. 'A call for you, sir,' said the lieutenant. 'On the red scrambler.'

'Thank you, Hodges.' The Brigadier turned to Colonel Rutkin and Wing Commander Withers. 'If you'll excuse me,' he said. He indicated, with a wave of his hand to them, the flashing light on the red scrambler phone in the cubicle. Brigadier Wallace listened for a moment on the phone before leaning out of the cubicle to beckon Rutkin. 'It's for you, Rutkin,' he said. 'I'll be damned if it's not some damned Kraut called Bretzler on the other end asking for you. How the hell did he get on this security line, I'd like to know. Is this some damned POW you're working in cahoots with, Rutkin? I warn you, Rutkin, you're going to have to be very careful working with these damned turnabout Kraut blighters, I tell you.'

'Oh, I am, sir; believe me I am.'

# 17

The month had turned nasty, so that in the lofty, roomy, interior of Lindwell Hall it was extremely cold. Major Drummel had taken to wearing his greatcoat and scarf indoors, hung open over his uniform. He tugged the coat front close as the hall door was thrown open by the wind. Captain Falzoni came in carrying a wooden crate partly wrapped in sacking. It looked like a heavy load, judging by the stoop of his back. Putting his shoulder to the back of the door, he attempted to push it against the persistent wind, but the latch wouldn't catch. 'If you could give me a hand, Major,' he said over his shoulder to Drummel.

The Major stepped over to secure the latch. He looked at Falzoni's load. 'So you managed to get one and fly it in, then,' he said.

'And sure as hell lucky to make it short of having our pants shot off from under us. The whole damn operation was touch and go. The plane badly shot up – more bagel-sized holes in it than in an old kosher mama's bakery in the Bronx -- one engine gone – the undercarriage fucked with only one wheel down – we were burling round like a damned ballet dancer when we came in on the landing strip. Those air base guys at Harrington sure near lost a control tower, the way our plane was wallowing in the air. Maybe those Pyrenees partisan guys got their dates wrong – thought it was party night for a good old hogging shoot-out with Jerry.'

Falzoni walked over to the hall table and planted his load down on it with a dull thud. Pulling the sacking away, he began prising the crate open with a jack-knife. With a mixture of impatience and frenzied relief from his life-threatening experience, he ripped the crate planks away. The bright polished wooden box stood alone. They both stared at it for a few moments.

'It's larger than I thought,' said Drummel. 'I hadn't imagined the Enigma machine to be as large as that.'

'Maybe that's because it's *not* an Enigma machine.'

'It's *not*? What is it, then?'

Falzoni leaned over the box to open its lid and scan over the inner assortment of wheels, rotors, levers and 'things' he couldn't put a name to. 'It's a Geheimschreiber cypher machine, codename Sturgeon. Used by the Wehrmacht HQ top brass for relaying interdepartmental messages. You won't get one of these in a U-Boat or a German trawler. They're too hush-hush to be installed outside of Germany or German-held territories. If this cute baby doesn't give us some useful military gen, at least maybe it'll let us know what general is taking the morning off for a haircut.' Falzoni patted the box. 'It's a lot more complicated than the Enigma machine. It can have up to twelve rotors, compared to the Enigma's four rotors. Let's see – this one's got two, four, six, eight, ten – ten rotors. God knows how many thousand or million tra-lah-lah permutations, or whatever they're called, that makes. Mind you, this is a home-made, half simulated version of the machine, put together by those clever wizard Polish intelligence people. God knows how they managed to do that?'

'Possibly that's attributable to the fact that pre-war Polish engineering had close links with the German engineering industry – Siemens especially, on which this model would appear to be modelled. That would allow for them, on the Polish side, to construct something of their own design,' said Drummel. The Major's own pre-war experience in the engineering and manufacturing industry was apt to have him bring forth these interesting little points of information from time to time.

'You don't say, Major. How about that.'

Drummel wasn't sure if the Captain's last remark was a mocking one. To cover his air of uncertainty, he took on a brisk air of duty. 'We have to get this over to Bletchley Park, pronto. Let their genius-minded mathematicians get to work on it.'

'That's going to be one hell of a bother, driving along your narrow country roads this time of night. Bad enough with the road signs removed, but in the darkness, I might as well hitch a ride on one of Jerry's passing planes and fly straight there, cutting out all the twisting and turning. Why can't you have straight roads in this land, like we have back in the States?'

'No problem. I'll assign Sergeant Rivers to deliver it. He knows the way there. He does the route regular.'

'Thanks, Major, but I'd prefer to take it there in person. Having flown all that way, dodging all those tracer bullets and ack-ack flak, I may as well complete the last leg of the trip.'

'I'll assign Rivers to accompany you.'

'Have it your way, Major. That way we can both keep an eye on each other.'

'I shall do that.' The Major turned and strode off to find and assign Sergeant Rivers.

Falzoni called out to Drummel's back receding along the long hall. 'Tell the Sergeant not to buckle his belt on too fast. I want to grab me a coffee first – and some good old forty per cent proof Kentucky mouthwash.'


'Not flying? What do you mean I'm not flying out?' Monica Redfern, now officially switched on in her role as Monique Berac, was truly exasperated. 'Do you mean to tell me that I've spent weeks racking every bone in my body jumping from balloons and aeroplanes, and learning to cheat, destroy and kill, only to be told that it's all been for nothing?'

Selena Leighton-Lagrishe shook her head in patient correction of a misunderstanding. 'I didn't say you weren't flying out. I said you would not be flying out in *this* plane. She pointed to the Wellington bomber, shrouded in the darkness like a sleeping flying dragon, some fifty yards from them. They were standing outside the personnel block adjacent to the small control tower of the Harrington SOE air-field.

'If it's not that one, what *am* I going to be jumping from?'

'You're not jumping from anything. It's a last-minute change of plan. The Wellington is not suitable for this operation. We've just received last-minute info that we have to make an urgent pick-up. So we can't use the Wellington. It's all right for parachuting into enemy territory, but not for pick-ups.' The Wellington, Lancaster and Stirling bombers did indeed serve well for dropping agents off, but they were not suitable for landing and taking off in small unprepared fields. 'You'll be flying out in the Lysander. That one there,' said Selena.

'Where? I don't see anything except that great thing,' said Monique, meaning the Wellington.

'It's behind the Wellington. It's very small. Just room for the pilot, and you seated behind him. We may as well go over, if you've got everything and you're ready.' Selena cast a quick once-over inspection glance at Monique to check if she *was* ready. She saw that Monique had her transmitter, weighing less than 40 lbs, disguised as a simple suitcase. Good. As they moved off, heading for the planes, two other figures came out of the building behind them, to follow them. Alphonse Palpiere and the pilot.

Like a sparrow dwarfed by an albatross, the small Lysander sat alongside the massive Wellington. Manufactured by Westland Aircraft, the small plane was fitted with a single Bristol Mercury air-cooled radial engine, and had its wings mounted high on top, glider-style. The landing gear was fixed, with large streamlined spats over the wheels. These covering structures had stub wings that could carry a 500lb bomb or four 20lb bombs. Because of its smallness, The Lysander was ideal for photographic reconnaissance and daylight observation of artillery behind enemy lines. But this was not a bombing operation. The .303 Vickers machine-gun had been removed from the rear cockpit for the civilian passenger. Only the two forward-firing .303 Lewis machine-guns, mounted in the wheel fairings, remained in place for protection.

Selena and Monique reached the Lysander first, joined moments later by Palpiere and the pilot. 'I can't guarantee that it won't be a bumpy trip,' said Selena, judging by the plane's size.

'It'll be bumpy, all right, and *cold*,' said the pilot. 'And we only have a compass and map for navigation. So we need the moonlight for getting us in the right field.'

'Thank you so much,' said Monique. 'That sounds very reassuring – I think not.'

'But it will be a very swift switch,' said Selena. 'You'll just have enough time, when you land, to get out before we pick up our contact in your place to take off again to fly him back to London for debriefing.'

'Who is it?' said Monique.

'I can't tell you that, as you well know,' replied Selena.

'So I won't have time to check my lipstick in my mirror,' joked Monique nervously.

'No, you won't have time for that,' replied Selena, perhaps a little too solemnly. 'It's all so quick with these last-minute alterations. And the location has been changed as well. You're not going to Mologne now – you're going to --- ' Selena turned to Palpiere. 'Where is it they're supposed to land now?'

'A tiny field just outside the village of Bouleau,' said Palpiere. He looked apologetically at Monique. 'Sorry, but we have great difficulty contacting the Resistance reception committee to arrange exact pick-up times and places. You must remember that these men are at great risk, defying the night-time curfew imposed by the bastard Boche when they make these arrangements.'

Listening to these foreboding details, Monique was experiencing a two-way swing of feelings, from excitement, to last-minute withdrawal nerves. All the while she was absentmindedly stroking a section of her left sleeve. It was where a small .25 calibre Webley and Scott semi-automatic pistol nestled in a secret pocket inside the sleeve. The silencer for it was concealed in the right sleeve. Selena noticed this nervous tell-tale action and waved a forefinger slowly at Monique to warn her. Monique quickly pulled her hand away from her sleeve.

'I am thinking how you have a great advantage over the men,' said Palpiere to Monique. 'While men are being taken away and used for forced labour, by the Boche, the women are free to travel anywhere on trains, trams, bicycles, with explosives and guns hidden under the bread and --- and ---les legumes --- in their innocent baskets.' Palpiere found it necessary to continue his advice like a grandfather to a child. 'And do not forget not to look right when crossing the road – look left. Yes, yes, you shake your head at this simple advice because you know it. But it is simple things like this that are so easily forgotten, *because* they are so simple. And these simple mistakes cost lives. We have already lost one agent, arrested and no doubt shot, because of this very mistake of not remembering.' Palpiere was about to continue with his lecture, but Selena warned him off with a faint shake of the head not to go on, lest he should upset Monique too much.

The pilot shifted, to step into the conversation. 'I think we can climb on board, if we're ready. Yes?'

Monique's jovial chirpiness seemed to have drained out of her in the last moments of getting into the plane's rear cockpit, and if it had not been for the darkness, her face would have shown an uncharacteristic grey grimness. At the pilot's OK from Control, the engine exploded into life with a shower of sparks and great coughing of fumes, sending the propeller swirling into violent rotation. Taxiing round and away from the Wellington, the Lysander moved down the runway.

Standing there, one with hands clenched in her pockets, the other with hands opening and closing by his side, they watched the tiny shape leave the ground and go off into the sky until it was lost from their vision in the darkness. Neither of them said a word to the other as they turned and headed back to the personnel block.

<h1 style="text-align:center">18</h1>

With his last patient gone, Dromyrk spared a few minutes more going over the case notes before closing the file and putting it away with all the other files and swivelling round in his chair to face the wireless. Turning it on, he tuned in to the BBC concert broadcast. Bartok's Violin Concerto No 2 with its pulsing allegro non troppo notes pierced the room's silence. It was not the same Bartok piece that Tildi had played, but it was similar enough to bring to mind the very magic of her playing. Dromyrk sat there  mesmerised, listening to the evocative melody. The years fell away as he let the soft notes play with his memory and his emotions.

She had come to Stockholm that weekend as part of the Leipzig Light Symphony Orchestra to play in the City Concert Hall as well as giving her own solo performance. Dromyrk could only recall it as being an exquisite solo rendition. It created the perfect opportunity for her to meet his parents. He was eager for her to meet his parents. The men had taken to her more smoothly than the ladies. Dromyrk had tried, as best he could, to hide his inner disappointment at his mother's cool reception of Tildi. The Oedipus gauntlet cast down to challenge many a son. Otherwise, everything else was perfect. Tildi was perfect; her playing was perfect; the weather was perfect. Dromyrk smiled in appreciation of his own euphorically misted memories.

But Tildi's skill with strings was not confined to the violin alone. She surprised everyone, Dromyrk especially, when she had expressed an eager request to accompany the men on their intended afternoon's fishing on the lake outside home town Uppsala. Dromyrk, his father and grandfather, had welcomed this. His mother had seen this as somewhat unladylike. So they had set themselves on the lake, three doctors and one violinist in two boats, Dromyrk and Tildi in one boat and his father and grandfather in the other boat. She had declared herself to be feeling so very safe surrounded by three doctors. Dromyrk could never have imagined at that time that the concept of safety could carry such a sinister Implication. She was better at fishing than he was, but he didn't care. With the two of them so close together in the limited confines of the little boat, everything else around him was purely idyllic. Time passed like a slow yawn. The summer sky had a heavy haziness of afternoon heat. Through this thick blanket of misty warmth there peered, rather than glared, like a myopic eye, a weak yellow disc that was the sun. Fishing lines, glinting as they swished through the air, matched the sparkling swarms of insects hovering over the water, while occasional voices echoed that of frogs croaking over lily-pads. Theirs was the perfect peace in isolation, so far from the lake sides, where all manner of complicated troubles lay beyond.

Dromyrk listened on dreamily, held in seclusion with the music and its memories. It took him several seconds to realise that he was not alone in the study. Abruptly drawn out of his soft reverie, and a little annoyed, he turned round sharply. It was Mrs Morton. He was familiar enough with her stance by the open door to see that she had come about someone outside. 'I haven't forgotten someone, have I? That was the last patient for today I saw, surely, Mrs Morton?'

'It's a new gentleman. He says he has to see you.'

'Didn't you tell him that he has to make an appointment?'

'He says it's urgent.'

'Indeed, I'm sure it is; as it invariably is in each individual case. But he still has to make an appointment. I'm sure you can manage to tell him that in your own precise manner, Mrs Morton.'

'I did, but he still insists on seeing you now. He seems to have been hurt --- just like Mr Guther. His throat is all bandaged up so that he can hardly speak.'

Damn! thought Dromyrk, in the bitter realisation of who it was waiting outside. Stalking, rather than waiting, was a more accurate word. 'Send him in,' said Dromyrk with a bluntness that totally surprised Mrs Morton. He swirled away from her, to turn the volume of the wireless up to a near-deafening blare. A defiant gesture against the unwanted visitor.

In the split second before Dromyrk's turning away, Mrs Morton could have sworn that she had seen what she had never ever before seen on the Doctor's face. On such occasions as these where the caller did not have an appointment, the Doctor always had a compassionate reserve of patience and understanding for the individual. But in this instance Mrs Morton had witnessed what could only be best described as cold grey hostility verging on violence.

The deep metallic gurgle of the four ton armoured car's 75hp Horch V8 engine  carried a menacing message not unlike a wild boar's roar approaching along the country road. Its 20mm cannon and 7.92mm MG34 machine-gun reinforced the message. The ominous sound caught the ears of Monique Berac and Rene Trepet, her Resistance contact walking beside her, putting them on nervous alert. Preceding the armoured car was a squat open-topped Kubelwagen staff car and in front of that, leading the patrol, was the BMW R75 military motor cycle and side-car with its own menacing MG34 machine-gun. As the patrol drew near and slowed down, the motorcycle swung round sharply across the road and stopped, blocking Monique's and Rene's way.

'Kettenhunde,' muttered Trepet quietly aside to Monique as they stood there waiting. Monique recognised the translation – chained dogs – as the nickname for the German military police, Feldgendarmerie. The nickname on account of the work that they did and also because of the metal gorget, a crescent shaped shield suspended on the upper chest by its chain round the neck. Monique ran her mind over her training to recall that this was an organisation that had received full infantry training and yet had extensive police powers. These military police units were employed with Wehrmacht divisions and higher divisions. Provided with various different detachments which are self-contained units under the command of a Wehrmacht division, they worked in close co-operation with Geheime Feldpolizei (Secret Field Police) and with district and town commanders. They served on every front in the war, and were often employed as regular troops in the front-line and involved in many desperate counter-methods and defences. One or more Feldgendarmerie battalion was attached to each Army battalion. Staff officers were responsible for maintaining order and discipline, for traffic control during large scale troop movements and maintaining traffic routes.

Truppen, or platoons, were attached to each Division or Corps, while Groups (Gruppe) were assigned to a field or local command, and separate units or sections assigned temporarily to specific duties for support. Monique's brain had been bombarded with details by her instructors so that she knew that a Truppe typically assigned to an Infantry or Panzer Division would comprise 3 officers, 41 NCOs, 20 men, 17 Kubelwagens and 4 trucks. Tasks, aside of basic traffic control, and maintaining order and discipline, would involve disarming, searching, collection and escort of POWs, as well as stragglers, supervision of civilian population in occupied areas, checking papers of soldiers on leave and in transit, carrying out street patrols in occupied areas, control of evacuees and refugees during retreats, border control and anti-partisan duties. Feldgendarmerie also had authority to pass through road blocks, check points, secured areas and were allowed to conduct body and property searches and obtain the assistance of any other military and civilian personnel. They had authority over every soldier up to their own rank whatever the service. In occupied areas their function was to carry out control duties at ports and airfields and administrative control of aliens. When superior Wehrmacht Divisions are advancing, they would follow combat troops closely and act and establish temporary town control and army stragglers posts; round up enemy stragglers and guerrillas and collect refugees and POWs. They would ensure civilian weapons were surrendered and organise civilian labour as well as erecting military and civilian signs. Responsible for overall troop discipline, the Feldgendarmerie rounded up deserters, controlled military traffic, and marshalled refugees and evacuated prisoners.

Monique was wary, and she had to admit, *nervous*, of the patrol in front of her. These were no ordinary soldiers. These were specially trained individuals whose inspection techniques went beyond that of the conscripted soldier. Trained at military school in Potsdam, their fields of instruction covered basic criminology, specific police powers, traffic codes, industrial codes, passport and identification duties, weapons drill and instruction and criminal police methodology. All this and more, they had drummed into her brain back at Lindwell. It was unsettling information to hold in mind.

The man in the sidecar, clad in shiny black leather coat, his face covered by great goggles and wind-blown grime around them, sat there stock-still but ready, beside his big machine-gun, tilted up at the sky for the moment. His companion got off the motorcycle. As he walked slowly towards Monique and Rene, the sun glinted on the silver chain and Ringkragen gorget with its eagle and swastika emblem. Every Feldgendarme was compelled to wear the Ringkragen on duty. Monique, with her recently sharpened observational powers, noted the emblem of police eagle and surrounding oak-leaf in orange thread, and swastika in black thread on the NCO's upper left arm. The size and shape of the holster at his hip suggested a Mauser C96 pistol to Monique.

'Ihre papiere, bitte,' said the NCO, holding out his hand.

Rene Trepet stepped forward first, holding out his papers, so as to give Monique a few seconds to collect her wits and understand what the military policeman was demanding. 'Hier sind meine papiere,' he said. The NCO took Trepet's proffered papers. Monique handed over her papers as well.

A man had got out of the Kubelwagen and walked towards them. An officer Monica noted by way of the fact that the left arm emblem had its eagle and oak-leaf in fine silver wire and its swastika in grey cloth background. That made him a Lieutnant. The holster on his belt was too snug to be carrying a Luger. It was more likely a Walther PPK. He held out his hand to the NCO at his side, all the while keeping his eyes on the pretty woman. The NCO passed the papers to his superior.

'Ihr name und Ihre addresse, bitte,' said the Lieutnant, still looking her straight in the eyes. He was testing her time and manner of response without any documents to help her.

'Monique Berac, dix-huit, Rue Vallane, Bonmaude.'

The Lieutnant held her beautiful face, with its beautiful blue eyes, in his long gaze, nodding slowly to himself all the while. Monique felt her inner tension rising when she saw the Lieutnant frown as he pulled her papers up closer, turning them round for scrutiny from a different angle. Not yet satisfied, he turned them round the other way for further sharp inspection. Monique could see that he was expert in his craft. She hoped to high heaven that the documents people back at Lindwell knew theirs better. He looked away, up at the sky, thinking of something for an eternal few seconds, then looked at her, then back at the documents. He stared for a long while at the ID documents before looking back up at their owners. She tried hard against her nervousness to give a warm seductive smile back to the officer. As the Lieutnant went on speaking in a broken mixture of French and German, Monique struggled to understand. She struggled more with the effort of refraining from the fatal gaffe of blurting out an apologetic 'sorry?' over words that escaped her. That was the number one cardinal sin her instructors at Lindwell had warned her not to make.

'Your home in Bonmaude is that way,' the Lieutnant said, pointing the way they had come. 'So you are travelling afar? You are travelling with Herr Trepet, who is married and not your spouse, as your escort, Fraulein?'

'Oui – Ja,' replied Monique.

'And you are coming back today?'

'Yes.'

'You would be well advised to return before curfew time.' The Lieutnant tapped the ID documents in his hand for a few thoughtful moments, meeting the nervous look growing in both their eyes with his own searching stare. At last he gave the papers back to the NCO to return to the two civilians, muttering a low remark to the man as he did so. Monique let out a quiet slow breath of relief. She fingered her headscarf, tied round her neck, with a coy disarming smile to meet the Lieutnant's long stare. He touched the peak of his cap in courtesy gesture.

Monique and Rene stood and watched as the two Germans went back to their vehicles. The motorcycle roared into life and the 'wild boar' growled once again as the patrol moved off. 'Heil Hitler,' said the Lieutnant, with outstretched arm as he passed.

'Merde a tout les Boches,' muttered Rene *sotto voce* behind a blank straight face.

# 19

Row upon row of young GI faces looked out from the GMC CCKW triple-axle 6x6 trucks, their helmet chin-straps swinging side to side, and mud-crusted wheels turning round and round as the military convoy made its way along the bleak south-eastern coastline of England. The dark green line of vehicles snaked its winding way through an otherwise motionless drab wintry landscape that seemed totally devoid of life, animal or plant. The empty, 'vacuum' effect, was on account of Allied Forces Operation Fireball. This required the systematically careful evacuation of civilian population from the area, without raising suspicion, for the sake of security.

'Fuck,' swore Captain Falzoni as he was hit in the teeth by Shenny Hitchpole's swinging chin-strap buckle as the 2.5 ton truck's massive wheel, with its 7.5x20 military tread tyre, bumped over a deep pothole. They were seated at the back of the truck, facing each other, leaning forward, elbows on knees, heads almost touching, in a serious tete-a-tete discussion over Hitchpole's marriage problem. Too late to catch Hitchpole at camp, Falzoni had joined the convoy halfway on its way down to get him. Falzoni was giving him a detailed outlay of the legal pros and cons that governed the situation's outcome and how he was dealing with it to his best professional judgement.

'Hell, skipper, I hope you didn't put that word in the letter. Those God-fearin' prayin' folks don't go in much for that kind of blasphemous talk none,' said Hitchplole with a wide grin. For all that his uniform said, metal helmet, carbine and all, Shenny Hitchpole's narrow, long-boned face, and the slow drawn-out southern accent couldn't hide the fact that he looked better suited to faded denim dungarees and pitchfork. At least that was how Falzoni saw him in his mind – just like Bretzler had said.

Falzoni slapped the long-legged farm boy's knee. 'You shame me, Shenny, old buddy. Would I screw my goddam piece of paper from Harvard that declares me Attorney at law, with a botch-up like that when every goddam word I write is costing a hundred bucks in fees? Not that you're paying even a lousy nickel for anything, anyway.' This remark embarrassed Hitchpole, so that he straightened up from his leaning position to sit back upright.

Falzoni saw this and slapped the other's knee again. 'Relax, buddy. I've crossed every t and dotted every I correctly; you're appeal is going to slide through swell. Everything is going to be fine --- short of you and the intended new Mrs Hitchpole skedaddling off to Vegas for a two-dollar chit that says the Hitchpoles are now 'hitched', and you go live in another state across the country as far away as possible from Alabama.' He caught the alarmed twitch in Hitchpole's face. So he slapped Hitchpole's knee again. 'Joking, buddy; just joking. It'll be O.K. Take my word for it.' This brought out a brighter expression on Hitchpole's face. Seeing this, Falzoni in turn blew out his cigarette smoke in relief of having done his duty, privately as well as 'officially'. Privately he had sent off Hitchpole's marriage annulment appeal to the States; 'officially' he had sent a letter to the intended new spouse informing her of this latest development. Included in this innocent personal news was Falzoni's deliberately 'accidental' mention of Hitchpole's unit being part of the 12th Army Group's general south-bound manoeuvre to the coast. He reinforced this message by reassuring the woman that she needn't worry about Hitchpole's fear of water, since it was only a short stretch of water from the English coast to the Pas-de-Calais. This innocuously 'careless' slipping out of information, normally seen as a breach of security, was Falzoni's covert ploy of leaking out misleading propaganda to catch the ears and eyes of Nazi agents in the States. Whether it was picked up in neighbourly gossip, or by anxiously sought snippets of news of loved ones overseas, in the town's gazette, every little trick, however small, counted in this war. It wasn't just Jerry's propaganda wizard, Goebbels, who could fool the masses with torrents of lies; we were hard-batting back our own brand of specially doctored double-talk to win the day – and next the war.

They talked on a while, Falzoni lighting and smoking his way through another cigarette and more reassurances to Hitchpole, before the conversation was interrupted by one of the soldiers remarking on top brass being up ahead. They all looked out. Sure enough, distinctly marked out as staff cars by their bright coloured pennants flapping in the breeze and drizzling rain, the two vehicles stood just off the road some distance up ahead. Standing by the cars was a small group of figures in Army issue trench coats and rubber ponchos watching the convoy pass by. Falzoni hurriedly stood up, telling someone at the front to signal the driver to stop. A young G.I. banged on the back of the driver's cabin. 'This is where I've got to leave you guys to get on with your lot and prove that all your boot camp combat training wasn't a waste of the drill sergeant's time. Go get 'em, guys,' said Falzoni, putting a leg over the tailboard. 'But cheer up. The weather's bound to be better across the water, where you're going.' He looked out at the rain. 'Better than this lousy English piss,' he muttered, regretting not having brought his own rainproof piece along with him.

Hydraulic brakes screeched and the truck jarred to a halt. Falzoni jumped down, stepping aside quickly to avoid being hit by the following truck before it had time to brake. The heads of the roadside observers swivelled round in unison to see what had caused the trucks' sudden stop.

Walking up to the group, Falzoni beamed a cheeky smile at Lt Col Bretzler, who was standing, as advisor, beside the General. Falzoni saluted the General.

General George S Patton, newly appointed Commander of FUSAG (FIRST US ARMY GROUP), returned the salute. A brazen scheme thought up and put together on paper by Allied intelligence services, FUSAG was a fake army consisting of 6 Airborne Divisions, 23 Infantry Divisions and 1 Armoured Division. To give semblance of a *real* army, a small contingent of soldiers were assigned 'FUSAG duties'.

'Well, Frank, what do you think? Would you say that he merited a pass?' said Bretzler, looking at Falzoni and then at the General.

Falzoni looked the General up and down in exaggerated open inspection. 'Hmm, I dunno, Bret,' replied Falzoni, in playfully feigned uncertainty. He looked the General straight in the eye. 'So what do *you* say, Bob? If we do stick a cute little star on your performance sheet for today's sham, do you think you can keep it up? It was only our own guys you hoodwinked today, but from now on you've got to fool Jerry's sharp eyes. If you don't, it'll be us who'll be goddam hoodwinked.'

The General was not offended by this casually offhand manner of address from a lower-ranking officer. This was because he was *not* George S Patton. He was, in fact, Robert Darnley, former Albuquerque insurance salesman, come small parts thespian, come administration pen-pusher in the Army's Catering Corps. Promoted from lowly private to three-star general in one giant leap. His facial resemblance to 'Old Blood and Guts', and his acting ability to take on the role of another character had earned him the important duty of decoy stand-in for the General.

'I think he's got your drift, with all its seriousness, Frank,' said Bretzler.

'I'm putting my all and everything into it, believe me,' said the 'General'.

'Yeah, well, just so long as you remember that this is going to be a lot more tricky than walking the boards on Broadway,' said Falzoni. 'Pull this one off right, pal, and the Old Man is going to be  commanding the whole goddam Division come see your brilliant debut performance on Opening Night. I'm holding you to that, buddy,' said Falzoni, now looking over at the cars, with a mind to getting out of the rain. 'Any room in there for an extra butt?'

'He has to wait until I get in first, doesn't he?' said the 'General', looking round at his adjutant, a young blond lieutenant whose aftershave competed with the wet rubber smell of his poncho.

'Correct,' said the adjutant, in succinct confirmation of protocol. 'You're always first to get in and then we follow you. But we'll wait until the convoy has passed, and then we can be on our way.' The lieutenant looked with affected concern at his watch. 'You still have to put in an appearance at the fuelling installation and then the supplies depot after that.'

'It's all right, I'll be mother,' said Malcolm Tewkes, taking the teapot out of the woman's hands. This was his polite way of shooing her out of the room so that he could continue with his talk on classified material meant for select ears only. Tewkes was from the Psychological Warfare Department of SHAEF (Supreme Headquarters Allied Expeditionary Forces). He stood there, in herring bone tweed jacket and suede elbow patches, watching her go out and close the door securely behind her, before turning back to the tea-trolley to pour out the tea. The front locks of his thick thatch of snow-white hair fell down over his brow as he stooped over the cups. Long accustomed to lecturing his Cambridge students with his back to them while chalking up mind-bending axioms in Socratic philosophical logic across the backboard, he poured into the cups while speaking to those behind him. 'As I was saying, if we're going to put a halt to Hitler's advance across Western Europe, we have to secure a foothold, so to speak, in Northern France; and the likeliest place for this would be Normandy, using amphibious craft.' Tewkes swung round to hand a cup to Doctor Dromyrk. 'Would you agree, Doctor?' He handed out tea to the others.

'We can't break Hitler's grip on Europe without getting our own forces into Northern France, by way of Normandy,' said Dromyrk. 'I would say that Hitler thinks that if we dared to mount an attack across the water, it would be at the narrowest stretch; that is, from Dover to Pas-de-Calais. Judging from his concentration of heavy armament in that southern region, it seems fairly probable that any plans he has of sending out his own invading forces would be across that specific stretch of water. For Hitler to imagine that our attacking a different part of the French coast is a better strategy would be for him to concede that his infallible judgement is flawed.'

'In other words, that's not on — he wouldn't accept that — is that what you're saying?' Colonel Rutkin's words carried the usual faint note of doubt that he held on Dromyrk's own 'infallible' judgement over military issues, never mind that of Hitler's.

'More or less,' replied Dromyrk.

'We need to press on Jerry the solid idea that we are going to invade at Pas-de-Calais,' said Tewkes. 'With all the heavy armour he has concentrated in that region, it makes a most formidable force that would cost us heavy casualties. Indeed, we couldn't really be sure of securing victory. We must make sure that he is not tempted to move north; what force he does have to the north, we must try to spread as thin as possible along the coastal area in order to make our landing a successful operation. So we confuse Jerry with what will seem like a two-pronged attack --- in the north, Norway --- and Pas-de-Calais in the south. Both fake, of course. Poised in preparation for attack – one in Scotland – the other in southeast England.'

'All these false manoeuvres will require a credible front to them in order to fool the Germans,' said Dromyrk.

'I quite agree, Tewkes replied. 'We're hoping our bluff attack to the north is made to seem real by way of our letting false radio messages be picked up, as well as briefing our double agents with enough false information to pull the wool over Jerry's eyes. Their Abwehr can go on thinking that their spies have successfully infiltrated Allied intelligence networks in Europe. In fact, we've managed to nab most of the ruddy blighters and turned them round to work for us as double agents.' Tewkes held his hands clasped together to his mouth while pacing to and fro for a few seconds paused in thought. He let out a short sigh of releasing his thoughts. 'Although things are a little more awkward in the south – that is, with our fake manoeuvres south of here, in the coastal sector. Yes, I know I just said that we've rounded up most of their agents; well we have – but not all of them. Our activities in this area are thus still dangerously open to prickly German eyes and ears. Leaking out false radio messages alone is not going to fool them for ever. The situation must be made to really appear to be a substantial army assembling in battle readiness in the south –- across East Anglia – and of course, at Dover.'

'In short, the phantom force must be brought out into the open by the marching boots of a few soldiers to represent that whole army,' said Rutkin.

'Do we have the men to spare for such '*phantom*' tactics, thinly stretched across the battlefronts as you tell me they are?' Dromyrk asked. 'Or do we have the Americans to thank once again for providing the necessary human resources?'

'We are all agreed, ourselves and our American allies, that General Eisenhower has done the right thing by assigning Patton full command of the fake army, FUSAG,' said Rutkin. 'In spite of his disgraceful conduct of striking low-ranking soldiers, it remains that Patton is most highly respected as a general by Hitler and his High Command. By putting him in charge, to lead the Third Army's invasion of France, we put him in the spotlight, and so hopefully get Hitler to believe that we intend to engage head-on with his Panzers at Pas-de-Calais.'

Tewkes gave a smile of acknowledgement to Captain Jalwanowski. 'And of course, no less thanks to our Polish allies for their setting up a false chain of liaison between Free Polish forces and FUSAG HQ. This would leak out fake vital operational details on FUSAG's manpower, manoeuvre schedules and battle readiness.' Tewkes let out a short laugh, followed by an equally short cough to make up for his 'unduly' interrupting what he was saying next. 'And we haven't forgotten to take up the clever suggestion of bringing in civilian help for relaying false military information to deceive Jerry.' For personal indication he glanced across at Dromyrk.

'Yes, I mean by way of relatively innocent small snippets of ordinary news,' said Dromyrk.

'*Ordinary* news?' said Rutkin, openly puzzled. 'I don't quite follow you; how can any of this strictly classified material be *ordinary?*' Rutkin plainly had difficulty in putting one hundred per cent reliance on Dromyrk's advisory comments for military planning, derived as they were from a purely psychological root. Given the good Doctor's total lack of 'field experience', Rutkin couldn't help feeling an inner twinge of uneasiness at the thought of risking soldiers' lives on the basis of 'mind games' alone.

'I'm referring to nothing more complex than person-to-person neighbourly gossip in areas in the proximity of our supposed FUSAG' camps,' said Dromyrk. He paused for a moment's thought. 'Yes, and letters, too; yes, of course, letters to the local council --- letters in the local papers mentioning weddings and deaths, false and real, as well complaining about the disgusting unruly behaviour of American troops stationed in the area. Disturbing the peace of our good neighbourhood with their pub brawls, street fighting and even outrageously urinating into our gardens. After all -- "Over paid, over fed and over here." -- isn't that what they're saying?'

Sensing a rising difference of opinion between Dromyrk and the Colonel, Tewkes stepped in to stop it rising further. 'I think we are agreed on that being a plausible ruse. There is also ---'

'But surely this will not be enough to fool German aerial surveillance,' cut in Captain Jalwanowski. 'Whilst our giving out false information is for the purpose of getting them to *believe* in our fake manoeuvres, reconnaissance flights will let them *see* what the real situation is. Our figures say that FUSAG will be --- *is* --- the largest military force operating in the European theatre. So it has to give that impression, when seen from above.' Jalwanowski looked round at the others, anxious for a satisfactory answer.

Tewkes glanced at Rutkin, feeling faintly guilty at the knowledge he shared with him, but so far not with Dromyrk and the Polish officer.

With raised chin for indication, he looked over openly at Rutkin to take over.

'Ah, yes – well, we do have that matter in hand; we are dealing with it, be most assured, Captain,' said Rutkin.

'How, exactly?' said Jalwanowski.

'Yes, how?' said Dromyrk, also feeling a little left out.

'We have a significant number of our soldiers, along with American units, carrying out duties to represent the fake army, said Rutkin. 'We also have fake bases positioned along the south east area.

Fakes vehicles, tanks, trucks, jeeps made from plywood, cloth, inflatable rubber; as well as fuel dumps, ammunition storage, hospital tents, mess tents, toilets. The vehicles are carried by soldiers to different positions at night, and tyre marks are made on the ground with rake-style tools to  make it all look convincing to Luftwaffe  reconnaissance'

'We even have a false navy playing its part,' added Tewkes, wanting to regain his place.  'Whole fake harbour scenarios realistically being set up, thanks to the resourceful effort of our film studio props people. Massive jetties and oil docks floated on oil drums, with fuel storage installations and pipe-lines; whole complexes stretching -- from what I gather – for miles upon miles.'

In fact, southern England was a humming beehive of deception tactics, especially in the Kent and eastern Sussex areas; offshore waters bristled with dummy troop carriers, landing craft and even a small number of real battleships, whilst smaller vessels crowded inlets and creeks between the Thames estuary and Great Yarmouth. To create a convincing message of the massive building-up of naval and railroad traffic, the coastal area was dotted at night with fake lighting fixtures. All this to be picked out and, hopefully, fool sharp-eyed Luftwaffe pilots.

Rutkin tried to measure Dromyrk's thoughts from the expression on his face. As usual it revealed very little, if anything at all. 'Convincing enough?' he asked Dromyrk.

Dromyrk's response was a pensive slow nodding affirmative. 'Yes,' he said at last.

Well thank heavens for his letting that little lot out, Rutkin thought. Small miracles do happen.

While Tewkes continued with his lecture, Dromyrk's mind was preoccupied elsewhere. Dromyrk looked at his watch and suddenly stood up. 'You'll have to excuse me, gentlemen, but I have to be elsewhere.'

'Pigeon?' said Rutkin, using the codename for Harry Carswell, alias Obersturmfuhrer Krunz.

'No, I'm meeting him this afternoon. Time and place still to be arranged. At the moment, I'm having to see a patient.'

'Do you think he'll swallow all this information we're giving him --- our dummy version of it, that is?' said Rutkin. In his mind he wasn't quite sure which of the two he was less happy with – Dromyrk or the German spy. 'Can we rely on him not guessing our little game?'

'Since we've already had him relaying false information to his Abwehr masters, it would be tantamount to his signing his own death warrant for him to now tell them that this, and previous information, was false. Regardless of what good he has done so far, in their eyes, one mistake would suffice for an order to have him executed. If he should tumble to our ploy of using him, we threaten him with the choice of death from his German masters, or working for us as a double agent.'

'Right,' said Rutkin slowly. It was his turn to give a long pensive nod, unsure as he was of what he had just heard. As Dromyrk made to leave, Rutkin touched his arm to delay him. He looked up, with earnest request, as well as query, in his expression, at Dromyrk. 'Don't forget to let me or Colonel Bretzler know that time and place.'

'Of course.'

Rutkin was so far away in his thoughts, watching Dromyrk leave the room, that he did not hear Tewkes asking him if he wanted a biscuit with his tea.

20

Selena Leighton-Lagrishe paused for a moment to look at Hitler standing there without any trousers, his underpants spotted with miniature red swastikas. Pinned to the inside of her wardrobe door, it was a small card version of the larger poster she had got from one of the girls working in a War Office propaganda unit. Depicting an embarrassed Hitler, caught off-guard in his compromising position, it carried the cheering message of catching him with his 'panzers' down. The brightest thing in her wardrobe, it did nothing to lift her low-spirited mood. In dejected resignation she looked along the row of clothes hanging there. They were all so dull. All so very, very dull, she thought in her dull mind. She found it somehow strange how she had enjoyed their colours and designs before, but now they seemed so ghastly drab. Perhaps it was on account of her being clad in military uniform most of the time. It was also dull; but then it was an expression of change – of her getting on with doing something worthwhile – of her getting away from here – of her loosening the filial tie with Mummy and Daddy. She thought of breaking that bond compared with being drawn in closer to Brent. Her dwelling on this conflict of loyalties was eased by the distraction of noise from downstairs in the kitchen. Mummy, in one of her agitated outbursts that demonstrated her inner surlirness.

Selena sighed and turned slowly to look around her room. Everything was changing. Attitudes were going through a general shift, collectively as well as personal. Not just because of this horrible war, but also because of ---. She put a hand to her stomach, reasoning that it was her antenatal hormones that were having a beastly good time playing her up. But this logical rationale didn't lessen her morose mood any. Still feeling her stomach, she looked at her dresses, wondering how long it would be before none of them at all would fit her. Funnily, it gave her the odd feeling that she would be betraying them, after all their years of loyalty to her tastes. With a slight mental jolt, she wondered in turn how long it would be before Colonel Rutkin came to appreciate her 'delicate' situation. She hadn't told him yet. That would present problems of a different kind.

This morbid turnover in her mind made her pensive of her own looks. Was her condition making her increasingly unattractive, dull as she already was? Ugly, even? Looking in the wardrobe's inner mirror, she didn't like what she saw. Giving a faint sigh of resignation, she thought of how lucky other women were. Those glamorous Hollywood dames, Betty Grable and Rita Hayworth, with their 'Victory-Roll' hairstyles that were taking women by storm. Letting her hair down, she took two handfuls atop her head, trying to form twin crest-waves parting at the front, in the manner of that currently raging fashion. What a pathetic mess that was, looking back at her in the mirror. The blonde mass dropped back down in defeat. This moping wasn't doing her any good. Closing the wardrobe doors firmly, she turned and walked over to the window.

Peering down out of the window overlooking the back-garden, she managed a weak smile at Daddy happily preoccupied in his 'war effort' contribution of watering the vegetables growing on top of the corrugated-iron Anderson air-raid shelter. Churchill, himself, had rejected the Basal Diet that had been recommended by the Scientific Food Committee as a wartime diet for the public as being somewhat demoralising in its meagreness. So growing fresh food in your own garden soil was the next best thing. Her hand having absentmindedly wandered back to her tummy, Selena was once again drawn to more solemn issues. But with these problems looming up in the not too distant future, she decided to confront a more immediate one; that which was causing the unnecessary clatter of plates and pots in the kitchen downstairs. Her distraught mother's usual way of displaying bitterness. Selena stomped noisily down the stairs with a mounting resolve of anger to match that of her mother's tantrum.

Standing side by side, neither one acknowledging the other, the two women worked in heavy brooding silence over the long stone sink-top. Inner strife escalated with passing seconds. Selina jolted slightly as her mother, suddenly dropping the colander into the sink, turned to her. A priggish frown creased the mother's brow. It was meant to cast stern maternal disapproval on the wayward daughter. But Selena saw it as silly. 'What exactly was it that you said he does?' said the mother. She knew perfectly well what it was that Selena had said the American *Lieutenant* Colonel's occupation had been before he had enlisted in the US Army. But she liked to feign ignorance as an excuse to drag out what she considered to be sordid details much to her distaste.

Well familiar with her mother's tactics by now, Selena made no effort to hide or soften things in any way. Being boldly frank was the way to push the matter back in her mother's face. 'He was a jolly US Federal Marshal.'

'Would that be some sort of American policeman.' Still the pretentious ignorance.

'Yes, that's what I said --- a jolly good policeman,' replied Selena, hoping that her 'jolliness' was rattling her mother's righteousness.

'But how dreadful. How can you possibly allow yourself to become involved --- and get yourself into such a --- a --- with a policeman who's not even English!' She couldn't bring herself to mention her daughter's state of pregnancy resulting from copulation outside of holy wedlock. 'After all your dear father and I have taught you, and brought you up to be!' Upset as she was, she couldn't allow her eyes to stray anywhere near Selena's midriff.

Selena was greatly stung inside by her mother's pouring this insolence on her intimate act of love with the man she loved – and who loved her. She experienced a strange unwelcome emotion at  a moment's thought of questioning Brent's love for her. Why on earth was she thinking that? Was he cooling off in his feelings for her, of late? She was suddenly uneasy. Was she imagining this? Had she seen this in his behaviour when she'd told him that she was pregnant, or was it truly her hormones playing havoc with her emotions. Or her mother's callous words getting to her? More likely a combination of both.

'Am I to understand that he intends to continue in this occupation after military service, when the war is ended?

'I would imagine that to be a matter of his decision alone,' replied Selina with a darkening  irritation in her mind that surprised her. She was suddenly drained of her inner vigour. She was feeling very tired.

Her mother was unrelenting. 'But can you really believe that he will be taking you back with him to America when this is all ended? That's always assuming that he survives the war.'

'Mother! How could you!' The very thought of Brent being mortally taken from her pierced her chest. She was feeling more than hurt. She felt so fatigued, in mind and body, that she could lie down and sleep forever. 'I'm going upstairs to lie down and get some rest, Mother. I'm expected to report in for eight hundred hours tomorrow. Goodnight, Mother.'

But her mother held back her words tighter than a clam. Selena left the kitchen to its heavy silence cut by the solemn ticking of the pendulum wall clock.

Dr Dromyrk's hurried trip to Belsize Hospital to see his patient unfortunately turned out to be a wasted effort. Greeted on arrival by an expectedly sour-faced Sister Nolan, the report  he got from her was more sombre. Margaret Pomfrey had suffered a severe relapse, causing her to attempt harming herself, and had been put under heavy sedation. Dromyrk reckoned that with the patient's mind clogged with drugs, slowing it down, she would be virtually unable to be aware of, let alone comprehend, any questions he put across to her in a therapy session.

Seeing her in that condition was out of the question. Perhaps that was just as well, thought Dromyrk, with a faint twinge of guilt in rating less importance for his patient's welfare than he did for his next appointment. He thanked Sister Nolan and left.

'*Here*, you are saying, along *this* section of the waters?' said Krunz, flattening out the map with one hand whilst pointing to the said area on it with his other hand. The light was so poor in the squashed quarters of the back-room salon of the shabby little Pekham pub, that Krunz shifted to one side to let Dromyrk have a confirming look at the map.

Dromyrk leaned in to see. 'Yes, along here in the Channel. We have smokescreens covering the area, as well as ships checking the waters for mines. This in double purpose to prevent us being attacked before we are ready to launch our own attack from this point.'

'And what precisely do these two points represent, Herr Doktor?' said Krunz, rubbing the marked points with his forefinger.

'Ah, yes, those are oil patches, laid there by ingenious Admiralty planning. And if I remember correctly --- supplied through a host of pipes running down from the Dover cliff-head. Set ablaze by naval flares to stave off attack by German ships.'

'To be put out again, of course, when British ships are ready to mount their attack on the French coast *here* --- Pas-de-Calais.' Krunz drummed his two fingers on the map-points. 'Is that correct?

'Of course; it wouldn't make sense otherwise.' Dromyrk, in a touch of nervousness, wondered if he had put the last part of his remark across too hastily, making it sound as if it was for the wrong reason --- as if it was to convince the German of its credibility, rather than its tactical feasibility. Accustomed as he was to playing mind games, this new spy game, with all its dangers, was alien territory, putting him on edge.

Krunz looked up from the map, to bluntly stare Dromyrk in the face. Nodding his head up and down slowly for a few thoughtful moments, wondering what he could possibly see beyond what was not showing on that face. He looked back down at the map. Sweeping a hand randomly across the map as he tried settling his judgement on what was troubling him, he nodded again slowly. 'Most ingenious, as you say, Herr Doktor. Most ingenious, indeed.'

The salon door suddenly flew open with the grubby-faced barman walking in, causing both Krunz and Dromyrk at the same time to snatch at the map and fold it between covering newspaper pages.

'Can I get you gents anything else?'

Dromyrk was anxious to close the 'touchy' meeting with Krunz and get away, so he shook his head in decline at the barman's offer. But the German surprised him by ordering another glass of spirits and looking at him with a prompting: '*Another?*'

'Yes, all right; thank you,' replied Dromyrk, affecting a grateful gruffness in his acceptance.

The door closed behind the barman, who hurried away with his order for two more black market Glenfiddoch malts. Something that Krunz couldn't get his hands on too easily in his Fuhrer's glorious Fatherland. Dromyrk and Obersturmfuhrer Krunz sat back, away from the classified documents on the table between them, looking at each other, wondering what was going through the other's mind.

# 21

Mostly shrouded by cloud as it was, the moon gave off enough light to catch the gleaming steel of the railway line receding in a graceful curve into the distance beyond the trees. It was also enough light to catch the polished radiator grill of the Citroen car that was nosing cautiously out of the bushes in response to a moment's blink of torchlight from out of the darkness. The car returned the signal with a sharp flash of its headlights.

Suddenly it was not just the trees that stirred softly in the breeze. Materialising out of nowhere, a host of figures ghosted up out of the night to form a double line alongside the steel track. Monique Berac reckoned their number to be about over a dozen, as far as she could see, as she got out of the passenger seat of the two-door cabriolet. Three of them that approached her preferred to keep a tight grip on their Sten guns, rather than offering smiling handshakes for greeting. One of them, what appeared to be the leader to Monique, wore a beret, which was 'French' enough to not arouse suspicion and subsequent arrest by gendarmes operating on pro-Nazi terms in accordance with the Vichy Treaty in this region; but with the corduroy waistcoat and scarlet neckerchief, it struck Monique as dangerously conspicuous as Basque, hence, 'Maquis ' style.  In her briefing by Intelligence, before flying out, she had been made to understand that a fair number of these Spanish fighters were lending their strength to the Resistance movement. Originally engaged in fighting against General Franco's Fascist army in bitter civil war, half a million Spanish Republicans, upon losing their struggle, had fled to France to evade imprisonment. But their effort to escape prison was not completely successful. Marshall Petain, in compliance with Nazi policy, had repatriated most of them, whilst retaining the remaining contingent of 120,000 to 150,000 as political prisoners for slave labour for Compagnies de Travailleurs Estrangers (Companies of Foreign Workers). Roughly 60,000 or so of these had made their escape, so joining the Resistance movement.

Monique looked at the figures closing in around her – enigmatic dark shapes that revealed nothing but for the moonlight giving glints of steel in their hands. Weapons and sabotage equipment were supplied by the SOE in great air-droppings that the poor pigeon couldn't manage -- sub-machine guns, grenades, ugly but efficient Welrod silencer pistols, plastic explosives and their pencil detonators. As if this was never enough, Jerry's Mauser 98 rifles and MP 40 sub-machine guns could also be useful whenever they could be seized. Where need and opportunity presented itself, agents also would float down out of the overhead darkness.

The babble of unfamiliar foreign accents, especially in their rough provincial dialects, hit Monique with a blast as the Spaniard and one of his comrades, French it seemed, suddenly blurted out their words at the same time. A torrent of words in two different tongues together thrown at her and she couldn't understand either of them. So unexpected, it caught her off balance. She felt so embarrassed -- so naïve and stupid. This wasn't how it had been at Lindwell, where her lingual instructor had put everything across to her with properly accentuated vowels and consonants, giving little thought for uncouth rustic vernacular that varied with the locality. It made her feel shamefully out of step with those around her, so experienced as they obviously were in this very real dangerous game. It made her feel even more 'not with it' when she had expected everyone to speak in low clandestine whispers. Instead, they gave a clamouring of voices so loud that she could virtually see hordes of gun-wielding gendarmes rushing out of the undergrowth to arrest them. But the foliage around them stirred only with the breeze.

She pulled herself together at the sound of the car's driver-side door opening and clicking shut again. Rene Trepet came over to stand beside her. Picking her up outside his office, he'd put his foot down, making the 6-cylinder engine's carburettor gurgle out its 'juice' to hold them at 84mph top speed along the empty country roads, only slowing down whenever a vehicle that looked suspiciously 'official' came towards them. They'd had to stop twice at security check-points. That he was a respectable notary-public seemed to carry some weight with the check-point guards since the car and its occupants were passed through both roadblock inspections with relatively little fuss. She suspected that he had brought her along not just because she had to show saboteurs how to use the new bomb-detonators developed by SOE back-room boffins, but because he thought he was going to 'enjoy' seeing how she reacted at being thrown in at the deep end in this operation with all its perils.

'It's all right, give them time. They'll let you in when they get used to you. It's their way of sounding you out by being awkward.' Rene said this aside in a low voice to Monique whilst listening to the others' words, mostly enquiring, if not complaining, directed at this new woman. He measured uncertainty, if not total mistrust, in the faces of these hardened men who knew death through informers' betrayals. He saw this especially in the eyes of the Spaniard – codename Anjon, and leader of the cell. This was all Monique was allowed to know of him – nothing beyond that for the sake of security.

'Don't worry,' replied Monique, 'when Grandma Mela's goats were being awkward and not giving her milk, she promptly had them eating out of her hand, so to speak, so that the stubborn animals gave her what she wanted.'

Rene looked at the men clustered around them and then back at Monique. 'Let's be sure of one thing --- these men are rough-living, hard-hitting partisans --- not goats.'

'At least goats have an excuse for not trimming their beards,' joked Monique. But she seriously realised that this was something more than a personal chauvinistic bias against her joining the cell. Those political gurus back at Lindwell had warned her to possibly expect a lingering vein of anti-British sentiment in some quarters. This original resentment had arisen out of Churchill's harsh order to sink French naval vessels *and their French crews* at Mers el Kebir, rather than let them fall into German hands. With the liberated French general, De Gaulle, broadcasting from England, the message for his people to fight the Germans occupying northern France was rabidly taken up. But in 'unoccupied' southern France, where the wisdom of Petain was still respected, De Gaulle's call to arms had not been so readily heeded. Only when Marshall Petain's Vichy Government collaborated openly with the Nazi forces was there a falling away of resentment against the English --- perhaps more slowly in some remote instances.

Monique found her patience with Anjon dwindling. She had tuned her ears in sharp enough to the man's hoarse Catalan brogue to sense a  bickering attitude to everything she said. As she tried to continue describing the tricky details for applying the XL-2 detonator to the TNT, he scoffed the need for all that explosive as being totally unnecessary. 'So what do you propose we use in its place, senor?' she asked, not caring if her irritation was beginning to slip out. She looked round at Rene for the help she thought she was going to need if Anjon was going to hold things up by being obstinate.

Rene was liaison officer – 'messenger boy' – collecting and relaying important intelligence between the different cells and so knew next to nothing about the technicalities of field operations; what the hell did he know about handling ruddy TNT, or trinitrotoluene, as he believed she had called it? But he saw that he was needed to step in for the English agent if things were to run smooth. He repeated the woman's question to Anjon.

'We simply remove the connector plates on the outside rails,' said Anjon.

'Sorry, I'm not with you. How is that better than using explosives?'

'The Boche,' replied Anjon with deep guttural contempt, 'they are not stupid. They expect their trains to be attacked so they take precaution. They will have spare engine at the back as well as rails and materials to repair the damage to the track at the front. But if the outside connector plates are removed from the track on a mountainside stretch of the railway line, the whole train, repair materials and all, would be lost down the mountain. Paff! Like that.' He snapped his fingers and spat aside to prove his point.

'I have to admit there is merit in what he says,' said Monique, somewhat surprised at her own words. Her glance of agreement at the Spaniard brought out the man's grimly smiling row of broken teeth.

'Hmm, I suppose it does have its points,' said Trepet thoughtfully, his mind painfully caught between the two ideas. 'Unfortunately the nearest mountainside is over a mile back. Jerry's train will be here long before we could get to that point. It's too late. We stick to the original plan. So let's get on with it.' Trepet turned and walked off along the track, then stopped to scratch his forehead as a new thought struck him. 'There's something else. There's the town at the foot of that mountain slope.' Unlike the ruthless Spaniard, he was not of a mind to sacrifice – *kill* -- innocent people – *French* people -- just to get at the Germans. 'We'll consider using your idea some other time, maybe; but we do it this way for now. Come on, time's getting on.' He walked on.

Giving a resigned shrug, Anjon spat out a second time and beckoning his team to follow, started walking after the Frenchman. Monique stumbled over a sleeper beam, but regained her balance to hurry after those walking away fast in front of her. She barely had time to get into the car before Trepet was moving it off while she was still pulling her leg in and closing the door. His official position in town allowed him a privileged overlap of the curfew time, but that time was running out. Monique had come along solely as observer and explosives advisor on this, her first 'live' field mission. As radio operator, she had to get back and make her report. Radio operators, known in the field as 'pianists', had an average life expectancy of around six months since their transmissions were eventually picked up by German goniometer detection devices. Monique pondered ruefully over this frightful statistic – another 'gem' handed out by Lindwell experts – as they drove off. She couldn't deny that her feeling was one of relief at leaving before the fighting broke out. Perhaps she would feel braver next time. But would dying in a street-skirmish shoot-out be easier than being stood before a firing squad, after brutal torture by the Gestapo? She thought back on the harrowed state of those agents needing treatment by Doctor Dromyrk at Lidwell following their return from assignments. Monique smoothed the coat's creases on her lap to wipe this question from her mind.

Having planted the plastic explosives at their strategic points along the line, and connected the wires to the plunger-box terminals, Anjon and his team moved back, to hide as best they could among the shrubs and shadows alongside the track. They waited.

Nine minutes later than expected, they heard the rushing 62mph approach of the heavy SNCF 141.P Class steam locomotive. Two flat platform waggons with nothing on them were at the front. These were supposed to take the force of any contact mines on the track and so spare the rest of the train; these were followed by two armoured cars in their heavy steel plates. After this came waggons sprouting heads in steel helmets of troops looking out cautiously over the sides. Unoccupied as the southern region was purported to be, German 'personnel' still passed through it. Then came the waggon with rails and spare parts to repair any damage that may be done by any explosions occurring at the front. Finally at the rear, pushing all this, was the 144 ton engine. Since the explosives laid out on the track were connected by wires, to be detonated from afar, the two empty waggons at the front served no purpose.

Anjon nodded to the man lying beside him. The man pressed the plunger down with enough fiery passion to send the 144 ton mass of steel bucking up off the rails, and toppling over on its side, while waggon-pieces, as well as bodies, hurtled into the air in great blazing blasts of fury. Several seconds of screaming and wailing elapsed before angry German commands rang out --- to be drowned in turn by steady, concentrated, gunfire breaking out.

## 22

But for the large curve formed by the boiler suit pulled tight round the stooped figure's rear end, you wouldn't have guessed that it was a woman. She had no face – only a black plastic panel fronting her leather-hooded welding mask through which she peered closely at the fussily fusing metal plates. Like a great spluttering fountain of light, giant menacing sparks arched out in all directions, causing Colonel Rutkin to step back promptly as some came near to him, one just missing his face. 'Serves you right if you gets hurt, mister,' said a hard voice that belied the soft female form lurking beneath the welder's otherwise rough outer appearance. 'If you don't know where to step to keep out of the road, then it means you've no business being here. 'Ow did you get through the dock guard-room gate without a bloomin' pass, anyway, eh? You lookin' to get arrested then, mister?' The sparks suddenly cut out at the same time as the grim mask went up. Hardly any prettier than her grimy overalls, she at least had a friendly, if cheeky, smile.

Free now of the mask's protective visor, she saw the military uniform and understood. 'Right. So what do I call you, then – *General?*'

'*Colonel* will do.' Taking on what he considered to be an appropriately more friendly attitude to complement this dedicated worker, Rutkin looked down at what she had been doing, without an inkling of what it actually was. 'Fine work, I see.' He coughed to hide his ignorance. 'What exactly is it you're doing?'

Laughing at this question, she cast an outstretched arm round in one great sweep to take in the whole panoramic view of the naval dockyard, with all its tumultuous commotion, both on the quay and off the quay, involving great mountains of steel that comprised part of the country's fighting fleet moored to the mighty bollards lined along the quay's edge. Giant cranes and tiny specs that were men – and *women* – earnestly going about their tasks of making these great grey riveted monsters battle-worthy before sending them out to engage with, and hopefully, destroy the German Kriegsmarine's menacing sea-power of 'invincible' warships and deadly wolf-packs of U-boats whose underwater tactics were always difficult to predict and trace, in spite of our recent success of Bletchley Park cryptographers breaking some of the Enigma codes. '*Doing?* What does I *not* do's more like it. I does battleships, submarines, aircraft carriers – the whole bloomin' lot an' all. That's what I bloomin' does.' Searching in her pocket, to bring out a cigarette, she reached down for the blowtorch, to light the cigarette from the fierce hissing blue jet flame. She took a drag, then blew out the long train of smoke before continuing. 'Used to work in a wool factory before; easy work but boring compared to what I does now; this job's great.' Stopping to peel a tobacco flake from her lip, she went on. 'Cept now I can only see me boyfriend once a fortnight because of the long shifts – round the clock they are – twelve hours nightshift.' Another deep drag and blowing out of smoke. 'He works in a munitions factory; he's excused from the Army call-up because of his important job as Production Line Precision Inspection Manager. Mind you, I ain't sure if I likes the idea of him working there among five hundred women – all bloomin' cows, the lot of them, I bet.'

'Most commendable – most commendable,' said Rutkin in a typically dismissive tone that said he had wasted enough time on idle banter and his attention was elsewhere, in a hurry to get away and about his own important business. But he needed directions. He looked at all the milling activity of workers and sailors around him on the quay as well as steel beams and 'things' swinging around precariously on cables through the air. Rutkin wondered where best to ask for information; the sergeant in the guard-house hadn't been of much assistance. He didn't think that the welder would know either, but nevertheless on turning to her and about to ask her, he spotted the marine guard in white cap and white belt with holster coming along. The man also had a fierce-looking Alsatian guard-dog on a steel chain walking beside him. Rutkin wasn't sure how the dog would interpret his approaching its master directly and so hesitated.

The 'problem' was solved by a long shadow stretching out along the ground at Rutkin's feet. He turned round to see a tall Commodore Leighton-Lagrishe silhouetted against the afternoon sun. Just the person Rutkin was looking for. Even wrapped up as he was in Duffle-coat, scarf and gloves, the Commodore looked as if he could well do with several more layers of insolation against the cold, hugging himself and clapping his arms as he did. Clearly he preferred working indoors at the Admiralty to that of his experience, two years earlier, escorting our merchant ships on their ice-frozen Arctic convoy routes mainly to Murmansk and Archangel, with their precious cargoes of ammunition, tanks, fuel, planes and other much-needed material. These routes were particularly hazardous not solely on account of severe weather, but because of virtually guaranteed likelihood of German ships, planes and submarines patrolling the area. Constant Arctic daylight increased the danger from attack; alternatively, constant Arctic darkness could cause convoy vessels to lose cohesion and so wander perilously astray of their escort ships. The Commodore's Flowers-class corvette, *HMS Azalea,* having been sunk by a combination of U-boat torpedoes and a 'coup de grace' salvo from the massive twin triple-turreted 11"guns of the German cruiser, *Brunsmersch*, had  seen him sentenced to what should have been certain death in the sub-zero waters. Yet contrary to all logic, he had somehow miraculously survived the life-draining pull of the freezing black water. A mere eleven of the crew of ninety -- himself, Petty Officer Collins and nine ratings -- had been granted miracles that dark Arctic morning. This death-defying encounter had seemingly induced in him an acute aversion, if not phobia, of the cold. 'Ah, there you are, John,' said the Commodore. 'Don't you think you should be wearing your greatcoat or something on top of that in this wretched weather?'

'I'm all right,' replied Rutkin. Forever mindful of enemy 'ears' listening in, he took a sweeping look around himself. 'Is there anywhere better where we can talk?'

'Good thinking, John. Let's get in out of this damn cold before my ruddy whatsits freeze over and fall off.'

'Lead on,' said Rutkin, stepping carefully between piles of unfamiliar metal objects, to follow after the Commodore. He made a point of not bumping against a single column stack of three shining new depth charge cylinders. They looked different to him somehow.

Glancing back, the Commodore saw Rutkin pause with curiosity, and stopped to explain. 'Ah, yes, another little improved toy, courtesy of our American cousins. These clever beggars have special canted fins on them. This gives them a rotational motion as they go down, so causing them to stay close to the intended target.'

'I would have thought that our own depth charges do well enough on the job,' said Rutkin, feeling somewhat peeved by yet another American 'intrusion.'

'Ah, yes, well you see this is an important factor. We've since learned that those U-boat hulls can resist rupture from detonations occurring at a distance greater than about fifteen feet or so. The charges can be set for depths up to roughly six hundred feet. Estimated speed of descent through the water is about just over fourteen feet per second.'

'*Really?* You don't say,' said Rutkin. 'I stand corrected.'

'Yes, indeed,' replied Leighton-Lagrishe, chuffed with his little spiel of technicalities. He stepped forward to tap one of the cylinders with his knuckle. 'And its Torpex, not TNT; that's roughly fifty per cent more powerful than TNT.' He gave the cylinder another tap. 'All two hundred pounds of it.'

'Without doubt we have a lot to thank the United States Navy for in helping us fight our battles,' said Rutkin, in what sounded like a gruff tone to the Commodore. They walked on. The eyes of the marine guard and his canine companion followed the two men in silent scrutiny all the while. What looked like a string of sausages in the distance, zig-zagging its way between obstacles, was coming towards them. It was a trolley-train of 21 ft-long torpedoes, each with 750lbs of death-delivering TNT. Leighton-Lagrishe and Rutkin stopped, to let the deadly 'sausages' cross their path, on their way to being loaded onto the grey hulk speckled with rust spots that was just discernible as a tired A-Class submarine nestling low among the larger sister vessels dwarfing it at the far end of the quay.

They had no sooner stepped in through the door of the steel cabin that was the Quay Master's office, than Leighton-Lagrishe was making a beeline for the tubular cast iron stove. Taking a rod from the dirty wooden coal box, he prised open the stove's small door to look inside. Satisfied with the red glow he closed the door and returned the rod to its box. Turning around to face inwards, he remained standing in front of the stove with the warmth now on his back. He never thought of leaving some space to one side in the consideration that possibly Rutkin may have wanted to share some of the heat. 'So how did it go, then?' said Leighton-Lagrishe.

'As well as can be expected, I suppose.'

'You "*suppose*"? I gather then that all was not as it should have been?'

'We got the train, but we also sustained a greater number of casualties than we had reckoned for the operation. It seemed that Jerry was better prepared than we had thought. They had a back-up contingent of troops coming up fast along the line behind the first train. They engaged with our lot before they could finish with the first lot and get away.'

'So do you think Jerry was informed of the operation?'

'It's possible – but I don't think so?' replied Rutkin slowly, through a mind fuzzy with uncertainty.

'So what's the alternative, then?' said Leighton-Lagrishe.

'More likely a case of crying 'Wolf' too often. With the number of Resistance people over there having reached forty thousand or so, the rate of rail sabotage jobs carried out by them has been roughly over one hundred and thirty per month. That's no doubt getting Jerry's hackles up and causing him to mount appropriate countermeasure tactics.'

But the Commodore could see that something other than this was holding Rutkin's inner attention. 'How is Selena faring?' Now that the news of his niece's 'situation' was out, he could speak of it openly with Rutkin.

Rutkin gave a sharp glance at the Commodore, surprised at the apparent reading of his mind. He needed several seconds to gather his thoughts on that problem. '*Selena*? Hmmm --- ye-e-s,' he said in a slow pensive voice. 'You've hit it right on the nail with that question --- a *bent* nail at that. The plan to send her out as Miss Redfern's handler in the field is now out of the question ------ totally aborted.' An awkward cough. 'And that's not a pun. Her parents would never settle for that, heaven forbid. In the active field, her condition makes her an absolute liability. As if the medical aspects of it aren't enough --- with a child to worry about, she would never withstand the pressure of interrogation were she to fall into the hands of the SS. This according to Doctor Dromyrk's opinion.'

'And the replacement? Presumably you have a stand-in for such unforeseen contingencies?'

'The good Doctor, himself, could be the very answer to that. We've given serious consideration to the idea of him going out in Selena's place. He was, after all, responsible for building up Selena's psychological fitness for the task. So he does have an awareness of what's involved in that aspect of the game. Besides, his knowledge of our strategies is limited to what we feed out to him, and nothing beyond that. There's also the advantage of him being Swedish, therefore neutral – of his having worked in Germany, with a somewhat unique 'association' with Hitler – as well as having the Abwehr believe that he is currently working for them in collaboration with their agent, Carswell, alias Obersturmfuhrer Krunz.'

'And *is* he?'

Rutkin didn't answer the question, and the Commodore didn't ask it a second time. They both walked over to the large table that was normally used for inspecting large naval drawings and blueprints. The Commodore took a long folded sheet out from under his Dufflecoat and opened it out across the table, patting down the folds to flatten it. Leaning in over it, they sought out the exact co-ordinates and manoeuvre details for Operation Thor, along the coastline of Nazi-occupied Norway.

'He would seem at least to know what he's talking about, I grant you that,' said Leighton-Lagrishe while still peering closely at the map, its operational tactics just that 'short step' ahead of his nose as it moved to and fro across the paper.

'Who's that?' said Rutkin.

'Your psychiatrist chap, of course --- Doctor Dromyrk.'

'He wasn't my choice, let's be clear about that,' returned Rutkin, not bothering to hide the 'distance' that he still felt lingering between himself and the Swedish doctor. 'He was landed on me from 'above' --- PWD, to be exact --- and no questions asked – you know what I mean.' PWD (Psychological Warfare Department) had only just been formed that year and came under the responsibility of SHAEF (Supreme Headquarters Allied Expeditionary Forces) which was made up of American OWI (Office of War Information) operatives and British PWE (Political Warfare Executive) personnel. Rutkin seemed relieved at this open sharing with another of his uncertainty, if not distrust, of working close at hand with someone who was not of his military cloth or native to the land that he considered it was his duty to guard.

Leighton-Lagrishe sensed this, but made no comment to the contrary, be it because of his Anglo-Gallic lineage or otherwise. As far as he saw it, in this mad fiasco of a war, help from all flags but three was to be greatly appreciated. 'Are you seeing him to be a hindrance, rather than an asset, in our operations?'

'That remains to be seen.' A long pensive pause, followed by Rutkin's clamming up on further discussion on his personal prejudices; he'd said enough on that for the moment. He closed the matter with a blunt finalising: 'We'll see.'

'Like I was saying, all things considered, his prediction on enemy field movements in that area would appear to have been virtually spot on,' continued the Commodore. 'It would appear that he knows the workings of the German mind --- or one in *particular* – the one that matters. Hitler has taken in our false information like the dumb fish grabbing that hook. Our leaked plans have gone all the way to the top, through the High Command, with Hitler overruling the wiser judgement of his experienced generals in the field. He's gone and reversed original orders for his heavy Panzer Divisions in Pas-de-Calais to move north to Normandy; ordering them, instead, to stay put. In fact, the information we have coming in says that he's having all other forces head swiftly for that southern region. In all, with his messiah's intuition, he's coerced his generals into believing that we will, in fact, launch our attack at Pas-de-Calais.' Leighton-Lagrishe clapped his gloved hands together and rubbed them in open show of satisfaction. 'The seeds of our little ruse seem to be taking root and festering.'

Fake manoeuvres to fool Jerry were not confined to the land alone; extending beyond our shores, our RN vessels were making regular sweeps of the Channel for mines, whilst Mosquito bombers carried out lightning raids on and around Calais. This was a double ploy to persuade Jerry that just as we expected to be attacked across this stretch of water, so did we intend using the same convenient short distance for mounting our invasion of Europe. FUSAG had set up a special radio signals unit that had devised equipment capable of recording all messages traffic in advance, along with special equipment that made one transmitter's output simulate that of six transmitters; hence all the radio messages sent out by one divisional headquarters and its brigades could be sent out by one single wireless unit. That way Jerry would get the impression that FUSAG's forces were spread out over a great expanse, 'here, there and everywhere'.

'Things seem to be going according to plan.'

'Unless we're the ones being fed false information,' replied Rutkin in a negative tone that didn't exactly reflect the Commodore's optimism. Turning away from the table as he thought, he ambled  over to the stove. Putting a foot to the stove's door, which had opened slightly, he rammed it shut with a loud angry-sounding clank. If the Commodore was easily pleased, the Colonel wasn't.

Rutkin's pessimistic mood-dip didn't escape the Commodore's notice. 'Don't you ever accept anything without reading a double meaning into it, John?'

'If I did, they'd promptly have me relieved of my post.'

The Commodore gave a slow nod of resigned agreement to Rutkin's remark. 'I don't really see how I can fault that. You're quite right, of course.' He had his own cold recollection of what disaster felt like when things didn't go to in your favour. Chilling memories, black as those killing black waters. Giving a final scrutiny of the proposed operation plans, Leighton-Lagrishe folded the sheet up, and turning round to face Rutkin, held it up for him to see. 'Are you okay with this? I need to have our joint approval before I even think of handing it over to the Brigadier's SO2 Committee.' (SO2 was the Active Operations section of SOE.)

Rutkin didn't need a lot of thought to answer that one. 'If it's successful, we kill two birds with one stone --- we'll have put their heavy water production plant in Norway out of action, and at the same time reinforced Hitler's belief that we would never intend landing at Normandy'

'And if the Norwegian mission fails?'

'Like I've said, even a failed effort to sabotage the installation will in itself suffice to distract Hitler from our intention to attack him on his least expected, least guarded, flank,' replied Rutkin.

'Lives traded in exchange for deception. Sounds abominable however much we know it to be necessary.' The Commodore's morose words came out in a slow utterance that gave the false impression that it was a personal insight of shocking revelation. Which it wasn't. Not after four years of lives lost, it wasn't. 'The Committee, then? What do we say?' said the Commodore, waving the folded plans in the air, waiting for Rutkin's answer.

Rutkin figured, from what he had seen of late, that the Commodore had become a little too sentimental. Losing his ship and almost all his whole crew had done something to him. Induced in him some sort of survivor's-guilt. Dromyrk no doubt would know some long-winded expression for the situation. Perhaps it would help things if he put a quiet word Dromyrk's way for the Commodore's sake. But that could wait. Putting that issue aside, he nodded his affirmative to Leighton-Lagrishe. 'I'm satisfied with what I've seen of the strategic details. Go ahead and give the Committee our agreed green light on Operation Thor.' Rutkin turned and made for the door. He stopped, to look round at Leighton-Lagrishe. 'Do you have transport? My driver's waiting outside the gate with mine. Do you need a lift?'

'It's all right, John, I have to stay on here a little while longer to check on some developments. But thanks.'

Rutkin nodded and turned away again, opening the door. He paused yet again. 'My club, tonight,' he said over his shoulder, while holding the door wide open. Leighton-Lagrishe accepted the invitation promptly, not only because it was Rutkin's turn to pay for dinner, but more because the freezing wind blowing in through the doorway was cutting into him like a cold knife. Shivers ran through him.

# 23

Pulling aside the flapping tarpaulin to go inside, Lt-Colonel Bretzler found himself having to duck under and through a criss-cross spider-work of steel crossbars and stanchions forming the scaffolding that was holding up the great sheet. More responsibly, it also held in place the remaining inner half wall of what had been the basilica's east transept, with its side chapel, right-angled to the central nave. That whole side chapel had been reduced to rubble by nocturnal droppings far more destructive than that from pigeons --- namely Luftwaffe 4000lb Amatol bombs. Bretzler stood in the centre of the main aisle to look around for a moment at the church's dark interior. With the dark tarpaulin taking the place of stained glass windows, where the wall had been, the place was shrouded in greater darkness than usual. Bretzler felt a surprising long-forgotten reassurance from the hard wood of the pew end as he put a hand on it. How it was forever to be there, for you to lay a hand on. He genuflected and knelt down on the long knee-rest. An action that came automatically to him in spite of his not having done it for some time. Quite different from stepping over moaning, writhing, bodies to accept a cigarette from, and talking to, the chaplain in the field.

A fluttering sound overhead made him look up. No, it wasn't an angel come to collect him. Its wings beating the air feverishly, the little bird hovered to and fro, in desperate attempt to escape the curved stone entrapment of the ribbed vault roof. Trapped. Just like him.

That thought made his mind jump. Why on earth did he make that association? But he couldn't kid himself. He had to concede to the fact that he had been having some strange feelings concerning the wedding. Some people would have said straight away that it was a plain case of him getting the old 'cold feet' syndrome. But he didn't think it was that. True, he had been having strange emotional tremors of hesitance – even uncertainty – over the idea of tying the matrimonial knot with Selena. That admission embarrassed him for a second. He wasn't sure what was bothering him.

Shifting up off his knees, he sat back on the dark oaken bench to marshal his thoughts. His mind went to Frank Falzoni and his carefree ways – everything easy come, easy go. Like that great horde of G.I.s with their boisterous ways of what they thought was 'fraternising' with the English. A lot of those guys were marrying their dames. Bretzler rubbed his cheek slowly at this thought. Was this what was niggling him? That he was possibly getting married because of the baby, or more cheaply, because it was the trendy thing to do? Following the flow of the current floodtide?

Sure enough, hundreds, indeed, thousands of servicemen were 'hitching-up' with British women. Feeling run-down by austere living conditions imposed on them by war, the country's people were seeing this incoming wave of young Americans as virtually one would see and welcome that biblical 'manna from heaven', with no shame in holding out their hands for all they could get --- and that was before you counted the kids. Always having more money to spend than our boys in khaki and attired like generals, this affluent demeanour that typified the American G.I. caught many a woman's eye. Their great outpourings of cookies, gum, candy, nylons, cigarettes, comics and other eye-popping, hitherto unavailable, commodities was enough for many a young women to pledge her troth to that man of her dreams.

Bretzler wasn't forgetting that English women could all too often be seen as traitors by their own folk when they dated American servicemen. Nor was it a secret that Uncle Sam was not particularly enthusiastic about U.S. servicemen marrying and bringing their foreign brides home to live in the States. Many of his top generals saw family responsibility as constituting a distraction to their young soldiers, whose primary duty it was to fight, so imposing restrictions for its prevention on servicemen. Bretzler was acutely aware of this from all those diplomatic induction lectures, otherwise better known as 'Keeping in with the British by keeping out of trouble', given by the Unit's PR Officer, Major Hennely, and falling mostly on deaf ears. But inasmuch as it irked him to admit it, there was something solid to think about somewhere in all that lot. With this damn war raging on and on, that Old Grim Reaper was ticking the names off his list faster than that race track bookie flip-checked your dollars before handing over your winnings. He shrunk back from the idea of Selena being a widow, giving birth to a child that would never know its father.

Or was he just being stupid? Heck! He thumped a hand down on the pew in front to shake off his morbid mood. A small greying head, over by the pillar, turned round to see what the noise was. Bretzler tried to crack an apologetic smile at her, but the old lady turned away quickly in rebuff. His need to quell a rising frustration had him reaching into his pocket for a cigarette. On second thoughts, better not to. Not in here, under the Chief's roof. This had him looking over to, and noticing for the first time, the empty confessional, its dark red entrance curtain drawn back, in open invitation. That was another thing he would have to see to soon before the big day. Not just for Him Upstairs. For Selena's sake as well. She was anxious to do everything by the book from here onwards, after their having torn several pages out of it by way of their naughty pre-emptive night of passion. Her old man didn't seem to be too bothered by it all; but that dragon-mouthed woman who was to become his mother-in-law was well in league with those flamethrower guys on the front line.

He saw them just a moment just before their voices reached him, loudened with the opening of the vestry door. Selena and the priest in his flapping black cassock. It wasn't the Fr O'Malley that Selena had introduced him to at her house. This one was smaller, with balding head and round bespectacled face befitting the Pickwickian image. And just as loquacious, it seemed. He was doing all the talking while she listened on in that 'obedient' mindful manner of hers that pleased generals and juniors alike. As they approached up the aisle, Bretzler got up and went to meet them halfway. Smiles flashed with Selena introducing Colonel Bretzler and Fr Trelawney to each other. Whilst Fr O'Malley would still be the celebrant for the Mass and wedding ceremony, urgent parochial business was unavoidably demanding his presence elsewhere. So Fr Trelawney had kindly consented to step in and help the couple through the rehearsal ceremony.

As they talked on, Bretzler got the impression that Selena was using the conversation to distance herself from him, taking cover behind the semi-formal flow of words. She barely spared a glance to look him in the eye. But when she did, it wasn't her looking at him. Not the warm loving woman that he held deep feelings for. His growing uneasiness was not helped by the 'jingly' nerves state he was experiencing over the wedding virtually rushing in on them. He wondered if she was reading similar cold mood changes in him. Strangely unfamiliar moments of awkwardness between them grew into minutes, until they were rescued by a timely interruption. All heads turned towards the commotion.

Falzoni, of course. Who else, but Frank all on his own, could create a ruckus that sounded like the Boston Bears in that unforgettable hell-hollering last game scrum before the team folded in '40. And, as usual, he was late as well. The tarpaulin bulged and twisted where, lost for a moment behind it, Falzoni was punching, swearing, and finally finding his way through it, into the church. Soaked with the morning's heavy downpour, the tarpaulin gave a generous helping of its rainwater to him so that he stood for several seconds shaking it and wiping it off his sleeves. Feeling a bit drier and having cursed the lousy English climate enough, he was all smiles again. He joined them in the central aisle. 'Don't the churches in this country have doors?' he said. 'Instead of leaving us to fight our way in through a square mile of canvas.'

Fr Trelawney's explanation in his thin high-toned voice didn't seem to be catching the Captain's ear, so that Bretzler stepped in. 'Much as the English love their tea, Frank, those bags piled up at the front door are not tea-bags. The UXB guys are defusing one of Jerry's bombs that didn't go off.'

'It's sure going to be one heck of a pun if they get their wires crossed. Death's counting its seconds down only half a ball-throw away, and you're still letting people in here? Hell --- sorry, Father --- but you guys are sure playing it cool, even if it is His house.' Falzoni cast a glance heavenwards to carry his message. One could only hope that it was heard.

Conversation stopped with their attention drawn to the heavy pounding of boots on the stone-flagged floor approaching from the nave's east end. Walking up to them in black helmet with its white ARP letters and overalls covered in brick dust, the warden held up his clipboard in indication to the priest. Trelawney excused himself politely from his group and went to join the warden. 'We've managed to identify all but four of the total dead of nineteen, Father. It would help if you could tell us if they are your parishioners or not, even if you can't identify them. That would help, Father. Your deacon was caught directly and must have taken full force of the blast. We only managed to identify his scattered parts from his dog collar: sorry, his clerical collar.' Fr Trelawney looked at the dull brown booklet attached to the warden's clipboard. It was a morbid list of casualties, live and dead. Instead of inspecting the names of individuals, as the warden had wanted him to do, his eyes kept straying to the different columns listing the hospitals and mortuaries, mainly in Putney Vale, where human beings, living and dead alike, were reduced to mere impersonal case numbers. Other columns showed injuries inflicted on these innocent civilians to be severe enough to require immediate on-the-spot amputation. Some injuries were so horrific as to consider those injured, but alive, less fortunate than those killed outright.

Fr Trelawney pointed at a number of names. 'Yes, these ones are of this parish.' He pointed at another two names. 'But I'm not able to place these two. Perhaps they were just visiting and came in to attend the Mass. My memory fails me in my old age. We'll have to check the register.' Fr Trelawney excused himself a second time from the group. He would be back shortly to go through the rehearsal ceremony with them, after he had helped the warden with his unpleasant task.

Summing all this up, and thinking of Falzoni's initial remark about 'doors', Bretzler turned to Selena. 'Why have we chosen this church to have it in, anyway? Isn't there one we can have it in that's still in one piece, and not about to fall down around us?' He looked around at the bomb damage while he said this to emphasise his point. Pausing to lean his head in closer to hers, he put his hands on her shoulders. 'Are you all right? You seem to have been a little' – he hesitated for a moment to find a way of saying it – 'a little bit far away and out of the picture, the last few days.' He wondered if he should say what he wanted to say. But he went on. 'Do you think that maybe we're doing all this in too much of a rush, with the fuss over all the arrangements getting you down?' There, he'd said it, and caution be damned.

She deeply wished that he had not said that last part. It confirmed her dreaded suspicions on how he had been behaving recently over their coming wedding. She couldn't help feeling that he was cooling over the idea of them getting married, and sensed his slowing down, if not stepping back from it all. This touched her coldly inside, just like it had been making her feel distanced from him over the last week. But his firm hands on her, and his eyes and breath so close to her fired her inside with a great surge of determination. She wasn't going to let him slip away that easy. Pulling on a great reserve of inner strength, she forced a warm smile into her face. 'Mummy couldn't possibly have imagined her daughter being married anywhere else but in this very church. Saint Anselm's Basilica has been the Leighton-Lagrishe family's place of worship for generations. Having the wedding elsewhere would have been virtually inconceivable as far as Mummy was concerned.'

'Quite,' said Bretzler bluntly, not knowing how to follow on from that without the risk of contradicting her mother's iron ruling.

Selena smiled at Falzoni. 'And don't worry, Frank, with you as best man, your bridesmaid partner, Harriet, is my own choice. You'll like her.'

'I'm sure as heck glad to hear that, Selena.' said Falzoni, not hiding his relief. 'No disrespect to your swell old lady. But as you mention, where is she, this cute doll of a partner of mine? Shouldn't she be here, helping us go through the fancy steps of the wedding and all its do-dahs?'

Selena consulted her gold watch on its slender strap round her slender wrist. 'Yes, she should be here by now. I don't know what's holding her up. She does have a habit of being late for appointments.'

Bretzler looked at Falzoni. 'There you are, Frank, you're both bound to be right soul buddies, with you both sharing that same habit.' The stiff atmosphere that had held them minutes before had lifted, with the feeling that something other than a 4000lb German bomb had been defused.

'And while we're waiting for Father to come back,' said Falzoni, 'do you think you could lend me fifty bucks, Brent?'

'How about forty?'

'Sure, that'll do; you can owe me the ten.'


With the deep drone of its four Bristol Hercules 14-cylinder radial engines reverberating in the sunny afternoon sky, the massive frame of the Avro Lancaster circled round in preparation for landing down on 263 Bomber Squadron's Merton Dale airfield. Weighed down by the body-load of a great mammoth, but moving with the graceful lightness of a giant gadfly, it came round in a declining arc to eventually straighten out and finally touch down on the landing strip. Flight Lt Guther looked on with mixed feelings as the plane rolled past heavily on its huge wheels. He felt thrilling pride at the potential punch it could deliver, vying with pangs of guilt over the searing memories of that disaster that he had been near enough to see, but too far away to prevent. If only he had not strayed away from his flight escort position. If only. He'd watched helplessly from his distance, seeing the plane he was supposed to protect 'snap' in two halfway along the fuselage, exploding under the impact of a 109 Messerschmitt's cannon bullets streaming into it like frenzied hornets. A tiny human figure had fallen from the spinning wreckage-pieces, looking comically stupid with its tragically futile flailing of limbs in the merciless open sky. The falling figure's scream, muted by distance, wailed its horror aloud inside Guther's head. He had only known the navigator, Tony Hawkins, but none of the rest of the crew.  They'd shared  the same 1900 cc V-twin-engine Morgan three-wheeler between them  at RAF Morely training camp. Poor bloody, Tony.

But the propeller blades coming to a jerking halt was the only action that this plane had seen. Guther could see this from the plane's overall pristine gleam of 'innocent' newness. Twin-barrelled .303 Browning machine guns gleamed along the fuselage, poking up idly skywards in the Frazer Nash mid dorsal dome turret and over the bomb-aimer's position in the nose and in the Nash & Thompson FN20 tail turret. It was another fresh delivery from the factory by the ATA (Aircraft Transport Auxiliary) lot. This conclusion was confirmed with the pilot stepping down and pulling off the leather flying helmet to let fall, and pull a stroking hand through, long tresses of blonde hair. A female ATA pilot.

Where male pilots were urgently needed for combat duties, women were now engaged in their place to ferry military planes across the country. Restricted from flying in combat, and from landing on aircraft carriers, women were otherwise responsible for delivering as many as up to thirty eight classes of aircraft from place to place. These gallant women were trusted with delivering their planes, factory-fresh to active service airfields, or battle-torn to Maintenance Units for general repairs and reinstallation of damaged weapons. The need for this auxiliary service was so great that a totally clean bill of health was not compulsory. It virtually sufficed for you to have one arm, one leg and one eye. If you had these, you were in. You had to be able to fly something bigger than a kite, of course ----- and have 500 hours of solo flying experience under your belt.

That was why Guther was here. Grounded from fighter escort duties by the camp's MO, Group Captain Melrose, he was anxious to get back into the air some way or other. It was 'Doc' who had referred him to the psychiatrist on the clinical basis that whilst his physical state was 'passable', his faculties were otherwise questionable. That meant that his name wasn't going to be chalked up on the Operations board for the foreseeable future. The nagging fear of being cramped in that narrow cockpit all alone, facing death rushing on at him at over 300 m.p.h, was keeping him back. He accepted this bitterly. If he could fly a larger plane, with a much greater protective fuselage and wing structure around him, perhaps that would chase away his inner bogeyman. But hope fighting with doubt wasn't settling his mind any.

Nervously preoccupied with these gloomy thoughts, he couldn't think for a second what it was that he was bending and scraping with his thumb-nail in his pocket. He pulled it out to see. It was his small blue Permanent Pass card, giving him official leave from camp during off-duty hours, with the option of being in uniform or civilian apparel. That brought memories of a different sort flooding back. They were of those early days when young inexperienced minds were not yet etched with scars that one was fated to carry later. The very elation of pulling himself up into that bright yellow Tiger Moth for the first time, after months of learning navigation and signalling at Initial Training Wing. With its 29ft wings and 23ft fuselage made of canvas, wire and 'sticks', the Moth gave him his first feel of the air, climbing up into the sky at 673ft/min, to a 13,000ft ceiling, behind the swirling blades of its purring De Havilland Gypsy 4-cylinder piston engine. Learning to bank and turn like a bird came easy as cake --- with help of that instructor in the rear seat. But he left the comic book Biggles image behind when he progressed from biplane to monoplane at the Operational Training Unit. Now capable of flying at 210mph in the Miles M.9 Master fighter trainer with its 715hp Roll-Royce Kestrel engine, he got to grips with the serious aerobatic tactics necessary for gunning down enemy planes, whilst at the same time avoiding having his pants and plane shot out from under him. With instructions being all fun and excitement, and your only worry being that of the sausages growing  cold  when  you  ran  like  hell  for the NAAFI canteen after a training stint, those were truly halcyon days.

Guther broke off from his quiet reverie when he saw the figure coming out of the control tower building, to look around, before moving off slowly in his direction. The casual splay-footed gait and at that distance, the red blot of a moustache, was enough to identify him. Phil 'Ginger' Burkiss always took his time. 'Hi, Guthy', cried Warrant Officer Burkiss, still yards away. 'What the hell are you doing away out here, in this ruddy wind? Let's go back inside and get ourselves a mug of tea and muffins. Warm ourselves up.'

Guther didn't seem to favour this suggestion and turned away, affecting a long stare at the long wind-sock flying horizontal in the strong current. 'No, I'd rather stay out here in the fresh air, if you don't mind.'

But Burkiss could sense a diffidence of sorts was putting Guther off from going indoors. Probably a state of after-shock nerves; and that bloody Quasimodo face of his making him shy away from company. Especially official company. 'Yes, all right. But let's get over to the other side of the field, and we can stand in the shelter of the mess block , out of the way of the wind.'

As they walked off towards the corrugated round-backed Nissan hut that housed the pilots' rest-room and canteen, Burkiss looked askance with re-kindled curiosity at Guther. 'Were you being serious with what you said the other night in the Crown? Or was that just the beer talking? Dog's piss wouldn't have tasted any worse, I can tell you that.'

'No, I meant what I said.' In fact Guther had been asking Burkiss to do him a favour and wangle him a way into flying non-combative missions for the ATA.

Burkiss stopped to stand and look enquiringly at Guther. 'Yeah, but are you up to it, my old son? '

'I've notched up my fair share of kills. Fully accepted by the CO.' Guther looked down at his leg, giving it a double slap. 'And you can forget about this being a bother. I'm not the only one who hobbles about like a penguin. It clearly doesn't bother Douglas any having two tin ones, as you well know.' He was, of course, alluding to the now iconic Squadron Leader Bader.

Burkiss didn't appear to be fully swayed by Guther's words. The gold ring on his finger winked in the sunlight as he put up a hand to finger his moustache while he took a moment to think. 'Sure, sure, but I was thinking more along the lines of what with the --- you know ---,' he said, putting a finger to his head to carry his meaning , '--- the old noddle, an' all.'

'Come on, Phil, you owe me one.' Guther swung round to look pointedly at the Lancaster. 'I can fly one of those, and crates like it, no bother, I assure you. All I need is for you to do your bit setting up the secondment papers. You can do it. I know the drill. All I need is your signature along with your official stamp.'

Burkiss stepped back, taking a deep breath to openly demonstrate his state of heavy concern. 'Jesus Christ, old man, you don't seem to appreciate the enormity of what you're asking. We're liable to be court-martialled if we're caught signing false transfer papers.'

'*Unofficial*, not false.'

'Yeah, that distinction will make all the difference, I don't think. But I suppose we can only give it a try, heaven help us.' Burkiss put on what he considered to be one of his best looks of compassionate thought. 'Hmmm, I'll look into it and see what I can arrange.' A cheeky cough preceded another two-finger stroking of the ginger moustache, before he spoke. 'Of course, I'm can expect that an appropriately handsome remuneration will come my way for my part in smoothing out any rough patches in administrative protocol. Yes?'

'Don't worry, Phil, you'll get your money' Guther knew full well that Burkiss was giving a show of holding back in his pretence of considering possible impending difficulties only because of the money. He had every faith that Burkiss could take care of the necessary paperwork safely. It was what the man readily did all the time, be it with or without official seal. Burkiss didn't give a hoot about being stripped of his badges in dishonourable discharge for violation of King's Regulations, Clause 29, Sub-Section 7, so long as the money balanced it out. One of his varied desk job duties at HQ was that of fixing up, and keeping records, of liaison meetings between the services. So he was forever involved in implementing changes by writing up amendment clauses in interdepartmental memos. Hence he was comfortably in his element arranging underhand deals in return for fat backhanders.

If Guther hadn't known this, he wouldn't have bothered to 'accidently' bump into Burkiss at the Crown that night. In fact, at that point of their meeting in the pub, Burkiss was just finishing setting up an unofficial contract with a freelance journalist to have exclusive rights to publishing Bomber Command operations material when suitable in the future, as well as possibly some visits to airbases.

Guther had thought that he had seen the journalist before somewhere, but couldn't recall where. Then he remembered later. It had been when he was on his way to Doctor Dromyrk's place. The man had stopped him to ask for directions. It wasn't the face that had stirred Guther's memory. It was the man's scraping voice and the iodine-stained bandaging round his neck.

# 24

'Not long to go now, Skipper. We'll be able to get a whiff of their flippin' onions before long,' said navigator/bomb-aimer Flt Sergeant Colby into his rubber mouthpiece, the words carried along inter-communication lines to beat the massive din of four Bristol Hercules 1,375 h.p. engines, to reach the pilot at the front of the 87ft Stirling bomber. His leather-helmeted head bobbed with encouragement as he added, for the rest of the seven man crew: 'Not far to go now.' But the crew was accustomed to Matt Colby always being 'miles' out with his calculations, so found little joy in his words.

'I'll believe that when I see it, Flight Sergeant,' returned the pilot, Flight Lieutenant Fromes, in his usual dull unemotional voice.

On and on the plane raced at its cruising speed of 200mph, tearing through the darkness that was dotted with millions of stars, without hitting one single one of them. Gunner Royle made his stumbling way along the plane to reach, and hand, Colby a mug of ugly-looking black tea that was spilling out of it with the plane's swaying motion. 'Here, Matt, you great Aussie bastard. Seeing as we're *nearly there*, as you say, you'll have plenty of time to drink your tea without worrying about spilling any of it on some poor Frenchman's head.'

'If there's any of it left,' said Colby, shielding his precious maps with one arm, while taking another spillage of the 'tea' on his other arm. 'Don't worry, Jim, I wouldn't dream of wasting a drop of your bloomin'

Pommy tea on a bloomin' Froggy, seein' as they only drink wine.' Taking the mug, Colby turned back to the serious business of peering closely at the silver 'splashes' constantly changing shape on the dark screen of the 10cm S-band H2S radar panel. Newly installed earlier that year, with its Nash & Thompson rotating ground scanner for locating targets, it was the RAF's latest answer to better all-weather day and night bombing. 'Thanks,' he said over his shoulder to gunner Royle. 'I'll let you get back to that pea-shooter of yours.'

'You heard him, Royle. Get back to your post, pronto,' cut in the Skipper's voice. 'You can never tell where Jerry is out there. I'm not having this mission shot up just because you've decided to play char-lady.'

'I'm on it, Skipper.'

The sonorous lull of seven airmen sitting still, waiting patiently, nervously, to reach their target, continued with its guaranteed monotony. Nothing changed, the engines giving out their mind-grinding roar all the while, the long fuselage and 90ft of wings rocking and dipping in battle with the buffeting wind, the propellers slicing great thirteen foot diameter circles in the air, to cut a way through the night.

Then at last they saw it. It was as deceptive a first sighting as you usually always expected at this height, where reality was twisted by the disorientating darkness cloaked all around you. Still some distance away below them, it looked like a giant black shirt with two rows of shiny white buttons. It was lights to guide them over the stretch of field they were going to fly over and make their drop.

Despite it being larger than the Lancaster and the Halifax, and its being armed with eight Browning machine guns, the Stirling was relieved of bombing duties and relegated to SOE missions, dropping supplies for the French Resistance. It also served as a high altitude control plane for guiding Mosquito bomber/fighters to their low level lightning strike targets, mainly off the Dutch coastline. These were Heinkels carrying V1 flying bombs ready for launching from the air.

As was usual before making a drop, Flight Lieutenant Fromes wanted to get a feel of the angle and height needed for curving round and down safely over the illuminated area, which from this height, looked dauntingly tiny. Things weren't helped any when you considered that dropping zones continually moved from place to place for the sake of avoiding detection by the Vichy police who, in lightly armed patrols, constantly monitored the countryside for such clandestine activities. If heavier armament was deemed necessary, a German military contingent would be called in. There wasn't any time for practice runs. They had to do this and be gone in one swift smooth action. No hanging around for 'Vive la France' salutes and blown kisses. The Flight Lieutenant prepared to take the plane in for its now-or-never daredevil swoop.

Shifting controls to tip one wing's ailerons down, and the other wing's ailerons up, he had the enormous juddering frame banking steeply over to starboard and going down. They levelled out straight, homing in towards the target. 'Bay doors opening now,' said Fromes in monotone voice.

The two bomb-bays magically obeyed the command, opening their doors.

'Say when,' said Fromes to aimer Colby.

'Nearly – nearly – nearly – NOW!'

Down below, standing in the field, Monique Berac's forty minutes of anxious waiting exploded into a thunderous interruption of noise and action. The night's stillness and deafening silence was broken with the ground seeming to vibrate from the ear-shattering roar of the monster bird's great engines, as it swept down and in overhead. Monique hadn't imagined that she would have been so frightened; but she was. Fear of being crushed into the ground by this terrifying great thing was a natural enough reaction to have in the circumstances. Quiet, empty, space of the night was now full of this awesome thundering black mass seemingly filling up the whole sky with its titanic structure, its lights out making it more menacing.

Four flaps opened down to let the long belly disgorge its 'entrails'. Down, down they floated, like long tubular seeds each carried on long tendrils of a black pappus. They were coming down on them everywhere, and Monique, looking up, turned round in a circle, trying to see how many they were.

The four engines screeched out a higher note as the plane, shed of its load, started to climb up and away into the darkness as swiftly and as smoothly as it had come in. Mission completed, its next scheduled route was across those waters, over those white cliffs, and onwards to base at RAF Station Bentville. Hopefully the Luftwaffe would not seek to intercept their homeward flight.

Watching the Stirling rapidly recede into the distance, along with its diminishing roar, Monique's realisation of the plane's obvious destination gave her a momentary pang of envy. A wistful thinking of how safe it had been back there, at Lindwell, in spite of all the scratches and bruises she had collected, and all that rude shouting from Sergeant-Major McCulloch and Sergeant McAllister she had endured in her gruelling training. Not a shade on the minute-to-minute knife-edge business she was involved in now. She tried to shut the six-week life expectancy of an agent statistic out of her mind. Standing there staring, her mind was held in distant memories.

'Watch out!' The frantic cry broke into her thoughts at the same time as the hands seized her by the shoulders, to fiercely pull her backwards. Just in time to avoid being hit by the great tube thudding down into the ground beside her. Seconds before the great area of parachute flopped down beside it. 'For God's sake, Berac, didn't I tell you to constantly be on your guard. If you really want to be killed that much, I'd expect it to be by the bloody Hun, and not by one of our own supply packs. If it wasn't night-time, I'd say that you were daydreaming. For God's sake pull yourself together. Try and remember that this is an important job we're on. We've enough to worry us over our possibly running into a Police, or even a German, patrol, without you giving them a hand. Please, please, try and not fuck things up. Can we trust you to do that?'

Jolted out of her admittedly foolish inner preoccupation, Monique felt a surge of anger rise in her at Trepet's sharp chiding. But she thought it more sensible to say nothing. Especially since he had been right about her 'not being fully there on the job'. And he had saved her from a nasty sore knock on the head, if not from death. She busied herself detaching the trailing parachute cords from the metal supply canister.

Rene looked down the length of the clearing where the flaming torches were being put out. Every second that the lights stayed on was one moment closer to being discovered by a patrol. They had to move fast, getting this over and done with lest their operation was routed. He walked over to where Monique was trying to open the long cylinder that had almost hit her. Kneeling down beside her, he leaned in to give her a hand with the stubborn catch. 'You'll understand, if I was a little sharp there. You're not the only one who's nervous,' he said to her.

'Who says I'm nervous?' Monique felt a little silly in hoping that the hollow tone in her voice was not betraying her tingling state of nerves. Active in the field on a dangerous night operation for the second time, she was once again expecting the darkness to be flooded with sweeping searchlight beams and loud megaphone announcements ordering them to lay down their arms or be shot. But the only noise ruffling the night's thick stillness was the low murmur of the others commenting over the supplies they were unloading. She realised that another sound, long drawn out like that of a steam engine, was her own tense breathing through her nose.

Not looking at her, Rene smiled to himself as he spoke: 'We're *all* a little nervous, believe me.' With a determined effort, loaded with a fair measure of annoyance, he wrenched the canister's door open. 'And not a moment too soon,' he exclaimed, throwing the metal lid back. 'And with damn nuisances like this holding us back, who can blame us for being a little on edge and keeping an ear open for the Hun's marching jackboots.'

As they leaned over the dark opening to inspect the tube's contents, the fresh 'green' smell of country air was invaded by a whiff of something else; that peculiar to heavily-oiled metal. Guns. Weapons of different size and calibre. Sub-machineguns and pistols, revolvers and automatics, automatic and bolt-action rifles, Webley, Smith & Wesson, Colt, Browning, 9mm, 0.38 and 0.303 calibre. Anything that could be used against the enemy was welcome, be it factory new, or old with a 'bloody' record.

Rene didn't bother to examine any of the weapons individually, instead, handing them blindly one at a time to Monique for her to transfer to the coarse farm sacks that they had brought with them. In spite of his hurry, he spared a moment to pause and look around him to see how the others were progressing with their lot. Speed was of the essence. The sooner they got this lot cleared away, the greater their chance of living to see another day. He turned to Monique, who had taken his stalling as an opportunity to look at an American air-cooled Lewis light machine gun. She was fiddling with the drum magazine.

'Something wrong?' he asked.

'The ratchet teeth seem a bit loose in engaging. Could lead to jamming. It's certainly seen its action. Not sure for how much longer, though. You could always use it as a club, I suppose.'

'Your expertise extends to weapons, as well as explosives then, does it?'

'I was a good little girl and paid attention to my instructors, as well as doing my homework.'

'Let's get on with it,' he said, turning back to the cylinder. 'After we've unloaded this lot, we've still got to clear away the containers and parachutes, and bury them in the woods. We can't afford to leave a single blade of grass in the field disturbed enough to alert the police.'

Promptly putting the weapon into the sack, she held out her hands to him, waiting for the next item to be passed to her.

# 25

**MILICES REVOLUTIONNAIRES FRANCAISES**. The bold words on the card, held a few inches from her face, stood out to catch Monique Berac's attention, as they were meant to, with their brazen message. A fascist-style double-headed axe in the left corner, together with the words **Brigade Speciale,** running along a diagonal red white and blue strip, helped to reinforce the card's authority. The squiggly signature below the man's photograph was barely legible, made more so by the smudged ink ring of authority stamped over it.

Affecting a fake surprised reaction at the card's sudden presentation, Monique made a deliberate point of almost spilling coffee from her minuscule 'thimble-size' cup. But she had already summed up what he was from a covert side-glance at him through the glass door when he opened it to come into the Chien Noir bistro. His uniform of blue jacket, trousers, beret and brown shirt had identified him as a Milicien; a member of the pro-Vichy paramilitary force formed earlier, with German assistance, in January, to put down the insurgent French Resistance. Monique noted how the man, in open gesture, rested his hand for a moment on the polished leather open-style holster which held what looked like to her to be a Spanish version of a Smith & Wesson revolver. From what she remembered of her Lindwell details, the pistol probably used French Ordnance 8mm cartridges. The man's left arm sported a German Army Wound Badge, indicating his honour of past service with a German military unit. All in all, not a man to be toyed with.

'Papers,' he said brusquely, deliberately leaving out 'mademoiselle' that would have made for a Frenchman's politeness. He obviously wanted to sound as hard as his German counterpart. Holding his head back, he looked down at her, watching her, as he slowly pocketed his warrant card. Monique sensed that he actually wanted her to be difficult so that he could demonstrate his official power. And power he had. But she'd practised her 'native' accent over and over again so that it would be good enough to get past him as she answered his probing questions. Whilst doing so, she tried to remember Dr Dromyrk's lectures on what he had called 'body language', and what facial expressions to pose and where to focus her eyes for different situations. She hoped that she was doing it all correctly as he had told her to do.

Since the Milice operated alongside, but separate from the Vichy Police Force, its actions were not governed by civilian law and so went beyond the limits stipulated by judicial ruling. It could virtually do what it wanted – and it did. With Secretary General Joseph Meurmont as its Chief of Operations, it was free to carry out executions and assassinations, as well as helping to round up Jews and anti-Vichy insurgents in readiness for their transportation to labour camps in Germany.

Feeling the man's eyes digging into her, and knowing how his lot, with legal approval, freely resorted to grim torture in the process of extracting information from prisoners, Monique wasted no time in handing over her ID documents. In the eyes of the French Resistance, the Milice was considered to be more deadly than the Gestapo and the SS. With Milice agents being full-blooded Frenchmen with natural knowledge of districts and their dialects, and knowing who were Nazi collaborators and who were not, they proved to be a formidable thorn in the side for the Resistance to deal with. In its more heavily armed capacity, the Milice was officially called the Franc-Garde.

Monique could see that the man was disappointed in not finding any fault in her papers as he gruffly handed them back. He would very much have liked to take this pretty woman in for searching and interrogation. She shivered inwardly at the thought of his hands wandering all over her body and stripping off her clothes. Monique's face had been the only one the man was unfamiliar with, so there was no need to question the others sitting there, eyes down, in stone-faced silence. There was a lightened air of relief all round when he left. Pausing outside, he turned to look back through the closed glass door for a last moment's scrutiny at Monique. With his hand still on the door handle, it looked as if he was going to come back in. She held her breath until at last he turned and walked away to join his comrades parading across the small square with their blue and silver banners. Their noisy incoherent rabble was music to her ears with it dying down as they moved off to finally disappear round the far corner.

If Monique had not been caught off-guard by the Milice man, she was, on the other hand, certainly a little surprised by Rene Trepet's entrance into the bistro, now returned to its hubbub of cheerful chatter, now that the 'merde' had gone. It wasn't so much because of his somewhat surreptitious coming in by a back door, but because of the person he had brought with him. She had been duly informed that Selena Leighton-Lagrishe was no longer going to be her Case Officer in the field, owing to the little 'bump' of trouble that she had landed herself in. She knew Selena was being replaced. But this came as a total surprise.

Dr Dromyrk greeted Monique with his customary polite nod and smile. He waited for Trepet to be seated before sitting down himself.

Ordering three Gautret cognacs, Trepet used a few moments looking round the room, smiling at faces he recognised, to ready himself for discussing things with Monique and Dromyrk. Having now worked with Berac, he knew how her mind worked and so could handle her. But a consultant psychiatrist, that was something different altogether. Odds were that following the Docteur's logic and train of thoughts would be a more convoluted passage, with more than a few sharp corners to turn. And he wasn't even English. A Swede, in fact, from what he'd been told. Valued in SOE covert intelligence circles not only for his professional expertise, but also on account of unique personal knowledge of 'German things'. Exactly what this was, Trepet had no idea. No-one had told him, so he waited with a burning curiosity. But from the short time that he had known him, he had learned that Dromyrk tended to be very much taciturn, and so had the feeling that the details of that particular subject would not be coming his way just yet, if at all.

'The invasion, it is still on, yes? This is correct?' said Trepet to Dromyrk, keeping his voice down so as not to be heard away from their table.

Dromyrk looked down at his cognac for a moment before looking across at Trepet. 'As far as I know – as far as any of us are aware of – nothing has been ultimately agreed upon so far. But yes, as far as preliminary planning has progressed, the prospect of our mounting a cross-channel assault is fast becoming a reality. As well as our American allies sending in their OSS agents on specific operations, we're also sending in small teams – ninety three, in fact, – composed of three agents, American, British and French, with the task of bringing together a co-ordinated front in preparation for an invasion.' Previously, Resistance groups had been scattered, lacking the punch a united effort could give. It had taken the co-ordinated set-up of the Communist lot to demonstrate the strength that could be derived from merging isolated small groups into a larger fighting force.

Trepet raised his glass to Monique and Dromyrk, in salute at this news. 'We are indeed gathering our separate fighter groups together to join the Conseil Nationale de Resistance, now that General DeGaul has taken over as its president. With one great united front, we can at last push the Boche out of our country for good.' Rene raised his glass again in a toast. 'General DeGaul.'

'General DeGaul,' said Monique, raising her glass.

Dromyrk didn't want to darken the Frenchman's shining iconic image of DeGaul by saying that the General tended to be a right pain in the arse with his obstinacy during discussions with Allied commanders. Keeping tempers down between Eisenhower and Montgomery was one thing; but bringing in DeGaul to make a bickering threesome, was virtually a guarantee that plans were not likely to advance from square one without him demanding 'conditions'. Only after a measured degree of patience was it possible to persuade DeGaul to order his countrymen to sabotage vital transport and communication installations in preparation for the intended broadside assault --- Operation Warlord --- on the French coast. Dromyrk held up his glass: 'General DeGaul.'

In the midst of their confident toasting, Monique couldn't help thinking back on her moments of bated breath only minutes earlier. 'Can we afford to be that confident? I mean with the enemy so close on our heels, virtually shadowing all our movements; I mean the Milice, not the Police – the Milice. I was questioned by one of them just before you came in.'

Both a little puzzled, they looked round at her, waiting for her to expand on her remark. But nothing followed. She was relying on Rene, with his better in-depth knowledge of the situation, to take it from there. Realising that Monique was handing over to him, he took over. 'It's a nasty reality we'd much rather believe wasn't true; but it is, so has to be dealt with. And there's a great lot of them; we reckon going towards twenty --- maybe twenty-two --- thousand, roughly; and growing.' He saw Monique's faint look of dismay and gave a sad smile at the bitter truth that she had apparently not grasped until now. 'It's not just our people who believe themselves to be fighting for the right cause. Pre-war right-wing politics, helped along by Vichy government promises of employment, regular pay and generous food rations, holds the Milice people in an iron grip. With German occupation lowering food rationing to what you can only call starvation level, it's not something we can ignore.'

'And a powerful incentive for collaborating with the enemy,' added Dromyrk solemnly.

'Along with the fact that petty criminals joining the Milice automatically have their sentences commuted and are exempted from slave labour duties.' Trepet shifted his glass around in thought for a moment. 'There's also the motive of personal revenge, of course, where we've had no choice but to resort to brutal methods of threatening and extorting information from otherwise 'innocent' family members of Milice operatives.' Possibly with a slight feeling of guilt, at this late admission, Trepet tapped the table hard and sat back upright. 'C'est la guerre.'

Monique looked at Dromyrk, watching him watching her, measuring her taking all this in. The coupling between Dromyrk and Monique was perhaps an ideal one, where the Case Officer had to act like a shrink with his patient, handling his agent's situation problems with a calm professional control of emotions; at the same time as sectioning off a corner of his mind to resolve operational problems with cold logical decision. Monique certainly couldn't forget her many long sessions with Dromyrk. How he'd painstakingly taught her how to behave naturally in nerve-rackingly unnatural situations; how to establish, with lightning reflex, an air of innocence and convincing pretext if caught being where she shouldn't be; in all, how to survive under constant close surveillance and preliminary interrogation without breaking down.

But this would be her one and only meeting with the Doctor. After this, as her Case Officer, he would be liaising at a distance. Rene would be acting as buffer, carrying messages between Momique and Dromyrk. This way Dromyrk's very existence would remain totally unknown to other Resistance agents and their cell networks. Hence, neither 'end' of the set-up could inform on the other owing to complete lack of knowledge.

Discussion was agreed to be exhausted when the glasses were no longer taking in refills. 'We'll leave separately,' said Trepet, rising from his chair. 'Docteur Dromyk and I will go back the way we came; through the backyard outhouse and out through the side gate into the alley --- thanks to Gerard.' He gave a glance of appreciation to the haggard old face behind the bar. He looked down at Monique. 'You can wait for five minutes after we leave before you go out the front way. Okay?'

Monique nodded 'Okay.'

When Monique stepped out of the bistro and started across the square, she was conscious of the many eyes following her movements. Two of these eyes were those belonging to the uniformed figure with the metal Ringkragen gorget shining on his chest, sitting at an iron table outside a café on the square's far side. Lieutnant Grunvald Klanner, of the Feldgendarmerie. As he watched her pretty figure move across the square, his mind sifted through his stock of memories. Searching systematically, he suddenly found it. Nodding slowly, he smiled his satisfaction. 'Berac,' he said slowly to himself. 'Monique Berac.' He looked to the café's doorway. 'Hubber!' he shouted.

The doorway stayed vacant for several seconds before Obergefreiter Hubber appeared, drawing a backhand wipe across his mouth to dry it of beer. He went over to stand by the Lieutnant.

The Lieutnant got up, pointing at the Corporal's holster. 'Prime your Mauser, Hubber, and follow me on foot, at a discreet distance.'

'Where are we going, Herr Lieutnant?'

'To follow a suspect.'

Hubber scanned the people all around him in the square. 'Which one is it?'

But the Lieutnant was already walking away at a casual pace. He answered back over his shoulder: 'Brown coat, pretty red beret and two very pretty legs.'

# 26

'And you, pal, can go fuck a ham pie.' Captain Falzoni threw the strong suggestion, with its coarse wisdom, at the two-fingered brush-off from the sergeant driving the US Army Catering Corps supplies truck as it moved off, picking up speed, to recede down the road on its way to 6th Marines Base Camp G, outside the village of Oakston Lun. As far as Falzoni saw it, it was those poor Green Beret rednecks who would lose out by not reaping the rewards of his proposed deal.

'Oh, you are rude, Francesco; such a naughty, ever so naughty, rude American boy.' said Harriet Jocelyn Wilhelmina Covington, looping her arm round Frank's arm, to hug him in close.

'Last time I heard it, my name was Frank, honey.'

She pulled him in closer to kiss him playfully on the cheek. 'Oh, but Francesco is ever so much more romantic, so much more *attractive*.' She gave his cheek another peck.

'You reckon so? Well, I guess that must be why my dear old *padrina* --- godmother --- Antonia planted great slobbering kisses all over my face when I was making my First Holy Communion; half drowned me in her saliva.'

Seemingly unable to remove her face from Falzoni's, she caressed his 'ever so romantic' Latin cheek slowly with hers. 'And did you go on to become a lovely little angelic altar boy after that?' she whispered to him softly.

'And you figured out that last bit of holy truth all by yourself, did you, honey? I reckon with your quick wits on our side, we can sure as hell match Jerry's tricks any day.'

'Oh – you – are – wicked,' she whispered, the words coming out one at a time, between adoring licks of his 'attractive' ear. Harriet could virtually hear the wheels turning in Francesco's mind, with him already seeing the dollars pouring in from another one of his 'sure as hell' schemes. When Harriet had turned up at St Anselm's that day to rehearse for Selena's wedding ceremony, she had expected the best man, a Captain Falzoni, to be another shy bespectacled dullard, as typified the intellectual side of Selena's circle of friends. But the light that had exploded on her first seeing him had well and truly made up for the church's dark interior. She had taken to him instantly, totally captured by his bursting-with-life healthy all American image, dazzling uniform and his confident extrovert manner of projecting himself on you. She'd pushed that wonderful film's Rhett Butler character out of her mind.

Shaking off annoyance from his verbal tussle with the sergeant, Falzoni turned to Harriet to give her his full attention. Freeing his arm from hers, he put it round her to pull her in close. Selena had predicted correctly when she'd said that Frank would like Harriet. He did. She was certainly his type of doll; fun-loving without being too crazy, and scoring over Selena with 'double points' that stood out a mile. With that going for her, he could overlook the fact that she hailed from the same snooty crowd that Selena belonged to.

Feeling the thrill from Francesco's warm breath on her face, Harriet playfully ran her finger along the rainbow strip that was his campaign ribbon on his chest. The bright nail stopped at a bright colour. 'So what's this one for?'

Falzoni looked down to see what colour she had picked, putting his hand over her pale finger, and feeling it soft and smooth in his own broad hard fingers. 'Let's see now; that one, honey, was for a little friendly get-together with Jerry's Afrika Korps lot, near the little dung-fly-infested village of Bir Jadid, on the Moroccan coast; where the passing bullets gave you a better shave than your razor  did, and you hoped that your guardian angel was watching over you, protecting you, instead of wandering off for a lunch break of bagels and bananas in the shade of a palm tree, among farting camels. '

'And does Colonel Bretzler have these colours too?' But the colours Harriet was really interested in now were those of Falzoni's eyes.

'Hell, yeah, Brent has his colours as well, but a little different from mine.'

'You and he are what I believe you Americans call 'good buddies'; is that the correct term?'

'Right on the nail, honey. Yeah, you could say that we've shared the mud on our boots over one heck of a trek.' Falzoni took his hand from hers to run his finger along the ribbon as he thought back over their battles, forgetting Harriet for a moment.

'But he's not a lawyer like you, is he?' said Harriet, wanting to get Falzoni's attention back.

'Brent was already established as a marshal, roping in crooks on the run across the States, when I was just swopping my Yale faculty fraternity sweater for a collar and tie, to join the district attorney's team as a glorified junior, handing out case files to seniors, when I wasn't counting paper clips. You could well bet that the Jap Admiral Nagumo's Aichi E13A planes had barely returned from Pearl Harbor, when Brent would have been virtually collecting his bayonet and M-1 Garand carbine from Stores. Two months later, close on Brent's heels, you could bet that I was handing the paper clips over to some raw junior, so that I could enlist at the nearest recruiting office. Not that we'd yet crossed paths at that early stage.'

'So when *did* the two of you meet, to forge your unbreakable comrades' bond?'

A broad smile broke out on Falzoni's face, just short of giving way to a chuckle. 'Do I see a green tinge coming into those beautiful eyes of yours?'

'A green *what?*' Harriet dew back from him slightly. Don't be silly. Whatever gave you that idea?'

Frank let out a quiet laugh. 'If you must know, it was a chance meeting in a crater.'

'You don't mean that volcano in Italy, do you? Selena told me you were both fighting in Italy; naughty girl that I am, I forced her to tell me, knowing that she wasn't supposed to.'

This time Frank allowed himself to sway back with laughter. 'No, honey, not that kind of crater; I mean a damn great hole in the ground created by an exploding thirty pounder artillery shell. Some dumb recruit on the field-gun practise range was, for some God-only-knows reason, getting his co-ordinate points wrong and firing in our direction. At me and Brent, can you believe it? If Brent's lightning reflex hadn't had him diving into that crater, and pulling me with him, I wouldn't be sitting here with you now.'

'Oh, don't say that!' said Harriet, throwing her arms round Francesco's neck to yank his head in closer, and taking over from Padrina Antonia by showering his face with a deluge of hysterical kisses.

As they clung together, it occurred to Frank that if she was turned on so much by his battle experience details, by how much more was she likely to be turned on if he was to show her the scar he carried from his Palermo scrape. But indoors, in a comfy room, was a better place to be doing that, than here, in this freezing cold jeep, in the depth of the rural countryside, with its freezing God forsaken English weather. And it wasn't just the jeep's engine that would need a crank-up to get it going; his Falzoni 'stallion' balls were likely to become 'frozen assets'. Frank inwardly cursed the fact that he'd had to come out here to meet that goddam supplies truck; for all the good that had done. Frank didn't think taking Harriet back to a base backroom bunk for some fun, like the other guys did, was an idea that would get anywhere if he had put it to her. She was too classy a dame for that. And she shared her posh Kensington apartment with two other high society dames, so that was out of the question too. He raked his mind for a 'quiet' hotel, among those he was acquainted with, for one that would not be too seedy to meet Harriet's approval. She did tend to be pernickety in her tastes, as he supposed a lady of her class should be. Thinking through this, Frank was suddenly distracted by the figure looming up in his wing mirror. Seeing the figure's red cap, he sighed in dismay. 'What the hell does he want?' he muttered in low-keyed annoyance.

The military policeman waited for Falzoni to move the plastic window flap aside before poking his head in at them. 'Everything all right, sir?' he said. 'Stuck out here, all on your own. Engine trouble?' Switching his enquiring look from the Captain to the woman, he knew full well what the score was; but he kept a straight face, where a broad knowing smile could have come out. He left that sort of crude behaviour to his Yankee counterpart MPs.

'Is something wrong?' whispered Harriet, clearly worried.

Frank waved down her alarm. 'It's okay; nothing to worry about.' He looked at the MP. 'Everything's fine, Sergeant. Don't let us keep you back from your patrol duties,' he said in a voice that he thought would sufficiently hide his annoyance and his wish to be rid of the interfering bastard.

It didn't. Not showing *his* annoyance, the MP stepped back smartly to make room for someone else. 'Someone here to see you, sir.'

From the dark grey saloon that had drawn up and parked behind the jeep, a figure was walking up to them. The man stooped down to look inside the jeep. Falzoni recognised the guy as 'Walker', an obvious alias, from US Army Intelligence. 'Needed the Sergeant's help to track you down,' said 'Walker'.

'Yeah?' said Falzoni, waiting for the important stuff to come out.

'Pigeon's flown the nest.'

That was important enough for Frank. He turned to Harriet. 'Got to step out for a second, honey. Boys' talk.' Not waiting for any remarks from her, he got out and got into the other car to talk with 'Walker'.

'Pigeon', codename for Obersturmfuhrer Krunz, had been handled by Dromyrk up until now. But now that the Doctor had, himself, 'flown', it seemed that Krunz's movements had been monitored somewhat carelessly, with the result that he'd gone to ground. They'd goddamn lost him!

When Frank got back into the jeep, Harriet felt that he had forgotten her, him showing only a hard smile, in place of his previous affectionate advances that had now seemingly evaporated. The engine coughed into life and had them moving off, before Frank had the politeness to speak. 'Sorry, honey; fun-time aborted,' he said in a preoccupied serious tone that Harriet was not familiar with. 'Got to go bird-watching.'


The car seat creaked as its shadowy occupant shifted to look in the rear mirror, as a vague 'shifting of darkness' indicated a figure emerging from a lane. Scrutiny held for a few seconds and then relaxed, with the brain registering friend, not foe; it was a bobby. The policeman walked at his normal slow pace along the South London street in its inky blackout darkness, alone in his nightshift patrol, but for the spasmodic thudding and flashes of bombing far across the city. 'Hello, what have we got here, then?' he muttered, as much to himself, as to the cat that was walking along the low garden wall beside him. He was referring to the vehicle parked further up the street. It didn't look like one of their regular patrol cars. 'What do you say we go and have a look, eh?' The cat replied by wagging its tail, watching the policeman cross the street and walking more purposely towards the car.

Down slid the car window slowly. The constable looked at the Special Branch warrant card and then gave it back smartly. 'Thank you, sir. I was just checking to -----'

'That's all right, Constable. You did the right thing. Can't be too careful, can you?'

'On a special job, are you, sir?'

'Yes, we are.' Impatience was coming into the man's voice, him wanting to get rid of the policeman. He didn't want unnecessary public attention to ruin the operation.

*We?* The policeman looked about but couldn't see anyone else. 'Can I possibly be of help, sir?' he asked eagerly. Leaning forward to offer a further suggestion of help, the constable almost had his nose cut off by the window shooting up. He got the message of the man's thumb jerking back sharply, telling him to clear off up the street and out of the way.

The man continued to wait in the car, the minutes seeming like hours in his restlessness. Then suddenly he was no longer alone. An ash-grey saloon had ghosted up out of nowhere to park inches from his rear bumper. A tall lean figure in red-tabbed Army greatcoat and cap got out the car. Colonel Rutkin knocked on the rear window of the front vehicle. He turned to look behind him as Colonel Bretzler, in short US Army overcoat, and slim garrison cap with officer's black and gold piping and ends smartly standing up back and front, came up to join him.

The Special Branch man got out of his car. 'All briefed and ready when you are, Colonel,' he said.

'Are your people all here, Superintendent?' The words had barely left Rutkin's lips when figures were growing out of the brickwork shadows, where only the night had been a few moments ago. Coming out of the darkness from all directions, the sinister shapes flitted down the street with a common direction in their stealth. Converging around the target address, they melted once more into obscurity, to await the signal to move in.

'So can we move in now, please?' Rutkins' statement, polite as it was, had a steely command in its tone of authority.

'Right! Moving in now!' With the Superintendent stepping forward sharply, body shapes in the gloom of the unkempt garden suddenly shifted in unison, to gather around the building's front door. 'Some of us are suitably armed, I take it?' The Superintendent looked around for confirmation of this. Heads nodded.

'You can sure count me in on that one,' muttered an American voice.

With the power vested in a single sheet of paper from the Yard supporting them, there were no guilty feelings over smashing the front door in. The hall was in darkness when they rushed in, so that the

Superintendent switched the lights on without closing the door, either forgetting, or not bothering about blackout regulations. 'Right, get on with it,' he said to the men. 'I want this place searched thoroughly, working our way up from the cellar ---- check if there's a cellar --- and work up from there or from the ground floor to the roof. Look under the slates, if *necessary*.' This last word seemed to bring out some annoyance in the Superintendent, so that when he glanced round at Rutkin and Bretzler, the look in his eyes put the blame for all this on them. His loud shouting of orders continued as the men dispersed into side-rooms. 'I want every crack and knot hole gone over with a toothpick until we can count the maggots. Pull up the floorboards; tear off the wallpaper; maybe one of the cockroaches you find will speak German.' He stopped for a breather. 'And someone bring me the landlord.'

Finished shouting at his men for the moment, the Superintendent turned to face the two Colonels squarely. 'And anything of importance we do happen to find, you'll be taking that, I suppose?'

'Yes, that's correct, Superintendent,' said Rutkin. 'We'll take care of that side of it, as you agreed.'

'I'm not sure I remember agreeing to anything, really, except to that of having my team race out here at short notice.' The Superintendent playfully scratched his head to demonstrate his puzzlement.

'And your guys are doing a swell job,' cut in Bretzler, where he saw possible friction arising between the other two.

'What I don't understand is why you're hunting him down if he's working for you as a double agent.' The Superintendent paused for a moment's mental re-shuffling of the 'cards'. 'Let me guess, he *was* working for you as a double agent, but he's done one over on you with his being a *triple* agent all along, right?' He couldn't help letting out a little smile at his military colleagues having egg on their faces from being outwitted.

Rutkin gave a small embarrassed cough. 'That would appear to be --------'

'You got it right on the nail, buddy,' said Bretzler, cutting in again to save face for Rutkin. 'Truth is, we're pitched against some smart guys in their Abwehr over there.' He looked around at their surroundings, wall to wall, to ceiling. 'They've certainly done their homework, mapping out a whole string of safety houses, run by Nazi sympathisers. This joint is just one of them. That allows an agent to move along the line to the next safe address and escape arrest when our lot start closing in on the old known address.'

Conversation was interrupted by them being approached by a very angry man in a dapper striped three-piece and red bow tie. It was the landlord, no less, with mounting indignation giving the cheeks a tinge nearing that of the tie. 'What is the meaning of this? I demand an explanation for this outrageous intrusion of my property. And what about that door that you've left hanging on one hinge? That will have to be paid for by you.' But the words, in spite of their pretentious fury, failed to hide the feebleness behind them that the man felt, knowing that his game was up.

'Bag him,' said the Superintendent bluntly, in no mood to waste time explaining his actions where he felt no need to, considering that the circumstances verged on treason.

'What do we charge him with?' said the officer holding the landlord by the arm.

'Don't worry, you'll find something; you can be sure he'll have so many black market deals on his hands, you can have him for exceeding coal rationing. Take the bastard away.' In spite of being disgusted with the man and his kind, the Superintendent prided himself on not having laid a single finger on him, unlike those New York cops he'd seen in films. Seeing the man being taken away, he turned to the American. 'No doubt your lot in the Brooklyn precinct would have beaten the prisoner to a pulp with their night-stick batons to get him to talk. '

'No, in fact, they leave that to the bail-bondsmen and marshals, to get better results using their point three eight calibre Colts, a safe distance away from the precinct,' returned Bretzler, with a soft mocking smile. 'That way, bad  publicity  is  avoided.' He glanced round at Rutkin to share his joke.

The Superintendent stared hard at Bretzler, wondering how many little boxes you had to tick to separate fact from fib in the American's words. He shifted towards the doorway and its door hanging 'wounded' to one side. 'I've got to go. I've done my bit getting you into the place on my official warrant, so I'll let you get on with it, looking for whatever it is you're looking for. Some of my officers will stay behind to give you a hand. Good luck.'

Rutkin and Bretzler nodded their appreciation of the policeman's help.

Bretzler looked round at Colonel Rutkin. 'You can go as well; I know you have a lot to deal with elsewhere. I'll look after things here.'

'How are you going to get back?' said Rutkin, remembering that they had come in the same car.

'I'll beat one of these good English policemen to a pulp with my point three eight calibre Colt to persuade him to give me a lift.'

Rutkin wasn't sure if he should share Bretzler's humour in mocking the Superintendent and English policemen that far. He walked out the front door, while Bretzler mounted the hall stairs, two at a time, with a burning hope that he could find something, anything, of importance that Krunz had left behind in his haste to escape.

'I got held up,' said a familiar voice from below, in the hall. 'Goddamn bomb-holes in the road holding up the traffic.'

'And before you ask me --- no, I haven't got fifty bucks to lend you --- not even for myself,' said Bretzler.

Now that the prey had eluded the search, there was no longer any need for stealth, so that car doors slammed shut loudly, to match the bomb banging, and the cars raced off at tyre-screeching high speed. But the bombs continued their noise for a long time after that.

Round the corner at the far end of the street, the constable stopped short of colliding with the man coming out of a dark alley. 'I'd see and put a scarf round your neck for extra cover. Bandages are all very well, but it doesn't do to expose open wounds to this cold weather,' he said to the man. The man nodded, and holding up a hand, supposedly in gratitude for the 'medical advice', turned and walked away.

'Mind how you go, sir, with all this debris lying about. And you can't be too sure either what nasty characters you can come across in these blackout nights. Rob you blind, they will.' The man didn't answer. 'Goodnight, sir,' said the constable, a little peeved at getting no response and being left all alone again on his boring patrol.

# 27

'Mind the head.' But Rene Trepet's warning came a second too late.

Coming down into the dimly-lit cellar, carefully watching where he put his feet on the narrow wooden stairs, Dr Domyrk didn't notice the gnarled oak beam until his head gave it a generous thump. Stepping down onto the stone-flagged floor, he was not spared the inches to allow him to stand upright, having to stand with a stooped back, to avoid banging his head a second time on the low ceiling.

'I know, it's a bit cramped,' said Trepet. 'But hold on, maybe we can do something about that.' Putting his arms around a fat slatted wine press, with a grunting effort, he lifted it off its bench, to stagger round under the weight and place it down on the floor. Looking round at Dromyrk, he held out a hand, inviting him to sit on the now vacated bench. Dromyrk sat down. That was much better than ending up with a strained back. Removing the empty wine bottles from a wooden box, Trepet stood the box on its end and sat himself down on it. 'There, I think that's a little better.'

Dromyrk looked around the shadowy subterranean surroundings, taking in the atmosphere. Primitive was the word that came to mind. With uneven, very roughly hewn rock walls that had shiny rivulets of dampness trickling down them, this was plain enough. Dromyrk rubbed his head where it was still sore. And with that ever so low ceiling with its damned beams pressing down on you, perhaps *furtive* was more fitting.

Trepet watched Dromyrk's inspection of the cellar, smiling and just managing to hold back his laughter at the other's annoyance where his head hurt. 'I'd much have preferred for us to meet in my office,' he said, 'but with the recent step-up of ID inspections by police and Milice in public places, this is safer. You're lucky to get away with them accepting that your own skin is not counterfeit.' Although with the 'Jew' situation scourging the country as it did, that was not so much a joke as it sounded. He had not intended anything anti-Semitic in the least, seeing the connection only as an afterthought. But he wondered if the Docteur had read his thoughts from the remark. The woman, Berac, had as much as hinted, if not actually saying, that the Docteur was capable of this. He fidgeted with a splinter on the box end for a moment, to slip under what he imagined was Dromyrk's mental radar homing in on his mind. From the way his secretary had passed Dromyrk's telephone message on to him that morning, Trepet had instantly sensed that Dromyrk's visit would be something more than the routine operations report followed by a casual cognac or two. Far more. And he was right. So he had chosen this place for its secrecy to match the urgency. Dromyrk had not kept him waiting either, arriving as he did, just short of helping Trepet lift the heavy marble slab that concealed the cellar entrance.

Searching through his pockets, Trepet brought out his packet of Gitanes cigarettes. He held them out to Dromyrk. But the nearest Dromyrk ever got to smoking was having an incendiary bomb warning poster put up on the outside wall of his London residence. He shook his head at the offer.

Shrugging his shoulders, Trepet put one in his mouth and lit it. He took a long draw to get the first taste that morning, then blowing out slowly, used the time to gather his thoughts while looking the Doc over. Whilst it was true that their work took in a myriad of character types from varied occupations, Trepet nevertheless had been sparked with curiosity when first informed that this brilliant mind specialist would be joining them. Again, Berac had proved useful here with her careless innuendoes. *Mon Dieu!* Don't those instructors in England know how to train their agents to refrain from giving away 'harmless' information in their small talk – how to be tight-lipped. Anyway, according to the woman, the good Docteur had once worked for the Boche, no less. That fact, if it was true as she said, was worth a thought or two. Trepet blew out more smoke slowly as he turned this aspect over in his mind. For *that* particular point, he didn't care if the Docteur *was* reading into his thoughts. He noted that for the indoor medical practitioner that Dromyrk was, the man carried himself with an active outgoing image, with the stature that spoke of relatively good health for his age. Quite the man of contrasting parts.

Trepet had to blow out a tobacco flake before speaking. 'Melia, my secretary, got the impression from your phone message, that you were anxious to see me.'

'You'll recall that when we last spoke, the subject of major concern was that one which we forever fear.'

'That of having a leak in our security? Yes, the possibility of that has been on my mind a lot since then.'

'Alas, it is now a fact,' said Dromyrk gravely, leaning across with a sheet of paper in his hand for Trepet to take. 'Suspicions confirmed beyond a doubt.'

'Really?' Trepet tried not to sound too much like being one step behind in this new development. 'What exactly am I looking at? I recognise these co-ordinates and their operation times; and these names --- hold on – these three names – they don't belong to our cell; they're from the adjacent cell along the line, cell PLUTO. Are you saying that one of these is spying for the enemy?'

'In agent Berac's last three mission transmissions, specially encrypted material was included, without her knowing, I may say, and deliberately put about along differing routes so as to allow one of them to reach the enemy. The only ones who could have known of that secret information and passed it on to the enemy are those in your hand.' Dromyrk didn't let on that he had suspected that there was a leak from the time Colonel Bretzler had said mentioned this back at Lindwell Hall.

Trepet coughed. 'But *I* knew of those transmissions and their operational details. *My* name's not here. I suppose you could add it to the list.' Trepet looked across at Dromyrk. 'The same applies to you, Docteur; you also knew; and *your* name's not here.'

'Granted,' said Dromyrk, his searching eyes, not breaking their hold, unsettling Trepet.

A fresh line of thought gave Trepet a means of eluding the Docteur's scrutiny. 'I believe you worked for the Boche at one time, did you not? In Berlin, itself, in fact. Am I correct?'

'A purely medical situation.'

Trepet's spirits gathered momentum in his bid to pick a chink in the Docteur's personal armour. 'But didn't you in fact actually work with that bastard H----'

'On purely *medical* grounds – like I've just said.'

But Trepet wasn't giving up on the subject that easily, now that he thought it to be possibly useful. He picked away at another stray tobacco flake on his lip. 'Your country's neutrality must have made things easier for you, that is, with your not having to fight German soldiers; allowing you to work and fraternise freely with what was France's mortal enemy at that time  -- and still is.' As conversation continued along the 'German line', Trepet played on the point that Dromyrk's passport neutrality gave him relative ease in moving about enemy territory. This was giving Dromyrk ideas along a different vein that were stirring up a mixture of guilt and excitement feelings. As agent Berac's handler, the thought of him leaving her on her own – deserting her in the field – stung him with guilt; this was balanced with going to Germany to find Tildi, making his spirits soar.

There was a sudden change in the pattern of sound above them, with its falling away of voices. A stillness cut by the sharp sound of a single voice --- an impromptu ID inspection. Dromyrk looked up, at what was going on above them, and back at Trepet. 'If it were either one of us, would only one of us be leaving the cellar – and would that person be arrested or *welcomed* by the police?' Dromyrk gave a smile that didn't hide its serious probing concern. He wasn't carrying the Webley issued to him by Amoury at Lindwell, despite his protests; but he read the signals that Trepet had a 'loaded' pocket, and that he was wavering over the need to bring the weapon out.

With only the silence and its hanging questions pulsing away between them, they stared long and hard at each other.


Cobblestones on their own were awkward to walk on; wet with rain, and they were a bother; but cobblestones, wet from rain and on a steep slope, and they became an absolute hell. And it had been raining. So Monique Berac cursed quietly to herself as she wobbled and slipped on the unkind surface of this street that wanted to dive, rather than lead, as other decent streets did, down into the mountain town of Chardonne. Why did all these foreign towns have to be built on slopes, she moaned to herself. All right, so her grandma's place was also on a hill, but you got up and down the hill by way of a dirt track, not cobblestones. The only bother there was that you had to avoid stepping on dung in the dark. She'd have come into town by an easier way, if she could have borrowed Trepet's car. But it seemed that he was busy with whispers of a security leak. So she'd taken the bus that went along the mountain road, to be dropped off above the town. Monique's irritation was balanced with a faint humour at the thought of what her mum and dad would have made of the new habit of swearing that she'd developed. But then she'd learned to do a lot of nasty things, including how to kill in cold blood with her bare hands, since her recruitment into SOE. Now she was on another assignment that could see her arrested and shot, if things went wrong.

As she made her unsteady way down the treacherous incline, something odd caught her attention in a house window. It couldn't be – but it was. What she had mistook to be an ornamental piece had shown itself to be alive with its jerking head movements. A live chicken, no less, standing on the windowsill behind the glass. With food being scarce, hoarding livestock in one's house was understandable. Monique went over to the window to have closer look at the bird as it lifted a leg in majestic slow motion.

Hinges moaned out their agony aloud as the door beside Monique opened. A surly-faced head poked out round the door jamb, followed slowly by the rest of a large body in dirty collarless shirt and braces. The hard face lines wrestled themselves into a more amiable expression for greeting the pretty girl --- and for doing business. 'Mademoiselle would perhaps like to buy an egg?'

Knowing the severity of food shortage and its strain on rationing, Monique realised that this was not as outlandish a remark as it sounded. It also meant that in these circumstances, the price of an egg would be steep. 'No, thank you,' said Monique cheerfully, stepping aside, to be on her way.

But the man stepped in front of her, blocking her path. 'Mademoiselle does not think my chickens lay eggs of good quality?  She insults me and my chickens, thinking they are not of healthy stock?' There was unmistakable hostility rising in the man's voice.

Monique wanted only to be cordial and not cause a street scene in a silly argument over chickens that could possibly lead to something more serious. At all costs, she had to keep a low profile and not become tangled with municipal authorities who could well pass her down the line to a locally-stationed SS unit. 'I'm sorry, but I don't have any money, Monsieur,' she said, hoping that would satisfy him and let her be on her way.

But the man gave a grunt of disbelief, reaching out to take a hold of her coat sleeve. He rubbed the sleeve slowly with his thumb, feeling its rich fabric. 'For someone who has no money, Mademoiselle dresses very well.'

Her wits raced to beat this. '*On me*, I mean,' she said with a playful smile, tapping her pockets to show him what she meant. 'I don't have any money *on me*, Monsieur.'

This seemed to bring a lighter mood into his eyes. It also caused his grip on her sleeve to tighten, she noticed. There was no hiding of the animal pleasure showing in his face as he openly inspected her from head to foot, and then up again, savouring the goods. 'Mademoiselle can always pay *another* way and not worry about money.' The dark eyes came closer to her with their horrible leer.

Monique ran her mind over the tricks of the trade that Sergeant McAllister had shown her in her unarmed combat training. But she also remembered him telling her not to blow her cover by drawing unnecessary attention to herself. To put down this great lecherous hulk who was easily more than twice her weight, here in the street, would be doing just that. Looking round quickly at the window, she cried out: 'What's that?' With him turning round to see, she used his moment of distraction to yank her sleeve free from his grip and made off down the slippery slope, cursing again, this time gleefully, as she slipped and stumbled over the wet cobblestones.

With the slope eventually levelling out, she was at last in the main body of the town. There was a marked preference for back passages, away from the heavy volume of babbling crowds and roaring German army truck engines. She wanted to keep away from prying eyes. And yet not even down these narrow dark alleys, away from the blinding glare of wider sunlit thoroughfares, could she be sure that she was not being watched. As she made her way along the long winding alleys, she passed between lines of market stalls, open street traders and doorways, where bartering was done with the tongue at Gatling-gun speed, while the eyes searched elsewhere to snatch away your secrets as you passed by. With the din of buyers' and sellers' haggling competing with the braying of donkeys, Monique gave up trying to test her ear in picking out differing dialects around her  It was market day, and people came in from many far away districts to trade their wares.

After ducking under clothes-line after clothes-line stretched across the way, there was suddenly no more need for Monique to shield her carefully combed hair from flapping sheets. The passage had opened out into a tiny square. Two short dumpy palm trees enclosed by a knee-high circular terrazzo wall claimed the square's centre. Small metal tables and chairs sat outside the cafes on the right side and the far side of the square. A medley of food smells drifting out from the two cafes played with her nostrils. She was tempted by the food, but she had to complete her important assignment first, before she could allow herself to even think of sitting down to have something to eat. Perhaps it would be all right to have a quick coffee. That would calm her nerves. She could easily believe that no matter how experienced one was, no matter how many missions one had completed, this nervous feeling never went away completely.  She sat down at the iron table with its red-chequered tablecloth.

The beaded curtain across the doorway parted and a waiter came out wiping the table-top with his cloth and bending over Monique to take her order. She ordered a small coffee. And small it *was*, so much as to mimic a large thimble. When the waiter placed the cup down, he also placed a napkin close to it. Monique saw that it was soiled with pencil marks and pushed it away across the table. The waiter pushed it back to her. The 'contest' between them was repeated. A little piqued at what seemed like rudeness on the part of the waiter, Monique pushed the napkin away again with a firmness that she hoped the waiter would respect and leave it at that.

He didn't push it back, but fidgeting with it, and glancing meaningfully at it, he looked at her asking: 'Mademoiselle's eyes are very well, yes?' With her plainly not grasping what he was getting at, the waiter gave up. Slapping his cloth over his forearm, he disappeared through the beaded curtain and into the dark void beyond.

Puzzled by all this, Monique pulled the napkin closer to look at the markings. They were definitely not letters of any kind. But staring thoughtfully at them, it occurred to her that the squiggly, distorted lines roughly resembled a pair of spectacles. *Spectacles*! Eureka! So that's why he had asked after the state of her eyes. This is what Dr Dromyrk had inferred when he had emphasised the importance of always being ready to take in 'what is not there' in a moment's exploding insight. With the message getting through to her hitherto slow brain, Monique succeeded in scalding her mouth gulping down the coffee, in her haste to get up and hurry from the square.

Retracing her steps back through the streets and alleys, she searched and searched, all to no avail, to the point of exhaustion and the thought of giving up. And then she saw it. Through the window of the small pharmacie; further back in the shop interior, suspended high in the air, a larger than normal pair of wire-framed spectacles. The chemist shop doubled as an optician's. The door opened with a pleasant 'ting' of its bell as Monique went in to enquire about having an eye test.

Taken through to a back room, Monique barely had time, beyond being seated, to look around, before she was engulfed in total darkness. Reflexes had her tensed to defend herself when she sensed a movement extremely close her. A side light came on somewhere making her relax a little. She tensed again as a strange metal appliance was swung round and near to her face. Bristling with knobs, dials and 'things', it looked as if it could have done well in a medieval torture dungeon. The man, now seated on a stool beside her, fitted the phoroptor to her face, somewhat like a giant iron mask, so that she could see through the two lens apertures. With one eye's vision blocked, Monique read out the letters on the illuminated panel on the opposite wall. For a, she said P; for h, she said L; for c, she said U; for e, she said T; for m, she said O. The man's mind registered PLUTO. Lights came on and the eye test was abruptly over. Monique wasn't charged for the test; but when she left the shop, her coat was minus one of its detachable hollow buttons.

Her assignment completed, Monique's mood was much more lightened, so that she felt free to mix with the people around her, as she wandered aimlessly about the town. Even the contingent of German soldiers stationed in the town didn't seem to be occupied in a particular operation, so that they also were wandering around as aimlessly as her. But with the crowd of people that flowed around her being speckled here and there with the dull grey of German uniforms, she hadn't noticed, indeed, wouldn't have recognised, that one of the off-duty soldiers walking innocently along was Obergefreiter Hubber, trailing her, as Lieutnant Klanner of the Feldgendarmerie had instructed him to do.

The cold night breeze sent the tin can rattling along before it in an unsure meandering path rolling in and out of the gutter. Stopping and starting again, its erratic clinking cut the night's silence to carry Krunz's mind back to a time of his responsibility of a different kind; as when he had helped in his father's metal-works business workshop, amidst the satisfying sound of tools impinging on steel, shining and beautiful. Hammered and honed as like those blades of the valiant Siegfried and Lohengrin. As would his father forever intone to encourage him in his craft as well as the country's glorious folklore. That was long before the British and the Americans started dropping bombs. Only two sections of storeroom behind the workshop had survived the bombings. And that number was two more than any of his family had survived. Not that he was harbouring personal grievances. In his present work for the Fuhrer, he was not allowed to let personal feelings to come between him and his duty for the Fatherland. People's feelings must be directed collectively for the benefit of the State; and the Fuhrer *was* the State. Strict Abwehr discipline decreed that all his mental energy should be channelled into the fulfilment of his mission. Emotions had to be restrained in their lateral wanderings, to be directed forward as a sharpened point that would pierce the enemy's armour. His failure to observe this ruling would see him put before a firing squad.

Krunz was on foot, and doing his travelling at night, in order to keep a low profile, rather than use the Underground or take a bus. Now that he had been 'rumbled' by the country's accursed security, he considered using the public transport service to be a great risk. Moving on from his last safe house at Putney to the next one along the line should have been an easy shift for him, except that intelligence operations commanded by Colonel Rutkin had intervened, failing to snare him by only minutes. With police and security teams across the city alerted to his situation, he had been forced to lie low during daylight hours.

Hour upon hour of hiding among the ruins of a partly bombed school had been worrying as he listened to the voices of men searching among aftermath rubble. He couldn't tell if they were looking for him. Even if they were looking for bombing casualties, how would they react if they came across him? According to emergency plans, when darkness fell he was required to go to an agreed point, where he would be picked up on the hour, over three hours, and taken to the next safe house. He hadn't been able to be there on the hour any of the three consecutive times, so his 'collector' hadn't been able to hang around for fear of arousing suspicion. Instead, he had resorted to the secondary measure of leaving directions in a previously agreed dead-letter box.

Krunz had walked many miles as a boy, delivering and collecting for the family business, and then for his toughening-up in training with the Fuhrer's Youth Movement. But walking also kept his body fit for action. Taxi drivers had eyes and ears and minds for recalling their passengers, and their passengers' destinations. In compromise, he had let himself be driven from the last cell's location in Putney, to be dropped off several streets away, which was a good ten minutes walking distance from where he was heading now. This way, the taxi driver didn't know the exact address of the cell he was seeking and so could not be of any help to the police or intelligence people.

The night air was cool after what had been an unusually warm day; but Kunz could barely suppress a cynical smile at the puniness of what the British called warm, compared to those sunrays burning his semi-naked body as he worked on holiday, on the vine-terraced slopes of the Rhine Valley. Turning into the right street at last, he put his map away in his pocket. It was a long street. Counting down the house numbers, he was worried whenever a door, or several doors in succession, didn't show any. He didn't want to attract attention by knocking on the wrong door, even if only to ask for directions. The number he was after finally presented itself.

Krunz knocked twice, once, and then twice again. After a long pause, a thin sliver of light sliced the darkness as the door opened a few cautious inches, and guarded suspicion looked out.

'This is number seventy-nine,' came the slow, suspicious words from the slim suspicious face looking out at him. 'Is this the number you're looking for?'

'Only if it is not a number I'm *not* looking for,' replied Krunz, nervously completing the coded exchange, with the forever present fear of walking into a trap.

'Let him come up,' said a voice that Krunz recognised as Landor Salmerssen's, speaking from the top of the hallway stairs.

Krunz stepped inside and the door shut out the light, to let the darkness reclaim its secrecy of the night.

28

The house was fronted by lichen-velveted walls with gateposts pocked by metal stumps where the hinges had been. These no doubt, having gone, as in England, to feed the hunger of the ever so devouring war effort. The house seemed to be unscathed, being a safe distance south of Berlin and so escaping the bombing. A dull grey gravel footpath leading up to the house looked bright against the dark mass of decaying plants abandoned all around it. Strangely pleading line marks on the walls' inner surfaces were all that remained of trellis frames for climbing plants that had been mercilessly ripped off. Brown splotches of rust gave memory of where the nails had held the wood captive. Just like those nails two thousand years ago on that Mount, Dromyrk thought. An odd thought perhaps, but that was only one of many odd, more *questionable*, things going on.

He rang the doorbell. After many minutes of waiting, Dromyrk was on the point of leaving and was turning away, when the door decided to reward his patience and started to open. The woman, in her sixties, looked very tired; the housekeeper most likely, worn down very much by her never-ending chores about a large rambling property. Dromyrk held out a card to identify himself, explaining as he did that he had come to see his former mentor and colleague, Professor Bernheim; his words were wasted on the woman who, having done her lot in opening the door, walked off to continue with her cleaning, picking up her mop and bucket at the far end of the hall and disappearing through a door beneath the heavy baroque wooden staircase.

Left standing there alone, wondering what or to whom he should apply himself next, Dromyrk became aware of a faint strain of music drifting out to him from a far off room. It sounded like Schuman, and on gramophone, judging by its tinny quality. The strains suddenly loudened, as a door was opened, letting the music out. The music cut out. Several seconds of what Dromyrk just made out to be low footfalls, before the figure was framed on the doorway on his left. Just like he had magically appeared in that other doorway twenty-eight years ago. Neither of them had words to fill the seconds that they stood staring at each other. True, fashion had long changed from formal morning coats and diamond-studded cravats; but it wasn't just the clothes. Inasmuch as he had been shorter than Dromyrk then, the Professor presented a more shrunken image now, having thinned and seemingly weighed down with stooped rounded shoulders. But a steely strength was discernible still, hanging on stubbornly as it shone out from those blue eyes.

Coming together and shaking hands came easier than finding first words. 'We'll be more comfortable going to the inner parlour,' said Bernheim. 'Maria will prepare a warm beverage for us.' Leading the way, Bernheim moved with a slow shuffling gait replacing his former stalwart stride. Pulling his cardigan tighter around himself, Bernheim turned round to look at Dromyrk. 'Normally I would ask you to take off your coat; but perhaps it would be more convenient for you to keep it on.' He gave a quiet laugh. 'Things being as they are, our coal supply is a little limited.'

Feeling the chill in the hall around him, Dromyrk guessed that the said parlour would be the only room in the house to have the warmth of a lit fire. The same as in his own house. 'As is mine, in London,' he said. 'As is mine.' A cold solemnity of feeling caught his inside at what he'd just said and the thought of what he'd left behind in England. To have fled there from here all those years ago, only to have come back here again. It ironically mirrored the patient suffering a relapse. Luckily the Professor had his back to him as he led the way, so was not able to read his mind, from seeing his expression. But he did say over his shoulder to Dromyrk: 'Ah yes, *London*.' As always, his short utterances held that lingering tone of underlying inference that had you wondering what part he had plucked out of the thoughts that you imagined were yours alone.

Originally a spare room, the parlour had been assigned its new role because its smallness allowed a moderate fire to be enough make it warm and comfortable to be in, unlike the house's larger rooms. They lowered themselves into two old scarred leather armchairs that had seen better days. 'You've come a long way. Doctor Dromyrk. And not just across the water,' said Bernheim, sitting back and tapping his chair's armrests as he studied the other's face.

'And all thanks to you, Professor.'

They both laughed to clear the nervous air between them. Going back through old clinical cases of patients helped this. Holding back on the primary reason for his coming here that was biting away at his patience, Dromyrk hung on, lending an ear to the Professor's renewed arguments over cases where their diagnoses and prognoses had clashed. As senior, the Professor's opinion had always carried through. It mattered little that this difference in rank was gone and that they were now 'equal'. With other things at the back of Dromyrk's mind, and the Professor having a better memory of cases than him, he didn't push his views beyond polite opinion. Besides, many of these individuals would no longer be with us; some escaping from wretched mental turmoil by passing away through natural causes; others by a new life threatening source called bombing.

They paused in the course of their discussion as the housekeeper, Maria, came into the room carrying a tray bearing two cups that gave off twirls of vapour, and a plate of what looked like hard maize cakes. Dromyrk amusedly thought they looked as if they could possibly break one's teeth, smiling as he did in appreciation at the woman bending down to place the cups and cakes on a low table between their chairs. 'Milk with the addition of honey,' said Bernheim, taking up his cup. 'Remote and isolated as we are, we nevertheless not only elude the ravages of war, but we also at least have better access to nature's beneficial products.' He looked up at his housekeeper. 'Thank you,'

As the woman straightened up and turned to go, Bernheim called her back. She leaned in close over him so that he could whisper in her ear, partly deaf as she was. Dromyrk's mind flashed back to the time that he'd seen the Professor do that to quell the patient's anxiety, in the first few minutes of their meeting. All the years that he'd worked with Bernheim, in spite of the Professor's brilliant expertise of teaching, he'd never quite acquired this skill, or *gift*, of rendering instant subsidence of the patient's escalating hysteria. It would perhaps have served well on one of those sessions when he was attending, on his own, Hitler in one of his frenzied moods. The image of that individual brought Dromyrk's mind back into the room and to his reason for coming here.

With the woman having left the room, they drank on quietly, Bernheim waiting, Dromyrk wondering. After several minutes, the woman returned, handing the Professor an envelope and then leaving them again. Bernheim placed the envelope on his chair's armrest. He left it there, and went on drinking his warm beverage. Dromyrk went on drinking his while looking at the envelope, wondering if it had anything to do with what he was after.

Unable to withstand the tension of waiting any longer, Dromyrk made to speak.

'She is unwell,' said the Professor, anticipating the mental shift of another, like he always did.

Dromyrk felt a deep inner pang, as he admittedly knew he would, at that sombre information. He pointed at the envelope. 'Is that ---'

'The address; yes.' Berheim took up the envelope and held it out for Dromyrk. Getting up promptly and taking it, Dromyrk sat down again. While Dromyrk was occupied opening the envelope and reading the notepaper he'd taken from it, Bernheim continued with his information. 'Lebensborn (fountain of life) clinics, the Nationalist

Party's idea of promoting the growth of the Aryan race by setting up these official venues for healthy young men of pure Aryan stock to have sexual intercourse with healthy young fraulein of pure Aryan stock, for the eventual producing of healthy young children of pure Aryan stock. In reality, high-class brothels provided for officers' weekend pleasure. Men driven by their carnal lust who cared little for the 'strict' genetic requirements that permitted entrance to these, what can only be called, morally questionable establishments. Which generates no surprise, really, since the plaudit for original concept belongs entirely to Reichsfuhrer Himmler.'

Dromyrk was somewhat upset by Bernheim's words, unsure and worried at how it could have been brought on at the mere referring to Tildi. He shrunk from a dreaded suspicion of how it could implicate her. 'And you are certain of this? There is no room for dou ---'

'Most assuredly so.' The Professor sounded as solid, as he seemed certain, of his facts and went on to give more. 'As far as we know – or are *permitted* to know -- there are some fourteen or so of these '*clinics*' stowed away in quiet parts of the country, safe from the aerial bombardment besieging our larger cities and towns.'

Dromyrk couldn't believe his ears. He refused to believe his ears. 'You're saying that Tildi --- ,' he struggled to find 'admissible' words, ' --- *entertained* these men?'

'Was there a *choice* for her? With the threat of her father being taken away in the infernal slave labour programme for political dissidents, to eventually die of fatigue and malnutrition, God knows where?' Bernheim shrugged his shoulders to this.

Dromyrk looked down for a moment, pulling a hand across his face and giving a long sigh as he took this in. He looked up again at Bernheim. 'And the mother?'

'Alas, tuberculous meningitis, nineteen forty-two. Small blessing that her suffering was short.'

Dromyrk was shaking his head at this last piece. 'And to think that only last year, one year later, there was a breakthrough in this area.

From the scant snippets of information one catches from the American Army doctors, an antibiotic, streptomysin, has been developed that is apparently having some degree of success in combating the virus. I gather that soldiers as well as civilian patients are presently being administered with this treatment.'

Seeing Dromyrk's distress, Berheim gave a deep sigh at the thought of what he still had to say. 'Whilst the clinics were originally used for the procreation of perfect children through normal copulation, later developments sought artificial means, by way of genetic experimentation to achieve this more directly. A concentrated study was made of the translocation of chromosomes in the embryo specimen cells, for which human contributors were needed – over and over again.'

'Guinea-pigs!' said Dromyrk bluntly. 'And Tildi was one? Is that what you're telling me?'

Berheim nodded his head slowly in straight-faced confirmation of the grim facts.

Dromyrk's face darkened, as did his mind. 'With your knowing of all this --- all these precise details --- am I to understand that your knowledge was first-hand? That you were there giving your consent?'

'Given your personal ties in this and your heightened emotion, I can well understand your asking what would otherwise be a most offensive question.' Bernheim took a moment to settle his own roused feelings. 'There is an inevitability of these things finding their way along the professional grape-vine. Unofficial copies of records reached me and I was consulted for an opinion. My absolute condemnation of what was clearly a grotesque infringement of medical ethics was plainly stated to the point that I resigned from my post. This gesture of protest on my part could easily have seen me being sent away, like Tildi's father was. But I was spared this woeful penalty providing that I consented to retire and live quietly far away from the capital.'

After a silence of several long seconds, Dromyrk looked searchingly at Bernheim. 'Why have you done all this, Professor? I mean you keeping a file on Tildi, so to speak?'

Stretching his arms out on the arm rests, Bernheim sat back and smiled at Dromyrk. 'I knew that that eager-to-learn young doktor who had fled this country in great haste wouldn't be able to resist returning to resolve his situation.'

'And do you see me resolving that situation?'

'Personal resolve depends on how much pain one can accept as the price of putting the situation to rest --- *forever*.' Bernheim paused to look with faint warning in his eyes at Dromyrk. He pointed significantly at the notepaper Dromyrk was still holding. 'You're not going to be happy at what you find when you go there. *If* you go there. If you consider it wise.'

'I'm going there, be most assured.'

Conversation couldn't have lightened in mood even if they'd tried. Which they didn't. There was no point. To have tried salvaging some good cheer from the bleakness that their talk had descended into would have been futile, with a hollow-faced pretence putting the lid on it. With inner foreboding of unpleasantness over what he expected to find when he met up with Tildi, and knowing that he and Professor Bernheim would not meet again, Dromyrk said his farewell with open sadness. He walked out the door and away from the house without looking back.

# 29

There was a pig in the bus somewhere. She knew there was. She could hear its snorting, or perhaps squealing was more accurate. It must have been a small piglet. And it was, when she saw it poking its tiny pointed pink snout out between the lapels of the woman's coat. Monique giggled to herself for thinking for a moment that it was 'something else' peeping out from the woman's chest. Having carried out her assignment, only for the second time on her own, Monique was feeling her confidence grow, and that was making her inner tension fade away. She looked around at fellow passengers, mostly returning home from the market, happy with what they had bought, or with the money they had saved not buying anything. Or maybe she was just bestowing this feeling on them because she herself was feeling cheerful.

A movement outside the bus caught the edge of her vision, to make her look round. Her spirits dipped when she looked out the window. The motorcycle, with its gleaming parts and the gleaming helmet of the Feldgendarmerie rider, sliding smoothly past at its slightly greater speed, put Monique on the alert again. Her inside jumped when the goggled face looked up in her direction, seemingly straight at her in particular. She would have jerked her head away in reflex, but for the instructions that to do so was a sure sign of guilt. Holding the man's stare for a controlled moment, she turned her face away slowly as if unconcerned. But she watched him out of the side of her eye.

With a great roar of its 26h.p.745 flat-twin engine, the motorcycle suddenly accelerated to shoot off past the trundling mass of the bus and away on ahead. But it didn't disappear completely. Monique stood up to look along the length of the bus and through the windscreen to watch its progress. It was holding a steady position some thirty metres or so along the road ahead of them. It looked to her as if they were being escorted. As far as Monique knew, the bus wasn't scheduled to stop anywhere between here and Mont du Laf, the route terminal. If she made the driver stop to let her get off, the bike rider would know all about it and come back to investigate. Monique fretted over what to do next.

When the bus came to a halt at the town terminal stop, Monique let the other passengers surge to the door before her so that she would be less conspicuous getting out into the small crowd. But when she stepped down out of the bus, the people who would normally have stood there talking for several minutes suddenly scattered like frightened sheep at the approach of the 'wolf'.

Lieutnant Klanner walked up to stand before Monique and give a polite bow of the head instead of the Nazi salute. Obergefreiter Hubber stood behind him, his Mauser holster open, should his assistance be needed. 'Mademoiselle Berac,' he said in friendly greeting, 'we meet again. As you would say in your beautiful English language, your game is up. As much as I would like spending this lovely afternoon with you, discussing your country's wonderful pastoral literature, it is my duty to hand you over to the Schutzstaffel (SS) whom I fear, alas, are apt to prove to be somewhat less appreciative of this cultural wealth.' He looked round at Corporal Hubber. 'You have called them?'

'Ja, mein Herr Lieutnant.' Hubber brought his wrist up smartly to consult his watch. 'Ten or twenty minutes, they said.'

Nodding his satisfaction to Hubber, the Lieutnant turned back to Monique to take her by the elbow and walked along the street with her. 'In the meantime, we can spend what little time we have waiting, to talk over England's lyrical masterpieces and enjoy a cup of exquisite French coffee.' Heading for a table outside a café, they both sat down, while

Hubber stood at ease several tables away. When the SS unit eventually arrived to collect its prisoner, Lieutnant Klanner insisted that it waited until he and Mademoiselle Berac had finished their coffee. He made a point of taking his time.

Interrogation at the SS headquarters was gone through swifter than Monique had anticipated. She had set herself ready for what she feared would be a painful ordeal, physically as well as mentally. It was a surprise, instead, to be locked up alone in a cell only after basic questioning over relatively non-vital material. Monique got the impression that they didn't consider her to be that important to their investigations. All the information Monique could have told them if she'd been broken by their torture, they already knew. They had their reliable source of information from an informer, or informers, somewhere else along the line. She was important only as a means of demonstrating the Fuhrer's long-reaching arm of retribution. She would be executed at dawn.

And dawn couldn't have come any sooner in a single life. Too soon, in Monique's fright-frozen brain. Never before would she have felt such regret at the sight of that golden disc rising up to make what would be another glorious sunny day. A day she would never see. Those twelve men standing there in a line, they would see the day out; and many more. They would write to their wives, sweethearts and mums. She would never see Mummy again. Oh, Mummy, Mummy! Two strange noises, she came to realise, were those of her own sniffling and swallowing hard in her mounting anxiety.

The officer strode up to her, to offer her the option of a blindfold. She accepted, not wanting to look straight at what was going to bring her life to an abrupt end. The world went black as it was put on around her head and over her eyes. A sharp command rang out for rifles to take aim. She felt the warm liquid run down between her thighs in a soaking rush of shocked release.

'Feuer!'

A thunderous explosion of mind-wrenching, mind-blocking gunfire. Silence. It took a millionth of a second to appreciate that it was automatic weapons that had fired, not rifles primed to fire one single bullet. This conclusion came a millionth of a second after she realised that she was still alive.

'Berac? You are very okay? You are safe; we have killed all the bastard Boche.' Someone pulled her blindfold away. It was Anjon, the Basque guerrilla cum Resistance fighter standing there, his face barely an inch from hers, checking to see that she was all right. It didn't matter that his breath carried a horrific stench and that his yellow broken teeth made you want to puke; to her at this moment, his ugly face was the most beautiful thing she had set her eyes on in her whole life.

'Do you reckon on taking that thing with you, then,' said Bretzler, referring to the football that Falzoni was squeezing and turning over and over again in his hands, in an action that was as monotonous as them sitting waiting in the car was.

'Don't suppose I'll be taking it with me anyhow, I guess,' replied Falzoni, pulling his arm back, ball in hand, in a silent practise throw. 'I played real swell in college. Sure had those girls squealing. Maybe I could have become something, if the old man hadn't continued to shout in my ear about what he never had, what my elder brothers never had, but what I *did* have, which was the opportunity to study hard to become a hack lawyer. Which I did.' Falzoni slapped his own forehead, shaking his head in mock regret. 'The mad things we do to please others, eh, Brent,' he said, looking round at Bretzler.

'And you're still set on going in?'

'Well, you heard what Rutkin said, and we were all agreed, weren't we? With Dromyrk having gone AWOL, one of us has to be over there in Europe to keep a finger on the intelligence pulse when we finally go in. Who knows, maybe I'll come across that belt of mine that I lost over there,' Falzoni joked, even although Palermo would be a far distance from where the coming Operation Overlord was going to take them in Europe. He handed the ball back to Bretzler. 'You can have this. I'm not sure you'll have a hand to spare for it, with both of them occupied dealing with Rutkin, the kid, when it comes, and Selena. How is she doing?'

Bretzler's eyes took on a distant look while he rubbed his chin slowly in faraway thought. 'She seems to have sunk into a gloomy sort of negative withdrawal situation. Not exactly what I would have expected of her, since she's normally a strong-minded person. And if that's not enough, her doctor is seeing problems that are going to make it a difficult birth. He didn't make it quite clear what these were. I'm not sure if he knew himself; or maybe that's just my subconscious excuse for not wanting to know the gruesome details.'

Falzoni punched Bretzler's arm playfully. 'You're being too hard on yourself, Brent. All in all, I say you can keep it. I'll stick to staying alive dodging Jerry's Panzer shells.'

A sudden pinpoint of light stood out in the darkness ahead of them. 'There it is,' said Bretzler, handing the ball back to Falzoni and shifting to get out of the car.

'Where?'

'*There*, in front of you, Bonehead. Let's go.' Getting out of the car, they walked quickly towards the figure flashing the torchlight signal. 'Have they got him?' Bretzler asked the Special Branch man.

'No, not yet, Colonel, but it shouldn't be long. Dogs are being brought in to help.'

'So let's go get him,' said Bretzler, glancing round at Falzoni. 'Coming, Frank? You can practise your football shots later.' They worked their way down the heavily wooded slope towards an abandoned cottage, with dark figures on both sides of them helping scour the undergrowth. As they approached a well-braided police officer, the man turned round. 'Help is on its way, Colonel. The van with the dogs should be here any minute now.'

'If we had some more damn decent light, we wouldn't need any damn dogs,' muttered Falzoni in groaning voice, annoyed at the muddy soil and wet branches ruining his trousers.

Barely one hundred yards away soft wind carried the sound of the search to Krunz's ears. Snapping twigs and voices trailing out through the air for several seconds and then stopping. And starting up again in recurrent cycle. They seemed to be coming after him from his left. But wait – a babble of voices rushing through the empty air said that they were also moving in from the right. And dogs as well, from the sound of it, coming up at a fast pace from the rear. He had thought that he had been making fast progress through the wood; but they seemed to be moving faster. Change of tactics was called for. Krunz looked around for cover. He listened for his stalkers as their voices and movement through the undergrowth became more audible. Footsteps slowed down and shifted around in the same spot, seemingly unsure of what way to go next. 'Maybe it would be a better plan to split up into two lots; and get the job done quicker,' said Bretzler's voice across the darkness. 'We'll work our way down on this side.'

'We'll make our way along this side and up towards the road,' said a policeman's voice. 'And for God's sake, somebody go and tell them to bring those dogs over this way, and be quick about it!'

Krunz listened as footsteps started up once more only to stop again, as a close search hovered in its bit by bit progress nearby. Footsteps faltered and twigs snapped here and there, confusing Krunz's keeping track of exactly where his stalkers were. The sounds began to move away and then stopped. They moved up and down the slope a short distance, and then back to the opposite side of where Krunz lay hidden. Krunz's nerves jolted him inside as a stick rasped along the top of a coarse stone, in a sweeping stroke near his head. Otherwise, he didn't shift an inch. An inverted view of a helmeted head moving warily over his covered hiding-place had Krunz holding his breath as the policeman looked to see if he had disturbed anything with his stick.

'Anything?' said an American voice.

'Difficult to see. Nothing, by the look of it,'

'We've wasted enough time here. Let's try over that way,' said Bretzler's voice.

Krunz listened to this, lying rock-still only feet away in a hollow that was concealed by bushes. Breathing out more freely, now that the sound of his pursuers was distancing itself down the hill, Krunz got up on his knees to look round about and then moved off in the opposite direction. He had to find a way of getting himself out of this mess. Making good progress stumbling less and less through the undergrowth, his spirits began to rise. They took a dip when he suddenly noticed that some of the trees in front of him were of the silver-buttoned kind. Turning round to change his direction of escape, he was confronted by a great monster of a dog baring its teeth, snarling menacingly as it blocked his path. To add insult to his dismay, it was a German shepherd. Krunz braced himself as the dog came closer and was about to leap up at him. A sharp cry rang out and the dog stopped, stepping back in obedience to its handler's command. A cordon of police formed round him.

'Well, well, if it isn't our Herr Krunz, himself,' said a sergeant, stepping up to take Krunz by the arm. 'Taking a walk in the Black Forest, were we? Sorry to disappoint you, if we only had a teeny patch of woods to offer you.' Krunz held his silence in defiance. The sergeant, just about to say something else, stalled to look past Krunz to to see that someone was approaching from that direction. It was the American Colonel. 'We've caught the blighter, Colonel,' he said.

'All right, Sergeant, you can let us take care of this Kraut,' said Bretzler, stepping up to the policeman who was still holding Krunz by the arm. He saw that the Sergeant was a little unsure about the question over who had the jurisdiction for making an arrest. 'It's okay, buddy. Don't let our different colour of uniforms bother you. Your boss will tell you that he's to be handed over to us so that we can put a boot up his ass to get him to play ball proper with us.' Bretzler looked round at the Special Branch officer that was walking up to them. 'Isn't that right, Superintendent?'

'That's quite correct,' said the Superintendent, not hiding his reluctance in conceding to this fact. Especially considering the American's cheeky jibes the last that time they'd met. 'Do as he says, Sergeant, and let the good Colonel have the prisoner, like he's requested.'

Bretzler looked at Krunz, giving a head jerk to tell him to move. 'I don't know if Gute Nacht has the same idiom in your lingo, buddy, so I'll just say it's '*goodnight*' for you!'

'Auf Wiedersehen fits the bracket better, I'd say,' said Falzoni, drawing his forefinger across his throat to signify the spy's ultimate '*goodbye*' through execution.


She turned and started, shocked at his unannounced presence. They stared at each other in a tense long silence, their minds suspended in the surprise confrontation. He saw that Tildi had thinned, the skin gone sallow, and her mouth shrunken with a dryness of lips that had somehow lost their former bounty. Most unfamiliar of all were her cheeks, drawn in with a sullen pale tightness of reserve that he found he didn't like to acknowledge. She pulled her shoulders in tight, turning in sharp reflex away from him, sheltering within herself somewhat. This stung him. It even alarmed him a little, to find her so alienated from him – from herself – the person she had been. Her shrunken form, like a shrivelled leaf removed of its living freshness, and her mentally starved state, gave her an ugliness that both shamed and frightened him in his having to admit it. But those eyes. Where once they would have held you with their captivating drawing power, they were now shrinking back inwardly. Dromyrk saw that they were shutting him out. Respecting her wish for the moment, he pulled his eyes away from hers, looking around, anywhere, at anything, to give her shocked thoughts a few moments of escape.

Four dull brown bare walls with their depressive air now replaced what he remembered of that happy family house atmosphere in Achendorf. All those pictures that should have been on the walls; that one with him, father, grandpapa and her holding the fishing rod, standing beside the lake that day at Uppsala. He snapped out of his wandering thoughts.

It took no great effort for him to see that her inner damage was deep. Prolonged incarceration on its own would generally suffice to commence inroads to upsetting a mind; but Tildi's being submitted to horrific physical abuse through 'medical experimentation' over this period was wholly contributory to her mental breakdown. On his arrival at the clinic, Dromyrk had asked to see Tildi's medical history. But the nurse had refused his request because of his not being family; not even if he *was* a doktor. He doubted that this was the real reason for his not being able to inspect what he suspected to be most questionable material. But he didn't push the issue. He was treading on perilous enough grounds, as it was, with him being in the country itself.

Like those many patients he treated for this problem, she would not respond to his words. But this was not one of those patients; this was his Tildi, and for the first time since he was a young inexperienced hospital intern, he was slightly numbed with his approach to the patient falling flat. She simply sat there, isolated from him in her silence. To overcome the personal relationship that was interfering with his treating her illness, it was imperative that he saw her as just another patient, and not as the woman he had so dearly loved long ago. He relaxed, settling himself into his mode of playing the silent game with the distanced mind before him. His words were few, with the waiting between them long. Those eyes, like bleak fading lights, stared back long and hard at him. Their twin message, boring relentlessly into him, was that he had brought this soul-scarring injury on her when he had deserted her. Short of making him squirm inside with guilt, the thought was pushed to the side of what was now his medical task of relieving her mental suffering.

The silent battle between them was interrupted with the door opening and the nurse coming in. She had barely the time to announce the presence of two men who had come to see him, when they appeared immediately behind her, moving her, *pushing* her, aside, to come into the room. He guessed what they were, before they produced their credentials, along with limp hand-flapped back-at-the-shoulder salutes, in reverent emulation of their beloved Fuhrer's manner of 'friendly-nice-man' greeting. Gestapo.

But they hadn't come to arrest the good Doktor. With his personal prestige as former consultant to the Fuhrer preceding him, they were here to 'accompany' him to Berlin. Hitler, in one of his frenzied throes of dementia, had summoned him for help. With the war turning against Hitler, so crushing the invincible Messiah-style power that he'd believed himself to possess, and his generals now openly questioning his decisions, his mind was being battered into a corner.

As Dromyrk was being escorted from the room, he heard Tildi blurt out in a weak voice, what sounded like, 'You won't come back.'

Turning half round, in the grip of the two men, he said, 'I will be back, Tildi, believe me, love, I will be back.'

But he hadn't heard her properly, as he realised when she repeated what she'd said. 'Don't come back!'

It wasn't until the following day, whilst waiting in the Reichschancellery for his appointment with Hitler, that Dromyrk received the message that Tildi had killed herself. As far as was known, she had used a piece of glass from a broken window to cut her own wrists. She had bled fatally before she had been found. His facial expression remained as it was at hearing this. Not a single twitch of body movement registered to the eye. But his inner reaction rivalled the erupting volcano. The fury pulsing through his brain could only be measured in the strength of his pounding footsteps as he was escorted along the corridors to the Fuhrer's stateroom. Dromyrk's life-long pledge to the Hippocratic Oath was rent into a million pieces in his storming mind. He was inflamed with a new resolve to fulfil.

He would rid the world of all this genocidal horror. He would destroy the monster that was responsible for all this horrific killing, all these deaths, Tildi's death. He was going to kill the Fuhrer. That shrapnel wound twenty-eight years ago hadn't killed him; mustard gas in a later field engagement hadn't killed him; assassins' bombs and bullets hadn't killed him. But he would definitely kill him. When he went into that room, if that monster was alone, he would kill him. Even if the room was overflowing with generals crowding around the bastard, he'd still kill him --- with his bare hands.

He would kill Hitler.

# 30

**5<sup>th</sup> June, 1944. D-Day** fast approaching by the hour, with not a precious second lost where Allied Forces were building up a massive assault front, land, sea and air, to be unleased in all its might on  Hitler's Waffen-SS to stop its brutal iron boot march across Europe.

'If we can just go over that lot once again, just to check,' said the Stores-duty corporal, looking at the equipment laid out before them on the long counter. He walked along slowly beside the counter, touching individual items between glances at his clipboard as he read them out. 'Three days E rations, three days B rations, two morphine needles, two first aid kits, helmet, chute, boots, MK1 rifle, gloves, reserve cute, Mae West, three blocks of TNT, canteen of water, two smoke grenades – orange smoke and red smoke, a forty-five caliber Colt automatic pistol, one gas mask, trench knife, two cans of machine-gun ammo, that is, six hundred and seventy rounds of point three o three ammo and sixty-six rounds of forty five ammo, two bandoliers, six fragmentation grenades, one Hawkins mine to blast Jerry's Panzer tracks to hell, one blanket, one entrenching tool  --- and see here, there's two blasting caps taped on the outside of the steel part to ---' The corporal broke off with an apologetic look at Captain Falzoni. 'But then I reckon you don't need tellin' a spike from a spoke. Sorry, Captain.' He continued along the line. 'One Gammon grenade, one waterproof poncho, two cartons of cigarettes and that's about it.'

'I think we can skip the helmet, rifle and automatic; I've got my own,' said Falzoni. 'How about some more cigarettes in their place?'

'Can do, Skipper. Sure can do.' Picking up the three items and putting them back on their shelves, the corporal disappeared down an aisle, returning promptly with extra cigarettes for the Captain. Falzoni turned round to look at Brent Bretzler stepping over to him.

'I suppose you'll be needing me to help you shift that gear, Frank.'

Falzoni gave a broad grin to Bretzler. 'We don't want to keep the old moaner waiting too long.' Frank was referring to Colonel Rutkin waiting outside in the jeep, in much of a hurry to get to SHAEF HQ for Supreme Allied Forces Commander General Eisenhower's final briefing on the Normandy assault. Rutkin had already spoken with Ike that morning, sharing the General's attention with other Chiefs of Staff, as well as members of the press, as he made his inspection tour of the south coast, speaking to and shaking hands with young fresh-faced anxious-mothers' sons preparing to board their troop ships. With the General's whistle-stop tour taking him everywhere, it followed that 'HQ' was where and when you were lucky enough to catch him.

'It's a bit of a jump, if you'll forgive the pun, you dropping in on Jerry by parachute, Frank; considering that our mode of attack with the Armoured Division was always by land or sea.'

'Get's me there a lot quicker than all our guys who've been waiting for hours and days in their trucks and tanks, anxious to get on the move and see some action. It's time we quit stalling. And saying that, if you could just grab that lot of bandoliers, ammo and explosives there, Brent, I'll take the rest and we can get going.'

Somewhat reflecting Falzoni's words, 'miles and miles' of tanks, trucks, jeeps, bulldozers and other military vehicles lined the roads, crawling along bumper to bumper in a snail-paced five miles an hour military convoy. It made his driving past them and avoiding oncoming vehicles awkward. This was worsened when the moving convoy was periodically guided round long sections of parked vehicles by precise stiff-arm signalling from stiff-faced no-nonsense MPs. Bored soldiers' faces stared back at the solitary jeep, lucky as it was to be whizzing by. 'See what I mean,' said Falzoni, throwing his remark at Bretzler sitting beside him. 'Poor bastards; God knows how long they've been sweating their guts out waiting to get on the move. At least they have all the time, stuck as they are on their asses, to get their coffee, or should I say *tea*?' he said, glancing in the rear mirror at Colonel Rutkin. Bretzler and Rutkin followed his words, looking out at the white Women's Institute tea-waggon that served as a veritable oasis for the stranded soldiers who were queueing up at its open hatch, eagerly holding out their tin mugs. But whilst the public had long become accustomed to the Army's rehearsal manoeuvres in the streets, there was something this time in the overall soldiers' behaviour, their tensed attitudes, that said that this was the 'real thing' – that the grand march was underway.

Falzoni gave another glance in the rear mirror. 'If you could perhaps give me a brief rundown on the situation, Colonel? With the curtain about to go up on the big show, and me walking the boards in Act One, so to speak, I could well do with some more details.' He gave a cheeky smile at Bretzler. 'I'm spared the worry of not being there to bring up a young kid and show him how to pitch the ball.'

'And I won't have to worry about going broke shovelling mountains of dollars to a bum hustler.'

'Like you say, Captain, your action is in the forefront of the general D-Day operation,' said Rutkin. 'You'll go in with your own 101$^{st}$ Airborne Division, accompanied by the 82$^{nd}$ Airborne Division, along with our own 6$^{th}$ Airborne Division. As a vanguard force, it will be your task to take control of vital tactical points and ports – Cherbourg, especially -- and hold them until our ground forces come ashore from amphibious craft. You must fight your way through German resistance, to join up with our ground troops, to form a strong broad front. You have to attack and destroy vital strongpoints and installations immediately west of the beach, and so put German coastal defences out of action. We need you to capture crossroads and bridges that flank our landing areas – two points especially -- Pegasus Bridge and Sainte-Mere-Eglise.'

Rutkin gave a concerned frown at his watch, and then looked in front of them, at the potential threat of traffic hold-ups. 'Time is vital,' he said, openly worried. 'Flights are scheduled for no later than twenty-one hundred hours; our ships will set out shortly after twenty hundred hours. It is vital that we arrive before the tide rises to cover obstacle barriers. We have a number of midget submarines there to guide our troops in. So we must hurry.'

'Unless Ike changes his mind again,' said Bretzler quietly.

Where the original launching of the invasion had been set for the 31rst of December, '43, General Eisenhower and General Montgomery had agreed to put the date back through dissatisfaction with proposed landing plans. They had deemed an assault strength of three main divisions supported by two secondary divisions to be dangerously inadequate. Increasing the strength to five divisions, with airborne section getting three additional divisions, along with more landing craft necessary for a wider land invasion front, called for more time to allow for manufacture. So the date was put back to the 1rst of May '44. Final assault strength saw 39 divisions, comprising 22 American divisions, 12 British divisions, 3 Canadian divisions, 1 Polish division and 1 French division. A total of over one million brave soldiers ready to march, blood, bullets and bayonets, against the Nazi regime. Eisenhower next proposed the launch date to be the 5th June. Alas, bad weather over the Channel had Ike now saying that we attack tomorrow.

Rutkin stared back at the American, irritated by his forever bringing up negative points, but more so, fearful that they could well prove to be accurate predictions. His attention went back to Captain Falzoni's situation. 'Schedules all going to plan, our SAS and Commando units should already have been putting their mischief about sabotaging enemy radar stations before you arrive, Captain.'

'And you can count on our US Rangers having done their bit spiking Jerry's guns at Pointe-Du-Hoc, to help lay out a welcome carpet for you and your parachute to land on, nice and clean, Frank,' said Bretzler jokingly. The jovial air faded a little on Bretzler's face as he thought of conflicts elsewhere. One hundred and fifty-eight thousand of our troops against fifty thousand German troops seemed to put the odds in our favour; but how many of our young guys had never ever pulled a trigger before enlisting, compared to the battle-hardened Hun ever so ready to kill. Landing at the Omaha beach, our raw young men of the 1rst and 29th Infantry Division would have to face one of the Wehrmacht's crack infantry units, the 352 Infanterie-Division.

'With eight thousand planes and five thousand ships, we have the largest attacking force in history, without a doubt; a most formidable force, said Rutkin triumphantly.

'Their Panzer units are also *formidable*,' said Bretzler, in a thoughtfully slow warning tone. 'If we're to believe reports, one of their Tiger tanks alone knocked out twenty five of our tanks.'

But Rutkin wasn't having his moment of triumph stolen by Bretzler. 'We have to take into account the ----'

Falzoni suddenly waved a hand to stop the conversation so that he could listen for something. 'Listen. Can you hear it?'

'Hear what?' said Rutkin.

'Listen,' said Falzoni again, tilting his head to listen above the sound of the engine as he looked up at the grey sky. Rutkin and Bretzler followed his action, also looking upwards, listening. It grew nearer, louder. They heard it. The now familiar gurgle of an approaching 'doodlebug' flying bomb. The ominous sound suddenly stopped overhead as the engine cut off, letting the V1 dip its nose and begin its devilish downwards rush. Their vehicle somersaulted high into the air, under colossal impact from the bomb explosion, landing yards away with a metal-crunching crash.

'Give me a hand over here! One of them's still alive,' cried the ARP Warden to those around him, as he frantically set about pulling apart the mangled wreckage of the US Army jeep. A group of Rescue Team men hurried over to help. The surviving soldier, barely alive with horrific injuries, was trying to get through with incoherent mutterings to the Rescue men. But they were unable to understand the garbled cries of pain, more so because of the rich American accent. Ignoring what they couldn't understand, the men got on with their vital work of searching among the rubble for life – or death -- in another typical night-long shift, in this never-ending war.

# EPILOGUE

30th April1945, Hitler committed suicide in his private room in his bunker. Nine days earlier he had summoned the doctor to the bunker in the hope of at last being relieved of his harrowing depression. Held in captivity for 336 days, the doctor refused, as he had done many times before, to help the Fuhrer. He was summarily executed by strychnine injection and his body incinerated outside the bunker. A soft breeze wafted Dr Dromyrk's ashes in a northerly direction that was towards his homeland.

# ACKNOWLEDGEMENTS

For their invaluable aid to my writing this novel, I thank the following:
C Ponting
John Keegans *The First World War*
Martin Gilbert
Robin Cross *Hitler: An Illustrated Life*
Paul Roland *Nazis: An Illustrated History*
Jon E Lewis *World War II*
Pilot Officer Roger Hall 152 Squadron RAF
Richard Hillary 603 Squadron RAF
Donald Burgett US 101st Airborne Division
Alan Moorehead
Barry Turner *Countdown To Victory*